THOSE WHO
DARE

PHIL WARD

GREENLEAF
BOOK GROUP PRESS

Published by Greenleaf Book Group Press
Austin, Texas
www.gbgpress.com

Distributed by Greenleaf Book Group LLC

For ordering information or special discounts for bulk purchases, please contact Greenleaf Book Group LLC at PO Box 91869, Austin, TX 78709, 512.891.6100.

Design and composition by Greenleaf Book Group LLC
Cover design by Greenleaf Book Group LLC

Cataloging-in-Publication data (prepared by The Donohue Group, Inc.)

Ward, Phil, 1947-

Those who dare / Phil Ward. -- 1st ed.

p. ; cm.

ISBN: 978-1-60832-040-0

1. World War, 1939-1945--Campaigns--Western Front--Fiction. 2. Soldiers--United States--Fiction. 3. Special forces (Military science)--Great Britain--Fiction. 4. Special operations (Military science)--Fiction. 5. War stories, American. I. Title.

PS3623.A7342 T45 2010

813/.6   2010920421

Part of the Tree Neutral™ program, which offsets the number of trees consumed in the production and printing of this book by taking proactive steps, such as planting trees in direct proportion to the number of trees used: www.treeneutral.com

TreeNeutral

Printed in the United States of America on acid-free paper

10 11 12 13 14 15   10 9 8 7 6 5 4 3 2 1

First Edition

Abbreviations:
Orders and Awards

Bt—Baronet
CB—Companion of the Bath
CMG—Companion of the Order of St. Michael & St. George
DFC—Distinguished Flying Cross (Royal Air Force)
DSC—Distinguished Service Cross (Royal Navy)
DSO—Distinguished Service Order
GCB—Grand Cross in the Order of the Bath
KCVO—Knight Commander of the Royal Victorian Order
MC—Military Cross
MVO—Member of the Royal Victorian Order
OBE—Order of the Empire
VC—Victoria Cross

SPARTANS

PROLOGUE

24 May 1940
Calais, France

LIEUTENANT JOHN RANDAL, AN AMERICAN VOLUNTEER SERVING IN the British Army, stood on the deck of the S.S. *City of Canterbury* as the ship pulled into the empty war-ravaged port of Calais and prepared to dock. Surveying the wild scene before him, while keeping one eye cocked on the sky to track the Heinkel 111 bomber that had already made one attack run on the ship, he was wondering what he had gotten himself into.

The port city was in flames. Tall plumes of smoke rose from all points around the city. To the west, oil tanks were on fire, casting a cloud of black smoke that draped over the town like a shroud. Artillery fire or bombs had damaged nearly every building.

On the dock a full-scale riot was taking place. A rabble of mutinous French soldiers were in open revolt as they attempted to force their way to the head of the queue, desperate to board the *Canterbury* for her return trip to the UK and safety. A thin khaki line of determined-looking Royal Marines held back the mob with bayonets fixed on the business end of their Lee-Enfield rifles. "One riot, one Ranger, eh, Lieutenant?" the ship's first officer observed sardonically, making reference to his passenger's regiment, the Rangers, as Lieutenant Randal prepared to make his way ashore armed only with a regulation swagger stick.

"You sailors read a lot of Westerns?"

"Skipper has a sea chest full of the bloody things."

The mayhem grew as the *Canterbury* slipped into her berth and began lowering the gangplank. Her escort, the destroyer HMS *Wessex*, began laying down a pattern of depth charges just outside the entrance to the harbor, providing rear security. The speckled, blue-gray Heinkel 111 thundered over again, dropping a string of bombs off the starboard stern quarter of the *Canterbury*. The tremendous detonations sent white-topped geysers of dirty green seawater seventy-five feet into the air.

Lieutenant Randal watched the bomber roar past, regretting that he did not have so much as a pistol to shoot back.

Machine gunners from the Rifle Brigade, stationed on board for just such a contingency, were blazing away at the bomber. The Green Jackets, as members of the Rifle Brigade were often called, propped their Lewis guns on steel drums, the ship's railings, or any other solid object that might serve as an expedient antiaircraft mount. Tracers crisscrossed the sky while hot brass danced across the steel deck. The Green Jackets did not hit a thing.

Down on the dock, a column of stretcher bearers carried up wounded soldiers to be loaded aboard for the short trip across the English Channel. Behind them, a tidal wave of panic-stricken civilian refugees and demoralized troops from a mishmash of routed allied units flooded the streets, making for the dock. The fleeing refugees and retreating soldiers were running out of real estate, and they were frantic to find any means to evade the German panzer juggernaut bearing down on Calais.

A boat was the only hope left, and the *Canterbury* was the only ship in the harbor. "The natives definitely look restless," the first officer opined. "Enough of the blighters headed for us to swamp a bloody aircraft carrier."

"Run many 'repelling boarders' drills?" Lieutenant Randal inquired, flicking his cigarette over the rail, never taking his eyes off the rapidly swelling mob.

"Negative. How do you suppose those blokes will take it when they find out this ship is under strict sailing orders not to allow anyone on board except the wounded?"

"Hope the Marines don't take ten."

Intermittent long-range artillery shells started coming in and exploding randomly. When the shelling began, the French stevedores on the dock quickly determined that their services would be put to best use elsewhere, and they decamped, making the business of unloading the ship a challenge. The Heinkel 111 came back around to make another run. Outside the harbor the *Wessex* exploded, broke in half, and started to sink.

Meanwhile, the casualties on the stretchers stoically smoked cigarettes, ignoring the pandemonium swirling around them, and tried to avoid looking at the bodies that had been stacked on the dock in a neat row and covered with greenish-gray cargo packing tarps.

Making his way down the gangplank, Lieutenant Randal glanced back across the Channel. He could actually see the faint white cliffs of Dover.

The first officer called out, "Good luck, Yank."

Lieutenant John Randal had been assigned as a replacement officer to the King's Royal Rifle Corps, a regiment of the line that was in fact a battalion, frequently called the 60th Rifles. The KRRC was the parent unit of his territorial regiment, the Rangers. They were assigned to 30 Brigade, which also contained the Queen Victoria's Rifles, the Rifle Brigade, and the Third Royal Tank Regiment—and that was the sum total of all he knew about the current military situation in Calais except for what he could see.

By any measure, the circumstances Lieutenant Randal found himself in on his first day in France could accurately be described, as it was to him by the harried brigade major he reported to, standing at the foot of the gangplank, as a "sticky wicket." The 30 Brigade officer briefed him right there amid the bedlam on the dock. He did not mince words.

"Lieutenant Randal, you are to take command of a combined detach-ment of two twenty-man scout platoons—one each from the Rifle Bri-gade and the 60th Rifles—plus a five-man signals detachment of Royal Marines. Your mission, in short, is to screen the right flank of the approach to Calais.

"Here is the situation," he continued. "The Germans are driving hard on the port city with two divisions, the First and Tenth Panzers, supported by five squadrons of Stuka dive-bombers acting as aerial artil-lery. The panzers have raced two hundred fifty miles across France in a lightning advance, and they're closing fast on the roughly four hundred fifty thousand British, French, and Belgian troops who have fallen back on the coastal town of Dunkirk, thirty miles away to the east, in hopes of being evacuated by the Royal Navy. All the Germans have to do now is cut their way through 30 Brigade here at Calais, make a right hook to get at Dunkirk, and it is war over.

"When Calais falls, the fate of the British Expeditionary Force men not already rescued from Dunkirk will be sealed.

"Initially, 30 Brigade was ordered to re-embark and return home, then that order was countermanded, and we have now been ordered to dig in and hold here at Calais to prevent the Germans from getting through to Dunkirk. Our task is to buy time for the forces trapped there in order for them to be sealifted back to the UK. We are to be the Spartans to the BEF.

"Buy us as much time you can out there, Lieutenant. Every minute is precious. I do not care how you go about it. Shoot from behind trees, that sort of thing. You Americans are good at that, what? Anything you do will be a great help."

Considering that the Spartans had died to the last man, it was not what Lieutenant Randal considered an auspicious analogy to use in describing his new combat command. But one thing came across loud and clear—the troops at Calais were expendable.

Given the mad way the British Army had of designating their units with the free use of the words "corps," "brigade," and "regiment," it would have been perfectly understandable for the German commander to have the impression he was going up against a formidable fighting force at Calais. The truth was, give or take a few men, it was defended by approximately three thousand fighting men of a decidedly mixed lot, the Rifle Brigade and the King's Royal Rifle Corps being two of the finest regiments in the army.

In the Wehrmacht a panzer corps was exactly what it said it was—thirty thousand men plus—and one of Germany's toughest, XIX Panzer Korps, was storming in full blitzkrieg straight toward Calais.

Spartans, hell, thought Lieutenant Randal as he headed off to locate his new command.

Lieutenant John Randal found his men on the outskirts of the bombed-out town. The troops were clearly not thrilled when they learned they were to be assigned an unknown officer of uncertain ability, and a Yank to boot, though in the 60th Rifles it was a tradition to have Americans serving. The men would have much rather been back with their regiments under their old trusted platoon commanders who had unceremoniously been pulled out, along with most of the senior noncommissioned officers, and reassigned elsewhere.

A quick survey of his command revealed that the men had rifles, a scattering of revolvers, no transport, very little ammunition, and one day's rations. Mortars had all been discarded because not one unit in 30 Brigade had anything but smoke rounds for them, and no one could think of any good reason to be firing smoke at German tanks.

Between the two Green Jacket platoons there were a total of six corporals and one baby-blue-eyed King's Royal Rifle Corps sergeant, Mike "March or Die" Mikkalis, who looked as hard as you might expect of a man who had acquired his moniker during a previous tour in the French Foreign Legion. The signals detail was in the charge of Corporal Mickey Duggan, Royal Marines. All told, there were forty-five men.

Wasting no time, Lieutenant Randal assembled the troops, and taking note that the mood was ugly, said casually, "Well, men, I guess you're wondering why I called you here today."

Behind him in the distance a mottle-camouflaged Messerschmitt 109 raced low down the road at treetop level, strafing the hardball—red tracers ricocheting off the asphalt—while a salvo of six artillery rounds screamed overhead and slammed into the burning town. The troops cut their eyes at each other in disbelief at the lieutenant's opening remark, and there were a few faint snickers of laughter—the first any of them had heard since landing in country.

"Our mission is to screen the right flank of the Calais defense zone." Lieutenant Randal cut straight to it, all business now. "We will be operating against the Tenth Panzers. To accomplish that mission our only tactical option is to take up positions far enough out that we can trade space for time."

The Riflemen and Marines sat in a semicircle staring holes through their new commander. They did not like the sound of the assignment. Every man present was a prewar professional soldier, and they all had an idea of what it meant for them.

Unfazed by the open hostility, Lieutenant Randal continued, "I spent the last two years chasing Huk bandits in the Philippine jungles. My plan is for us to operate like guerrillas. There was a legendary American general called the Swamp Fox who specialized in irregular tactics. He thought it was a good idea to run away to fight again another day. We'll call this lash-up Swamp Fox Force. We're going to hit and run."

The men muttered among themselves, but there was a noticeable reduction of tension in their mood. "Maybe the Yank knows his stuff," Lieutenant Randal overheard one of them comment hopefully.

"One can only wonder, mate. 'E don't look like all that much to me."

"'Ow do you trade space for time?" a troubled cockney voice inquired. "Sounds like one of 'em standard IQ questions."

"Fire and fall back, you idiot," Sergeant Mikkalis snarled. "Silence in the ranks."

"Take charge of Swamp Fox Force, Sergeant," Lieutenant Randal commanded, paying no attention to the chatter. "Send a party to the dock to appropriate all weapons and ammunition from any troops re-embarking to go back to the UK."

"All, sir?"

"All the ammunition. We won't need many extra Enfields, but don't let a single Boys antitank rifle, Bren gun, machine gun, or radio of any kind board the *Canterbury*. I want all the grenades and any explosives you come across."

"Sir!"

"Send another party into town to appropriate rations. I suspect you can forget about going through proper military channels. Send everyone else out to commandeer motor transport. We'll need motorcycles for every man who can ride one; seize any lorry or civilian vehicle that looks like it might be useful. Scrounge as much fuel as it's possible for us to carry with us."

"People are not going to like it, sir."

"Don't take no for an answer. There's no reason to be overly polite—if any foreign military or civilian attempts to interfere, shoot 'em."

"Sir!" barked Sergeant Mikkalis with a gleam in his strange pale eyes. He had no idea if the new officer knew his job or not. He rather doubted it, but like all military men, he dearly loved to be given assignments with the words "appropriate," "commandeer," and "seize" in them. As icing on the cake, the men of Swamp Fox Force had been authorized to shoot to kill in the performance of their duties, and Lieutenant Randal had said it as though he meant it.

The troops perked up. For the first time since arriving in France, they had been given clear, concise orders and a plan they could understand: one that fit the capabilities of the Rifle Brigade, the 60th Rifles, and the Royal Marines down to the ground.

"Assemble in one hour behind the sand dunes just south of here. I'll be there making a map reconnaissance."

Lieutenant Randal wisely elected not to mention anything about Spartans.

When the men trickled back from Calais, where they had executed their orders with a vengeance, they were in a higher state of morale. The simple act of doing something rather than sitting around waiting for the unknown had had a good effect.

Lieutenant John Randal assembled the troops, and with two Marines holding the map up for the rest to see, he used his swagger stick as a pointer to give a detailed briefing on the area in which they would operate.

"Our mission is to buy time. We're going to accomplish that mission by attacking, inflicting casualties, and then immediately disengaging. Our objective will be to shoot bad guys from concealment, break contact, move out rapidly, find another concealed position, and shoot more. Under no circumstances will we ever stand and fight.

"We're going to break Swamp Fox Force down into six teams, each with a designated sniper and led by a corporal. Sergeant Mikkalis, make it happen. Have the automatic rifles and machine guns evenly distributed."

"Sir!"

"I'm planning to go kill some Germans," Lieutenant Randal concluded, studying the semicircle of Riflemen and Marines coolly. "Any of you men who want to can come with me. Those who don't are released back to your units."

The announcement caught the troops off guard. The British Army was not known for being a democracy, especially in the middle of a battle it was in the process of losing. There was a long, uncomfortable silence, and then three of the men stood up and trudged back toward Calais.

"'E's bloody crazy—Yank's lost his ruddy marbles," one departing soldier commented to two others, loud enough for the assembled group to hear. "Calais ain't the bleedin' jungle."

"Anybody else?" Lieutenant Randal demanded; no one moved. "All right then; saddle up and prepare to move out."

As the remaining men shook out their equipment, Sergeant Mike "March or Die" Mikkalis came up to Lieutenant Randal and handed him a Browning P-35 pistol with a lanyard attached and a tan leather pouch containing two spare magazines. "Thought the lieutenant might like a weapon. Took this off a Belgian officer wearing enough gold braid to be an admiral. He ran off before I could get the holster to go with it, sir."

Pulling the lanyard over his neck, Lieutenant Randal racked back the slide of the pistol to chamber a 9-mm round, then carefully lowered the hammer and tucked the weapon into his leather belt.

The former legionnaire carefully took in every detail of how his new officer handled the Browning. Sergeant Mikkalis knew you did not handle a pistol the way the lieutenant did without years of practice. "Brand-new, sir, never been fired, only dropped once," he said.

"Thanks, Sergeant. Now, if you'll pick out an Enfield rifle for me, I'll feel fully dressed."

"I would be delighted, sir."

In the sergeant's professional military opinion, the Rangers officer had pulled off a neat piece of soldiering. In a little over an hour, the lieutenant had managed to take a mixed lot of leaderless, dispirited troops and transform them into volunteers for a hazardous mission. Sergeant Mikkalis had never seen it done any better.

"Alright, listen up," Lieutenant Randal ordered the men of Swamp Fox Force, moments before they departed the assembly area. "Keep in mind, a panzer division is not the solid phalanx of armor it appears to be when you see it drawn on a situation map. Lightly armed reconnaissance troops of motorcycle scouts, sometimes accompanied by armored cars, travel out in front of the main force. Behind them come light tanks, followed by heavier tanks with mechanized panzergrenadiers interspersed throughout the column to provide rapid infantry support.

"We're going to force the tank units to stop and deploy the panzergrenadiers as often as possible. Dismounting a tank to check out a threat or deploying the accompanying mechanized infantry to conduct a road sweep takes up time and fatigues the troops—especially if they take casualties while doing it. And, we're going to make sure they do.

"I want you to shoot down the motorcyclists and dismounted infantry from as long a range as possible. Use the Boys rifles to engage the armored cars and thin-skinned vehicles. Don't bother shooting them at the panzers. No matter what they told you in training, the .55-caliber antitank rounds will only bounce off. However, the Boys are sure death to any command car, troop transport, or truck at up to a mile."

The German Mark III tanks posed a serious challenge. Swamp Fox Force did not have any weapons able to knock one out at standoff range.

"We can't kill a tank, but you snipers are going to go after the tank commanders. If the Germans are ever stupid enough to carry fuel cans strapped to the outside of the tanks, you Boys gunners can go for those.

"To get stationary targets, we're going to bury steel helmets in the road, make them look like antitank mines. The tankers won't be able to ignore 'em. When the column stops to investigate, you snipers take out the tank commanders standing in the turrets. The rest of you men, engage the troops on the ground with the automatic rifles and machine guns. We fire 'em up, break contact, pull out, and start all over again.

"Any questions?" Lieutenant Randal wrapped up his briefing. "All right then; let's go do it."

Two hours after receiving the designation "Swamp Fox Force," a forty-six-man gypsy caravan bristling with assorted weapons and trucks of British, French, and Belgian manufacture pulled out of the sand dunes and headed west, embarking on a vicious little private war where no quarter would be asked or given.

Swamp Fox Force moved directly into the attack, struck unannounced, hit as hard as it could, then disengaged quickly and departed the area at a high rate of speed to a preplanned fallback position. At the designated rally point, Lieutenant John Randal's men gathered around while he briefed them for their next mission over a 1:50,000 contour map and sketched out a new scheme of maneuver in the dirt with a borrowed bayonet.

Lieutenant Randal had a natural aptitude for tactics, a gift recognized in his first year of ROTC and later improved on at the U.S. Cavalry School. In the Philippines, while serving in the 26th Calvary Regiment, he had been carefully tutored by two long-service master sergeants who, appreciating his talent, had expended the time and effort to put the final polish on those tactical skills teaching him how to "out-guerilla" the elusive Huk bandits. Now he simply married up his cavalry training with those guerrilla tactics. The combination was deadly.

The trick, Lieutenant Randal knew, was to find a way to pit his troop's strengths against the enemy's weakness. Swamp Fox Force's strengths were surprise, speed, and violence of action. The Germans' weakness was their predictability.

The Tenth Panzer Division was essentially road bound. The Calais area was laced with canals and soft marshy ground that channeled the approach to the city. The terrain and the fact that the Germans were driving on Calais as straight as an arrow made it easy for Lieutenant Randal to anticipate their moves. He assigned a sniper or Boys antitank rifle team to contest every crossing where the sunken roads intersected the channels.

Had the Swamp Fox Force had any demolitions to blow the small bridges spanning the canals, they could have halted the German column or at least seriously slowed it down. As it was, Swamp Fox Force was little more than a speed bump to the mighty Tenth Panzers.

At night the Germans laagered, making inviting targets. Lieutenant Randal organized teams of his men, one of which he led personally, to infiltrate the laagers and attack the tanks with improvised Molotov cocktail firebombs.

"Takes a brave bloke to crawl into an enemy position in the dark and strike a match, sir," one Rifleman remarked upon hearing the orders.

"Anyone else want to say something stupid?" Sergeant Mikkalis growled.

Lieutenant Randal knew that the Tenth Panzer Division's only real vulnerability was its tail. The Germans had an armored tip of tanks on their columns, immediately followed up by a stream of hundreds of thin-skinned vehicles, mostly trucks, transporting all the fuel, fitters, and supplies necessary to maintain a tank force in the attack. Following behind the trucks, the next echelon of transport, to Swamp Fox Force's surprise, turned out to be horse drawn, even in a modern panzer division. Horses were soft targets.

"A tank outfit is like a spear," Lieutenant Randal explained as he drew a diagram of a long lance in the dirt with another borrowed bayonet. "All the steel is up here, on the point.

"What we're going to do is leave one element here under Sergeant Mikkalis to harass the spearhead while the rest of us swing wide behind it and do our best to shoot the wooden shaft clean off."

Immediately upon conclusion of the briefing, Lieutenant Randal, with half of his men, set out on a long-range deep-penetration raid to attack the fifteen-mile-long supply train traveling along behind the Tenth Panzers. Mounted on the Norton model 16H motorcycles Swamp Fox Force had appropriated in Calais, they cut around far to the rear of the armored tip of the column, arriving unannounced and unexpected in the division's soft, unprotected caravan.

The motorcycle raiders shot up whatever they happened across: bivouac areas, mess tents, truck convoys, POL stations, canteens, horse-drawn wagons, artillery caissons, motor parks, water distribution points, latrines—anything of military value. The Swamp Fox Force's targets of choice were the five-ton fuel tankers that blew up with a satisfying orange mushroom fireball when strafed with tracers. The guerrilla fighters would appear out of nowhere, strike fiercely with guns blazing, and then tear away on their Nortons, leaving a trail of death and destruction in their wake.

Lieutenant Randal's private little war was to hit and run, cavalry style—irregular warfare at its very best. His troops kept banging away at the enemy lines of communication long into the night and throughout the next day. The rear-area raids were devastatingly successful.

Although the Swamp Fox Force attacks were not much more than a minor annoyance to the Nazis, the raiders had nevertheless destroyed a few tanks, more than a few trucks, a fair number of horses, and enough troops to have the Germans glancing over their shoulders. The victorious storm troopers of the panzer divisions had been looking forward to wrapping up the campaign, going home, pinning on their medals to impress the *Fräuleins*, and enjoying the perks lavished on combat veterans by a grateful Third Reich. Not one of them wanted to get killed at the very end of the most brilliant blitzkrieg in modern history.

The Tenth Panzer Division began to proceed with uncharacteristic caution. Understandably, the division had already begun to lose some steam, even without the harassment dished out by Swamp Fox Force. The German vehicles were at the point where they needed to take a pause to conduct a major refit. Two hundred fifty miles is about as far as an armored force can advance before hitting a maintenance wall.

The German High Command's reaction to Swamp Fox Force was swift. The order came down: "Speed up the advance. Shoot anyone who impedes progress. Do not take prisoners."

ME-109 fighters flying at treetop level attacked first, firing their machine guns indiscriminately into the columns of civilian bumper-to-bumper traffic clogging the few avenues leading into Calais. The wrecked civilian vehicles blocked the roads.

Next, gull-winged Junkers-87 (JU-87) Stukas, circling above like rabid bats, dive-bombed the massive traffic jams created at those choke points. Then JU-88s, operating in the role of high-level saturation bombers, zeroed in on the tall pillars of smoke caused by the dive-bombing, cruised over, and toggled their heavy bomb loads indiscriminately into the trapped masses of helpless civilians.

On the ground, elements of the Tenth Panzer Division rolled up as soon as the bombing stopped and machine-gunned anything not wearing a swastika. A wholesale massacre was taking place. Men, women, children, horses, cows, goats, pigs, chickens, dogs, and cats littered the roads. The civilians were dying in the tens of thousands. The western approach to Calais became a highway of death.

At night the Luftwaffe dropped parachute flares over the roads to allow the strafing, bombing, and machine-gunning to continue the slaughter without letup. Survivors of the onslaught lay screaming, hideously mutilated with appalling injuries. In the hot sun they suffered terribly and died badly. Terrified men, hysterical women, and traumatized children milled around in dazed confusion.

In the midst of this butchery, the remnants of the battle-tested Swamp Fox Force assembled in a small, isolated copse of elm trees. They had been fighting all day.

Lieutenant John Randal rapidly issued new orders. Concerned that the men might have started to become overconfident after their recent successes, he casually mentioned, "One of the Huks we captured bragged, 'It's hard to kill a mosquito with a sledgehammer.'"

"Bloody cheeky," growled Royal Marine Corporal Mickey Duggan as he crammed fresh ammo into a Bren magazine. "But as we've been demonstratin,' the bandit 'ad a point. What did you 'ave to say, sir?"

"Not if you hit him with it."

The German Army swung a giant sledgehammer, and although they did not hit the mosquito, they smashed everything else.

Pressure can crush a stone or turn it into a diamond. Swamp Fox Force was down to fewer than twenty effectives. They were dangerous men.

On the morning of 29 May 1940, the word came through to try to escape if they could after completing one last task; it was to be every man for himself. The officer commanding 30 Brigade, Brigadier Claude Nicholson, was preparing to surrender the garrison to put an end to the slaughter. Calais was done for.

Incredibly, the lightly armed 30 Brigade, with help from a hard-fighting Swamp Fox Force, had held up the First and Tenth Panzer Divisions for four priceless days. Because of their sacrifice, the evacuation of Dunkirk was assured. The Riflemen fought like cornered lions. Virtually every man had been killed, was wounded, or would soon be captured.

Lieutenant John Randal received orders to blow a humpbacked bridge over the last major canal west of Calais before escaping. A sapper sergeant arrived in a truck loaded with the first explosives they had seen. It took three hours for the sergeant in the Royal Engineers to place the guncotton demolition charges.

At that point, Swamp Fox Force attempted to halt the flow of refugees streaming over the bridge. They could not make them stop. First, shots were fired into the air, and then the few remaining Swamp Fox Force fired at the refugees' feet, even wounding a few. Nothing worked. On they came: a press of old men and elderly women, mothers with small babies, families fleeing together, French and Belgian soldiers in uniform who had thrown their weapons away, and military-aged men of indeterminate origin with short haircuts in civilian clothes. The crush of desperate people stampeded, forcing their way over to safety, even though there was no safety to be had. No boats were waiting for them, and none were coming.

Stukas arrived and began strafing the fleeing column. German Mark III tanks advanced on the bridge, indiscriminately firing their cupola-mounted coaxial machine guns into the packed crowd, chopping people down. Pandemonium broke out.

The beleaguered sapper sergeant appealed to the Swamp Fox Force commander. "What am I to do, sir? I was bloody well never trained for anything like this!"

"Blow it."

"I bloody wired it. You bloody want it blown, you bloody do it, sir!"

Lieutenant Randal twisted the charging handle immediately. The bridge erupted in black smoke as the string of charges popped in rapid succession, dropping the structure, still jam-packed with screaming people, into the canal with an impressive splash. Even for the battle-hardened veterans it was a horrific sight.

Rounding up his surviving troops, Lieutenant Randal headed for the coast. When they reached the beach at dusk, they turned and drove straight toward Calais. An oily cloud of smoke obscured the city. Every building seemed to be burning. A lazy string of JU-87 Stukas curled in, releasing their ordnance, one bomb after the other, rolling into their attack run with their dive sirens wailing. Artillery rounds were falling sporadically and panzers were randomly firing their main guns into the town. Every German soldier with access to a mortar was stonking rounds downrange as fast as he could drop them down the tube. Calais was coming apart at the seams.

Just outside of town, as night began to fall, the Swamp Fox remnant abandoned what was left of their vehicles and patrolled on foot to the dock in a tactical file formation, with Lieutenant Randal pulling point. Dangling from his neck was a pair of Zeiss binoculars he had taken off a dead Nazi colonel. A Luger P.08 and a Walther P-38 were crisscrossed on their black leather belts across his chest, and an MP-38 machine pistol on a strap was hanging, muzzle down, from his right shoulder. The Browning P-35 that Sergeant Mike "March or Die" Mikkalis had given him was on its lanyard, stuck into his belt. German stick grenades were tucked into every pocket.

The Swamp Fox Force commander was unrecognizable as the young King's Royal Rifle Corps replacement lieutenant who had strolled off the *Canterbury*, swagger stick in hand, only four days earlier. It would not have been possible to guess his age within ten years.

The night was pitch dark as the men approached the dock. No ships were visible in the harbor, and the dock was being swept sporadically by searching machine-gun fire. The odd artillery or mortar round plopped into the bay. As they made their stealthy approach march, Lieutenant Randal ordered his men to tear down a wooden fence.

"I want every man to carry the largest plank he can."

In the dark they reached the west side of the dock, moved down under it, and waded their way out to the very end, where they found about forty men from assorted 30 Brigade units hiding. Corporal Mickey Duggan, the last surviving Royal Marine in Swamp Fox Force, shone his flashlight to seaward and began to signal.

To everyone's great surprise, a response came back right away. The Royal Marine and the unknown light blinked back and forth for a time. "Sir, I am in contact with the armed yacht *Gulzar*," Corporal Duggan said. "She is willing to come in to try and pick us up, but the skipper says he is not going to come to a stop. He wants us to climb up on top of the dock and jump aboard as he sails past the end of the pier."

"Signal 'can do.'"

Each man dropped the plank he was carrying, and with some of the other men who elected to come with them, climbed up the wet, slimy, barnacle-encrusted wooden pilings, struggled up onto the dock, and lay prone, hoping to avoid the intermittent bursts from the German machine guns. They did not have long to wait.

HMY *Gulzar*'s skipper was a master mariner. True to his word, he brought the yacht in close, slow and steady, braving the automatic weapons, the artillery, the mortars, and the unknown. Forty-seven men made the leap. They were the last evaders from 30 Brigade to make it out of Calais.

Lieutenant John Randal slept the whole way back to Dover.

SMALL-SCALE RAIDING

1

COMMANDOS

LIEUTENANT JOHN RANDAL DISEMBARKED AT DOVER TO FIND A mob scene of returning soldiers from Dunkirk at the dock that was almost as chaotic as he had found in Calais the first day he landed—the only difference was, nothing was actually blowing up.

While he had been in France, the famous American radio war correspondent for CBS, William Shirer, had reported live from London that, in his opinion, the Germans would storm the British Isles within three weeks. U.S. Ambassador Joseph P. Kennedy cabled his boss, President Franklin D. Roosevelt, that he concurred with the CBS time estimate and was highly skeptical of Great Britain's chances of survival. Invasion fear was gripping the nation. The British were being bombed, blacked-out, and rationed. Times were ominous: All the news was bad, and even the most optimistic description of the military situation was bleak.

Since no one was expecting him, Lieutenant Randal released the survivors of Swamp Fox Force back to their units and flagged down a Tilly with staff markings. "Take me to the station," he told the corporal behind the wheel. "I can grab a train from there."

The next morning at 9th Battalion "Rangers" King's Royal Rifle Corps headquarters, Lieutenant Randal was debriefed and sent on a two-day leave. When he returned, there was a message instructing him to contact a certain Lieutenant Stone at MO-9. It was marked EXPEDITE.

Lieutenant Randal read the cryptic note several times. He asked a battalion clerk, "Any idea what 'MO-9' is?"

The clerk frowned. "No, sir, I can't say as I know." He picked up a phone and dialed the number written on the message.

"MO-9, Captain Niven."

"This is Lieutenant Randal. I've got a message that says I'm supposed to call a Lieutenant Stone."

"No, sorry, Lieutenant Stone is out of the office at the moment. But stay where you are and a car will come round to collect you shortly."

"Roger that, sir." Lieutenant Randal hung up the phone thinking Captain Niven's voice sounded vaguely familiar.

The car arrived within the half hour, driven by a cheerful WAAF who seemed eager to please but who, like everyone else, had no clue what MO-9 was. When they pulled up in front of the gray stone building, the WAAF handed him a slip with a room number written on it. Lieutenant Randal located the place, which turned out to be a spacious three-room suite where men and women, in both uniform and mufti, were constantly coming and going. He found somebody who pointed out Captain Niven, and he immediately realized why the voice on the phone was so familiar: This was David Niven *the actor*.

"Lieutenant Randal, sir," he said, saluting.

The mustached captain returned his salute. "Oh, yes, you must be the American chap. You're here for Stone?"

"Yes, sir."

The phone on the desk rang; the captain turned and picked it up. "MO-9. Captain Niven? No, sorry, he's not here at the moment. Can I have him call you?" Captain Niven flashed a smile and a wink at Lieutenant Randal. Whatever MO-9 was, it seemed anything could happen here. Lieutenant Randal clicked on.

Captain Niven jotted down a name and a number and replaced the phone in its cradle. "Right, then. Come along, Lieutenant; I'll take you to Stone. He's expecting you."

"I wasn't aware you were in England, sir," Lieutenant Randal said as they walked.

"Oh, absolutely. Hollywood was becoming rather a bore, don't you know? When the shooting started, I wanted to go back to my old outfit, the Highland Light Infantry, but they were still peeved at me for resigning my commission to become an actor. Imagine! So I went into the Rifle Brigade instead. I'm on temporary assignment as liaison between MO-9 and a new raiding group we're putting together."

"Knowing the Green Jackets, I'm sure they would say you traded up, sir."

Captain Niven laughed. "Quite so, Lieutenant, quite so! Now, here's Stone. If you'll take my advice, believe about half what he tells you—and less than that if it involves women."

"I'll keep that in mind, sir."

Lieutenant Terry Stone had a phone to his ear. "Lieutenant Stone? No, sorry, he's out at the moment. Have him call you back, first thing."

The officer stood up and stuck out his hand. "Lieutenant Randal? Good to meet you at last."

The American shook Lieutenant Stone's hand, wondering, for a moment, if "Terry Stone" was a cover name: The tall officer, wearing the insignia of the swanky 2nd Life Guards Cavalry Regiment, was a dead ringer for the swashbuckling Errol Flynn.

"You wanted to meet me?"

"After that show you put on outside Calais? Everyone around here wants to meet you."

"I see."

Lieutenant Stone gave him a broad smile. "How'd you like another crack at Jerry, old stick?"

"What might you have in mind?"

"My boss will explain it to you over lunch today at White's. Can you fit it into your schedule?"

"Do I have a choice?"

"Well, actually . . . no."

In the car, Lieutenant Terry Stone produced a beautiful sterling silver cigarette case with the regimental crest of the Life Guards on it. He offered a

Player's Navy Cut, and Lieutenant Randal accepted, pulling out his battered, much traveled Zippo lighter with the gold crossed sabers of the U.S. 26th Cavalry Regiment on the front. He lit his smoke, then Lieutenant Stone's.

"Nice lighter," the Life Guards officer said.

"Function is beauty."

"Quaint notion, that."

Lieutenant Stone gave him a quick background briefing on the officer they would be having lunch with, Lieutenant Colonel Dudley Clarke.

"The thing to keep in mind is that the colonel might best be described as a mildly eccentric military genius of the first water. He has one of the best minds in the army, even if he is a 'cannon cocker.' He's also something of a practicing wild man. I accompanied him to Norway, and it was one cliff-hanging adventure after another—I do not exaggerate. We invaded the country all by ourselves in a little rubber dinghy cast out of a seaplane . . . but alas, that's a story for another time, don't you know. Makes one exhausted simply thinking back on it.

"Colonel Clarke was serving as the military assistant to Field Marshal Sir John Dill, the chief of the Imperial General Staff, when he dreamed up the idea to form a raiding organization to carry out amphibious raids on the French coast. Clarke was born in the Transvaal, so naturally he was inspired by the Boer commandos. In fact, that's exactly what the colonel has named his new force—Commandos. He told the field marshal his idea, Sir John mentioned it to the prime minister later that same evening, and the plan was approved the very next day. Mr. Churchill wants to raise five thousand aggressive men of the hunter class to fall on the Germans like, as he so colorfully puts it, 'leopards.'"

"Leopards?"

"Well, it's Churchill, don't you know. He has a certain style, what? Anyway, MO-9 has been created to coordinate raiding operations. Sound like something that might be of some interest to you, John?"

"You have my attention."

"Excellent. I think you are going to enjoy the colonel. He's a funny old bat, terrific to be around—but a rapier wit at the same time. Lately, he's been engaged in a running battle with the War Office to be allowed to wear the South African Service Ribbon. Claims he qualifies because he was in theater during the Boer War. Would've been a year old at the time, I believe."

"Had any luck?"

Lieutenant Stone shook his head, grinning. "By the way, have you heard the latest news? Hot off the press: Italy has finally come in."

"On our side?"

"In a word—no."

When they arrived at White's, the elderly hall porter informed them, "Colonel Clarke is waiting for you in the small side room."

"Thanks, Groom. I know the way," Lieutenant Stone said.

Lieutenant Colonel Clarke was wearing a pair of Royal Flying Corps pilot's wings prominently on his blouse. Lieutenant Randal knew there was a regulation prohibiting the wearing of RFC wings on an Army uniform. Apparently, the colonel didn't concern himself with rules he didn't care for; he made his own.

"Somewhat belatedly, Lieutenant Randal, I found myself assigned staff responsibility for the Calais operation," he said while still shaking hands, "and that is how your name first came to my attention.

"I drafted the text of the last 'no withdrawal' message to Brigadier Nicholson of 30 Brigade prior to its surrender. Staff had worked up a draft of a plan to order in the Canadian Division and try to hold the place before I came on board, but it all came to naught. What is your opinion? Would sending in another division have done the trick?"

"Nothing was going to stop the First and Tenth Panzers, sir."

"What a catastrophe. The pilot of a photoreconnaissance flight over Calais reported to me privately that the city looked like a holocaust. I doubt I shall ever forget him saying that. Terribly depressing, what?"

"He wasn't exaggerating, sir."

"I suspected as much. Thank you for your candor. Terry, be a good fellow and have Groom send in some sherry, won't you? And now to the business at hand. I trust that Lieutenant Stone has briefed you on the organization we are in the process of putting together. How do our plans to go raiding strike you?"

"Interesting, sir."

"Have you ever fired the Thompson submachine gun?"

"Yes, sir. I served four years in the U.S. 26th Cavalry Regiment. We were issued Thompsons."

"Were you now? Outstanding! I am planning to launch our first Commando strike somewhere in France in the very near future. There are, as it turns out, a whopping grand total of forty Thompson submachine guns, I am told, in the entire army arsenal as we speak, and no one seems to know very much about them. I am to be allowed to take twenty along on the raid. How would you like to instruct my troops in the use of them?"

"I'd like that, sir."

"Marvelous! You stick with Terry until the Thompsons arrive and take the opportunity to learn more about what it is we are attempting to accomplish. The prime minister has just sent out a missive that says he is looking for men of 'force, intelligence, and personality.' I dare say, among the three of us in this room, we have the requisite qualities to make up one complete 'leopard man.'"

Later that afternoon, back at MO-9, Lieutenant Terry Stone gave Lieutenant John Randal a detailed briefing on the proposed operation. The plan for the first Commando raid called for the raiders to strike at four different points along a twenty-mile stretch of the coast above Boulogne. For something that was supposed to be a starter mission, it sounded pretty ambitious.

To disguise the true nature of the operation, the idea was to sail from Ramsgate, Dover, and Folkestone, more or less simultaneously, and have the raiding forces rendezvous in mid-channel in the hope that by sailing in separate groups they would not arouse suspicion and thus tip their hand to the Germans.

"Not that I think we've got big worries on that score," Lieutenant Stone said with a shake of his head. "With France on her back and the British Army still reeling after the retreat from Dunkirk, I'd bloody well wager the last thing the Jerries are concerned about is the British Armed Forces conducting offensive operations anywhere on the continent of Europe."

Planning for the operation was hush-hush to the point of being absurd, prompted in no small measure by widespread paranoia that the Nazi intelligence apparatus was all seeing, all knowing. It all seemed melodramatic to Lieutenant Randal, but then, what could you expect with a movie star as liaison and an unabashedly romantic adventurer in command?

The army troops selected for the initial raid—No. 11 Independent Company, under the command of Major Ronnie Tod, Argyll and Sutherland Highlanders—were stationed on the Isle of Wight and were itching for a way to hit back. The Royal Navy, even though still fully occupied trying to pluck the last of the British forces out of France, reacted to Lieutenant Colonel Dudley Clarke's request to provide transport for the raid with a surprisingly cooperative attitude. The colonel told Lieutenants Stone and Randal that the assistant chief of the Naval Staff of the Admiralty had said, "So, the army wants to get back into the fight already? Best news in days. For that, you can have anything you like from the navy."

The admiral backed up his promise by appointing a real fire-eater, Lieutenant Commander J. W. F. Milner-Gibson, RN, to command the naval forces for the raid. The commander wasted little time; he had himself put ashore in France by small boat nine times to personally reconnoiter the proposed target areas. "You have to give Milner-Gibson credit," Lieutenant Colonel Clarke remarked. "I can't tell if he's a genuine workaholic or simply a man possessed of a death wish."

Pretending to be a war charity committee, the planning syndicate met wearing civilian clothes at a posh Grover Crescent townhouse owned by Lady Jane Seaborn, a wealthy widow who was away from the city.

"Colonel Clarke and Captain Niven are vying with each other for Lady Jane Seaborn's affections," Lieutenant Stone confided. "Without much success, from what I can tell."

"She must be loaded," replied Lieutenant Randall, "or really good-looking.

"In Lady Jane's case, the answer is both, old stick, though I believe the operative phrase one hears most frequently in describing the woman is 'drop-dead gorgeous.'"

2

LEOPARDS IN ACTION

LESS THAN TWENTY-FOUR HOURS AFTER THE OFFICIAL FRENCH surrender in a railway car outside Paris on 23 June 1940, a small raiding flotilla consisting of the 18-knot steam yacht HMY *Jamarna* and seven RAF crash boats set sail. Six of the air-sea rescue launches were commanded and manned by Royal Navy Volunteer Reserve personnel while the seventh, for reasons never fully explained, was crewed by civilian yachtsmen. Seated forward in the lead boat, Lieutenant John Randal pondered what he had gotten himself into. Though well intentioned, the naval preparations for this inaugural Leopard/Commando raid had pretty much been a shambles. You either use military skills or lose the capability, and unfortunately for this Royal Navy enterprise, amphibious operations had not been in vogue in the British military since Gallipoli.

It was well understood that flat-bottomed landing craft were necessary to place troops on a hostile foreign beach; there were none to be had. Lieutenant Commander J. W. F. Milner-Gibson was finally forced, as a last resort, to suffer the indignity of borrowing seven air-sea rescue crash boats from the Royal Air Force, of all places. Each launch was capable of carrying thirty fully armed raiders.

On board were the troops of No. 11 Independent Company, temporarily designated No. 11 Commando for this operation, under the command of Major Ronnie Tod. The troops were armed with exactly half the Thompson submachine guns in all of England.

Lieutenant Randal had thought Lieutenant Colonel Dudley Clarke was joking when he first told him there were only forty Thompsons in the entire country. If any self-respecting Axis spy had learned that startling piece of intelligence, he would probably not have reported it. In fact, no military observer from any industrialized nation would have believed it, considering that most South American banana republics had more automatic weapons than the Imperial Forces had at that moment. The mob in Chicago sure did.

When the Auto-Ordnance Corporation offered to sell its weapons to the British military prior to the war, the idea had been rejected outright on the grounds that "gentlemen do not arm themselves with weapons best suited for gangsters."

Due to a series of delays, the twenty Thompson submachine guns had arrived just before the mission launched. The weapons training program had been short and to the point. Lieutenant Randal demonstrated how to load loose rounds into the magazines, how to fit the magazines into the weapon, how to work the charging handle, and how to find the location of the safety and the magazine release. Not one single round was fired in practice before the "leopards" set sail.

The Operations Order called for RAF twin-engine bombers to buzz the four beaches where the Commandos would be coming ashore, to drown out the noise of the boats during their run in to shore. Lieutenant Randal had serious reservations about the air cover. What did the planners think was going to happen when the bombers buzzed in? His best guess was that the Germans in the vicinity would immediately stand to and man their antiaircraft guns. And they might take time off from their antiaircraft duties occasionally to smoke a cigarette and gaze out to sea. That would not be good; rapid-fire antiaircraft cannons cranked down to point-blank range would have a chilling effect on a small-scale amphibious landing. Sometimes you can over plan a thing.

Buzzing an enemy beach you were getting ready to land on was one of the worst tactical ideas Lieutenant Randal had ever heard.

Commander Milner-Gibson had sailed with the raiding party to act as its master navigator and to guide the main party, carrying in his lead boat, Major Tod, a contingent of No. 11 Commandos, and the three observers: Lieutenant Colonel Dudley Clarke, Lieutenant Terry Stone, and Lieutenant John Randal, who was really starting to regret that he had not spoken up to oppose the buzzing-the-beach part of the plan.

It got worse. Commander Milner-Gibson's compass failed. Despite having reconnoitered this stretch of coast on nine previous nights in search of a suitable landing area, he got it wrong. The main party sailed straight up to the harbor entrance at Boulogne. The commander realized his mistake when the lighthouse keeper, having heard the sound of airplane engines, turned on the light to see what was happening. At that point, Lieutenant Randal was fairly certain he wasn't the only "leopard man" having second thoughts about service in the Commando forces. The main party made a hasty U-turn and beat a retreat.

Meanwhile, instead of flying a combat air patrol high overhead, the RAF's Avro Ansons buzzed in low and tight and continued to zoom around just above the raiding force, doing everything but beaming a bright light on the little flotilla and announcing over a loud hailer, "Here we come." The pilots clearly had never provided air cover for an amphibious landing force before and had no clue how to go about it. Ordered to protect the Commando raiding party, they were determined that nothing was going to happen to those men—not on their watch.

"Now, this is what I call close air support," Lieutenant Stone remarked, tapping a Player's cigarette on his sterling silver cigarette case as one of the twin-engine aircraft blasted so low overhead, he could almost touch its belly. The Commandos ducked instinctively every time one of the planes thundered over.

If Commander Milner-Gibson's face, like that of the raiders, had not been blackened before the mission with charcoal from a burnt cork taken from a champagne bottle and roasted on the point of a bayonet, it would have been purple right now. "Ruddy RAF is giving away the show," he seethed. He was the maddest sailor Lieutenant Randal had seen in his entire life—and that included his time in the Army-Navy Club in Manila.

Lieutenant Stone leaned over and muttered, "I reckon our commander was something on the order of as furious as old M-G the day the first armored car arrived at the 2nd Life Guards to replace our beloved black horses."

The U-turn at Boulogne put the operation well behind schedule, but at long last the air-sea rescue launch carrying the command party slid onto the beach. Sand dunes were visible to the front. Major Tod and his men were up over the side and away in a flash into German-occupied France.

Lieutenant Colonel Clarke was under strict orders not to go ashore— a pretty difficult directive to follow considering that the boat he was in was beached as planned. He and his two lieutenants paced anxiously back and forth on the sand at the water's edge, awaiting developments. There was total silence all up and down the coast. No one was sure where they had landed. The second boat of their party had become separated and failed to land with them. Time dragged by. Originally, the plan allowed for three hours ashore, but the delay caused by the U-turn had cut that down to less than two.

Suddenly, a lookout called, "Aircraft, nine o'clock." In the dark they were unable to identify it, but the shadow of the aircraft's silhouette could be seen offshore, skimming low over the line of breakers behind them. Luckily, the Luftwaffe aircrew—if it was a German plane—did not seem to notice the Commandos. For all they could tell, it could have been part of their own air cover looking for something else to buzz.

Lieutenant Randal swung his Zeiss binoculars out to sea and thought he spotted the missing RAF crash boat. When he pointed it out, Commander Milner-Gibson barked, "Bloody E-boat, you fool!"

It was the worst imaginable scenario: a shallow-draft, extraordinarily fast, heavily armed enemy warship, capable of chewing the Commandos' unarmed air-sea rescue launch into matchsticks, showing up at the exact time and place when they were at their most vulnerable. But once again the main party's luck held. Like the aircraft, the German torpedo boat did not see them and disappeared into the night. Things were tense on the beach after that.

From the south came the crackle of automatic weapons fire and the *thump, thump* of hand grenades. The night glowed with Very lights arching into the sky all down the coastline.

"Those are Thompsons," Lieutenant Randal explained. "One of our raiding parties."

Unidentified aircraft thundered overhead.

"The show's started!" Commander Milner-Gibson shouted. Lieutenant Randal could hardly hold the commander's enthusiasm against him, but it was rather an awful lapse of noise discipline.

Major Tod reappeared out of the dark, carrying his Thompson submachine gun at the high port. He conferred anxiously with Lieutenant Colonel Clarke and Commander Milner-Gibson.

"With the heightened air activity of unknown origin and the possibility of an E-boat being somewhere out in the Channel behind us, now seems as good a time as any to call it a night and make for home," the colonel said.

"Heavily armed men heading this way," Lieutenant Randal announced in a loud whisper, interrupting the leaders' conference. "Bad guys!"

A Wehrmacht bicycle patrol, moving along the water's edge, had somehow penetrated the security perimeter set up in a half-moon around the air-sea rescue boat. Major Tod jumped to his feet with visions of the Victoria Cross dancing in his head and leveled his Thompson at the patrol. Unfortunately, his finger hit the magazine release instead of the safety, and the heavy, twenty-round magazine clattered against the shale of the beach, alerting the Germans.

The Nazis immediately opened fire and, being trained men, did not disengage their magazines until they ran empty. The first short burst from the German patrol leader's 9-mm MP-38 machine pistol knocked Lieutenant Colonel Clarke over the bow and back into the boat. Then, in the confusion of the moment, the Germans broke contact and fled, getting clean away.

Things happened very fast after that.

The rest of the landing party returned to the crash boat on the double, and re-embarkation began immediately. The German E-Boat came roaring back but blazed past at speed and kept on going, headed south. The angry sound of high-performance engines screamed overhead. Enemy? Friendly? Who could say? Commander Milner-Gibson made ready to put to sea.

Lieutenant Randal pounced on Lieutenant Colonel Clarke, who was bleeding profusely from the head. In the dark and the confusion of the night it was not easy to establish the extent of his injuries. Black-faced men were clambering over the side and into the boat with their weapons clanging. Somebody was taking a head count. The boat began to slide back out into the Channel.

"What's happening, John?" the colonel groaned.

"We're getting the hell out of Dodge, sir. Now, will you hold still while I try to figure out where to put the tourniquet?"

"But I'm bleeding from the head!"

"That's a problem, sir."

Lieutenant Colonel Clarke started laughing manically. "Who will ever believe this story? I create, name, recruit, plan, and get killed on the first amphibious Commando raid in modern history."

"You're not dead yet, sir. There's a pressure point directly behind and slightly under your jaw. Now, if you'll just press down hard and keep steady pressure on it, I think we can get the bleeding stopped. As far as I can tell, you're only nicked. I can't find any other entry or exit wounds, but they nearly shot your ear off."

"You make quite sure you back me up on the fact that I was in the boat at the time I was hit."

"No problem, sir. If anybody asks, I was sitting next to you when it happened, one hundred yards offshore."

The crash boat eventually linked up with the boat that had become separated from it. As the morning dawned golden, a flight of Hawker Hurricanes appeared in order to provide air cover and stayed with them the whole way back to Dover.

The Commandos sailed into a hero's homecoming. Ships at the quayside sounded their Klaxons, blew their sirens, and sprayed streams of water from their firefighting equipage. Sailors manned the rails and cheered Churchill's Leopards ashore, where they were met by the popping flashbulbs of the hurriedly assembled local press corps.

Not all the members of the raiding party fared so well on their return, they learned later. Due to the intense secrecy of the mission, when part of the flotilla sailed back into Folkestone, no one was expecting it. The exuberant fighting men had taken their young skipper's recommendation—"Splice the main brace, boys!"—at face value. They broke open the emergency containers of "medicinal" intended to revive shot-down pilots plucked from the icy waters of the Channel, and medicated themselves forthwith. The harbor authorities took one look at the boatload of dirty, armed drunks and arrested them on the spot, thinking they might be deserters. It took some doing before the misunderstanding was sorted out, though it was never clear what the men were supposed to be deserting from.

While they were waiting at the hospital for Lieutenant Colonel Dudley Clarke to receive medical attention, Lieutenant John Randal gave Lieutenant Terry Stone his opinion of the operation. It was not kind.

The colonel was sitting on a stretcher—in a fair degree of pain, covered in dried blood, clutching a bandage to his ear—listening to the exchange. "Do you have a better idea, Lieutenant Randal?" he snapped, finally.

"Sir, the Apaches, never numbering more than a thousand men total, raiding out of Mexico into the Arizona Territory, had over one-third of the entire strength of the U.S. Army chasing them for something like ten years. The Apaches seldom operated in groups of more than twenty-five or thirty warriors. Most war parties consisted of fewer than ten adult male Indians, the bulk being teenage boys."

"Your point is, Lieutenant?"

"What I think would be more effective, sir, is a small, lightly armed, self-contained raiding outfit of not more than one boatload of handpicked men. They could strike from the sea like lightning, be gone in an instant, show up unannounced somewhere else, then do it all over again, night after night. That's the way raiding ought to be done, sir. Guerrilla war, and plenty of it."

"What is your opinion, Lieutenant Stone?" Lieutenant Colonel Clarke asked.

"I should like to be a part of something like that, sir! Sea cavalry—only we ride fast boats instead of horses."

"In that case, gentlemen, I shall arrange for orders to be cut for you two to get started no later than tomorrow. Acting Captain Randal, you are in command, with Lieutenant Stone as your deputy commander as soon as I can release him from MO-9. Make something happen, gentlemen, and do it with celerity."

The colonel stifled a groan through gritted teeth. He gave Lieutenant Randal a thoughtful look. "Maybe you want to rethink recruiting from the independent companies," he said. "No. 11 did seem a trifle amateurish tonight. I would dearly love to know how that German patrol managed to infiltrate undetected through our perimeter."

"Lesson learned, sir," Lieutenant Randal said. "Just because a military unit thinks it's an elite force does not make it so."

The next morning the *London Times* screamed, BRITISH RAIDERS LAND ON ENEMY COAST! The people of Great Britain were euphoric.

Prime Minister Winston Churchill proved a trifle more fickle, as Lieutenant Colonel Clarke reported privately to Lieutenants Randal and Stone. According to the colonel's sources, the PM had penned across the bottom of his copy of the report—admittedly, a sanitized version designed to show in the best light possible an operation some described as "brilliant" and others "bold and daring"—the words, "Unworthy of the British Empire to send over a few cutthroats."

"Not the kindest assessment we might have wished for the very first Commando operation," the colonel ruefully remarked.

"It's a good thing he doesn't know what really happened," Lieutenant Randal said.

"John, is what you told me actually true, the bit about one thousand Apaches tying down a third of the entire U.S. Army for ten years?"

"That's what they taught us at the Cavalry School, sir."

"Hmm. Maybe instead of Commandos I should have named them Apaches."

3

PINPRICK

THE NEXT MORNING, ACTING CAPTAIN JOHN RANDAL, CAPTAIN
David Niven, and Lieutenant Terry Stone held a hasty council of war at
MO-9. They decided that Captain Niven would make arrangements for
a boat of some type to transport the new, small-scale raiding unit Captain
Randal had been authorized to raise. Captain Niven would also help with
the selection of a target for their first raid on the French coast because,
in his capacity as liaison officer, he had access to a variety of intelligence
sources.

"Sounds perfectly mad to me, chaps," the movie star pointed out
cheerfully. "You two are simply going to get yourselves killed. That said,
if I were to take a reduction to lieutenant, how would you feel about me
signing on?"

"Talk to Colonel Clarke," Captain Randal said.

"Blast! Already turned me down, actually."

"I would have thought the colonel would be more than delighted to
see you rubbed out, old stick," Lieutenant Stone said. "That would give
him a clear run at the ravishing Lady Jane."

"No such luck for him," Captain Niven said with a smile. "That is one match I intend to win."

Lieutenant Stone undertook to recruit the first draft of volunteers. The youngest scion of one of the great noble families of England, he was also its storied black sheep. His father, Captain Randal learned, was an earl who possessed what Englishmen admire the most in one another: mind-numbing wealth, conviviality, liberality, a sense of Empire, and blue-ribbon foxhounds. All that having been said, if Lieutenant Terry Stone had any limitations as a professional cavalry officer, he did not admit to them.

Volunteers had to come from somewhere, so Lieutenant Stone went to the Household Cavalry Brigade straight away. He came back in short order with the polo squads from the Life Guards and Horse Guards Regiments. Though the recruitment made him persona non grata with the colonels of both regiments for pirating their most prized sporting teams, it was an inspired choice, as Captain Randal soon learned.

The cavalrymen were extraordinarily fit, keen sportsmen, and extremely competitive in an aggressive, dangerous, hard-charging game. They were trained to think for themselves on the dead run and accustomed to acting on their own initiative while working together toward a common object as members of a highly disciplined team. Most of the polo players were also slightly older and more mature than the average soldier. It would be hard to imagine better raiding stock.

Captain Niven appeared one day with a tall, bayonet-slim Grenadier Guards sergeant major in tow. "Captain Randal, this is Sergeant Major Maxwell Hicks. The colonel has asked him to come down and have a look at your operation."

Major Hicks's Grenadier Guards were a no-nonsense outfit. They took the business of being the First Regiment of Foot seriously. Discipline, iron will, and a readiness to unhesitatingly carry out any order were their stock-in-trade. Tradition in the Grenadier Guards dictated that if a trooper was on time to a formation, he was considered five minutes late.

The Life Guards and the "Blues," as the Horse Guards Regiment was nearly always called, were good-natured rivals of longstanding, but to most people the only discernable difference was that one regiment wore a red coat and the other a blue one when on parade. The Foot Guards, on the other hand, held both regiments in slight contempt and referred to them generally as "Piccadilly Cowboys."

"They don't mean it as a compliment, really," Lieutenant Stone remarked, eying the sergeant major with a certain amount of trepidation.

It was not clear what Sergeant Major Hicks's role was intended to be, but it was a sure bet his presence was going to cast a wet saddle blanket on the high jinks of a bunch of polo-playing Piccadilly Cowboys recently turned Leopard Commandos with a license to play merry hell on the French coast.

In fact, Captain Randal suspected that was exactly what the chief of MO-9 had in mind when he sent the sergeant major down to them. Lieutenant Colonel Dudley Clarke was a conventional officer with an unconventional bent. History showed that a background like that often produced the best type of special forces operator. The commander of MO-9 was proving to be a hands-off leader able to delegate command and control and still find a way to place his mark squarely on the Commando units he organized—a formidable talent.

Sergeant Major Maxwell Hicks took in every detail of raid planning, but he did not have much to say. A target was selected and ten men were picked for the first raid. They brandished their antique Webley Mark V .455 revolvers and an exotic variety of bayonets—some almost as long as swords—and draped themselves with bandoleers of ammunition like Mexican banditos. Each man carried a .303 Short Model Lee-Enfield rifle.

Captain John Randal loaned Major Hicks his liberated 9-mm Walther P-38 and kept the 9-mm Browning P-35 his Swamp Fox Force topkick had given him. He wished he still had the MP-38 machine pistol he had captured outside Calais. Unfortunately, the military port authorities at Dover had confiscated it the moment he had stepped ashore.

All things considered, they were about the most poorly armed group of modern-day raiders ever imagined; some of the Huk guerrillas Captain Randal had operated against in the Philippine jungles had carried more individual firepower. The Commandos were definitely going to have to rely on the element of surprise because they couldn't do battle with the

Germans on anything like even terms. Bolt-action rifles against automatic weapons at night was not a fair fight.

The horsemen and the lone Grenadier Guardsman took turns painting wicked-looking camouflage stripes on their faces with theatrical makeup supplied by a stage actress girlfriend of Lieutenant Stone.

Captain Randal gave the men a final briefing and conducted an inspection. He ordered each trooper to jump up and down, checking for metal-on-metal contact: loose ammunition in a pocket, an untapped, slack rifle sling, or anything that might rattle. He checked each man's bolt-action .303 Mark III SMLE rifle to make sure that the magazine was loaded but there was *not* a round in the chamber; he didn't want an unintentional discharge to give away the show. He also looked for the signs of panic that they all should have been feeling but, never having actually been shot at before, were not.

His inspection completed, Captain Randal addressed the Commandos as a group, talking calmly and quietly. The troops gave him their undivided attention; they had heard a few things about the business at Calais. He told them they looked ready; he spoke of spirit, pride, dangerous enterprise, and a few other things. By the time he was finished, the men were so fired up, they were just about ready to start hacking each other with their old sword-type bayonets.

Then he led them aboard the racy, forty-foot civilian craft His Majesty's Yacht *Arrow*, commanded by Royal Navy Volunteer Reserve Midshipman Randy Seaborn, on which they would set sail for enemy shore. Because their hobnail boots would scar the deck, the men were banned from wearing them on board and instead wore rubber-soled athletic shoes and knee-high leggings. The Leopard Commandos were less than thrilled to be invading France in "bleedin' ballet slippers" as one Blues corporal was heard to complain indelicately.

Eighteen-year-old Midshipman Seaborn, the nephew of the widow at whose London townhouse the planning sessions had occurred, was just as green as the raiders when it came to battle, but he did have the dual advantages of coming from a seafaring family and commanding a yacht that he had a lot of experience with—because she had belonged to his parents before being called up for emergency war duty.

Royal Navy officers have three career paths to choose from: engineering, gunnery, and navigation. Midshipman Seaborn had chosen to specialize in navigation for the simple reason that it was a prerequisite for command. It was an intuitive choice because, as the midshipman explained to Captain Randal, the Admiralty, in its infinite wisdom, on occasion allowed reservists to command their own boats in the rare event when they were both mobilized. In this case, it was anticipated to be only a temporary tour of duty until the young skipper's orders conferring his regular navy commission came through. The paperwork was already in the pipeline.

"Randy may be a trifle young," Lieutenant Stone confided, "but he is as game as they come." Captain Randal knew he was going to need to be. The mission that night called for him to navigate across forty-odd miles of German E-boat–infested waters, land his passengers on a tiny pinpoint of a target, stand off a hostile shore while they carried out their clandestine mission, then recover the raiders and transport them safely home—all before the sun came up.

A stiff wind blew out of the northeast, which caused the sea to rise. The night was dark, with thick patches of high cumulus clouds obscuring what little starlight there was, complicating navigation. No one really blamed Midshipman Seaborn when he got lost.

Hours later and miles off course, the Leopards stumbled ashore through light surf, slightly seasick but ready for action. Leaving two men behind to secure the beach, the rest fanned out into a loose column formation with their weapons at the ready. They advanced cautiously on a road they thought—hoped—ran parallel to the beach, obscured by some sand dunes four hundred yards to their front. Their mission, hastily modified just before they hit the beach, was to cut the road and interdict enemy traffic—if any. They never reached it.

To Captain Randal's astonishment, almost immediately after wading ashore his team happened upon an open-topped Mercedes Benz–type Stuttgart German Army staff car parked hull-down among the sand dunes. Pulsating music from the car's radio, tuned to a station in Algiers, filled the night with the hypnotic beat of a primeval African drum song.

Floating on the sand like silent phantoms in their army-issue athletic shoes, the Commandos closed in and surrounded the staff car's unwary occupants. In disbelief, the men with the black-streaked faces observed Panzer General Ernest von Rittenhauser—one of Germany's finest, holder of the Blue Max and a recent recipient of the Knight's Cross—touch a champagne-filled silver chalice to the ruby-red lips of his companion for the evening, a plump, strawberry blonde French girl who appeared not to have very many clothes on.

The Commandos fell on the two of them like a pack of Churchill's proverbial leopards. Sometimes, Captain Randal knew, it was better to be lucky than good. The odds against anything as miraculous happening again in this war were at least a million to one. They sent the French girl packing and, with their captive in tow, set a course for England.

Alerted by a radio signal from HMY *Arrow*, the press was carefully stage-managed to be on hand for their arrival. Allowed unfettered access to photograph the return of the raiders to their hearts' content, the reporters were nevertheless strictly forbidden to interview the participants for reasons of operational security. The Official Secrets Act was cited.

As Captain John Randal and Lieutenant Terry Stone knew, the actual reason interviews were off-limits was because MO-9—meaning Lieutenant Colonel Dudley Clarke—wanted to create the impression that the operation was a carefully orchestrated snatch mission conducted in response to precise intelligence, specifically targeting Panzer General Ernest von Rittenhauser. The big lie was that the mission had been brilliantly planned and executed with split-second timing and uncanny precision. The last thing M0-9 wanted was for one of the participants to spill the beans: that they had been lost and it had all been a big, happy accident. Naturally, there was no mention of the French girl.

A news release that was a wonder of hyperbole and bald-faced lie—all carefully couched in clipped British public school understatement—was quickly drawn up by Captain David Niven and distributed to the press corps. The news release was remarkable only in that the reporters actually believed it.

Captain Niven had clearly mastered the art of stage-managing public relations during his time in Hollywood, a fact that was duly noted and that resulted in his being whisked off soon after to a super-secret signals organization known as "Phantom." There, it was hoped, he could put his talents to good work, fooling the Germans instead of the local citizenry.

The British public went wild with joy over the capture of the enemy general. Captain Randal and Lieutenant Stone were both immediately decorated with the Military Cross. Midshipman Randy Seaborn was awarded the Distinguished Service Cross, the Royal Navy's equivalent to the Military Cross. Sergeant Major Maxwell Hicks received the Distinguished Conduct Medal, Great Britain's second-highest valor decoration for an enlisted soldier. Each of the NCOs on the operation was granted the Military Medal. Every Commando trooper received a mention in dispatches that was denoted by an oak leaf cluster worn on his campaign medal.

Not a single shot had been fired in anger. It sure beat playing polo.

After such an enterprising start, the future of the Small-Scale Raiding Company, as Lieutenant Colonel Clarke dubbed them, was never in doubt. Prime Minister Churchill fired off a dispatch reportedly dictated through a blue cloud of cigar smoke while soaking happily like a plump, pink porpoise in his bath at Checkers. "This intrepid enterprise demonstrates the kind of bold thinking, brilliant planning, and rapid execution we have needed all along! Press on, Commandos!"

Midshipman Seaborn suggested to Captain Randal that they use his wealthy aunt's vast, isolated estate south of London as their base of operations because it was located on one of the narrowest parts of the English Channel. The Small-Scale Raiding Company repaired there, straightaway. Toward nightfall, all the Commandos would have to do was walk down to the private boat dock, climb aboard HMY *Arrow*, and go raiding. Only, as it turned out, it was not quite that simple.

4

RAIDING DOCTRINE

"WHAT WE NEED," CAPTAIN JOHN RANDAL, MC, INFORMED HIS TWO officers one day soon after their arrival at Seaborn House, "is a copy of the army's and the navy's raiding doctrine. There is no sense trying to reinvent the wheel."

"The Royal Military Academy, Sandhurst, is the place to look," Lieutenant Terry Stone, MC, offered. "I am one of its most distinguished graduates, you know. They say I hold the standing record for demerits in a single term."

"The Admiralty will have something," Midshipman Randy Seaborn, DSC, added. "My father works there. He can locate the material for us."

They both struck out. Neither the army nor the navy had publications on the subject. Captain Randal even went to the American Embassy in London to pay a call on the officer in command of the Marine guard detachment stationed there. He asked to borrow USMC tactical manuals on small-scale amphibious raiding operations—but came away empty-handed. The USMC's idea of amphibious operations was to establish a beachhead lodgment on a hostile shore—by force if necessary—and stay there until relieved or the enemy was dead. The U.S. Marines were not in the raiding business.

"Look on the bright side, old stick. No matter what we do, no one will ever be able to accuse us of violating official doctrine," Lieutenant Stone pointed out, "because there isn't any."

Captain Randal and the Small-Scale Raiding Company were forced to work up their own tactics. And they had to do it amid the frantic activity of the local military authorities, who were preparing a defense against the much-feared, highly anticipated German assault on England. Invasion paranoia along the English coastline was at fever pitch.

Sergeant Major Maxwell Hicks made his presence felt from the start. The first thing he did was to announce: "In the Grenadier Guards, if you're on time for a formation, you are already five minutes late. That policy is in effect as of right now."

The second thing he did was to restructure the rank nomenclature. The Life Guards Regiment and the Blues had some strange ranks, he pointed out to Captain Randal. For example, for some obscure reason, sergeant majors were called corporal majors, and Sergeant Major Hicks was having none of it. His logic was that they would eventually be recruiting men from other line regiments, and there was no sense confusing them when they did. Sergeants went back to being called sergeants and corporals became corporals. Interestingly, Captain Randal noticed, the cavalrymen made no objection.

The third thing Sergeant Major Hicks did was to suggest that the Small-Scale Raiding Company establish an eleven-day operational cycle followed by a forty-eight-hour pass plus one day of travel and administrative downtime tacked on the end.

"Work hard, play hard, sir," he said.

Captain Randal agreed.

This turned out to be an excellent policy, except for the men's custom of requisitioning any handy means of transportation they happened across to get them back to Seaborn House on time when their pass was about to expire. The local constable routinely rang up Captain Randal to make arrangements for the borrowed vehicles to be picked up, knowing they could be found scattered along the driveway in front of Seaborn

House. No serious attempt was made to stop the practice, however, on the grounds that it showed initiative on the part of the troops.

The Small-Scale Raiding Company began rehearsing landing exercises from HMY *Arrow*. Midshipman Randy Seaborn observed that on their initial raid they simply sailed up to the first beach they came to, eased the *Arrow* in, and waded ashore, being extraordinarily lucky in making landfall at a place that allowed them to pull in so close to the shallow beach that they did not even get wet above the knees. Not to mention their extreme good fortune in finding a carousing German general in flagrante delicto.

"It is not always going to work out like that, sir," the young naval officer said. As the men would shortly learn, this was the mother of all understatements.

They practiced rowing ashore in whalers, dories, cutters, and canoes before finally settling on Goatley dinghies as the craft best suited for their purposes. Nevertheless, the Commandos quickly discovered to their chagrin that they could not row ashore or back to the *Arrow* every time they tried.

The problem lay in the fact that the Small-Scale Raiding Company was composed of cavalrymen, not sailors or Marines. Transitioning from the hurricane deck of a polo pony to a seat in a tiny eggshell of a rowboat proved easier said than done. The flimsy little dinghies sometimes went round and round, and sometimes they tipped over. In fact, it was a challenge to offload from the *Arrow* into one of them while carrying arms and equipment without capsizing.

But even if they did manage to get themselves into the Goatleys without upending them, Captain Randal and his men were learning that it took a skilled boat handler to row through even light breakers. The men were all nearly drowned—or thought they would be—time after time after time.

Days turned into weeks. The Small-Scale Raiding Company trained and then trained some more, running endless exercises. After a while the troops hit a plateau in their level of skill. Unless the Commandos planned to spend all their time perfecting their boat-handling techniques—something they could not afford and did not want to do—they were never going to be better than talented amateurs.

They faced two formidable obstacles, however. The first was the English Channel, a notoriously unpredictable body of water. Even at the best of times it is choppy, and weather conditions tend to change minute by minute, making long-range planning a virtual impossibility.

The second was the Germans themselves, who were working fast and furiously to fortify the occupied French coastline just as the British were to build anti-invasion obstacles along theirs. Just as Midshipman Seaborn had said, the Small-Scale Raiding Company would not be able to count on being able to land on the first beach they came to. The Commandos were going to have to learn how to land in rough, out-of-the-way places where the heavily armed gentlemen of the Third Reich did not expect anyone to come calling. That kind of seamanship, as it was becoming uncomfortably clear, was a job for highly trained professionals.

It was cold, wet, frustrating, miserable work, not helped in the least by the fact that their proficiency level had peaked and was not improving.

In the evenings, all hands repaired to the tavern in the Blind Eye Inn, located on the tiny bay near Seaborn House, to strategize over fish and chips while drowning thoughts of their day's failures in drink.

The pub was always crowded with hard-partying fighter pilots from the two squadrons that were operating off a small grass airstrip located a few miles north of Seaborn House. One of the squadrons flew the glamorous Spitfires and the other the workhorse Hurricanes. The highest-scoring aces seemed to fly Hurricanes, but that did not keep the Spitfire pilots from asserting their natural superiority at every opportunity.

Fighter pilots had become the idols of the nation, accorded instant celebrity status and lasting immortality as the "Valiant Few." It was universally accepted that the RAF constituted the thin blue line: all that stood between King and Empire and the brutal Nazi onslaught. The fighter pilots drank like fish.

New pilots kept turning up at the Blind Eye practically every night, while many of the old familiar ones were conspicuous no-shows. So many of the fighter pilots were wearing the Distinguished Flying Cross ribbon on their uniforms, with its slanted blue and white lines, that the barroom seemed to tilt to the left.

The Small-Scale Raiding Company generally confined itself to a small corner of the pub, while the hard-drinking pilots swirled around them. The fighter pilots were a close-knit fraternity and seldom bothered to come over and introduce themselves. This may have been due in some measure to the lurid newspaper stories that appeared from time to time, claiming Commando units were filled to the brim with convicts recruited straight from prison. It was widely reported that the other ranks in the British Army were required to have a violent criminal record or be certified psychopaths in order to get in.

While nothing could have been further from the truth, the stories did seem to have a chilling effect on strangers and generally discouraged outsiders from striking up unnecessary conversations. This was fine with Captain Randal and his men.

There was one notable exception: Squadron Leader Paddy Wilcox, DSO, MC, DFC, a much-decorated, rotund, middle-aged Canadian World War I ace fighter pilot and former bush pilot. He flew the local air-sea rescue flying boat tasked with swooping in and picking up pilots and aircrew who got shot down in the Channel. The veteran pilot always wore a black patch over one eye when he was not flying.

"I say, old stick, but weren't you wearing that patch on your right eye last night?" Lieutenant Stone inquired of the squadron leader one evening when he strolled over to the Small-Scale Raiding Company table to introduce himself.

"Strengthens the eye muscles," he explained. "I rotate it. You lads are those pinprick boys," he went on. "You're the desperadoes who kidnapped a Nazi general! I've been watching you practice in your boats."

This announcement was met with stony silence from the Small-Scale Raiding Company/Leopard/Commando/Desperado/Kidnappers. At the end of a long, hard, frustrating day of cold, soaking-wet training, the men were not predisposed to welcome intrusion by any outsider, particularly some over-the-hill pilot dripping in medals. Besides, what they were doing was classified, even if they were not actually doing very much at the moment.

If the Canadian flier was put off by the lack of response, he didn't show it. Uninvited, he pulled a chair up to the table. "I have been observing," he repeated, "and doing some thinking. There is a small service I can provide that should be of interest to you."

"What might that be?" Captain Randal asked in the tone of someone who has just been solicited by an insurance salesman.

"When you fellows get through practicing paddling your little row-boats over here, my guess is you're going to go across the pond and paddle them on the other side. Now, the thought occurred to me that if you had some aerial photographs of wherever it was you were going to be paddling to over there, it might be of some help to you in your planning.

"So, if you were to let me know beforehand where that happened to be, I could maybe swing by there while I am out on my routine patrol, waiting for some of these bloody fools to get themselves shot down, and take a few pictures of your objective for you before I have to go do a rescue. I might even squeeze one or two of you Commando types into my cockpit before your mission and fly you over and let you do a visual reconnaissance of your target area . . . if you thought it might be any help."

"What was it you said you were drinking, old stick?" Lieutenant Stone asked, oozing charm, holding out his open sterling silver cigarette case full of Player's. "And if they don't have your brand in stock here at the Blind Eye, Squadron Leader, we'll be more than happy to send out to collect it for you."

"Something else," the pilot continued, leaning closer. "If you can paddle ashore from a yacht, what would keep you from paddling ashore from my flying boat? Most nights I have very little going."

"Could we do that?" Captain Randal asked with a raised eyebrow. "I mean, is it legal under international law?"

"During rescues, both sides routinely shoot at each other's air-sea rescue aircraft on sight—in the air and on the water. You won't find any red crosses on the sides of my ship. They're a waste of paint and only make a big, juicy target. Nobody is honoring them these days, not when it comes to pulling pilots out of the drink. There is nothing to prohibit you from launching a raid from my flying boat."

"I was not aware that the Geneva Convention failed to cover air-sea rescue!" Midshipman Seaborn said.

"Everyone wants to kill fighter pilots these days, lad—including me, most waking hours." He looked at the mob around the bar, shaking his head. "And to think I used to be one."

"A raid staged out of a flying boat . . . " Lieutenant Stone exhaled a stream of cigarette smoke, a thoughtful look on his face. "Now *that* has to be an original concept."

"Which is a good reason to do it," said Captain Randal. "We'd no longer be restricted to coastal targets the way we're limited now. And that, gentlemen, opens up a whole new range of possibilities."

It quickly became apparent that the Canadian aviator had talked his way into a sort of provisional membership at their table in the Blind Eye. Captain Randal quickly began to gather the impression that Paddy Wilcox was the Van Gogh of aviators: mildly eccentric, totally brilliant, and in a league of his own when it came to flying. As an unconventional pilot, he might just be the perfect match for Captain Randal's force of unconventional soldiers.

In the "War to End All Wars," Paddy Wilcox had flown Bristol fighters and shot down an impressive thirty-three enemy aircraft. Nowadays, the RAF refused to allow him to fly fighters because they classified him as being too old for frontline flying duty. The squadron leader was probably lucky the RAF let him fly at all, he said. "I fancy they wouldn't let me in the air, period, except that at the moment, multiengine, open-sea, amphibious landing–rated pilots happen to be in short supply."

At the bar a chant went up from a group of drunken fighter pilots. Two of them were having a chugging contest: Each intrepid though slightly wobbly birdman was working on a full pitcher of beer. Naturally, one was a Spitfire pilot and the other flew a Hurricane.

"What we really ought to do," Captain Randal said over the boisterous chanting at the bar, "is locate a Luftwaffe watering hole on the other side, like this one, and slip over some dark night and pay them a visit just before closing time."

"You may be on to something there, old stick," said Lieutenant Stone.

"The only problem with that idea, sir," injected Sergeant Major Maxwell Hicks in his gravelly voice, "is deciding whom to leave behind. As much as our lads hate fighter pilots, unless we can organize some way for every last man jack of them to go along, we are going to have a mutiny on our hands."

The table roared with laughter. Sergeant Major Hicks looked puzzled. Not known for his wit, he was being completely serious.

"I prefer Glenfiddich," Squadron Leader Paddy Wilcox announced, turning to Lieutenant Stone. "And now I'll have one of those Player's."

5

LADY JANE

CAPTAIN JOHN RANDAL HAD TO ADMIT IT: THE SMALL-SCALE Raiding Company had hit an operational wall.

Their daily struggles to master the rowing skills necessary to get the Goatley dinghies dependably launched, rowed ashore, and returned to HMY *Arrow* continued. Although the Commandos had significantly improved their small boat–handling abilities, they were still not able to achieve the level of proficiency necessary to guarantee they would not be drowned, be stranded on an enemy coast, or at the very least suffer a boat-handling mishap that would cause the raid to be aborted.

As if that weren't enough, Captain Randal had also learned that it was not possible, with the navigational equipment currently available, to designate a pinpoint target on the French coast, sail there in the *Arrow* at night, and locate it in time to go ashore, carry out their operation, and return home before daybreak.

On top of all that, the only weapons available were standard-issue .303 Mark III SMLE bolt-action rifles and Webley Mark V .455 revolvers, the newest of which was more than twenty years old; some were nearing fifty. So far, they had been unsuccessful in obtaining the modern Enfield .38s. The most generous thing that could be said about the weapons was that they were not suited for night-raiding operations. The German Army, on the other hand, was liberally equipped with assorted models of state-of-the-art machine pistols—all characterized by high cyclic rates—giving them clearly superior firepower. In any engagement in the dark of night, the Germans would always have the edge.

With all these circumstances working against them, Captain Randal and the officers and men of the Small-Scale Raiding Company were experiencing a period of high frustration and waning morale after getting off to a spectacular start. Pinprick raiding was proving to be considerably more difficult than it had first appeared.

Under the circumstances Midshipman Randy Seaborn's announcement that his aunt would arrive that evening and be in residence for a few days was not the most welcome of news. The last thing Captain Randal wanted right that minute was the added distraction of his naval officer's widowed aunt, even if she did own the property they were using as their base of operations.

The arrangement, Midshipman Seaborn informed his commanding officer, was for his aunt to meet them in the Blind Eye at the end of the day's training. If there had been any way Captain Randal could have prevented her coming, he would have.

He kept these thoughts to himself, however, as his officers and NCOs sat in their corner of the pub, the fighter pilots swirling around them in full after-action party mode. The Small-Scale Raiding Company troops were a subdued bunch as they waited; the day's training had been particularly awful, most of it spent being cold and soaking wet.

The instant Lady Jane Seaborn walked into the Blind Eye, the revelry came to a screeching halt. Every RAF pilot in the room abruptly stopped whatever he was doing to stare at the slim, green-eyed brunette in the simple white dress and heels, a raisin-colored leather handbag slung over her shoulder. Oblivious to the attention, she walked directly over to the table of Commandos.

Lieutenant Terry Stone stood up. "Boys, let me introduce you to Lady Jane Seaborn, Randy's aunt."

"Hello, Terry," she said.

"Aunt Jane," Midshipman Randy Seaborn said, "This is Captain John Randal, my commanding officer."

"It's a pleasure to meet you, Captain."

Whatever mental image Captain Randal had of a grieving widow, Lady Jane Seaborn wasn't it. He took the hand she offered and felt the firm grip. He knew in that instant that he would never be satisfied with another woman for the rest of his life. And that was too bad, because he also knew she was way out of his league. Randy Seaborn's aunt was the best-looking woman he had ever laid eyes on; she had the world's greatest smile.

Suddenly, he realized she must be the woman Lieutenant Colonel Dudley Clarke and the actor Captain David Niven were jousting over. He had never made the connection, but one thing was certain—as advertised, she was "drop-dead gorgeous."

"Aunt Jane works for British Intelligence, sir."

"What do you do for intelligence?" Captain Randal asked after they all were seated again at the table.

"I could tell you, John, but then I would have to . . . well, you understand."

"Sorry," Captain Randal stammered, embarrassed by his gaffe. He was not entirely sure how to address her. He vaguely remembered he had heard somewhere that she was a baroness. At this stage of his life he had exactly zero personal experience with female members of the peerage. And . . . had she just threatened to kill him?

"Just teasing," she said. "Actually, all I've been doing is attending an endless series of training schools." Lady Jane Seaborn smiled again, lighting up the room as brightly as if she had popped a Very pistol flare right there at the table.

"I've been trained to parachute out of an airplane, sabotage a factory, operate a clandestine radio, derail a train, pick a lock, eliminate a sentry with a hatpin, set up a dead-letter drop, and I can kill a German attack dog with my bare hands, to name a few of the tricks my firm has been teaching me."

The men at the table were silent. What could you say to a beautiful woman who has told you something like that?

Lieutenant Stone, however, was able to rise to the occasion. "Maybe you would like to come along on our next raid, Lady Jane. We can always use a school-certified dog killer."

"Have you actually parachuted, Aunt Jane?" Midshipman Seaborn asked.

"Yes, I have. The people in my firm are required to be parachute qualified. You should all try it. The capability might come in useful someday. I can make the arrangements if you like."

The thought of jumping out of an airplane gave Captain Randal butterflies.

"Now, John," Lady Jane Seaborn said, turning to him and looking at him levelly with those vivid green eyes, "I want you to bring me up to speed on what you lads have been doing. I hear things haven't been going so swimmingly down here. Perhaps I can be of help."

Captain Randal felt hypnotized. Only one other woman in his life had ever had such a dramatic effect on him, and that had been a long time ago, back in his senior year of high school when the student teacher in his English literature class was Miss UCLA.

Afterward he thought he probably should not have, but he proceeded to lay out for her all the problems the Small-Scale Raiding Company had encountered, starting with navigation and ending with its critical lack of firepower.

Lady Jane Seaborn sat listening intently, smoking a Player's Navy Cut that every man at the table and half a dozen of the fighter pilots had attempted to light the moment she took it out of her cigarette case.

When Captain Randal finished, she asked, "Have you ever heard of the Royal National Lifeboat Institute?"

"No."

"It operates along the coast," Midshipman Randy Seaborn explained, "rescuing ships in distress at sea or run aground during storms, at risk of breaking up."

"Lifeboat Servicemen are unquestionably the best rough-water small-boat handlers on the globe," Lady Jane Seaborn said. She flicked her ash into the tray on the table and then stared Captain Randal straight in the eyes. "I recruited eight of them for Randy's crew and brought them down with me. They're at Seaborn House settling in right now. In the future, you shall not have any more problems rowing to and from the *Arrow* in any weather."

It grew very still at the table. She had just addressed their most secret fear, the one they never talked about: being left stranded in enemy territory after a raid, unable to paddle out through the surf. In one neat move, Lady Jane Seaborn had endeared herself forever to the officers and men of the Small-Scale Raiding Company.

She gave the American officer a small smile. "Randy also mentioned to me that you were reduced to wearing your issue athletic training shoes and leggings because British Army boots have metal cleats and he will not allow them on board the *Arrow*. Are you familiar with an establishment called Purdy's, John?"

Captain Randal shook his head.

"Well, the people there tell me that waterfowlers often wear a lightweight, rubber-soled, canvas-topped lace-up hunting boot. I took the liberty of obtaining two pairs for every man. You may find they are just the ticket for your line of work.

"Also, I brought along a medical officer from the RAMC," she continued. "He's going to put all of you through an intensive course of first aid, at the end of which you will be qualified to receive your St. John Ambulance Certificate."

Lady Jane Seaborn turned and looked the Small-Scale Raiding Company's commander square in the eye again. "Which reminds me, is it really true, John, that you threatened to tie a tourniquet around Dudley's throat the night he was wounded?"

Like a bolt from the blue, the magnificent Lady Jane Seaborn had landed in their midst, and things were never, ever going to be the same for them again. To everyone's surprise—and Captain John Randal's great disappointment—she was gone the next day.

First aid training began. The Lifeboat Servicemen from the National Lifeboat Institute were infused into the crew of HMY *Arrow* and began to cross-train as Commandos. As advertised, they were boat handlers without equal; they considered rough surf to be their playground.

The waterfowler boots turned out to be the best piece of military footgear any of them had ever worn.

The men of the Small-Scale Raiding Company, like all soldiers Captain Randal had ever met, were happiest when acquiring new skills and being issued new and functional gear, as well as when their unit obtained a fresh infusion of personnel with high-grade special qualifications, particularly ones they could all see an immediate, pressing need for. Morale, which had ebbed to an all-time low, shot back up in very short order.

One day while the troops were on the lawn practicing the tying on of splints and performing other feats of imaginary emergency first aid, a Rolls-Royce towing a small Silver Stream camper/horse trailer pulled up at Seaborn House. Lady Jane Seaborn was at the wheel, and out from the passenger side stepped a tall, white-haired cowboy wearing a long-fringed buckskin jacket. Accompanying him was a pleasantly plump young woman in a chic purple and yellow cowgirl costume.

"Howdy boys," the old cowboy called across the top of the car. "Are y'all ready for some R&R?"

No one really knew what that meant, but every man within hearing distance enthusiastically agreed that he was ready for some.

Lady Jane Seaborn made the introductions. "Lads, this is Captain 'Geronimo Joe' McKoy and his associate, Miss Lilly Threepersons. They have come to provide you with an afternoon's entertainment: Captain Geronimo Joe's Traveling Wild West Show and Shooting Emporium."

Some of the Commandos were detailed to help unload the trailer and set up the little traveling ring. Geronimo Joe's directions and running commentary, expressed in language as colorful as his appearance, made it seem as if the Ringling Brothers Circus had come to town.

Five overstuffed chairs were carried out on the lawn and set up for the officers, Sergeant Major Maxwell Hicks, and Lady Jane. The rest of the troops arranged themselves on the grass around the ring.

Captain McKoy rode into the ring on the back of an elderly palomino named Slick. The old cowboy with the Buffalo Bill–style pure white hair performed every riding trick in the book while Slick—who knew his routine so well he appeared to be half asleep—loped around the little ring, never breaking stride.

Miss Lilly narrated the performance, identifying the captain as having fought Apaches, scouted for the U.S. Cavalry, charged up San Juan Hill with the Rough Riders, and fought crime along the Mexican border as an Arizona Ranger. If he had done everything she described, Captain Randal calculated, he'd have to be at least 102 years old!

As Miss Lilly tossed glass balls into the air, the captain shattered them on the run with bullets from his matched pair of ivory-stocked, silver-plated, beautifully engraved Colt .45 Peacemakers. He shot from the saddle; he shot lying on Slick's rump; he shot hanging under the old palomino's neck; he shot standing up in the saddle. Right- or left-handed—it seemed to make no difference to Captain Geronimo Joe McKoy. The pistols blazed, the glass balls shattered, and Slick went round and round the ring.

Sitting next to Captain Randal in her big easy chair, Lady Jane Seaborn appeared to be having the time of her life. She was thrilled by every trick. "Is he not simply wonderful?" she laughed, clapping her hands in glee. "I love him!"

"Captain McKoy?"

"No, *Slick*! I've never seen such a quarter horse before. He's marvelous."

The white-haired entertainer finally gave the palomino a break. He dismounted with a flourish and slapped the horse on the rump. Slick trotted out of the ring to uproarious applause.

One of the Commandos called out, "Smoke 'em if you've got 'em, Slick."

Captain McKoy broke out his lasso and proceeded to perform every rope trick known to man. When he got tired of his rope, he strapped Miss Lilly to a turntable that looked like a giant roulette wheel, put on a blindfold, and threw knives at her as she spun around, outlining her body with quivering hilts. Then Captain John Randal had to go out in the ring and have the obligatory cigarette shot out of his mouth. Standing in front of his troops and Lady Jane while clenching the cigarette in his teeth and hoping the old Ranger would not pick that exact moment to develop palsy gave him an instant migraine.

Finally, Miss Lilly Threepersons introduced the grand finale as the "Whispering Death." She and Captain McKoy set up a large, shiny square of tin on an easel. The cowboy showman flourished a .22-caliber Colt Woodsman semiautomatic pistol in each hand. The pistols had long, strange-looking cylinders attached to the barrels. Taking careful aim, he emptied one pistol at the tin square and then he switched the other pistol to his right hand and emptied it.

For once his shooting skills seemed to have deserted him. As he changed magazines, it became clear to the audience that the bullet holes were scattered all over the place. The men who had been cheering him on throughout the whole show grew quiet. From the looks they were exchanging, it was clear they thought any one of them could have done just as well . . . and British soldiers were well known for being rotten pistol shots.

But Captain Randal had not even noticed the erratic pattern of the bullet holes. All that registered with him was that the Colt .22 pistols had not made a sound louder than that of a match being struck. He had never seen anything like it: silent pistols. He leaned across Lady Jane Seaborn and said to Lieutenant Terry Stone, "We've got to have some of those."

Lieutenant Stone nodded, apparently equally impressed. "Absolutely, old stick. Just the ticket for sentry elimination . . . provided, of course, we can ever manage to locate a German sentry."

When the sharpshooter had reloaded the silenced pistols, he suddenly emptied them into the tin, one after the other, with blistering speed. The random pattern of bullet holes magically transformed into the capital letters J. S.: Jane Seaborn. The troops were instantly on their feet, cheering as Captain Geronimo Joe McKoy swept his white Stetson off his head and made a grand bow.

Captain Randal was the first person to shake Geronimo Joe's hand. "Gettin' a head start on the war, huh, John?" the old entertainer said, clapping the younger man on the shoulder. "I reckon there'll be a lot more of us Americanos over here soon enough, a-killin' Nazis. How'd you like the show?"

"A lot of fun, Captain. All these troops are cavalrymen from the Life Guards and Blues Regiments, so you were performing for a critical audience."

"You don't say. I'd a' probably been real nervous if I'd a' knowed everybody in the whole crowd was a genuine hoss soldier."

"Captain McKoy, about your silenced .22's . . .We could use some quiet pistols in our line of work."

"Step into my office, John," the showman said, gesturing toward the Silver Stream trailer. "Lady Jane told me you boys had yourselves a gun problem down here. She thought I might be able to help. Why don't you tell me about it?"

McKoy listened intently, chewing on the end of a long, thin, unlit Cuban cigar as Captain Randal outlined the Small-Scale Raiding Company's armament. He nodded when Randal was finished.

"John, Lee-Enfields make excellent battle rifles, but they ain't never going to do for what you boys need to use 'em for. Now, I reckon if you were to give me some time, I could come up with something that'll solve your close-in-shootin' problems as good, or maybe even better, than a Thompson submachine gun. How's that sound?"

"That would be great, Captain."

"And I can slick up your Webleys, too. They're good service revolvers, ain't nothing to be ashamed of. But they need a little gunsmithing to smooth 'em out some. Probably the best thing I can do for you is something you most likely never even thought about. And that's to run your boys through some real intensive shooting drills specially designed to make 'em better combat pistoleros—so they hit what they aim at. That's something sadly overlooked in most all armies these days: marksmanship. My rule is, when you pull a trigger, make sure a bad guy falls down dead. You'll find it's a great firepower equalizer. It don't matter how fast the opposition's wonder gun is a-spittin' out hot lead and missing if you plug 'em through the liver on the first shot."

"What might you have in mind, Captain?"

"John, you give me three weeks and I can have your boys shooting them Webleys like they was John Wesley Hardin."

"Is tomorrow too soon to get started?"

"Why don't you let me have a couple a' days to tune up the men's handguns first?"

"Just as long as you promise to teach me how to shoot my initials, Captain. That's some trick."

"Had much experience handlin' pistols, John?"

"A little."

"Well, then, all you have to do is: Watch the front sight close, touch her off, and adios. Take your time in a hurry. It'll be my pleasure to teach you and your boys all I can."

Sitting in her Rolls-Royce before she drove off, Lady Jane Seaborn said to Captain John Randal, "Looks as if you've made progress on some of your problems, John."

"Thanks to you, Lady Seaborn."

"Call me Jane, won't you?" she said in her smoky voice. "Now, the navigation issue is another matter entirely. I have no idea how to help you there, and neither does anyone I have discussed the situation with. By the way, John, I have to ask: How did you ever manage to sail straight over and capture General von Rittenhauser the way you did?"

"We were lost."

The lazy, million-dollar glamour-shot smile she gave him with her head cocked back as she put the Rolls into gear and drove away was stunning. After all the first aid training they had been doing, Captain Randal seriously considered lying down on the grass, elevating his brand-new, rubber-soled, canvas-topped raiding boots, and treating himself for shock.

Captain Geronimo Joe McKoy was as good as his word. He taught the Commandos combat pistol craft, and he proved to be a world-class instructor. The first thing he did was to repeat the shooting portion of his exhibition, this time armed with a pair of the tuned-up Webley revolvers. Then he drilled the men exhaustively from dawn to dusk for three solid weeks as they learned to shoot their reworked pistols. The troops ate it up.

The knowledge that they were now able to shoot better than any group of Nazi storm troopers they were likely to encounter—unless maybe they ran into the German Olympic pistol team late some night—gave the

Commandos a sense of confidence that carried over into all areas of their soldiering.

Lesson learned, Captain John Randal took note: A man who thinks of himself as a gunfighter is a superior soldier. It had been a good day for the Small-Scale Raiding Company when Geronimo Joe McKoy showed up.

It had been an even better day, Captain Randal decided privately, when Lady Jane Seaborn adopted the Small-Scale Raiding Company as her pet project. The woman clearly knew how to identify a problem, craft a solution, and make it happen.

But . . . why was she going to all the trouble?

6

TO BLOW A TRAIN

DESPITE THE SMALL-SCALE RAIDING COMPANY ACQUIRING NEW men, equipment, and skills, a feeling was growing that if anything could possibly go wrong on an operation, it was going to go wrong.

It did not sound like a difficult thing to load into a boat, cross twenty to thirty miles of the English Channel at night, and land on the continent of Europe, preferably somewhere in enemy-occupied France. In actual practice, however, it was turning out to be harder than anyone ever dreamed.

Night after night they went out in HMY *Arrow*, and night after night something unanticipated occurred, causing them either to abort the operation entirely or to make landfall but to be disoriented and have only a short amount of time ashore before they had to sail for home or risk being caught at sea in daylight. The dawn fighter sweeps that the Luftwaffe routinely flew over the Channel would make being spotted at first light tantamount to a death sentence.

Late one night in the Blind Eye, Lieutenant Terry Stone hit their problem squarely on the head: "Even when nothing can go wrong, something always manages to."

Some of their problems would have been laughable if they had not been so deadly serious. For example, one night the *Arrow* stood offshore in an area ringed by a treacherous necklace of semi submerged rocks that would rip the bottom out of any boat unlucky enough to brush up against them. Midshipman Randy Seaborn had carefully pointed out a landmark ashore for Captain Randal to guide on. Using his Zeiss binoculars to avoid the rocks during the row in, he led the landing party on its way.

The powerful Zeiss glasses were a splendid piece of German precision engineering. Being Wehrmacht issue, however, they were not fitted with the spray shields standard in the Kriegsmarine and the Royal Navy. Consequently, the glasses soon misted over on the trip in to shore, rendering them useless.

End of mission . . . because of a lack of two inches of hard rubber.

The times when they did make it ashore, their small teams were seldom able to accomplish very much. The Commandos were still armed with outdated revolvers—even though they were now dead shots with their finely tuned Webley .455s—but they no longer carried rifles at all, having substituted canvas bags full of hand grenades. The few chance encounters they had with German patrols were minor, inconclusive affairs, with both sides quickly breaking contact.

The discouraging fact was that the Small-Scale Raiding Company did not have much to show for its nearly continuous efforts. Weather, winds, tides, and a lack of sophisticated navigational equipment were their major concerns. So far, the Nazis had been virtually a non-factor.

The one bright spot was that ship-to-shore boat work was no longer a problem. The Lifeboat Servicemen had a phenomenal ability to handle small boats in all water and weather conditions. In fact, their attitude was, the rougher the better. The Royal National Lifeboat Institute men were routinely tasked to operate in much worse weather than anything the Commandos would ever dare to brave. They saw their assignment to the Small-Scale Raiding Company as easy duty—with the occasional occupational hazard of being shot at.

Locating a pinpoint target at night was proving to be impossible, given their lack of equipment and the present state of their training; they simply could not do it. Initially, Captain Randal and his officers assumed that navigation was hampered by a lack of accurate intelligence; all they ever had to work with was grid coordinates taken off a map sheet. When Squadron Leader Paddy Wilcox started photographing targets for them and taking selected Small-Scale Raiding Company personnel on aerial reconnaissance flights prior to their operations, the thought was that they would naturally find it easier to carry out operations on targets of their choosing.

To their chagrin they soon found that simply because they had a dedicated target, had reviewed photos of the target area, and had flown over and eyeballed it beforehand did not mean they could hop aboard the *Arrow*, sail over, and raid it. The Commandos still had to find the eight-digit coordinate, a tiny pinpoint, in the dark and fog; they seldom could.

All was not wasted, however. The officers and men of the Small-Scale Raiding Company were becoming extremely proficient at launching long-range, independent operations, even if they virtually never worked out as planned. Forced by circumstances to be self-reliant, they were learning from their mistakes, working through them, and gradually developing ways to solve their operational problems—except for finding the desired target.

"The problem with our navigation is that we are trying to find minuscule targets located far away from major terrain features, such as lighthouses or ports," Lieutenant Stone expounded one evening in the Blind Eye, restating the problem constantly on everyone's mind. "We do not have any equipment other than a compass and a chart to work with. We can't get a fix on the stars in the amount of time we have because it is nearly always cloudy or foggy. We don't have the luxury of waiting for the weather to clear so we can take our bearings. And we can't simply aim for a permanent terrain feature or big beach because we know all of those will be guarded or mined; we have to go for some rugged, out-of-the-way objective the size of a dog yard in the middle of London. We're never going to find them the way we're going about it."

"Being issued any sophisticated navigating gear is out of the question," Midshipman Seaborn said gloomily. "In this war, anyway. Maybe the next one."

"Could be we're going at this the wrong way," Captain Randal offered. "If we can't find the pinpoints, then maybe we ought to quit looking for them."

"Good idea, old stick," agreed Lieutenant Stone, sounding dejected. "Then I can go back to my regiment and be packed off straightaway to the fleshpots of Cairo. I could use a tan."

"No, listen up." Captain Randal cut him off, an idea beginning to crystallize. "There are two types of targets. Point targets and—"

"Area targets," Lieutenant Stone finished his thought. "You may be onto something. Where are you going with this?"

"What's an example of an area-type target we could raid?" Captain Randal asked.

"Railroads," Sergeant Major Maxwell Hicks replied almost immediately. "They run right along the coast in a number of places. It's impossible for the Germans to guard them for their entire length. We could blow a railroad at any point on the line."

Leaving their drinks unfinished on the table, the Commandos stood up, paid their tab, drove straight back to Seaborn House, broke out charts of the coast of France, and started searching for coastal rail lines.

A likely target rail line was quickly located and an operation laid on for the next night. The company was placed on alert for the mission, and the raiding party was designated and all personnel briefed. Captain Randal ordered the *Arrow* to be made ready.

When the appointed hour came to sail, the weather conditions were only marginally favorable, but that didn't discourage anyone. At the last minute, Midshipman Seaborn's grandfather, Vice Admiral Sir Randolph "Razor" Ransom, VC, KCB, DSO, OBE, DSC, arrived and requested permission to accompany them in order to observe their night's work. The Razor was sixty-three years old and long retired, but who was going to refuse him? Not anyone on the *Arrow*.

The old admiral donned his foul-weather gear, and once he was on board, the yacht slipped the dock right on schedule. The sky turned green, then black. The rain came down and the swell rose. The *Arrow* slammed ahead, with waves the size of small houses breaking over her. The wind was south Force 7, the sea was very rough, and squalls followed one another, their howling winds slinging sheets of icy rain at the yacht. Those who were not seasick to the point of prostration were practically incapacitated with fear.

HMY *Arrow* rode fairly well, but the acrobatics she performed amid the huge, gray-green waves were nothing short of heart-stopping. The men on the tiny ship were taking a heavy pounding. Shortly, the wind was gusting to Force 9 with high seas, heavy swells, and cutting rain.

Admiral Ransom appeared to be thoroughly enjoying himself.

The *Arrow* stood on. Time seemed to stand still. The big green waves kept rolling in, threatening to smash the yacht into kindling. At the crest of each wave, the *Arrow* stood up on her tail like a tarpon trying to shake a hook, then slammed down into the trough, fought her way up a wall of water on the other side, arced over the top, and plunged down the far side. She repeated the whole death-defying act over and over and over again, for hour followed by excruciatingly long hour.

After what seemed like a lifetime of pure gut-wrenching, seafaring terror, the lookout on the bow sang out, "Enemy trawlers, Green One Five." Due to the optical illusion experienced at night at sea, the Nazi ships looked a lot closer than they actually were.

There appeared to be four, or perhaps it was five, German L-lighters; it was hard to tell in the dark and the swell because it was possible to see them only from the very top of the waves. The Germans immediately challenged with the letter B for Baker. Naturally, no one on the *Arrow* had any idea of the countersign. In less than one minute, the Germans figured that out and opened fire at a range of approximately 1,500 meters.

Their fire was quite accurate, with 2-pounder shells bursting in deadly bright flashes overhead and 20-millimeter cannon rounds the size of flaming onions screaming in. It is not much fun to be shot at by machine guns firing bullets the size of fully grown onions, and since the *Arrow* had nothing to shoot back with, the young skipper immediately gave the order to make smoke.

The volume of enemy fire perceptibly increased. Burning orange pumpkin-sized 2-pounder cannon shells blazed down both sides of the *Arrow*. The only thing worse than being shot at with bullets the size of onions is being shot at with shells the size of pumpkins. Within five minutes, however, the smoke screen began to take effect, completely obscuring the German trawlers from view and, all hands sincerely hoped, hiding the yacht.

Five minutes is an eternity to be engaged by high-velocity, rapid-firing cannons. Shortly after the smoke screen took effect, Midshipman Seaborn ordered the smoke making stopped so they could try to reestablish the exact location of the enemy trawlers. The unintended result was that German sailors reacquired their target and responded by increasing their volume of fire, this time adding 4-inch guns to the mix, aimed at randomly selected points within the smoke screen. These large shells were bursting approximately six feet above the water. Screaming shrapnel punctuated every detonation. The 4-inchers made the experience of the flaming onions and blazing pumpkins seem inconsequential.

"It is always darkest," Lieutenant Stone remarked philosophically, "before pitch black."

Midshipman Seaborn restarted his smoke generator and executed a couple of skillful maneuvers. The second smoke screen and the *Arrow*'s radical tacks somehow seemed to bewilder the German gunners on the trawlers. Their shooting slackened briefly as they realized they had lost their target once more. Then, by chance, amid the smoke and confusion, one L-lighter accidentally fired on her sister ship. After the odd round back and forth, the German ships suddenly engaged each other all-out in a ferocious blue-on-blue encounter.

A relieved band of Commandos, sailors, and Lifeboat Servicemen watched the raging blizzard of tracers blazing back and forth as the German trawlers enthusiastically shot it out among themselves. Midshipman Seaborn eased the yacht away to the south-southeast unnoticed.

"Now that is what I would call friendly fire," Lieutenant Stone declared as they slipped away into the night.

"Those trawlers sure carry a lot of heavy firepower," Captain Randal observed in awe.

"Nicely done, Midshipman," Admiral Ransom said to his grandson. "A shame we have no torpedoes!"

Thirty minutes later HMY *Arrow* made landfall. All hands able made ready for inshore operations. On the yacht's small bridge, every officer studied the shoreline intently through binoculars. Captain John Randal's Zeiss glasses were sporting recently retrofitted, battleship gray hard-rubber spray shades.

The shoreline was extremely rugged, and the Commandos had absolutely no idea where they were. But because the railway ran parallel to the coast for nearly thirty miles in this area, it really didn't matter much. The *Arrow* was bobbing less than a mile offshore; from that vantage point the men could see a solid black mass that appeared to be a rock face rising out of the water to a height of approximately three hundred feet. If it was a giant rock, then the train either had to run around it or go through it. Should there be a tunnel, it would be the perfect place to set the demolitions. In the event the railroad tracks ran around the rock, then setting the charges on a curve would be almost as effective.

Midshipman Seaborn eased in the boat to within a cable's distance of the rock. Captain Randal and Lieutenant Stone climbed down into the dinghy being held in place against the side of the *Arrow* by the Lifeboat Serviceman who was waiting to row them in. Both officers were carrying 50-pound packs of guncotton explosives.

It was a short pull to shore. Thankfully, the winds had dropped to calm. The moon came out, rat-cheese yellow and one-quarter full, adding an eerie element to the night's business.

The rock cliff was not as steep as it had appeared from the deck of the *Arrow*. The climb would have been fairly easy had it not been for the side effects of the awful voyage and the heavy packs the two were lugging. The slope was steep enough that there was zero likelihood of a German patrol being out on it. They might be up there on top, though.

As they worked their way up the incline, Lieutenant Stone whispered, "What were you thinking back there when the trawlers started shooting those gigantic balls of fire at us, old stick?"

"I was wishing I was home, snug in my bed."

"At Seaborn House?"

"California. You?"

"I was regretting not having taken my father's advice to go into the foreign service instead of the army."

"Wanted to get you out of the country, did he?"

Near the top of the cliff they found a railway tunnel. Both men dropped their packs and crawled to the mouth to investigate. There were no guards they could observe, either at the entrance of the tunnel or patrolling the tracks.

That was fortunate, because they were only equipped with sidearms. In his shoulder holsters Captain Randal was wearing a pair of short-barreled, 1899-issue Webley Mark V .455 revolvers with round bird's-head grips and smooth-as-butter actions, thanks to Captain "Geronimo Joe" McKoy. Secured by a lanyard around his neck, and tucked into his belt, was his Browning P-35.

Lieutenant Stone was carrying the private purchase Mauser Broomhandle pistol his grandfather had taken to South Africa with him as a young subaltern during the Boer War. The Mauser had the Stone family crest inlaid in sterling silver on the grip.

In terms of weapons technology, with the exception of the Browning P-35, the two Small-Scale Raiding Company officers were two wars behind the times. A light at the far end of the tunnel emitted a dim, yellow glow. Pulling the Browning out of his belt, Captain Randal signaled for Lieutenant Stone to stay put while he went forward to investigate.

It was chilly and damp in the tunnel. With his heart pounding in his throat, Captain Randal crept down the tracks. When he reached the far entrance, he could see that the light was some sort of signal beside the right-of-way. Luckily, there were no guards at the far entrance to the tunnel, either. Quickly making his way back, the captain reported, "There's no one there. That's a signal light. Let's set these demolitions and get out of here."

"Why not just lay the charges inside the tracks?" Lieutenant Stone said. "We can scrape away enough gravel so the guncotton doesn't stick up above the rails and then cover it with a thin layer."

"Good idea."

Suddenly, they heard the sound of someone approaching.

There were a few seconds of high melodrama until they discovered it was the Razor crawling up the slope to observe their actions on the objective. Accompanying the admiral was Corporal Jack Merritt, an exceedingly competent Life Guards trooper. When the Small-Scale Raiding

Company commander pulled him aside and demanded in no uncertain terms to know what was going on, Corporal Merritt merely shrugged his shoulders. The Razor was a law unto himself.

Captain Randal set the charges, laying the dual-pressure ignition studs flush with the underside of the track. Next, he connected the main charge. Then, with delicate care, he put the detonators in place.

"Fire in the hole," he said softly to the others. It was not the correct thing to say under the circumstances, because he was not going to detonate the charges—the train would take care of that when it came along—but he did not know what the correct terminology was, due to the fact that the Small-Scale Raiding Company's demolitions training had been sadly lacking.

"Move out, gentlemen."

Instead of making for the beach, Admiral Ransom produced a small flashlight with a red filter, turned it on, and proceeded to carefully inspect every inch of Captain Randal's handiwork. One would have thought he was a lane grader on a training exercise rather than standing in a railway tunnel in enemy-occupied territory. Lieutenant Stone suddenly grabbed Captain Randal's arm and pointed. The yellow light had flashed to green. None of them knew exactly what that indicated, but they hoped it meant a train was coming.

"Time to go, Admiral!" Captain Randal said tersely.

The men beat a hasty retreat down the cliff and climbed into the two waiting dinghies. With a few powerful strokes, the Lifeboat Servicemen had them back to the *Arrow*. As soon as the dinghies were hauled on board, Captain Randal turned to his ship's commander. "Let's get the hell out of Dodge, Randy."

"Aye, aye, sir!"

They were half a mile out to sea when the dark shadow of a long train could be seen snaking into the tunnel. Within seconds, a startling blue-white flash erupted from the shoreline, followed by the rolling thunder of a muffled detonation. Seconds later, brilliant red-orange flames shot out both entrances of the tunnel. Powerful secondary explosions soon followed and cooked off for some time.

"I daresay we've just blown up some kind of ordnance supply train," Lieutenant Stone crowed, for once unable to conceal his excitement. "Carrying bombs for the Luftwaffe or ammunition for the coastal ack-ack, I shouldn't wonder." The muffled secondary explosions continued booming until the *Arrow* was well out of sight of land.

The celebration on board was enthusiastic, though short-lived. When the winds picked back up, the return voyage was even worse than the trip out—with the notable exception of the absence of enemy trawlers.

"Do you reckon this would qualify as one of those lightning-quick Commando strikes we read about in the papers?" Lieutenant Terry Stone asked as they stumbled weakly off HMY *Arrow* and onto the dock at Seaborn House.

"I thought tonight was going to last forever," a wobbly Captain John Randal responded in a high-pitched voice, sounding every bit as sick as he felt. "I never want to go through anything as awful as that again for the rest of my life."

"You have to admit, though, blowing up that train was bloody fantastic! Why not get the map out right now so we can select another stretch of railroad to attack?"

"Okay, Terry, only you're going to have to help me make it up to Seaborn House first. I'm about to slip into a coma."

The next morning a motorcycle messenger arrived with sealed orders. Captain Randal scanned the dispatch briefly and handed it to Lieutenant Stone. The Life Guards officer read it and looked up.

"Well, John, so much for blowing up more trains anytime soon. It seems we're off to learn the gentle art of military parachuting."

PARACHUTE SCHOOL

7

RINGWAY

THE BRITISH NO. 1 PARACHUTE TRAINING SCHOOL, OPERATING AS
"Central Landing Establishment" for the sake of secrecy, was located at
the Ringway civil airport in Manchester.

Just who, exactly, anyone intended to fool with an obscure cover name
seemed open to question, especially with the No. 2 (Parachute) Commandos jogging here and there in their distinctive little round, padded jump
helmets and with snow-white parachutes cracking open continuously over
lovely Tatton Park. Certainly it was not the Abwehr—the German intelligence service. However, No. 1 Parachute Training School was located far
enough away from the London area that it was hoped the Luftwaffe would
not interfere with their training operations.

Visiting the Central Landing Establishment was like entering another
world. The grounds had been nicknamed the "Circus." Everything moved
on the double all the time; danger seemed close at hand.

Lady Jane Seaborn—dressed in the uniform of a lieutenant of the
Royal Marines, which she had lately taken to wearing—met the officers
and men of the Small-Scale Raiding Company on the outskirts of Bench
Hill and escorted them to their quarters. Driving her Rolls-Royce was

the newest addition to the raiding company's roster, Royal Marine Private Pamela Plum-Martin, who looked as though she belonged on a billboard, wearing a swimsuit and advertising suntan lotion, more than in the Royal Marines. Where Lieutenant Lady Jane Seaborn had recruited her from was anybody's guess; she didn't elaborate.

The other ranks were quickly marched off to barracks at the Airborne Force Depot while the officers bunked in at ivy-covered Hardwick Hall.

Captain John Randal felt a stab of apprehension as he swung down from the cab of the truck and hoisted his gear over one shoulder. The idea of actually jumping out of an airplane sounded totally insane. Captain Randal was afraid of heights, or at least he thought he was. He felt as if he were being sucked along out of control and was far from sure he really wanted to go through with the whole thing. No—he *knew* he did not want to go through with it. Who in his right mind would jump out of a perfectly good airplane? Answer: No one. Captain Randal was beginning to feel trapped.

Every man in the company, including Midshipman Randy Seaborn, the crew of HMY *Arrow*, and the eight Lifeboat Servicemen, had volunteered to attend. Even Squadron Leader Paddy Wilcox had insisted on coming along, claiming he needed to understand "every aspect of parachutage." No longer flying air-sea rescue, he had volunteered, at Lady Jane's suggestion, for the secret intelligence organization she worked for so that he could become the Small-Scale Raiding Company's pilot.

Captain Randal couldn't remember whether the idea of becoming parachute qualified was his or whether Lieutenant Lady Seaborn had simply arranged for the training and he had been swept up in the moment. The parachute wings she wore on her sleeve may have had something to do with it; they were impossible to ignore. She had them, he did not, and there was no getting around it.

Little details like qualification badges can drive a soldier to attempt feats he normally would never consider. Captain Randal couldn't explain it—even to himself—since it didn't make a lot of sense. He just knew the wings were a powerful incentive in the military.

"The school commandant is waiting to see you in his office," Lieutenant Lady Seaborn said, producing one of her tremor-inducing smiles.

"I shall be back in three weeks to attend the wings ceremony when you graduate, John. Do try to have fun."

The Royal Marines lieutenant looked truly magnificent in her new uniform, which consisted of highly polished riding boots, jodhpurs, a perfectly tailored blouse, a khaki shirt and tie, and the glossy bill of her officer's hat pulled down low, shading her vivid green eyes.

Lieutenant Lady Seaborn stepped into her idling Rolls, and her beautiful driver stepped on the gas. The Rolls roared out the gate, spewing gravel.

"Do you think that's an official Royal Marines uniform she's wearing?" he asked, staring after the car.

"How could one know," Lieutenant Stone said, "having never actually seen a woman Royal Marine before?"

"Do you Brits call Marines 'leathernecks' like we do in the U.S.?"

"Yes, we do, old stick. Though, in this case, I should recommend against it."

Squadron Leader Louis Strange, DSO, MC, DFC, was a highly decorated ace fighter pilot from the last war, during which he had achieved the army rank of lieutenant colonel. He had come back on active duty in the Royal Air Force during the late, great trouble only to find that, like Squadron Leader Paddy Wilcox, he was considered over-the-hill for combat flying. To Squadron Leader Strange's total amazement, after a period of active service in France as a staff officer before the evacuation, he found himself in command of the Empire's first parachute school.

He did not have any previous experience with parachutes other than having wanted one in the last war. A good-looking, trim, silver-haired officer with a neat, clipped mustache, Squadron Leader Strange seemed most pleased to see Captain John Randal, though a trifle disappointed at the same time.

"Welcome to the Central Landing Establishment, Captain." The commandant gestured toward a chair. "You have elected to waive the parachute-packing phase of the course, I understand. Lady Seaborn has informed me that, since you are in the process of organizing your own rigger detachment, you will not require that particular block of training."

The rigger detachment was news to Captain Randal, but before he could say anything, the squadron leader continued.

"Most unusual woman, Lady Seaborn. Knew her late father, you know. Fellow practically *invented* money! Women in the Royal Marines—I never even realized they had a women's auxiliary! What have we here, Captain? Small-Scale Raiding Company, very hush-hush, top-priority orders straight from Combined Operations Headquarters.

"And your roster . . . You have with you one army officer, one navy officer, twenty-two soldiers, four sailors, eight National Lifeboat Servicemen, and one slightly long-in-the-tooth Canadian squadron leader. Unorthodox to say the least, old chap. You are the advance party, I take it?"

"No, sir."

"Blast! I was hoping for more."

"More, sir?"

"More trainees. The prime minister has decreed that five thousand parachutists will be raised this summer. To accomplish that, ah, shall we say *ambitious* task, the RAF has given me this excellent facility here at Ringway and six aging Mk III Whitley bombers converted to become parachute droppers. What the RAF did not give me were enough instructors, so we are being forced to cross-train instructors from the Army Physical Training Corps to teach our parachute school curriculum. All of which is completely irrelevant, of course, because we do not have five thousand volunteers to train.

"Picked men are all the rage, but they have to be picked from somewhere, and the army really does not want us raiding its established regiments. Regimentals' COs resent their best men volunteering out for what sounds like more glamorous duty.

"To make matters worse, the men we are getting in from No. 2 Commando are beginning to become somewhat resentful. They volunteered to be Commandos, expecting to see immediate action raiding the French coast, only to learn that all they are doing for now is training or being used in guinea-pig demonstration jumps to recruit more volunteers for the Airborne Forces."

"I see," Captain Randal said, wondering where, exactly, this interview was heading.

"And so, Captain, I was hoping you would send us your entire unit."

"The exact strength of the Small-Scale Raiding Company is classified," Captain Randal explained. "There's going to be a party of eight Lovat Scouts assigned to us, arriving at the end of the week to start training in your next cycle. For your planning purposes, after that you should not expect many more people from the Small-Scale Raiding Company."

"Lovat Scouts, eh? The premier snipers in the army and some say the best stalkers in the world. You've an eclectic mix men of men, I must say." The squadron leader nodded. "Well, then. Mad keen to be a parachutist, are you? You shall be jolly glad to jump out of those old Whitleys, I can assure you. Flap their wings like bats. Obsolete as dinosaurs. Do not ever land in one!"

"I see," Captain Randal said again, feeling slightly whipsawed.

"Oh, and just for the record, I command the school," Squadron Leader Strange continued, "and Major John Rock, Royal Engineers, is in charge of the military side of things. It is a bit of an awkward command structure. Not entirely sure why the RAF is responsible for training army parachutists. Our job is to stay in the air, not fall out of it, don't you know. However, it all seems to work. Do they do that in the American Army, too—things that do not make sense?"

"I'd have to say that, in my limited experience, yes, sir, they do."

"Thought so. Well, you are going to do ground week here at Ringway to prepare you for the physical and psychological reactions to the shock of parachuting. Then you progress to transition week to teach you how to operate all the specialist equipment and to familiarize yourself with the techniques incidental to jumping safely out of an aircraft in flight. And finally, you will progress to jump week, where you will make two jumps from a tethered balloon and five more from our beloved Whitleys.

"The main thing for you to keep in mind, as a future commander of parachutists, is that special emphasis must always be placed on the exploitation of an opportunity through great fitness, intensive training, careful organization, and detailed planning. Always, you, the leader, must have an eye for the main chance. We strive to provide you with a foundation for that here at Ringway. Do you have any questions, Captain? No? Well, good luck and happy jumping."

As Captain Randal stood up to leave the room, the squadron leader added in a sincere tone, "Congratulations on your recent award of the Military Cross. Got your teeth into them early. Good show. I cannot fathom why an American would want to come over and join in our fight, considering the desperate straits we British presently find ourselves in. But speaking for myself, I am glad to have you here. If you should encounter any problem, any problem at all, come to me anytime. The strategic importance of airborne operations is enormous. Not to mention that jumping from a balloon or an airplane develops courage, the decision-making process, resourcefulness, and the ability not to lose one's head in an emergency; it also tests will power and teaches men how to make quick decisions in case of complications."

No kidding, Captain Randal thought as he walked out the commandant's door. *I'm going to need every last one of those qualities just to have the guts to strap on the parachute.*

8

GROUND WEEK

TRAINING STARTED BRIGHT AND EARLY THE FOLLOWING MORNING. Actually, it started prior to bright and early; it was still dark and would be for quite a while.

"Wake-up call, sir," the orderly announced, flipping on the light switch in the room Captain John Randal and Lieutenant Terry Stone shared in Hardwick Hall.

"Things always look darkest before pitch black," the Life Guards officer groaned, rolling out of bed.

The uniform of the day was navy blue physical training, shorts worn under gabardine trousers, jumping jackets, and boots. It was cold and damp when they assembled for training. The training cycle was designed for syndicates of sixty men. There were six Whitley Mk III parachute troop carrier aircraft, and ten men wearing parachutes were all that could be squeezed into a Whitley—it was not rocket science.

Because the Small-Scale Raiding Company did not total sixty men, the empty slots were filled by men from No. 2 Commando under the command of Lieutenant Percy Stirling, 17/21 Lancers, who were just starting their parachute training. Both groups of men, Commandos and

"Raiders," as the Small-Scale Raiding Company men were beginning to be called, had been training hard and were confident they were in excellent physical condition.

As Captain Randal and the others quickly learned, however, they had not reckoned on having Army Physical Training Corps personnel assigned as PT instructors.

The instructor cadre jogged up to the formation of Commandos and Raiders in perfect cadence, moving like a team of well-disciplined robots. They were wearing skintight white tee shirts, and each instructor had wide shoulders and a tiny waist. The PT instructors looked as if they were on temporary duty assignment from Mount Olympus.

The chief instructor was a ginger-haired sergeant named Roy "Mad Dog" Reupart, who had a way with words: "Welcome to hell," he said in a conversational tone.

Then he dropped down and knocked out fifty one-armed push-ups while the rest of the instructor cadre, standing at parade rest, counted them out in unison. It took a long time for the count to reach fifty. In mid-air, Sergeant Reupart switched arms and knocked out another fifty.

As he watched the performance, Captain Randal reflected that one of the worst things that could ever happen to a trainee was to draw a PT instructor called Mad Dog.

Standing beside him, Lieutenant Stone said, "Uh-oh."

"You men are here to learn how to jump from an aircraft in flight!" the chief instructor shouted as he leapt to his feet. "Now, am I going too fast for anyone?"

No one breathed a word.

"Outstanding. I can tell we are going to get along perfectly."

In fact, their relationship went straight downhill from there.

To get their blood circulating Sergeant Reupart led them on a five-mile run. The men didn't know it was going to be five miles, though; no one bothered to tell the troops how far they would be running, and from the shape the cadre was in, it could be fifty miles or five hundred.

After the run came an hour of PT, with the instructor cadre all over them, screaming insults, driving them to go "Harder, faster, harder, move, move, move, go, go, go, drop and give me twenty-five!" The only consolation was that the trainees got to use both arms for their push-ups.

The PT was followed by an obstacle course, followed by another run, followed by climbing ropes, followed by another run, followed by a freezing-cold swim—fully clothed—in the pond, followed by more PT.

There was a break for lunch and a change into dry clothes, and then it started all over again. Apparently, the idea was to find out who really wanted to be a parachutist. Captain Randal was fairly certain Mad Dog would be disappointed to learn the real answer to that question.

There was a walk-run, a cross-country run, a one-mile dash, and a seemingly endless speed march. Then they did something called a "knees high" run. In between, there were countless push-ups for infractions, real and imagined.

"How many days are in a training week?" Lieutenant Stone gasped during a break between bouts of push-ups.

"Six, I think."

"We are all going to die, old stick."

They never walked anywhere; every move was on the double.

The instructors were sticklers for proper military etiquette but that did not stop them from singling out the officers for special attention. "Get those bloody knees up, Captain! You look like you are going backward, sir. Drop and give me twenty-five! Are you in pain, sir?"

The only trainees who caught more flak than the officers were the NCOs. Sergeant Major Maxwell Hicks paid the highest price of all. The privates would have enjoyed it had they realized what was happening, but they were being hammered too hard to notice.

Next, it was on to the sawdust pit. The sawdust looked soft, but the students quickly found out it wasn't. After an hour in the pit doing exercises, strong men were weeping in agony.

Captain Randal swallowed what seemed like about half the sawdust in the pit, and the other half found its way down the back of his shirt. He was so weak from exhaustion by the end of the PT period that he was having a hard time crawling over the eight-inch-high sandbags surrounding the pit.

"Give me twenty-five, sir! You look like a dying cockroach!" There was no escaping the eagle-eyed Sergeant Reupart. He was everywhere and had eyes in the back of his head.

An hour seemed to last a day; a day seemed like a week; and the idea of surviving until the end of the week was a frame of reference so distant in the future as to be totally unfathomable.

After the evening meal, a formation was held in the large gymnasium. A flight lieutenant named John Kilkenny stood at the front. He was from the RAF's Fitness Branch—an entirely different terrorist organization from the Army Physical Training Corps—and he announced that he would be teaching them the single most important thing that they would learn in the entire three weeks of Parachute Training School: how to fall. As Captain Randal and his men soon found out, falling was an advanced art form.

Flight Lieutenant Kilkenny had made a study of falling and had developed what he called the Five Points of Contact Resulting from a Parachute Landing Fall. He shortened it to "the parachute landing fall," but the trainees came to know and love it simply as the "PLF." First, he showed them film footage of German *Fallschirmjägers* in an actual combat jump. They were flinging themselves headfirst out of a Junkers-52 troop transport, arms outstretched like Superman. The Nazis looked as though they were literally raring to go get the enemy down below.

The way the German RZ-1 parachute worked, there was a terrific opening crack and then the jumper hung down, limply bent at the waist, dangling from the rigging attached to a D-ring centered on his back. It looked very uncomfortable in the movie and made the German paratroopers appear slightly ridiculous and somewhat helpless: two descriptions Captain Randal suspected no one in the audience had ever before considered applying to German paratroopers. With no way to reach up to control their descent by manipulating their risers, the Nazi jumpers had to ride it in face first all the way.

The German method called for the parachutist to make either a forward or a backward roll, though how they expected someone hanging down and bent in half with their arms almost touching their toes to make a backward roll was not clearly explained.

Most of the *Fallschirmjägers* landed by making a bone-jarring, full-body slam into the ground face-first. Dust flew up, and some of them actually bounced once or twice. To the trainees watching the film, it looked as though the German landing really hurt. A few men just lay there, stunned, as their parachute canopies collapsed down around them before the camera cut away.

"Have to be tough to be a German paratrooper," Lieutenant Stone observed, loud enough for everyone in the room to hear and laugh nervously in response.

"Men of steel," agreed Lieutenant Kilkenny. "Let me point out: Steel will snap. Metal can develop fatigue. What you are watching is exactly *how not to land* after jumping from an aircraft in flight. I have made a study of the subject, and I have determined that it is better to be a man of rubber than a man of steel. That is precisely what I am going to teach you to be: rubber men.

"You will be jumping the X-type parachute that deploys canopy last, providing the jumper with a soft opening rather than the back-breaking snap of the German chutes. Your harness is designed so you sit in it like a saddle and ride it down easy, feet first."

"Now you're talking, old stick," Lieutenant Stone called out, speaking for the cavalrymen in the audience.

The movie projector came back on and showed British parachutists spilling out from under a Whitley Mk III, their X-type parachutes gently plopping open, and the jumpers riding to the ground sitting in the upright position. Every man in the room cheered. It did not require a trained eye to see the difference.

"Now, utilizing the parachute landing fall I have developed, you will land on the balls of your feet, remembering to keep your feet and knees together; swivel; then roll onto your calf, thigh, buttocks, and small of the back, keeping your head down and chin tucked in on your chest. With your elbows touching together on your chest, the inside of the forearms covering and protecting your face—fists side by side together, touching the front rim of your jump helmet—you will roll over, limp as a dishrag, and land as light as a feather."

All the men cheered again, though it did seem like quite a lot to remember and execute. Especially considering that you had just jumped out of an airplane traveling at least one hundred miles per hour and you probably had less than twenty seconds, while descending, to decide what type of PLF you were going to attempt, to think about getting all the moves right and performing them in the proper sequence—all the while knowing that the instant the toes of your boots touched the ground on the drop zone, if you got it wrong, very bad things were going to happen to certain major bones in your body.

The PLF was further complicated by the fact that the speed of impact was about that of jumping off of a two-story building without a parachute. There probably would be other distractions taking place, when they did it for real—like people shooting at you.

The film cut to the drop zone where the British parachutists were coming in for a landing, sitting in the saddle of the parachute harness and doing all the things that the flight lieutenant had described. They landed, more or less, like leaves falling gently from a giant oak tree to the ground. The Commandos and Raiders cheered loud and long.

Flight Lieutenant Kilkenny did not mention to the group that quite a bit of footage taken at a number of different drops had been edited and creatively spliced together to present the many soft-as-a-feather landings the film showed. The PLF is one of the most difficult military skills any soldier will ever try to master, all things considered. But when it works, it is a thing of beauty.

The next five days were a blur of running, practicing the PLF, push-ups, practicing the PLF, sawdust pit PT, practicing the PLF, climbing ropes, and practicing the PLF. By the end of ground week the trainees were becoming reasonably proficient at running, doing PT in the sawdust pit, climbing ropes, and doing push-ups.

Mastering the PLF was proving to be a challenge.

9

SUNDAY

SUNDAY WAS NOT A TRAINING DAY. BUT THE OFFICERS AND MEN of the Small-Scale Raiding Company were so beat up and dispirited by the ferociousness of the first week's training, they were barely able to muster the energy to do much more than lie around their quarters. Religious services were only sparsely attended. No one went sightseeing.

The good news was that not a single Raider had dropped out, which to Captain John Randal seemed like some kind of a miracle. To a man they were stunned at how demanding the training had been.

The troops lay around their barracks, painting themselves and each other in the hard-to-reach places with orange Mercurochrome. They looked like orange zebras. Each and every one agreed it was, without doubt, a good thing that the British Airborne Forces had gone to all that trouble to develop the soft-as-a-feather, rubber-man landing technique. Imagine how brutal the first week would have been without it.

The Raiders were banged up from head to toe. It was not uncommon to see officers and men in the mess hobbling around with an arm, a leg, and even their whole torso encased in plaster. Parachute training was dangerous business. The problem, they had all discovered, was that even though each man had five points of contact, they seldom ever landed on any of them. Not only were they bruised on the places where the five points of contact were reputed to be, but since they also practiced front and rear parachute landing falls (where there were not supposed to be *any* points of contact), they were also banged up front and back from not being able to swivel fast enough to the right or the left in order to land on the approved school-solution five points.

The consensus among the Raiders was that their opposite numbers— the poor bloody Nazis training to be German paratroopers like the ones in the film—must really be hurting after their first week of parachute school. Practicing to land on your face had to be really tough training!

One lesson learned came through particularly loud and clear to Captain Randal: The Small-Scale Raiding Company had not been working on physical conditioning nearly enough. It was obvious that putting in excessively long hours to improve their military skills, as they had done, did not equate to training intelligently to be in top physical condition. Lack of conditioning was a mistake he did not intend to repeat in the future.

The irony was that the British Armed Forces needed to raise some five thousand parachute-qualified troops. Why, then, did they make their best effort to murder outright the few who did volunteer? Captain John Randal knew somewhere in this madness there had to be a lesson to be learned; he just couldn't figure out what it was.

Major John Rock came by Hardwick Hall to deliver a sealed telex from the Ringway message center to Captain Randal and to invite him on a tour of the training facilities that they would be using during transition week. The message read:

```
TO CAPTAIN JOHN RANDAL
COMMANDING
SMALL-SCALE RAIDING COMPANY
ON COMPLETION OF PARACHUTE TRAINING YOU WILL
RECEIVE AUTHORIZATION FROM COMBINED OPERA-
TIONS HEADQUARTERS TO INCREASE THE STRENGTH
OF THE SMALL-SCALE RAIDING COMPANY TO FOUR
OFFICERS AND FORTY-FIVE MEN EXCLUSIVE OF
```

NAVY, LIFEBOAT INSTITUTE AND RAF PERSONNEL
STOP YOU AND TERRY HAVE BEEN PROMOTED ONE
GRADE EFFECTIVE FRIDAY LAST STOP
CONGRATULATIONS MAJOR STOP HOPE YOU ARE
ENJOYING YOURSELF STOP
SIGNED
JANE SEABORN
CAPTAIN
ROYAL MARINES

"Captain, Royal Marines," Major Randal laughed, handing the flimsy sheet to the newly promoted Captain Terry Stone, who was reclining on his bunk with his boots propped up on his duffel bag. "That was quick. What do you want to bet she has date of rank on you?"

The brand-new captain quickly scanned the telex. "I would have to hazard that the peerless Lady Jane has found the experience of being a mere lieutenant a trifle tedious, old stick," he mused. "Probably the only way she could think of to justify having herself promoted was to arrange for us to be promoted, too. I say, let's hope she has ambitions to be a general of Marines. That would make us both field marshals."

"Terry, I've heard there's never been a Life Guards officer promoted to major general in the history of the regiment. Now why might that be?"

"Life Guards tend to flame out around the rank of lieutenant colonel. There are two schools of thought as to why that's the case. Some—mostly Life Guardsmen—point out that we are all so rich, we tend to retire early to manage our vast estates. Our detractors, on the other hand, make the claim that we are all so inbred, we do not possess the requisite brains to be general officer material."

He raised himself up on one elbow and gave Major Randal a look of appeal. "Make sure you don't do anything to discourage the good captain of Royal Marines in her ambitions for rapid advancement, John. She is my only hope."

"Maybe the War Office recognized our superior leadership skills?"

Captain Stone gave Major Randal a look that forced a laugh, despite his bruised ribs. "Okay, you're right. It had to be Jane. But what makes you think I can do anything to encourage or discourage her?"

"I hate it when that happens." Captain Stone rolled his eyes. "It's always such a letdown when you discover your commanding officer is an idiot."

Major Rock had been listening to the exchange, but the look on his face clearly indicated he understood little of what was being said. Both Major Randal and Captain Stone were careful not to allow him to see the contents of the telex.

"Good news, I presume?" he ventured.

"Terry and I just got the word we've been promoted," Major Randal explained.

"Jolly good! Congratulations are in order and all that. I have a spare set of crowns I'd be delighted for you to put up, and you can give your pins to Captain Stone. Afraid you won't find anyplace else around here to obtain new officers' rank insignia. We can stop by my quarters before I take you on the cook's tour and get you kitted out straightaway."

"Thanks, Major."

"You get to call me John, now—John."

As they walked across the Circus after stopping by his quarters, Major Rock explained that the second week of parachute school was to consist of "synthetic training" to gain proficiency in "exits" and "air control." What that meant, neither Captain Stone nor Major Randal had the heart to ask.

"Aperture drill takes place in here," he announced as they strolled into a huge hangar. A neatly raked sawdust pit ran its length. Towering above the sawdust stood a row of dummy midsections of Whitley fuselages mounted on wooden trestle legs. They looked like huge praying mantises. Quite a bit of praying did, in fact, go on in those mock fuselages.

"From a tactical standpoint, the trick is to exit fast," Major Rock explained, leading them up the wooden stairs into the belly of the apparatus. "The faster the exit, the closer together the stick of paratroopers lands on the drop zone. The closer the jumpers land together, the faster they can assemble and carry on with their mission."

The hole in the bottom of the floor of the mock-up looked a lot smaller than Major Randal thought it would. Really, it was more of a funnel than a hole; it was three feet deep.

"What's that?" he asked, pointing to the fresh paint that was thinly covering some suspicious-looking gouges on the far side of the exit hole.

"Teeth marks. We touch them up at the end of every day's class. No sense spreading unnecessary alarm and despondency to the students, what?"

"You'll want to make sure you don't look down when you jump," Major Rock went on, "or you'll inevitably lean forward and hit the far side of the hole. We call it the 'Whitley kiss.' Not a good idea to lean backward, either. If you do, then you'll most likely clip the near side of the exit hole with the back of your head. That's called 'ringing the bell.' Hard to make a decent parachute landing fall if you're unconscious, what?"

"I see."

As they made their way around the hangar, Major Rock pointed out various pieces of training equipment. Then they walked outdoors and inspected the seventy-foot towers used to simulate a full parachute jump.

"As you know, Prime Minister Churchill has ordered that five thousand jump-qualified troops be trained and ready by the end of the summer training cycle," said Major Rock.

"Can you do that?" asked Major Randal.

"Well, actually, yes, we probably can. Provided, of course, that we are allowed unrestrained advertising for recruits. There is always a bit of resistance from the old establishment to new ventures, but then I would expect that in your line of work, you fellows have firsthand knowledge of how that plays out."

"Yes, but we have a way to get around it," Captain Stone replied, giving Major Randal a wink.

Captain the Lady Jane Seaborn, Major Randal thought to himself. *Our own personal secret weapon.*

"I imagine you do," Major Rock said. "Truth is, the army senior staff is quite keen on forming Airborne Forces. They want to raise parachute battalions, regiments, brigades, and even divisions.

"They actually imagine that all the Royal Air Force will have to do is fly parachutists and glider troops to the target area, drop or release them, and that's all there is to it: an instant, air-delivered field army smack in the enemy's rear—as if by magic.

"The RAF, for their part, rather resent being tasked to divert their already limited resources for what they see as supporting a purely army adventure."

"Interservice rivalry," Captain Stone said with a sardonic chuckle. "The one constant in any military environment."

"Personally, I believe the army is being a bit shortsighted about the amount of air force support needed to sustain an airborne army in combat," Major Rock opined. "My guess is the RAF will have to resupply any troops it drops until they link up with conventional ground forces. They'll also have to provide continual close air support until the airborne forces can get their artillery up and going." Major Rock shook his head. "That is my job, you know, to come up with how we are going to develop and execute a national command strategy of aerial envelopment."

"Sounds like a big assignment," Major Randal observed.

Major Rock nodded. "I have six weeks to accomplish what the Germans have been working on for six years."

"Good luck, old stick," Captain Stone said. "Better you than me."

"Oh well, enough of my problems." The major laughed. "Do you fellows have any place on your entire bodies that is not sore right now?"

"Only the five points of contact, which I have never landed on even once, I do not believe, unless it was by pure accident," Captain Stone admitted. "A thing should not be that hard for one to master."

"I'm black-and-blue all over," Major Randal acknowledged.

"Precisely. The problem is that while you have only five points of contact, you have two sides of your body, which really makes ten points of contact, and you never seem to be able to hit them. And that's why I say gliders are the way to go, the way of the future!" Major Rock got a twinkle in his eye. "You can tow two of them behind a bomber. No Whitley kiss, no ringing the bell, no bloody PLFs, and no parachutists landing, scattered from here to kingdom come, and hunting for lost equipment bundles in the dark behind enemy lines.

"What you do have, gentlemen, is a tightly concentrated combined-arms team, landed intact with exacting precision, armed, equipped, and ready to fight. You don't have to break up existing regiments to form special battalions—guaranteed to make the old-line military establishment really happy, by the by. You simply cram an existing regiment in gliders, and away you go."

"Then what are we doing in a parachute school?" Major Randal said.

"I would not have any idea why you are here, John. The only reason I am is because of orders. I constitute the only non volunteer in Airborne Forces history."

"You never volunteered?" Captain Stone asked in a tone of disbelief. "I thought parachuting was volunteers only!"

"Do you possibly imagine I would ever, of my own volition, jump out of a perfectly good aircraft in flight? We don't even use reserve parachutes. The whole idea is ludicrous! No, I do it strictly because I've been ordered to."

"Lady Jane volunteered us," Major Randal offered.

Major Rock shook his head. "Did either of you know that of the first twenty-one officers and three hundred twenty-one other ranks trained—all handpicked men, mind you, from B and C troops of No. 2 Commando under the able command of Lieutenant Colonel C. I .A. Jackson—thirty of them found themselves unable to screw up the necessary courage to jump, two were killed because of parachute failures, and twenty sustained injuries serious enough to render them medically unfit to continue the training? There is a special ward at Davyhulme Military Hospital devoted exclusively to the care of patients from Ringway. We keep the X-ray and orthopedic departments over there humming."

Major Randal looked at Captain Stone; Captain Stone looked at Major Randal. Neither of them could think of any suitable response.

Captain Stone gave their tour guide a sideways look. "Major Rock, it would probably be in the best interest of Airborne Forces if you made a dedicated effort to stay completely out of the recruiting end of operations."

Major Randal stared at the ground. "Parachute failures?" Right this minute he would have dearly loved to wring newly promoted Captain Lady Jane Seaborn's drop-dead gorgeous neck.

When Major Randal and Captain Stone were let off back at Hardwick Hall, they found an officer neither of them knew waiting for them in the lobby. He introduced himself as Captain Neil Fergusson from Combined Operations Headquarters and asked if there was somewhere that they could talk in private.

The three officers went upstairs and closed the door to Randal and Stone's room. The COHQ officer proceeded straight to the business at hand. "Colonel Clarke ordered me here to brief you on the latest Commando raid undertaken by Combined Operations. Consider everything I tell you regarding the operation as classified 'Most Secret.' Do not discuss what I am about to tell you with anyone other than your Small-Scale Raiding Company personnel, for reasons that will soon be readily apparent.

"Two nights ago, on 14 June, a Commando-type operation was undertaken against the German-occupied channel island of Guernsey. The troops involved were No. 11 Independent Company and elements of the newly formed No. 3 Commando. I accompanied the operation as an observer from COHQ.

"An officer who had grown up on Guernsey was attached. He was supposed to provide intelligence on the German forces' disposition. Additionally, the destroyers and RAF launches used to transport troops to the objective were degaussed in order to make them immune to magnetic mines. This had the unintended effect of throwing off the compasses of the launches being used to land the troops.

"RAF Avro Ansons were assigned to buzz the landing areas and provide a 'distraction.'

"The mission was a complete hash. The officer from Guernsey failed to provide any useful intelligence. One of the detachments from No. 11 Independent Company sailed to the wrong island; another experienced engine problems and had to return to its parent ship; and a third from No. 3 Commando, though landing at the correct location, had to get ashore wading in neck-deep water, resulting in the troops being severely exhausted by the time they reached dry land. No contact was made with German forces, but unfortunately, while the raiders were ashore, the winds came up, which caused their only dingy to capsize when it was time to return to their ship. One man drowned. That meant the only way off the beach was to swim, and three men had to be left behind when it was learned that they had exaggerated their swimming ability when volunteering for special service. They are now presumed to be prisoners."

"The prime minister is outraged, vowing that there will be no more Guernseys. He called it a 'silly fiasco.'" Captain Fergusson wound up his report.

"Buzzed the beaches again, huh?" Major Randal said, shaking his head.

"And good old No. 11 nearly invaded the wrong island," Captain Stone observed drolly.

"Colonel Clarke required me to inform you he believes that, in the future, more accurate intelligence and better training are needed for successful raiding."

"You mean like swimming lessons?" Major Randal asked.

"One could argue they would have been rather useful for four of the men, actually," Captain Fergusson replied.

"Sounds like Combined Operations," Captain Stone drawled, "is operating at roughly the level of the Keystone Kops."

Captain Fergusson departed, closing the door behind him. Captain Stone offered Major Randal a cigarette. "Do you reckon those Apache Indians you were telling Colonel Clarke about had this much trouble getting their initial raids into the Arizona Territory up and running?"

Major Randal lit his cigarette and took a deep drag.

"Probably not."

10

TRANSITION WEEK

WORD WAS THAT THE SECOND WEEK OF PARACHUTE SCHOOL WAS worse than the first. No one in the Small-Scale Raiding Company or any of the No. 2 Commando fillers wanted to believe the rumor could possibly be true. Hope springs eternal for men bent on flinging themselves out of perfectly good airplanes. In fact, the second week of the British No. 1 Parachute Training School initially lulled the students into a false sense that things were not going to be all that bad.

They were.

The weather was a repeat of the first week: rainy, foggy, and damp. As they gathered on Monday morning, the future paratroopers were a sullen and battered body of men. Sergeant Roy "Mad Dog" Reupart did not seem to notice. He showed up alone, minus the dreaded cadre of assistants. He called the formation to attention and then shouted, "At ease . . . Catch me if you can!"

He took off in a dead run from a standing start, spraying gravel. Taken by surprise, the Raiders and Commandos nevertheless bounded after him like the hounds of hell.

When they caught up with him a mile and a half later they found him leaning nonchalantly against the giant hangar where they would conduct synthetic training. His merry band of sadistic assistants swaggered from within the building.

Mad Dog announced, "You lads are going to have to do a lot better than this if you expect to become parachutists in the British Army."

As he lay on the ground breathing fire, Major John Randal decided that being in the British Army was the worst idea he had ever had in his entire life.

Captain Terry Stone groaned. "I think I coughed up a piece of my lung."

The RAF parachute instructor staff arrived and synthetic training began. Why it was called "synthetic" was a mystery to Major Randal; there was nothing artificial about it.

The subject of the first day was their old nemesis from week one, the parachute landing fall. They performed PLFs from ground level into the sawdust pit, from the three-step platform, and then from the five-foot platform. They performed them from the right side, from the left side, the front, and from the rear.

"Keep your feet and knees together!" the instructors shouted continuously. "Keep your feet and knees together!"

A small mistake when landing by parachute could have serious consequences, so the parachute instructors were meticulous. They were also utterly ruthless. In the harsh, cruel military school training environment where the idea is to learn and profit from repetition and pain, they were, quite simply, outstanding.

The Raiders and Commandos then climbed up onto a ten-foot platform. Four cables were strung from it to the ground, with wooden spars in the form of an "X" attached to the top of each cable. Four men lined up on the platform, each holding a pair of the wooden spars. On command, they lifted their feet up and raced down the cable at full speed, feet and knees together. On the command "Drop!" they let go of the spars and crashed into the sawdust, attempting to make a forward PLF, utilizing the five points of contact, while traveling at full speed and in about the same amount of time it takes a bolt of lightning to strike. Few succeeded.

"You look like a bloody sack of coal, Midshipman Seaborn! Get back up there, go to the front of the line, and try it again, sir!"

It began to slowly dawn on the students that transition week really was going to be worse than the first week. The harassment was much diminished, and the PT, while tough, was reduced, but the constant, unrelenting banging into the ground soon took its toll. The students were steadily being pounded to pieces.

Then the pace picked up a notch. After performing landings from the right and left sides off the ten-foot platform, to the students' disbelief they practiced PLFs from the rear, which were the worst. They came sailing down the cable backward with no way possible to turn their heads to see where they were going because, as instructed, they had their chins screwed down tight on their chests. Then, upon the command "Drop!" they had to land—feet and knees together, knees bent slightly and relaxed, elbows tucked in, almost touching on your chest, with fists facing inward, protecting your face—swivel either left or right, and execute a PLF utilizing the five points of contact. The whole exercise proved to be a little tricky.

"Virtually all my actual jumps have resulted in a rear landing," Sergeant Reupart confided during one of the breaks to a banged-up, disbelieving group of Raiders and Commandos sprawled out on the ground nursing their wounds. It was not what they wanted to hear.

Next they moved to another ten-foot platform where they lined up four abreast again, but this time they strapped into a parachute harness. On the command "Go!" they jumped off the platform, swinging back and forth, dangling down over the sawdust pit. It was about then that they noticed each harness was connected to a rope and pulley that was held, in turn, by an instructor standing directly behind each of the four students. Each student was individually given the order, "Prepare to land," whereupon the instructor released the rope simultaneously with the command, "Land!"

There was only a split second for the trainee paratrooper to discover whether fate had dictated that he was going to need to make a forward or a backward landing and to execute the prerequisite PLF. Most of the students smacked into the sawdust in a crumpled, tangled pile.

Then something strange happened that proved to be a moment of pure magic, though no one recognized it as such at the time.

As the senior officer, Major Randal was always the first man to perform each new training exercise. The next apparatus was a thirty-four-foot tower on which a simulated Whitley troop carrier fuselage had been built—the "praying mantises" Major John Rock had shown the Small-Scale Raiding Company officers the day before. It was designed to give the student a realistic experience of exiting through a simulated hole in a Whitley troop carrier while experiencing the feeling of height. The tower would also introduce the trainees to the "Whitley kiss" and "ringing the bell."

The thirty-four-foot tower was, in many ways, the most frightening training apparatus in the entire school. The rumor was that army psychologists had determined that height to be the best for inducing the maximum amount of fear in a student. Why that was so was difficult to say, but many graduates of No. 1 Parachute Training School claimed the apparatus was scarier to jump from than jumping out of an airplane.

While the Raiders and Commandos watched anxiously from below, Major Randal disappeared into the apparatus, accompanied by an instructor. As he was moving into the sitting position to exit the funnel-shaped hole, his haste, exhaustion, and high state of anxiety combined to make him slip, lose his balance, and slide through. When he tumbled out of the exit hole, he windmilled for a split second before being jerked up violently by the risers attached to the cable.

He also screamed.

British officers did not scream; it was simply not done. British officers were expected to keep a stiff upper lip even if they were being boiled alive in peacock oil—and that dictum included foreign officers serving in His Majesty's Forces.

Major Randal realized what he had done and managed to catch himself in mid-scream, turning it in to a garbled Rebel yell. The two No. 2 Commando troopers assigned to catch him were so startled by the noise that they let him sail right on past and plow full-speed into the turnbuckle at the end of the cable.

"That was the worst exit in Airborne Forces history!" the senior parachute instructor roared. "What was that sound you made, sir? It sounded like something one might expect to hear from a pregnant elephant."

"A Rebel yell, Sergeant," Major Randal responded in the most even voice he could manage.

"What, sir, is a Rebel yell?" the senior parachute instructor bellowed.

"A cry designed to strike fear and despair into the heart of your opponent, Sergeant," Major Randal answered defiantly, still dangling limply in the parachute harness.

"It sounded more like you forgot to cinch up your leg straps tight enough, Major. Spare us from any more Rebel yells, sir, if you please."

And that would have been the end of it. Standing up to the instructors even when one had committed a serious faux pas was considered good form, provided one's excuse—even if totally outrageous—was delivered with a straight face and serious demeanor. But no one reckoned on the reaction of nineteen-year-old Scottish Highlander, free spirit, and independent thinker Lieutenant Percy Stirling, 17/21 Lancers—the "Death or Glory Boys"—to the incident.

At this point in the training, Lieutenant Stirling had decided that he had taken all the harassment he was going to take from the instructors and was looking for a way to give some back. On the very next break, before the noon meal, he and his new best friend, Midshipman Randy Seaborn, approached Major Randal. After offering the major a Player's Navy Cut, Lieutenant Stirling proceeded straight to the main point.

"Sir, would you teach us how to do that war cry?"

"Sure, but why would you two want to know how to give a Rebel yell?" If Major Randal had not been so banged up, his alarm bells might have gone off right then. But, alas, they did not.

"Midshipman Seaborn and I have always been interested in military trivia, sir. Neither one of us has ever actually heard an authentic war cry like it before. Where did you learn how?" Lieutenant Stirling inquired, not lying—exactly.

At this point, Major Randal's internal alarm jingled. He suspected, wrongly, that the two young officers were having a little fun at his expense. "The high school I attended in Los Angeles had a Confederate cavalryman as the school mascot. At football games a trumpeter in the band would blow 'Charge' and all the students would give a loud Rebel yell."

"Would you teach us how to shout one, sir?"

"You *give* a Rebel yell," Major Randal answered carefully, not sure where this was headed. It paid, he knew, to be very careful when dealing with bright young officers. "You don't *shout* one; they're a sort of art form. No two are exactly alike, and there are a lot of variations."

"We would like to know how to give one, sir."

Major Randal took a drag off the Player's Navy Cut. He studied the two serious-faced bright young officers through the cigarette smoke. "Okay, if you insist. Like I said, there's a lot of different ways to go about it. The most common goes: 'Yeeeeeehaaaaaa!' You come down real hard on the 'h' in 'haa.'"

"Yeeeeeehaaaaaa!" Lieutenant Stirling yelled. Midshipman Seaborn quickly followed suit with a yell of his own.

The two looked at each other and grinned.

Then they went into the mess hall and Major Randal did not give it another thought . . . until just before the formation to recommence the afternoon's training, when he came outside and found the Raiders and Commandos gathered around the two young officers.

"That does not sound anything like the noise I heard the major make," one of the Commando corporals argued skeptically.

"There are a lot of different variations to the 'Comanche yell,'" Lieutenant Stirling explained. "No two are exactly alike."

"In that case, I am bloody well game if you are, sir," the hard-looking corporal announced in a tone of grim resignation. There was a rumble of determined agreement from the rest of the men.

At that point, Major Randal's alarm bells did go off, loud and clear. But by then it was too late. Airborne Forces history was about to be writ—large.

11

THE COMANCHE YELL

SYNTHETIC TRAINING PICKED BACK UP RIGHT WHERE IT LEFT OFF before lunch. The troops seemed strangely eager to get started. Major John Randal sensed their change of mood immediately.

Now that the Raiders and Commandos were familiar with each apparatus, they could train more efficiently in smaller groups. The syndicate was quickly broken down and dispatched to the various pieces of training equipment in the hangar. It did not take long to find out what the troops were up to.

"YEEEEEEHAAAAAA!" Lieutenant Percy Stirling let out a blood-curdling scream as he stepped off the platform of the swing-landing trainer.

"YEEEEEEHAAAAAA!" Midshipman Randy Seaborn yelled as he dropped through the hole in the Whitley mock-up tower.

"YEEEEEEHAAAAAA!" shouted Commando Jeff McKinsey as he executed a PLF from the three-step platform.

"YEEEEEEHAAAAAA!" Captain Terry Stone bellowed as he raced backward down a cable.

"YEEEEEEHAAAAAA!" sounded off Lifeboat Serviceman Matt Pinkney, standing in line at the ten-foot platform, just because he felt like it.

The parachute instructors were caught off guard by the initial wave of yelling. True to form, they quickly recovered and swung into action in a frenzy that resembled ants whose nest has been imperiled. The instant a yelling trainee hit the ground they swarmed all over him, doing some pretty heavy-duty screaming of their own.

"What is that noise? A Comanche yell? Drop and give me twenty-five!"

The yells—in Cockney, Scots, Canadian, Welsh, and the other rich and varied accents of the Commonwealth, plus that of one lone American—echoed throughout the hangar.

It was a defining moment. A quantum shift in momentum had taken place in the blink of an eye. Troop morale blasted sky-high.

Men who had spent the last week feeling like victims decided they had had enough. Collectively the Raiders and Commandos closed ranks and forged into a close-knit team; it became "us against them." Major Randal's men were planning to show those parachute instructors that they could take anything the cadre could dish out and throw it back in their faces. Bring it on!

The parachute instructors immediately recognized the gathering rebellion. Being the trained professionals that they were, they knew exactly what they had to do. And they knew exactly how to go about it. They brought it on—hard!

Ten thousand—or maybe it was ten million—push-ups later, the enthusiasm for what the Raiders and Commandos had labeled the Comanche yell had waned substantially . . . but had not died out entirely.

A winded Midshipman Seaborn summarized the situation to an exhausted and battered bunch of Raiders and Commandos on the next break: "They can kill us, but they are not allowed to eat us."

"Ach, and what makes you so bloody sure, sir?"

"Because it is against the Geneva Convention."

Even though they were paying a heavy price for the yells, morale went up and stayed up. The Raiders and Commandos attacked the training like madmen. For the first time they actually started having fun. It required a special brand of soldier to absorb the kind of abuse they were taking, enjoy it, and ask for more.

"YEEEEEEHAAAAAA!"

"Drop and give me fifty!" The base number of push-ups had doubled.

"YEEEEEEHAAAAAA, Sergeant!"

"Make that a hundred!"

"Yes, Sergeant."

The Ringway parachute instructor staff was more than a little impressed—secretly, of course. There was no way the students could possibly win or even fight their way to a draw. Their effort was, at best, a forlorn hope. Everyone knew what the outcome would be: The Raiders and Commandos were going to be ground into dust. But that was what made it all so noble.

"Forty-five, forty-six, forty-seven, forty-eight, forty-nine—"

"Don't do it, lad—"

"Fifty! YEEEEEEHAAAAAA!"

"Give me fifty more, you bloody fool." And so it went for the rest of Monday and all day Tuesday.

On Wednesday three things happened to Major Randal. The first took place as one of his Raiders was knocking out push-ups for screaming the dreaded Comanche yell. Sergeant Roy "Mad Dog" Reupart made direct eye contact and gave him a clearly defined, slow-motion wink, keeping a perfectly straight face. It happened so unexpectedly and was so out of character that later Major Randal wondered if it was possible that he only imagined it.

Second, it occurred to the major that he was hitting all five points of contact on virtually every parachute landing fall. He was coming in fast, identifying what type of landing he was going to make, doing the correct things to get into position to make the proper landing, then twisting, turning, falling, relaxing, rolling, and bouncing right back up. The PLF was becoming automatic, exactly as it was supposed to.

Third, that evening Sergeant Major Maxwell Hicks pulled him aside for a private conversation. What he wanted to discuss was scouting the ranks of No. 2 Commando for recruits to help expand the Small-Scale Raiding Company to its newly authorized strength.

"Good idea, Sergeant Major, but don't make a big deal out of it," Major Randal advised. "Quietly let the word get out that we're going to be accepting a small number of volunteers at the end of parachute training school. We don't want to make it look like we're trying to poach No. 2's men, even though we are."

"I'm keeping a list of names, sir," Sergeant Major Hicks informed him. "There should be no shortage of volunteers. The men in No. 2 joined to see action. The lads realize now that forming a Parachute Commando is going to take a long time and consist of a tremendous amount of training, which is what they all volunteered to get out of in the first place."

"I can always count on you being one step ahead of me," Major Randal said. "What else have I not gotten around to thinking about yet, Sergeant Major?"

"We need to find some way to evaluate the No. 2 men in the other training syndicate, sir. There are bound to be some fine lads over there, and we don't want to pass up any likely candidates."

"I'll work on it," Major Randal agreed. "We're sure to lose some people when we travel to Achnacarry for Commando training. How many men do you think we should take?"

"Sir, the fact that we are only authorized a certain number of troops should have absolutely nothing to do with how many we decide to evaluate in order to reach our authorized strength. I recommend we take as many as we want, then make our selection slowly and carefully. We can always RTU the ones we decide not to keep."

"Sounds like a plan to me, Sergeant Major."

"There is something else I have been wanting to mention to you, sir," the sergeant major said with a thoughtful look on his face. "The lads have been making fun of the Germans ever since the night they saw the film of the *Fallschirmjägers* doing belly flops in their parachutes."

"No kidding? What do you make of it?"

"For the first time, sir, the Nazis do not seem quite so invincible. I believe it is a good sign."

"I think maybe you're right."

The next day, as soon as he had an opportunity, Major Randal had a quiet word with Sergeant Reupart, who listened carefully while the major explained that he needed some way to discreetly evaluate the men in the other training syndicate and why this was necessary.

"Next week is jump week, sir," said Sergeant Reupart. "I believe I can arrange with the senior Royal Air Force instructor to have some of your key people intermingled with the other syndicate so they can observe the students dealing with the stress of actual parachute descents.

"Also, I can speak to my counterpart over there and see if he has any recommendations on specific candidates for you, sir."

"Thanks, Sergeant Reupart."

"My pleasure, sir. You understand, of course, you are going to owe me."

"You can name your poison."

"In that case, sir, I shall make it happen."

The final exercise for the week was to make a descent from one of the two seventy-foot towers. The student jumper was strapped into a parachute harness, the chute was fully inflated inside a bell-shaped wire cage, and the jumper was hauled up to the top of the apparatus and released. Once the student had been pulled to the top and had released the safety line securing him to the apparatus, there was only one way to get down, and that was to drop. Although a fan system counteracted the fall of the parachute, the student jumper enjoyed the full sensation of what a real jump was like.

Releasing the safety line while dangling seventy feet in the air required substantial intestinal fortitude from the student doing the releasing. There was a lot of Comanche yelling as the Raiders and Commandos floated down to the ground. For once, the parachute instructors did not seem to take offense.

The tower jump was a serious exercise, and much to Major Randal's regret, two men—old originals from the Household Cavalry polo teams—came to see him that evening and requested to be returned to unit. They explained that they did not have a head for heights. The seventy-foot tower had been the straw that broke the camel's back and convinced them they did not have any future as military parachutists.

It was a bitter pill, but better to find it out now rather than later. Major Randal knew that just because a man did not have what it took to jump out of airplanes did not mean that he was not a good soldier. He wrote them both glowing recommendations and arranged for them to be allowed to transfer to the Commando unit of their choice or to return to their regiments.

The two were escorted from Ringway immediately.

Major Randal sat and reflected on his command as a whole. He was looking for calm, cool, self-assured soldiers. He wanted troops who could dig down deep inside themselves and be able to perform at peak performance level when the going got really tough: reliable people who could think on the move, adapt to rapidly changing situations, and improvise when things did not go according to plan. His Raiders needed the self-control to continue the mission when surrounded by total chaos; they needed to be men who never gave up. Major Randal knew that military skills could be taught; character could not.

In general, the hard training at Ringway was having a positive effect on the men in his company. From the original band of enthusiastic bunglers that started out on the first raid, they were gradually being transformed into a group of highly motivated professionals. The achievement was a slow, painful, polishing process, and it did not come without a price for some.

Major Randal had his eye on two men in particular. The relentless stress of the past two weeks had revealed personality flaws in them that weren't obvious before. One, the major noticed, tended to become belligerent when exhausted; the other constantly complained because he believed he was being singled out by the parachute instructors.

The Small-Scale Raiding Company commander was in the process of making up his mind whether the two would be invited to stay in the raiding company after parachute training school. It would be interesting to see whether Sergeant Major Hicks already had the two men on his list of those to be RTU'd. Major Randal was willing to bet money that he did.

If you are on time in the Grenadier Guards, you are five minutes late . . . Sergeant Major Maxwell Hicks never was.

12

JUMP WEEK

AS HAD VIRTUALLY EVERY DAY SINCE THEIR ARRIVAL AT THE
Circus, the first morning of jump week dawned heavy with fog. Parade was
at 0530 hours. The student parachutists had to spend a long time outside,
waiting for something to happen, which only gave them more time to
ponder the great unknown and unexpected.

"If you are not able to see the ground, there is no jumping," Captain
Terry Stone opined with the tone of a condemned man anticipating a stay
of execution. "I can barely even see all the way across this street."

Secretly, Major John Randal felt guilty about feeling so relieved by the
inclement weather.

Major John Rock pulled up in front of Hardwick Hall at the wheel of
his Humber staff car. He tossed each of them a long, sand-green denim
jacket. "Denison smock, just the ticket for parachutage. I took the liberty
of drawing yours, gentlemen, and having your rank insignia sewn on."

Major Randal and Captain Stone admired the three-quarters-length
jackets. The Denison smock was one of those great pieces of military
clothing that looked exactly right.

"These are prototypes. Afraid we cheated on them a bit," Major Rock added. "Captain Denison and I took some stills from that training film of Nazi paratroopers you saw, and he basically copied the German pattern. About the only difference is that theirs are camouflaged and ours are plain sand-green. Right now we do not have any camouflage material, but Captain Denison is experimenting with having three shades of brown camouflage splotches hand-painted on the smocks when we get them into mass production. The troops absolutely love them. We named it after Denison because he headed up the project. Besides, 'Rock smock' is not the best of names for a parachute jacket, ha-ha."

Major Randal liked his Denison smock the instant he put it on. It not only looked right, it felt right. "Where we headed?" he asked, as he and Captain Stone climbed into the Humber.

"Tatton Park," Major Rock answered cheerfully. "Your men will be transported in buses. It's about nine miles' distance. We could go a faster way and save about a mile and a half, but Lord Egerton refuses to allow us the use of the front entrance. Are you two stalwarts ready for your first jump?"

"In this weather?"

"We never cancel balloon jumps for anything less than a typhoon, and we have never had one of those. Besides, this pea soup might be a good thing after all."

"Why might that be?" Captain Stone asked from the backseat.

"When you are jumping from an airplane, the altitude does not seem real, somehow. The noise of the engines, the slipstream, the parachute popping open really fast, and the speed all work to distract your mind, and there is no sensation you are falling. Not the case with a balloon, gentlemen.

"Jumping from a balloon is a much more cold-blooded experience. It is tethered to the ground, they winch you up in a rickety, unstable, canvas cage in perfect silence, and when you leap out, you fall for four seconds before your parachute opens. You feel like a stone falling from the sky. You will be amazed at how long four seconds can be at a time like that.

"Then, too, the enhanced sensation of vertigo you suffer from the ride up in the basket contributes to the unpleasantness," Major Rock rambled on. "Quite frankly, the whole balloon experience is positively hideous.

"At least in this fog you should not be able to see the ground. I recommend you simply try to imagine you are sitting on the edge of a swimming pool and slip in to test the water. That should help—at least initially. Not to worry."

Major Randal looked over his shoulder at Captain Stone. The usually devil-may-care Life Guards officer had a sick smile pasted on his face. His skin color roughly matched that of his new parachute smock. He grinned weakly. "Remember, old stick: It's always darkest before pitch black."

The road to Tatton Park was narrow and winding. Creeping along in the dense fog, the convoy took nearly two hours to cover the nine miles. Major Rock regaled them the whole way with his adventures as the developer of Airborne Forces doctrine. "Can you believe some idiot actually submitted the idea we wear special jump boots with springs in the heels? The fool never explained how to walk in them after the landing. Besides, anyone mad enough to land on his heels will shatter every bone in his feet, ankles, and legs, all the way up to his pelvis, springs or no springs."

It was a long ride.

When they pulled into Tatton Park at last, the rest of their training syndicate was right behind them in the buses. Suddenly, a brisk wind picked up, and the fog blew away in a matter of minutes, leaving them to enjoy a pale sun that provided no warmth at all.

"So much for the bloody fog making things easier," Captain Stone muttered. "I would dearly love to put a throttle hold on Major John Rock, Airborne Pioneer!"

When it was Major Randal's time to draw his parachute, the WAAF rigger who issued it seemed more pleased to see him than was absolutely necessary. She flashed a radiant smile and gushed cheerfully, "Good morning, Major. Here is your chute. I packed this one myself, sir."

"How long, exactly, have you been packing parachutes?" Captain Stone asked as he slung his over one shoulder.

"The standard answer to that question, sir, is always, 'This is my very first day of on-the-job training.'"

The handsome cavalryman looked as if he had suddenly developed a gallstone.

"However, Captain Stone, I am not going to tell you that today because Captain Seaborn explicitly ordered me to make sure you and Major Randal received the VIP treatment. The truth is, sir, I am the best rigger in the business. Periodically, we are required to jump a chute we pack, and the one we jump is always chosen at random. You have nothing to worry about, sir. I would jump this parachute. As a matter of fact, if it does not work to your complete satisfaction, bring it back and I will issue you another, sir."

The men waiting in line to draw their parachutes all guffawed. Since they did not have reserve chutes, everyone knew a parachute failure was an automatic death sentence. Still, the WAAF rigger was a showstopper, and her confidence was infectious. The tension in the air ratcheted way down.

Whatever they're paying her, thought Major Randal, *ain't enough.*

He asked, "You mean Midshipman Seaborn, don't you?"

"No, sir, Captain Lady Seaborn."

"You know Lady Jane?"

"Yes, sir. Perhaps I should introduce myself, Major. My name is Karen Montgomery, soon to be *Lieutenant* Karen Montgomery, Royal Marines—the officer in charge of your parachute rigging detachment."

"Well, congratulations, soon-to-be Lieutenant," Major Randal said, reaching out and shaking her hand. "Welcome aboard, Karen. How'd you know who we were? There are a lot of officers in training, and Terry and I are not wearing name tags."

"Lady Seaborn gave me a description of you, Major."

"Must have been pretty good."

"Actually, it was easy, sir. Particularly after she informed me you would be accompanied by a Life Guards captain who looked exactly like the cinema star Errol Flynn."

Unfortunately for Captain Stone, a large contingent of Raiders and Commandos had gathered round the WAAF, panting like a pack of hungry Doberman pinschers eyeballing a piece of prime rib. To say the troops were bitterly disappointed to hear that she was destined to become a commissioned officer and therefore off-limits would be a major understatement.

To compensate, the men commenced ragging Captain Stone unmercifully. "Zorro!" someone called, and the damage was done. The men took up the chant: "Zorro, Zorro, Zorro . . ." In the British Army, when the other ranks liked an officer—and sometimes when they did not—they tagged him with a nickname. Forever after in military circles, Captain Terry Stone would be known as Zorro, even though Errol Flynn never played that role.

Captain Terry "Zorro" Stone turned as red as a beet. It was the first time any of them had ever seen him blush.

"I can see we're going to have a lot of fun with you, Lieutenant Montgomery," Major Randal said with a grin. "Let's go, Errol . . . I mean, Zorro. We've got a balloon to catch."

Captain Stone glared at the WAAF. "It's going to be a long war, Montgomery."

"Not if I packed your parachute incorrectly. Have a nice day, sir."

"Ooooooooohhh!" chorused the Raiders and Commandos.

She was really good. The class received the day's last lecture, the culmination of a mind-numbing series of presentations on parachute canopies, lines, risers, osculation, D-rings, quick-release switches, parachute landing falls, the five points of contact, and on and on and on.

Major Rock delivered the pre-jump briefing. "Men, today you will be jumping from a tethered balloon at an altitude of five hundred feet. The name of the balloon, for those of you who are interested, is Bessie. She was perfected for parachute jumping by the RAF Balloon Development Establishment at Cardington. You will be jumping an X-type parachute called a statichute. The canopy is twenty-eight feet in diameter and deploys canopy-last, activated by a static line . . ."

Major Randal had heard this all so many times before that he faded off. To be perfectly honest, he really did not care if his canopy deployed first, last, or sideways—as long as it deployed.

The order was given to "chute up." They were divided into jumping parties of four and numbered off one through four within each party;

Major Randal was number one in his party. Rank had its responsibilities as well as its privileges; he was going to lead the way, as usual.

There was a saying going around the parachute school to the effect that the brave men were actually the ones who were afraid, admitted their fear, fought it, and overcame it. Fearless men were not actually brave; they were merely fearless, and possibly stupid. There would be a lot of brave men on the ground and in the air at Tatton Park that day—and a few who would prove to be fearless.

Flight Sergeant Bill Beaverton, was to be the dispatcher. He gave each jumper a quick but extremely thorough inspection. Then the party climbed aboard the rickety canvas cage, one man to each side of the square, and crouched there, clinging desperately to the handles to avoid falling through the gaping hole in the floor. The jumpers were crammed like sardines into the surprisingly tiny and fragile basket. The canvas contraption was flimsy beyond belief; the idea that men would be sent aloft in it seemed criminal. Major Randal was momentarily outraged.

Flight Sergeant Beaverton was that rare individual who was a legend in his own time. He had made hundreds—some claimed thousands—of descents by parachute. A steely-eyed glance from him could send a chill down the spine of the toughest trainee. He stood at the end of the basket and hooked each man's static line up to the strap that hung down from a steel bar in the cage. After he connected the static line, he showed it to the jumper.

The student jumpers in the basket had the look of cornered rabbits. Major Randal hoped he did not look like a cornered rabbit. He felt as though he had been strapped into an electric chair, waiting for the executioner to throw the switch. Major Rock's description was dead-on: It was a horrible experience, and the balloon had not even left the ground yet.

Up, up, up went the skittish balloon, dancing like a kite to the harsh, monotonous grind of the winch playing out. The feeling of insecurity increased when the huge, ungainly airbag yawed from time to time, staggering about the sky like a drunken whale, causing the floor of the unstable canvas cage to assume a terrifying tilt that made the student jumpers feel as if the flimsy basket might collapse at any moment.

The ascent was totally demoralizing. No one on board except the dispatcher had ever ridden in a balloon before. None of the passengers would dare to even so much as glance at the hole in the floor, which took a tremendous amount of willpower on their part, considering that the hole took up virtually all the floor space and their legs were dangling out of it. Major Randal remembered one of the remarks that Major Rock had flippantly tossed out during the ride over: "Jumping from a balloon is exactly like committing suicide, with the strong possibility—which you sincerely doubt—that your attempt might fail."

He leaned over and whispered to Sergeant Major Maxwell Hicks, "I haven't heard a single man admit to being afraid yet. My guess is, ninety-eight percent of 'em are faking it and the other two percent are crazy. At the end of the training day, if you think any of our people fall into the two percent crazy category, RTU them before the sun goes down."

"My pleasure, sir!"

Abruptly, the moaning, grinding sound of the winch ceased. There was a tense moment of silence, broken only by the sighing of the wind through the balloon's rigging. From below came the grating blast of the horn from Major Rock's Humber staff car: once, twice, three times—the prearranged signal. It was the last nail in Major Randal's emotional coffin.

"Bessie" was at five hundred feet and had settled into a suitable position. The ground staff was satisfied that the cable was at a sufficient angle to ensure that the jumpers would not collide with it and become entangled on the descent—which implied that this must have happened sometime in the past. Real, primal fear set in. It was time.

All things considered, this was the worst experience Major Randal had ever suffered through—including Calais. The wind whistled through the overhead wires, the unstable canvas basket yawed in the breeze and danced sideways, and Major Randal's knuckles whitened as he gripped its sides.

Trying to ignore the hole in the basket's floor, he gazed out over the green expanse of Tatton Park. In the distance he could see the town of Altrincham and several tiny hamlets scattered across the horizon. Tatton and Rostherne meres and several smaller lakes sparkled in the distance like highly polished mirrors.

He shivered, unsure if it was from the cold or pure, raw terror. Even under fire he had never felt this type of electrifying, nonstop fear.

Flight Sergeant Beaverton was leaning over the side of the wobbly, unstable contraption, watching for the last and final signal from down below. Finally, the Aldis lamp blinked. It was showtime.

There was absolute, total, dead silence. Everything became perfectly still.

"Action stations, Number One!"

Major Randal sat rigidly, dangling both legs out of the hole and staring straight ahead to avoid looking at the ground. He was also being extremely careful not to accidentally slide out when Bessie skittered.

Before he had time to think, the dispatcher barked the staccato command: "Go!"

Major Randal went.

It never occurred to Major Randal as he fell that his parachute would open. He considered himself a dead man. He had his eyes clenched shut, in violation of everything he had been taught to the contrary, though he did not actually realize it at the time.

So, he was not surprised to feel himself falling, falling, falling, falling for a long time. It was what he had expected to happen. He fleetingly wondered if it would hurt much when he hit the ground. His life did not pass in front of his eyes, but he did flash to the night he had first met Lady Jane Seaborn, and he experienced a feeling of serene disappointment.

There came a gentle fluttering sound; he felt a mild jerk, then a heavier tug, and suddenly he found himself sitting easy in the saddle, floating down exactly as he had been briefed he would.

Wow, they told the truth!

A voice in his brain that sounded like his own screamed, *Check canopy!* an instant before a voice on the megaphone below barked, "Check your canopy, Number One!"

Major Randal opened his eyes, looked up, and saw the magnificent silk parachute fully deployed. There were no twists in the lines; he was not osculating. It was the most beautiful thing he had ever seen—ever! To the paratrooper dangling down beneath it, nothing beats the sight of a fully deployed parachute.

He felt an intoxicating thrill. The sky was the bluest blue it had ever been, and life was sweet. He had never felt so good. The experience was sensational.

"Lovely exit, Major!" he heard Flight Sergeant Beaverton shout down over the side of the basket.

But Major Randal had no time to attend to mere dispatchers; he was the Emperor of the Universe! This was the most outstanding single triumph he had ever achieved. Time stood still—for all of about ten seconds.

"Let's get those feet and knees together, number one!" Major Rock bellowed over the megaphone. "Prepare to land!"

Unlocking his knees so that they swung loosely; rocking back and forth; touching his legs together from his knees down to the soles of his boots; pulling his elbows in tight against his chest so they actually touched together; pulling his head down tightly, with his chin pressed hard down on his chest, Major Randal mentally prepared to land.

The ground suddenly blazed sideways beneath him. He felt a rushing sensation, the trees blurred out of the corner of his peripheral vision, and he felt a vague tinge of uneasiness as he remembered that landing was the really dangerous part.

WHAM! He was down and rolling, executing a textbook-perfect parachute landing fall better than any he had done in training. Everything came together—he was still alive. Unbelievable!

Major Randal could not restrain himself. He jumped to his feet and threw back his head.

"YEEEEEEHAAAAAA!"

"All right, Major, let's not have any more of those Comanche yells," Major Rock boomed over the megaphone. "This is not the Alamo! Roll up your parachute, turn it in at the assembly point, and draw another one. You have one more jump to make today."

Bring it on, Major Randal thought. *Airborne!*

13

GRADUATION

THE SECOND BALLOON JUMP WAS MUCH MORE FRIGHTENING THAN the first. Major John Randal would never have believed such a thing possible, but it was primarily because he knew what to expect. The ride up in the balloon was particularly terrifying because of the ground-induced vertigo. He must have been so scared the first trip, he did not notice it to the same extent.

It was a long ascent, and it seemed as though they were a mile high, or maybe two. The wait for "Go!" took forever. And it gave him time to think, which is really not a good thing for a novice, one-jump paratrooper to be doing.

On his second jump he managed to keep his eyes open. Well . . . almost.

Over the next three days, men of the Small-Scale Raiding Company completed a total of five jumps from ancient and decrepit Whitley Mark IIIs.

Jumping from a Whitley was a nightmare. Maybe not as big a nightmare as the balloon jumps had been, but a very real nightmare nonetheless. The Whitley converted bomber-troop transports, as advertised, flapped their wings like a pterodactyl. Actually, the flapping was an intentionally engineered design feature, but on every flight it seemed as if the wings were going to break and fall off.

The jumpers had to crawl down a long, dark, narrow tunnel inside the fuselage to reach the exit hole cut in the bottom of the aircraft. Five men sat on each side of the hole, leaning back against the skin of the airplane. It was cramped in the tight, claustrophobic space—the Whitley had been designed to drop bombs, not parachutists—and the close quarters were made worse by the fact that they were strapped in their parachutes and wearing their odd padded jump helmets. The jump helmet came in handy, though, when they bumped their way, headfirst, along the narrow tunnel in the dim light.

On Major Randal's first jump from a Whitley, Flight Sergeant Bill Beaverton crawled past, took the lid off, and straddled the hole. The dispatcher was wearing an intercom headset and listening to it intently.

"Running in!" he shouted to the student jumpers.

"About time," Corporal Jack Merritt of the Life Guards muttered anxiously.

"Action stations!"

Major Randal swung his legs into the exit hole and assumed the exit position.

The jump light turned green. The flight sergeant shouted, "Number One!" Then he slashed his arm down and barked, "Go!" Major Randal was more than happy to comply; jumping out of a Whitley seemed a lot safer than riding in it.

The next four jumps tended to blend together. To Major Randal's surprise, he got a strange kick out of being tumbled around by the blast of prop-wash turbulence created by the churning of the giant propellers during the exit before the parachute opened. He kept that piece of information to himself; no sense sounding like one of the fake tough or crazy brave.

Conquering fear was a rewarding intellectual challenge, he concluded. Jumping out of an aircraft in flight seemed to be ninety-five percent mental state and five percent technique. He reflected that most people simply would not be able to understand the mind-set of those who volunteered, and those who did jump found it virtually impossible to explain to non-jumpers why they did it. Major Randal knew he would never be able to explain his true feelings about the experience in any terms that did not sound totally insane.

Further, he was embarrassed to admit to himself that he had experienced a brief "jumping out of airplanes is what real men do" moment until it had occurred to him that Jane and Karen Montgomery did not fall into the beat-your-chest, he-man category. Furthermore, both of them acted a lot more casual about parachuting than he felt. Nonetheless, Major Randal was secretly pleased with himself for overcoming his fear of heights. It had not been easy. He would be proud to wear parachute wings.

A small ceremony was scheduled for after the last qualifying jump. Since everything done at the British No. 1 Parachute Training School was cloaked in secrecy, only a few outsiders would be in attendance. The officer commanding No. 2 Commando, Lieutenant Colonel CIA Jackson, Captain the Lady Jane Seaborn, Royal Marine Pamela Plum-Martin, and Captain "Geronimo Joe" McKoy constituted virtually the entire official guest list. Vice Admiral Sir Randolph "Razor" Ransom turned up at the last minute to watch his grandson parachute and to be there to pin on his wings.

Squadron Leader Louis Strange, the commanding officer of No. 1 Parachute Training School, sitting at the wheel of his Humber staff car, screeched up as Major John Randal was walking toward the assembly point to turn in his parachute after making his final qualifying jump.

"Climb in, Major!" he shouted. "We have a little surprise in store for you."

Feeling flushed with success at having just completed parachute school, Major Randal pitched his parachute into the boot of the Humber and climbed in, appreciating the ride. It was, he decided later, one of the larger mistakes he had made.

The squadron leader roared off the drop zone and headed back to the airfield at Ringway, traveling at breakneck speed.

"Have a nice jump?" he inquired.

"Perfect," Major Randal answered truthfully, beginning to let go and relax for the first time since beginning training three weeks before. "It went just fine."

"Outstanding!" Squadron Leader Strange actually reached over and slapped him on the shoulder. "Good to hear it. Then you won't mind making one more, a special demonstration jump for the class and the guests!"

"What?"

"Major, you have been selected to make a demo turret jump. When you land, we will pin your wings on right there. Should make a nice show for the crowd."

"A turret jump?"

The look on Squadron Leader Strange's face made him seem as innocent as a lamb. "This is your chance to show all the lads how parachuting should be done."

"Strange, you're not trying to get back at me for those Rebel yells, are you?"

"Rebel yells? Is that what your side shouted at Bunker Hill? Staff told me all that screaming your men have been doing was something to do with red Indians."

So much for historical accuracy, thought Major Randal, shaking his head. *What* is *a turret jump, anyway?*

It was a good thing he didn't know.

On Drop Zone Tatton, the entire class was formed up in their sand-green Denison smocks and padded jump helmets. The guests, staff, and dignitaries were seated in a small set of portable bleachers.

In the Ringway control tower, direct contact was maintained with the regional air-raid authorities to ensure the earliest warning in the event of hostile German aircraft approaching. At that very moment, high overhead, Major John Randal and Flight Sergeant Bill Beaverton were crawling down the long, narrow tunnel in a wheezing Whitley that was flying along, flapping its wings at just barely above stalling speed.

When they reached the tail of the aircraft, Major Randal realized that part of it had been cut out! More accurately, the rear machine-gun turret had been removed, leaving a gaping hole through which the wind came howling in. The hideous screeching sounded like something out of a horror show.

"You do not like heights much, do you, sir?" the flight sergeant asked conversationally as they inched forward. It was not really a question.

Ignoring the dispatcher, Major Randal was really curious about why the gun turret had been removed. The frightening, high-pitched, wounded banshee sound of the wind made him shiver involuntarily.

"Neither do I, sir, not really," Flight Sergeant Beaverton continued, matter-of-factly. "The thing is, it is not necessary to like it. You just have to do it."

The two men locked eyes.

"Here is what is going to take place, sir. You are going to crawl through the cutout and climb up on the little platform we installed outside where the rear machine gun used to be mounted."

Major Randal stared at him in horror-struck disbelief.

"Back out onto the platform, keeping your face toward me at all times. Hold on to the iron safety bar with your left hand and place your right hand on the D-ring on your chest. You may have noticed that there is no static line attached to your parachute, sir."

No, he had not noticed!

"When I give you the command 'Go,' reach over with your right hand—fingers extended and joined, elbow bent at a ninety-degree angle—grasp the D-ring on the left side of your harness in the palm of your hand, and with a sharp, vigorous motion, pull it as hard as you can. Then, quickly reach back and grab the safety bar again with your right hand to stabilize yourself in the upright position. It is okay if you drop the D-ring, sir; it will have come free in your hand.

"While you are stabilizing yourself, the canopy will be spilling out and deploying in the slipstream. When the canopy pops open and reaches the end of the lines, taking the slack out of the risers, you will be plucked backward off the platform. Make sure you let go of the safety bars at that point. Nothing to it, sir. Airborne!"

"Are you out of your mind?" Major Randal screamed at the dispatcher.

"Sir, if you think you are going to have any trouble pulling the D-ring, I can reach out and give it a yank for you."

"You're crazy!"

"One other thing, sir. When I complete my tour of duty here, do you think there is a possibility you might have an opening for me in the Small-Scale Raiding Company?"

On Drop Zone Tatton, Squadron Leader Louis Strange shaded his eyes and looked up into the sky. He picked up the microphone and it gave a shrill screech. "Now, ladies and gentlemen, we have approaching the DZ Major John Randal, MC, the famed American volunteer pinprick raider, aboard a converted Royal Air Force Whitley bomber. Shortly, Major Randal will be demonstrating what is known in Airborne Forces as a turret jump. Keep your eyes on the tail of the airplane."

All eyes turned to the lumbering bomber-troop transport as it was coming into sight, straight and level. A tiny stick figure appeared out the back. Suddenly, a burst of white silk spilled out and the crowd, especially the guests, said, "Oooohhh!" The silk streamed out farther and farther, then blossomed open into a full-blown canopy with an audible crack. The tiny figure was plucked off the tail of the Whitley, and the plane droned on.

It was a spectacular show. The Raiders and Commandos were cheering and the spectators screaming.

Major John Randal floated down as light as a feather. He could have made a stand-up landing, but he refrained; not because stand-up landings were prohibited, but because his knees had completely turned to jelly from pure terror and were simply too weak to support him. He bounded up, quickly rolled up his parachute, and jogged up to the reviewing stand.

Squadron Leader Strange made a grand show of pumping his hand, pounding him on the back, and congratulating him on his successful completion of training. At least that's what it looked like to the crowd. When he leaned toward Major Randal, however, what he actually said was: "Did you know, Major, that half my staff came to me and actually asked me to make those ridiculous Comanche yells a formal part of Airborne Training? The other half begged permission to volunteer for your Small-Scale Raiding Company. Just who do you think you are? I want you off this base immediately."

"What would it take, Strange, to get you to come down and go along on a raid with us some dark night?" Major Randal snarled. Both men had huge, fake smiles plastered on their faces for the benefit of the spectators.

Captain Lady Jane Seaborn pinned his wings on during the brief ceremony. "Congratulations, John," she said. "Welcome to the Airborne."

It had been three weeks since he had last seen her; she was even more beautiful than he remembered. The faint fragrance of her Cartier perfume smelled like vanilla. He was not able to think of one thing to say.

Later in the parking lot, the men of the Small-Scale Raiding Company gathered to load onto the buses. Captain Lady Seaborn had arranged to transport them to the rail station in Manchester, and then they were all off on a hard-earned ten-day leave.

Captain Terry "Zorro" Stone sidled up to Major Randal. Jerking his thumb at the sky, he said, "Was that as awful as it looked, old stick?"

"Don't even ask."

The Raiders were pounding each other on the back, proud as punch to have survived the tough training. They were officially paratroopers now: Jolly Green Giants in a world inhabited by Lilliputians.

As Major Randal and Captain Stone swaggered toward Captain Lady Seaborn's Rolls-Royce, it was difficult not to notice the glamorous Royal Marines driver, Pamela Plum-Martin, casually leaning against the driver's door, filing her long, most un-Royal-Marines-regulation scarlet fingernails. She looked exactly like a real-life Varga pinup girl dressed in a Royal Marines uniform.

Then they saw them: Stitched to her left sleeve were official-issue British parachute wings, the same ones they were wearing. The jump wings had not been there the last time either of them had seen her.

"Marine Plum-Martin," Captain Stone barked, "how many jumps have you made?"

"Seven, sir," the Royal Marine answered, looking up from her nails, not in the least ruffled by his challenging tone.

"When did you finish your training, Marine?"

"Last week, sir."

"And, pray tell, when did you start?"

"Last week, sir."

"*Last week!*" Major Randal and Captain Stone exclaimed in unison.

"Yes, sir, last week."

"That's right, boys," Captain Lady Seaborn said with only the slightest hint of a smile. "Pamela took the short course."

Major Randal and Captain Stone stared at each other. They were both in shock.

"The short course?"

"Done in a week," Captain Lady Seaborn said. "Five days, actually. I took it. The short course is reserved for senior officers and 'specials' getting ready to parachute behind enemy lines as agents for one or another of the hush-hush services."

"The 'short course'?" Major Randal growled the words through gritted teeth. "You never told me about any 'short course'!"

"You never asked."

While an outraged Major Randal and Captain Stone were standing there like two bulls blowing steam, looking at each other and feeling like complete idiots, Geronimo Joe McKoy limped up in his pointy-toed yellow alligator cowboy boots.

"That was a dang good show you put on up there, Major. Do you reckon they'd let me jump outta one of them balloons?"

REST AND RECREATION

14

TRAIN TO LONDON

THE TRAIN TO LONDON PULLED OUT OF MANCHESTER AN HOUR later with the Small-Scale Raiding Company on board. There were two first-class cars for the unit. In the first car were only two people: Major John Randal and Captain the Lady Jane Seaborn.

"I don't even want to know how you pulled this off," Major Randal said as he looked around at the rail car's plush accommodations.

"Quite possibly, the railway company had some reason to believe there were very important passengers aboard who had high-level, hush-hush business to conduct," Captain Lady Jane Seaborn responded in a composed tone, idly tapping the teacup on the table in front of her with her long, scarlet-tipped nails. Exquisitely poised, though slightly apprehensive at the moment, she planned to cover a lot of ground in the meeting they were getting ready to have and was not entirely sure how well what she had to propose was going be received.

"That explains the armed guards at the doors. For a minute there I thought we were under arrest."

"I did not want us to be disturbed," she explained. "I have found, John, that if a thing is stamped 'Secret,' most people tend not to barge in or ask many questions, particularly if there are armed guards barring their way."

"Right," said Major Randal, "questions like: Are you really sure this is official?"

"Precisely." Captain Lady Seaborn's eyes sparkled as she detonated one of her incandescent smiles. "You simply would not believe how easy it is to cut through red tape if you just say the magic word."

"The magic word?"

"In this case it was 'frogspawn,'" she said with a perfectly straight face. "I walked into the railway office in Manchester and discreetly whispered, 'Frogspawn,' into the managing clerk's ear. It does not mean anything, of course, but he did not have any way to know that."

"What did he do?" Major Randal asked, wondering if she was pulling his leg.

"First, he looked startled. Then he composed himself and inquired what he could do to be of service. I informed him that I required an extra first-class car on the train to London for the purpose of conducting a classified meeting in private and that I needed him to reserve the other first-class car for the officers and men of a very secret Commando unit."

"Frogspawn?"

"I could have said 'egg salad' or 'purple penguin.' Anything will work. I happen to like 'frogspawn.' The trick is to stand boldly on and not lose confidence once you make your play."

"You're one dangerous woman." He shook his head in admiration, not entirely sure he believed her.

"Yes, I am. Try not to forget it."

Captain Terry "Zorro" Stone and Sergeant Major Maxwell Hicks entered the car and walked down the aisle to their table.

Captain Lady Seaborn quickly demonstrated that she had not been idle while they had been "enjoying themselves" at No. 1 Parachute Training School.

"You received my telex to the effect that we have been authorized to augment the number of troops in the Small-Scale Raiding Company?"

"We did. I'm curious how Combined Operations Headquarters arrived at the exact number of officers and men," Major Randal said.

"It is the same as was recently established for a Commando troop under the new table of organization," she explained, unconsciously slipping into a clipped professional tone that had the unintended effect of sounding extraordinarily sexy. "You are not locked into that number. Consider it merely a starting point for administrative purposes.

"For example, I have arranged for a team of retired navy pensioners to take over the maintenance of HMY *Arrow*. They will free Randy's crew to rest between operations instead of having to worry about getting the yacht ready to put to sea again. The pensioners will fall under your command but do not count against your authorized troop strength."

"That's a great idea, Jane," said Major Randal, obviously impressed. He took out a Player's Navy Cut and offered her one from the pack. He lit hers, then his own.

"Well, it brings up the first item of business you have to decide today," she continued.

Captain Stone broke out his sterling silver cigarette case and extended it to Sergeant Major Hicks; they both lit up their own cigarettes and leaned forward to listen.

"Since the navy element has been expanded, it merits a more senior officer than Randy. As you know, he was due to be promoted to sub-lieutenant when his regular commission was approved. Well, it has finally come through, and his promotion party is laid on for tonight."

Captain Lady Seaborn gave Major Randal an inquisitive look. "You now have the option to bring in a more experienced officer . . . or you could promote Randy."

"Promote him to what?"

"Lieutenant—the equivalent of captain in the army," she answered, tapping the ash of her cigarette into the crystal ashtray on the table. "It would mean skipping sub-lieutenant. The Royal Navy is touchy about things like that. He's only eighteen. And his father may not be overjoyed with the idea of Randy staying on in the Commandos. He has arranged an assignment for him on HMS *Hood*."

Major Randal glanced at Captain Stone.

"Stick with Randy," the Life Guards officer advised. "He's bound to turn nineteen sooner or later. I say, beware the sailor you have never sailed with."

"Sergeant Major?"

"I agree, sir. The men are confident sailing with Mr. Seaborn."

"You need to understand, this is going to raise eyebrows," Captain Lady Seaborn said. "An underage-for-grade waiver will be required, but I have already made the necessary preparations in the event you decide to choose that option. Randy will become the youngest full lieutenant in the Royal Navy."

"Perhaps we can find Mr. Seaborn a seasoned chief petty officer," Major Hicks ventured.

"Probably should have done that a long time ago," Major Randal conceded.

"How is it going to feel, Jane, having a teenage nephew the same rank as you?" Captain Stone teased.

"I guess I shall just have to arrange to have myself promoted again," Captain Lady Seaborn replied smoothly.

Captain Stone gave Major Randal a knowing wink. "Hello, Field Marshal."

"All right, then, let's get Randy the waiver and work on locating a seasoned CPO for him," Major Randal said. "What's next?"

"There is a party planned tonight to celebrate Randy's transfer from the Volunteer Reserve to the Royal Navy and his promotion to sub-lieutenant. Everyone is going to be flabbergasted at this turn of events. The Razor will be there, which means half the Admiralty will turn out to wet down his grandson's new straight stripes. Randy's mother, Brandy, has made you, John, the guest of honor. Maxwell, you and Terry are both invited, of course."

"May I bring Mrs. Hicks?" the sergeant major asked.

"Absolutely, we would love to have your wife attend."

Major Randal's alarm bells kicked in. He and Captain Stone had made elaborate plans for their leave that did not include spending time with mothers and widows.

The dashing Life Guards officer had an inexhaustible supply of decadent, blue-blooded women of the fox hunting set whose first names all had three syllables—party girls who wore pearls and carried silver flasks in their purses. And they really liked Americans, particularly those serving in their armed forces now that England was standing alone.

The two Commando officers were literally chomping at the bit to get started, and it didn't seem fair for Midshipman Randy Seaborn's mother to force them to waste one precious minute of their leave time at a party where they would actually have to behave, especially considering they had just voted to promote her young swashbuckler ahead of his class.

"John, you and I have an intensive series of meetings scheduled over the next week," Captain Lady Seaborn continued. "Depending on how the initial contacts go, they could extend well into the following week."

Major Randal suddenly felt like one of those German parachutists in the film at No. 1 Parachute Training School, body-slamming onto the rocky drop zone.

"Meetings?" he said weakly.

"Combined Operations Headquarters has been authorized to raise ten Commando battalions. As we speak, they are in the process of forming and training all across the United Kingdom. No. 3 Commando even carried out a raid while you were in parachute school.

"We need to be very careful not to suddenly wake up someday to find ourselves absorbed by one of the new Commando battalions."

"We definitely would not want that to happen," Captain Stone agreed. "Not likely!"

"To avoid that ever occurring requires you to meet key people and to make the right connections," Captain Lady Seaborn said in an even tone, her eyes never leaving Major Randal's face.

"I hate meetings."

"John, it is imperative we establish ourselves before someone else gets there ahead of us. The early bird gets the worm."

"I see," Major Randal said, not having the slightest idea what she was talking about. It was obvious that Captain Lady Seaborn had been giving the future of the Small-Scale Raiding Company a considerable amount of thought. Once again, he wondered why.

"Tough luck, old stick," Captain Stone said, clearly sounding disappointed. "It appears Lady Jane has a plan. If there is any way to preserve our independent status, I for one am personally willing to do whatever it takes. This is the most fun I have ever had in the army—all operations, all the time. Will you be staying at the Bradford, Jane?"

"Yes."

"You can count on me to check in twice daily by telephone and not travel more than two hours from London in case you should happen to require my presence for any of your nefarious schemes," Captain Stone promised. He may have been a wealthy aristocrat and practicing playboy, but he was no dilettante. The 2nd Life Guards officer was the epitome of a professional British Army officer.

"But Jane, try really, really hard not to." He gave her a rakish smile.

"Thanks, Terry," she said. "There is one very special event I am hoping to arrange that you are uniquely qualified to attend. If I can organize it, you definitely need to be involved."

"Count me in."

"I thought rank had its privileges," Major Randal grumbled. He was surprised at how quickly Captain Stone had caved in and gone along with her scheme; he must actually believe Lady Jane knew what she was doing, and that was worth thinking about.

"There are a few other items we need to go over before we bring in the rest of the troops." Captain Lady Seaborn plunged on, wanting to move the conversation along while she was ahead.

Their much-anticipated liberty wrecked, Major Randal and Captain Stone sat there at the table smoking their cigarettes in stony silence. The two officers were sick. They took chasing women seriously.

Captain Lady Seaborn stole a glance at Major Randal, fighting the urge to smile. She was well aware the two officers had serious reputations as lady-killers. Her nephew held them in awe on that account.

"I have developed a new name for the unit," she announced, changing the subject.

"A new name?" Major Randal snarled. "What's wrong with the one we have?"

"Nothing, John, except it is somewhat confusing."

"It's *supposed* to be confusing; it's a cover name. Small-Scale Raiding Company has a nice ring to it, and it makes us sound like we have a lot more people than we do."

"The name also gives the impression of being limited," said Captain Lady Seaborn in an even, reasonable voice. "A company is a relatively minor military unit. Being designated as one limits potential for future promotion. 'Small-Scale' implies we are capable of only minor military tasks."

"By all means, we certainly would not want to limit any potential for promotion, that's for sure," Captain Stone said, giving Major Randal a nudge under the table with the highly polished toe of his boot. "Particularly for the officers."

"Here. I typed up the new name I propose in block letters so you can see it before you hear it," Captain Lady Seaborn continued, taking a folded sheet of paper out of her handbag and laying it out flat on the table.

The note read, STRATEGIC RAIDING FORCE.

"Whoa, that's good!" blurted Major Randal, momentarily forgetting his deep disappointment at having to cancel his leave plans.

"Extraordinary," Captain Stone said with genuine enthusiasm. "Sounds like we report directly to the prime minister."

"Most impressive, Lady Seaborn," Major Hicks added, sounding pleased. "The lads will like it."

"The name itself will be classified," Lady Jane explained. "We never use it except on documents that are classified 'Secret' or above. That gives us the aura of being very special, a hush-hush unit cloaked in mystery, not to be trifled with by middle-level officers or bureaucrats, because they will not be entirely certain who, precisely, we actually do work for."

"Clever," Major Randal said. She had his full attention now. "What will we call ourselves?"

"Raiding Forces," Captain Lady Seaborn explained, pulling a black tab embroidered in silver thread from her purse and laying it on the table. It read, in bold block letters, RAIDING FORCES.

"We'll wear it on our left sleeve. It'll look marvelous."

"Outstanding!" Major Randal exclaimed. "Absolutely first-class, Jane."

Captain Lady Seaborn's eyes sparkled with pleasure, and she was surprised at how pleased she felt that the major had complimented her idea.

"Raiding Forces is also a very subtle cover name," she went on. "Every time there is any kind of offensive operation, the troops involved are always described in the newspapers and newsreels as 'raiding forces.' No one will actually know who we are or what we have accomplished, but everyone will think they have heard of us.

"At the same time, the name 'Raiding Forces' does not give anything away. It could mean anything or nothing. German intelligence will never know what to make of a report that raiding forces have moved into a certain area or conducted an operation."

"You must have actually learned something in that posh Swiss finishing school of yours," Captain Stone said.

"I thought it might be appropriate for us to wear our parachute wings over our hearts, like the Royal Air Force pilots wear their wings, instead of on our sleeves the way Airborne Forces personnel do now," she continued. "They will look much prettier that way."

"Pretty is good," Major Randal said with a laugh. "What do you say, Sergeant Major?"

"As I mentioned, sir, the lads are sure to like the new name, and they will definitely appreciate being authorized to wear their parachute wings on their chest," he confirmed confidently. "A morale-building development, upon my word."

"Any more surprises?" Major Randal inquired, more delighted with the name "Raiding Forces" than he wanted to let on. It sounded crisp and professional: the kind of outfit the caliber of men they were looking for would want to be a part of.

"Oh, I may have something else up my sleeve. But right now would be a good time to bring in the lads," Lady Jane Seaborn said. She was beaming, well satisfied with the way the conference had gone.

Captain Stone and Sergeant Major Hicks went to the other car to collect the troops. When they were out of earshot, Captain Lady Seaborn said, "I hope you will not think it presumptuous, John, but I have taken the liberty to make arrangements for you to stay at the Bradford Hotel."

"Thanks," he lied.

"And John, if it's not too terribly much to ask, after I have ruined all your other plans, would you consider escorting me to Randy's party this evening?" she asked.

For once she did not sound entirely sure of herself.

That about caps it, he thought. *While Terry's hanging drunken horsewomen by their spurs off chandeliers, I get to babysit a grieving widow. How much worse can it get?*

What he heard himself say was, "Love to." He almost sounded convincing.

15

SHOTGUN

MAJOR JOHN RANDAL STOOD AT THE FRONT OF THE CAR AS THE troops moved in from the second car and took their seats. They all crowded in, and with the new men from No. 2 (Parachute) Commandos, it was a tight fit. The train was chugging steadily toward London.

"Men," Major Randal began, "I have some administrative announcements and then I'm going to turn it over to Captain Lady Seaborn. First of all, congratulations are in order for a job well done. Parachute school was sure a lot tougher than I expected it to be. You may have noticed that a couple of people are no longer with us. Good soldiers who completed the training and received their wings, but who did not measure up to the professional standard we require and so were not invited to continue. That's all that is going to be said on that subject."

There was dead silence in the car. The idea that you could be "invited out" at any time for simply failing to measure up came as a surprise. In the past, to be RTU'd, a man had to commit some major breach, quit, or be injured too badly to continue. As the realization settled in, the men in the room looked around at one another and nodded their approval. Only the best need apply; only the very best would be allowed to stay. They liked that.

"We lost some good people, but we've gained some outstanding men. Lieutenant Stirling and you new troops from No. 2 Commando who have been tapped to join our ranks, welcome aboard."

The troops in the railcar thundered their approval. Lieutenant Percy Stirling was wildly popular. The young "Death or Glory Boy" had acquitted himself well the last three weeks. When the going got tough, he kicked it into high gear.

The eleven men from No. 2 Commando selected to join them had been carefully handpicked. They came from some of the finest regiments in the British Army. Virtually everyone in the No. 1 Parachute Training School had volunteered when it was learned that the company was recruiting, but the men present now were the cream of the crop.

"The Small-Scale Raiding Company is no more," Major Randal announced. The car grew quiet. What could this mean?

"From this day forward, we will be known as the *Strategic Raiding Force*."

Whistles, Comanche yells, and other sounds of approval greeted the announcement.

"Our full name is classified. We are going to call ourselves simply 'Raiding Forces.' When anyone asks you what outfit you're in, that's what you tell 'em. This is the flash," Major Randal went on, holding up the black tab with the eye-catching silver stitching. "Captain Lady Seaborn came up with our new name and she designed the patch. She has requested that all Raiding Forces personnel be allowed to wear their parachute wings over their heart like pilots do, not on the sleeve. She thinks wings will look, ah, prettier that way. What do you think, boys?"

The Commandos cheered enthusiastically. Fighting men did like their badges. Major Randal remembered a quote attributed to Napoleon: something to the effect that he could conquer the world, as long as the French factories kept churning out enough ribbon for him to keep awarding decorations. From what he could tell, Captain Lady Jane Seaborn's stock had spiked to an all-time high.

"My first formal duties as Raiding Forces commander are pleasant ones. Royal Marines Karen Montgomery, front and center."

The parachute rigger looked wonderful in her brand-new Royal Marines uniform.

"You men know Marine Montgomery. She does professional work, which is a good thing, or there probably wouldn't be as many of us here having this little ceremony."

Everyone laughed.

"By decree of the King, or whoever, she has been commissioned a lieutenant of Royal Marines."

Marine Pamela Plum-Martin handed him the appropriate rank insignia and he pinned it on one epaulet while Captain Lady Seaborn pinned the other.

"In the U.S. Army it is traditional for a brand-new lieutenant to discretely slip a silver dollar to the senior noncommissioned officer present to buy his first salute. I do not believe you have that tradition in the British Army, but I would be proud, Lieutenant Montgomery, to return your first salute and not even be paid for it."

"Thank you, sir," the new Royal Marines officer said happily, and she snapped him a crisp salute, which he returned with a flourish.

"Next order of business. Midshipman Randy Seaborn, front and center. By order of the First Lord of the Admiralty—and with a little help in the form of a waiver for the age-in-grade provision—you have been promoted to lieutenant in the Royal Navy."

"You mean sub-lieutenant, sir," corrected the young officer.

"Nope. Don't forget, I'm your commanding officer, which means I'm never wrong. You skipped a rank, stud."

For a second there, it looked as though brand-new Lieutenant Randy Seaborn's first official act was going to be to faint dead away.

Not doing much to help his blood pressure, Royal Marine Plum-Martin moved in quickly with a uniform blouse that was sporting the appropriate straight gold rings on the cuffs, indicating the teenager's transition out of the reserves into the regular navy. The beautifully tailored blouse also bore the planks of a full lieutenant on the shoulders. She gave him a sexy wink.

"No more wavy-navy for you, Lieutenant," Major Randal said. "You're the real deal, now."

The men stood up and applauded. They kidded the young officer unmercifully about his navigation problems every chance they got, but they all knew that he was a good sailor in fair and stormy weather. More important, the Raiders all knew that when they returned to the beach at the end of a mission, he would always be there waiting to take them out. He was reliable, and that stood for something with these fighting men.

"Now, gentlemen, I'm going to turn the floor over to our beautiful patron, Captain Lady Jane Seaborn. As you will soon see, she has been slaving away diligently on our behalf while we were in training."

Captain Lady Seaborn stood to address the troops. "That was fun," she said, clapping her hands. Every man in the railcar laughed right on cue. At this moment, they would have laughed at anything she said, cheered, stood on their heads, done cartwheels, or whatever else they thought she wanted them to do. It was clear to Major Randal that the Royal Marines captain had the troops of Raiding Forces wrapped around her little finger.

"And now, Captain 'Geronimo Joe' McKoy has a surprise for you that I believe you are all going to especially appreciate."

Captain Lady Seaborn gestured toward the back door of the car, and right on cue, the former Arizona Ranger entered and sashayed down the aisle with a canvas gun case lovingly cradled in his arms.

Unzipping the case with a flourish, he pulled out an exotic-looking humpbacked weapon.

"Boys, this here is a 12-gauge Browning A-5 semiautomatic shotgun. The barrel has been cut back to twenty inches, and on the end is an improvised Cutts Compensator just like they have on the Thompson submachine gun, designed to reduce felt recoil and muzzle jump. The compensator also serves as a flash suppressor. The end has been duck-billed, which means she will throw a wide, oval, sideways pattern of shot rather than a circle. Makes for a nasty little alley sweeper," he added with a knowing wink.

"Notice the magazine tube has been extended to hold eight rounds. The U.S. Border Patrol came up with this idea a while back because they needed a lot more firepower than they had available at the time. Some good ole boys at Purdy's, which is a right nice shotgun outfit, took the specifications I gave 'em and modified us a whole passel of these here Nazi blasters."

Without fanfare, he stuck the barrel of the stubby Browning A-5 shotgun out the window of the train. They were passing a fair-sized pond when he began pulling the trigger.

BLAM BLAM BLAM BLAM BLAM BLAM BLAM BLAM . . .

Every round produced a pie plate–sized eruption and sent up a tall geyser of yellow-brown water.

When the empties had stopped rattling on the coach floor around the old Ranger's feet, he concluded, "This here modified Browning A-5 is my personal weapon of choice for fast, close-in work on dark nights, and is especially effective in tight quarters against multiple targets.

"I guarantee you she'll blow a hole big enough to throw a cat through in anybody you hit square with it. They ain't for shootin' skeet, boys."

Every man in the room was immediately on his feet, cheering at the top of his lungs.

Captain McKoy looked pleased. "Strategic Raiding Force . . . Now boys, that there is what I call a real 'bring 'em back dead'–sounding kind of outfit. First chance you get, I want each one of you to hose one of those Nazi Germans for me, personal. You ain't ever going to be outgunned again, not at night."

The men grinned at one another, clearly itching to get their hands on the Brownings.

"About thirty years ago, when I was a-operatin' against the Moros in the same Philippine jungles young Major Randal here cut his teeth on recently, a-huntin' Huks," the old Ranger continued, "the Moros had a bad habit of wiring themselves up real tight from head to toe with bits of telegraph wire until they cut off the circulation and couldn't feel no pain. They'd smoke a whole bunch of real powerful narcotic dope, then run amok wavin' their razor-sharp bolo knives. You could fill 'em full of lead, but they'd just keep on a-comin', dead on their feet. They chopped up a lot of good men that way. It pretty much took a spinal column hit to put one of those hopped-up fanatics down for the count, which ain't exactly all that easy to do when a wild man is a-swingin' a three-foot-long knife at you with evil intent.

"So I got me a 12-gauge Winchester Model 97 pump, had the armorer whack off the barrel and make one of these duckbill devices for it, and that shotgun never left my side the rest of the time I was over there. When one of them bad boys came at me, I'd just take dead aim at his Adam's apple and let him have it. Worked every time.

"Now, boys, let me tell you what; this here Browning is a much superior weapon. There ain't a Nazi made that's as tough to put down as a doped-up Moro religious fanatic with his testicles wired up tight—'scuse me, Lady Jane. Anyways, you can put that in the bank."

The Raiders stood up to cheer. They stomped their boots and gave Comanche yells for a long time. Geronimo Joe McKoy knew exactly how to communicate with fighting men; he was a master motivator and trainer. Major Randal, watching his troops closely, realized that not only were Raiding Forces personnel convinced beyond doubt that their deficiency in firepower had just been corrected; every man present in the railcar knew exactly where he was going to hold on target the very first time the opportunity presented itself.

The troops were going wild. Captain Lady Seaborn was not quite certain she was ever going to get them to settle down. When the Commandos finally quieted, she said, "Well, lads, there's not much one can do to compete with Captain McKoy; he is a rather hard act to follow.

"Marine Plum-Martin is passing out packets that contain your Raiding Forces flashes and additional parachute wings. You will wear the tab on the left shoulder of your blouse and your wings on the left side of your chest, above the pocket. There is a diagram in the packet that tells you precisely where they are to be sewn and gives you the exact spacing.

"When you return to duty at the end of your leave, Raiding Forces will immediately be traveling to Achnacarry Castle in Scotland for an intensive training program at the newly established Special Warfare Training Center.

"Congratulations on graduating from parachute school! Now go enjoy your leave, lads. Wings really get the girls, I'm told."

"YEEEEEEHAAAAAA!"

16

LONDON

WHEN THE TRAIN ARRIVED AT THE STATION, THE PLATFORM WAS crowded with men and women in uniform. Invasion fear was raging at fever pitch; the Battle of France had been lost, and the Battle of Britain had commenced. There was a sense of impending danger and urgency in the air as people went about on their appointed rounds.

The instant Major John Randal, Captain Terry "Zorro" Stone, Captain Lady Jane Seaborn, and Royal Marine Pamela Plum-Martin emerged topside from the underground station, a tall blonde wearing a luxurious full-length mink coat with the golden tops of champagne bottles peeking out of both side pockets stepped out of the crowd and glued herself to Captain Stone.

As Major Randal and the rest of them watched, the duo tangoed their way over to the curb where her racing-green Jaguar was parked. After tossing his bags into the bonnet of the stylish English sports car, Captain Stone waved a brave salute, climbed resolutely into the passenger side with the look of a man who has his work cut out for him, and with the blonde at the wheel, roared off into the city.

"Was that Monica Woodleigh?" Captain Lady Seaborn asked Marine Plum-Martin.

"Uh-huh."

"She was the one expelled from Westley for getting caught in the boathouse totally . . . "

"Uh-huh."

"John, you really are making the ultimate sacrifice if you gave up partying with Monica and her crowd to spend your leave attending meetings with me," Captain Lady Seaborn said. "Do you mind terribly?"

"If I had two choices—jump on Berlin, kill Hitler, win the war, and live to tell about it, or party with Terry for the next ten days—Hitler would be safe from me," he replied as the green Jaguar drove out of sight.

Captain Lady Seaborn and Marine Plum-Martin exchanged looks, but neither of the women said a word. They were both reasonably confident Major Randal was telling them the truth.

The hotel had sent a long black Rolls-Royce limousine, a silver "B" monogram painted on the door, to meet them at the train station. A uniformed chauffeur dressed in the traditional garb of an Indian Sikh, complete with a turban and sporting a full beard, helped them load their luggage.

Once they were on the way, Captain Lady Seaborn began explaining the drill. "We are going to drop Pamela off at the Bradford. She will supervise delivery of our baggage to our rooms, and then she has the rest of the day off to herself to prepare for Randy's party tonight. John, you and I are going shopping."

Major Randal could not think of one single thing he wanted to do less than go shopping in downtown London during the Battle of Britain. This day was going straight downhill. He heard himself say, as if in a trance, "Fun," and he managed not to sound bitter, even though in his mind's eye he kept picturing Terry tearing off in the Jag with the racy-looking blonde.

As it turned out, the shopping was not all that bad.

To his surprise, once they were alone together in the back of the limousine, he became extremely relaxed, almost to the point of becoming lethargic. Spending time with Lady Jane was having a strangely calming effect on him. Beautiful women had seldom made him feel that way.

The first stop was Pembroke's Military Tailors. Major Randal had never heard of the place; there was no reason for him to have. Welsh & Jefferies was the official King's Royal Rifle Corps regimental tailor, and besides, Pembroke's did not advertise. Admittance was "by appointment"; it said so right on the door. Pembroke's, he was to learn, produced the finest-quality military clothing made in England—and that meant, without question, the world.

When Captain Lady Seaborn swept through the doors of Pembroke's it was as if the queen herself had arrived. The staff flew into a frenzy as they all scurried to form a receiving line to greet her. She knew them all by name, and introduced each of them to a slightly bemused Major Randal. He did not fail to note that the staff seemed genuinely pleased to see her.

"Mr. Chatterley," she said grandly, "Major Randal needs the works."

"Whoa!" Major Randal exclaimed. "What's going on?"

"Would you give us a moment?" Captain Lady Seaborn asked politely. The staff vanished as if she had waved a magic wand.

She turned to him with a serious look on her face. "John, it is essential for you to make a good first impression on the people we are going to be meeting with. The cut of a man's uniform is vitally important. We British are funny about trivial things like the stitching on our military buttonholes, the exact shade of our Sam Browne belt, or the number of pleats on the back of a pair of an officer's leather gloves. While it may seem quite silly to you, that is how things are done here."

"Jane, can I afford this?"

She smiled. "My treat."

"You know I can't let you do that."

"John, you should know by now that money is not an issue with me. If your reluctance is about the cost, please try to understand that when you have the kind of wealth I was born into, money does not have quite the same meaning it does to others. I only spend for the best of reasons. In this case, we can reasonably say it is for the national defense.

"Besides, I've been so looking forward to surprising you today. Please be a good sport and don't let anything get in the way of me indulging myself."

"I've no idea what to say."

"I would like to show you around town and buy you anything I feel like without having to feel guilty. Please allow me this one day. It's been a long time since I've been able to do anything like this. We shall have great fun, I promise."

"Well, I wouldn't want to be a bad sport . . . " Major Randal gave her an uneasy look. "But what will people think?"

"They are going to see you have a rather nice Pembroke's-cut uniform. And being British, they will take you seriously right from the start."

"Okay . . . only you have to let me pay you back."

"Deal." Lady Jane's eyes sparkled as she held out her hand to shake on it. "I want you to be creative—surprise me. I think I should like to be surprised by you, John."

Captain Lady Seaborn made him feel more than a little crazy. He wondered if she had any idea of the powerful effect she had on him . . . *She had to!*

Not sure exactly what he was getting himself into, Major Randal shook her hand and said, "Did I ever tell you that you remind me a lot of my old high school English teacher?" He hoped he conveyed the image of a dowdy, matronly, wrinkled old schoolmarm with bad hair.

"She was able to get you to do things you did not think you wanted to do, no doubt," Lady Jane responded, without missing a beat.

"Let's do it, Mr. Chatterley," Major Randal announced. The staff reappeared from out of nowhere, and the tailor was all over him with tape, pins, and chalk.

"Mr. Chatterley, we are going to need you to whip up something quick for the major to wear to Randy's promotion party tonight," Lady Jane said. "Certainly you have something already started for some duke or field marshal that you can alter to the major's specifications?"

"Of course, Lady Seaborn, I am sure we can manage something," Mr. Chatterley assured her. He saw no need to mention that he had been working on a complete set of uniforms for Major Randal ever since Captain Lady Seaborn had had one of his spares delivered for just that purpose the day the major had gone off to No. 1 Parachute Training School. Unknown to Major Randal, this fitting had been set up almost a month ago, and even that was some kind of an all-time speed record for Pembroke's. Allowances were made during time of war, after all.

"I trust young Sub-lieutenant Seaborn found everything to his satisfaction?" Mr. Chatterley commented as he slipped a beautiful military blouse onto his new client. To Major Randal's surprise, it fit almost perfectly.

"We had to do some last-minute emergency sewing."

Alarmed, Mr. Chatterley looked up from his measuring to see if she was joking. Lady Jane Seaborn was well known for her sense of humor, though to Mr. Chatterley's knowledge, it had not been much in evidence since her late husband had been lost at sea.

"Major Randal nominated Randy to skip a grade, and he went straight to full lieutenant. He and his mother will be in to see you later today to have you sort it all out before his party tonight."

"Very good, Lady Seaborn."

Apparently, thought Major Randal, *"by appointment" does not apply in all cases—such as the Seaborn family.*

"Oh my," Mr. Chatterley said after a moment, "that should make Master Randy the youngest officer in his grade in the Royal Navy. I should imagine Admiral Ransom and Commander Seaborn are simply beside themselves."

"Neither of them have found out about it yet. Should you happen to see either Randy's grandfather or his father before tonight, mum's the word."

"You can count on my discretion, Lady Seaborn."

"There was never any question . . . Here are the insignia and wings that need to go on the major's uniforms, with written instructions and a diagram indicating where they are to be placed. He will also require a Military Cross ribbon."

"Hmmm!" Mr. Chatterley mumbled around the mouthful of pins clenched in his teeth. "You must be that pinprick raiding gentleman we have heard so much about . . . captured a German general some time back, as I recall.

"King's Royal Rifles—now that is a most appropriate regiment for you, sir. Raised in America during the French and Indian War—the officers trained under the legendary Ranger Major Robert Rogers. Sometimes called the 'Royal Americans,' later designated the 60th Rifles, then the King's Royal Rifle Corps. Mounted infantry for a time, I believe . . . Known as a thinking officer's regiment. The eyes and ears of the army, they say.

"Did you know, Major, my clients tell me it is more difficult to obtain a commission in the King's Royal Rifle Corps than in the Guards or Cavalry? And that includes the Life Guards and the Blues."

Careful to keep still because he was afraid of getting tagged by a pin, Major Randal moved only his lips. "Well, they took me. Must be scraping the bottom of the barrel these days."

"I doubt that, sir. It is tradition for Americans to serve in the King's Royal Rifle Corps. Let's see, now, for a foreigner to join the British Army, he must first enlist in a territorial regiment . . . The King's Royal Rifles have, I believe, six territorial regiments: the London Rifles, the Queen's Victoria Rifles, the Queen's Westminster Rifles, and the—"

"I was with the Rangers."

"You would be, sir. By any chance, do you happen to know that other American 60th Rifles officer who brought the last men out of Calais?"

"That would be me, Mr. Chatterley."

"You, sir? I was not aware there were any Rangers with the Green Jacket Brigade at Calais. I was under the impression the QVR were there."

"It's a long story."

"Most unfortunate what happened to the Green Jackets, sir. What a pity. I hope things were not as terrible as they have been made to sound, sir."

"Calais had its moments."

"I suspect it did, sir. Your exploit was quite commendable: bringing your men home at the end of the day after all was lost. Several of my clients remarked to me about it at the time. Quite a feat of derring-do, they said. About what you could expect of an American, not to know when he was licked . . . Only bright spot in a dark tragedy, I'm afraid, sir. What a pleasure it is to have you as a client of Pembroke's, Major Randal."

"Doesn't really count when you're saving yourself, Mr. Chatterley."

"You are being modest, sir. To the best of my knowledge, you are my very first Commando. From reading the newspapers, I would have expected you needed to have a violent criminal record, to be a cold-blooded killer, or to be a psychopath to qualify. You clearly do not fit that mold at all, Major. You are not from Chicago, either."

"I could go psycho at any time, Mr. Chatterley."

"Are you quite sure you are not going to want his autograph?" drawled Captain Lady Seaborn, sounding amused.

"I might, at that, Lady Seaborn. You have no idea how much bad news I have suffered through from my clients. We have had to replace quite a pile of army uniforms that were left behind somewhere in a big hurry by their owners, and more than a few for navy officers who lost theirs when their ships were sunk underneath them. Enormously refreshing to have someone in for a change who just wants a new one, someone who has spit in the eye of the Hun and gotten away with it—like a breath of fresh air, actually."

"Yes, I imagine you *have* heard your share of unhappy sea stories," Captain Lady Seaborn said.

"The war has been simply dreadful thus far, as you of all people well know, Lady Seaborn. The staff at Pembroke's do not like to think about anything unfortunate happening to the uniforms we create, or to our dear friends who wear them. Our clients are like our own family. That said, I am afraid we have some serious dry rot at the top of our military family tree. We need more officers like the major here: the kind who do not know when they are whipped, and keep fighting on."

Mr. Chatterley straightened up and took the remaining pins out of his mouth. "I can have this uniform delivered to the Bradford Hotel by six o'clock this afternoon. Will that be satisfactory, Lady Seaborn?"

"Quite." She rewarded him with one of her best smiles. "Which viscount are you going to hijack it from?"

"Lady Seaborn, you know we would never do anything like that. Besides, if we ever did, Pembroke's would surely never admit to it."

"Mr. Chatterley, do you happen to know Captain Stone?" Major Randal inquired.

"We have a Lieutenant Terry Stone of the 2nd Life Guards who is a preferred client, sir."

"Make sure you call him 'Zorro' the next time he comes in."

17

PARTY

THE BRADFORD HOTEL, POPULAR WITH CERTAIN MEMBERS OF THE wealthy and power elite, had been the London Headquarters of the Seaborn family for generations because of its convenience to Whitehall and the Admiralty. At least three government agencies that did not officially exist were within walking distance of the hotel.

Members of the families of three exiled heads of state, on the run from Nazi-occupied countries, were currently in residence. On any given night when the House of Lords was in session, a quorum of the lords could be found at the main bar off to one side of the lobby.

When the limousine pulled up to the hotel, a swarm of porters stormed the car. The front along the driveway was heavily sandbagged to protect the hotel from bomb blasts. Sentries in steel helmets, their bayonets fixed, manned posts at both ends of the drive. The combination of servants, sentries, and sandbag positions gave the handsome old building a surreal, battle-ready charm.

Inside, the opulent lobby glittered like a polished diamond. The effect was like stepping back in time to another century.

Without even the pretense of checking in, they were immediately whisked to a private elevator and zoomed up to the top floor. Captain Lady Jane Seaborn and her entourage peeled off and disappeared into a corner door.

One of the assistant managers escorted Major John Randal to his quarters, a three-room suite. Just inside the entry, standing at rigid attention, was a distinguished older gentleman in a tuxedo.

"Major Randal, allow me introduce you to Chauncy, your butler. He has served the Seaborn family for many years, as had his father before him."

"Nice to meet you, Chauncy."

"Sir!"

"You will find that your bags have already been unpacked in the bedroom," continued the assistant manager. "The room to the left is a fully equipped office. If you need it, the hotel has a secretary-stenographer on call twenty-four hours a day. We can also supply a courier service or cater to any special requirements along those lines that may arise during your stay with us.

"Is there anything else you can think of that you might need, Major?"

"How about a key to the room and a low-interest loan to pay for it?"

"Major, there is no key to the door. Chauncy or one of his assistants will be here to open it for you at all times. As for paying, you are a guest of Lady Seaborn.

"I see."

"Lady Seaborn instructed me to inform you that in the future, when you stay in London, sir, these rooms are to be your permanent residence."

"My quarters?"

"Yes, sir."

"You're kidding."

"Those are Lady Seaborn's instructions, Major."

The phone in the living room rang. Chauncy, the quintessential manservant, answered it on the first ring, "Major Randal's quarters."

The butler turned and held his hand over the receiver. "Lady Seaborn for you, sir."

Major Randal took the phone. "Hello?"

"John, are you finding your suite to your liking?"

"It's just swell. I'm getting ready to send Chauncy out to round up a dozen Nubian dancing girls. Do you need him to pick up anything for you while he's out?"

The butler had retreated to the far reaches of the room to allow the major privacy, but he developed a stricken look on his face when he heard what his new boss said.

"Just kidding, Chauncy," Major Randal called to him without bothering to put his hand over the mouthpiece. "Yes, Jane, I'd say things were pretty much to my liking."

Lady Jane gave a low chuckle. "You're going to embarrass Chauncy. And be careful what you ask for; you might get it. Your wish is his command, and he is extraordinarily capable."

"I promise to be careful."

Lady Jane laughed again. "Twelve is a fairly ambitious number of Nubians. Remember, you promised to escort me to Randy's promotion party tonight."

"Yes, I did."

"I am going to have a long, hot bubble bath and then dinner in my room with one of my girlfriends."

"You're taking a bubble bath with your girlfriend?"

"No, John—simply dinner." Lady Jane giggled. "Your things should start arriving within the hour. Take your time; the party does not start until eight o'clock . . . twenty-hundred hours for you Green Jackets, I believe."

"Can do. I love it when you talk military talk."

"Thanks again for today, John. You're a terrific sport. I really enjoyed myself for the first time in quite a long time."

As soon as he hung up the phone, he asked, "Chauncy, what do we have to drink around here?"

Major Randal pulled out a pack of Player's Navy Cuts and lit one with his old, battered Zippo. He sat down on the lush, overstuffed couch and propped his highly polished boots up on the coffee table. Without thinking about it, he rubbed the faded engraving on the backside of the Zippo lighter with his thumb. "Our Strength Is in Loyalty": It was the regimental motto of the 26th Cavalry. The days in the jungle seemed a long time ago.

"Get bombed often?" he asked Chauncy.

"No, sir. The Jerries have been going after military targets in the east end around the harbor area. The searchlight activity and ack-ack fire make quite the show at times."

"Really?" Major Randal answered, stifling a yawn. He suddenly felt extremely tired—all the hard training of the past weeks caught up with him, and he dozed off.

Chauncy carefully put out the major's cigarette and spread a light coverlet over him.

While the major slept, delivery people from various specialty shops started arriving with uniforms, boots, a Sam Browne belt, a holster for the Browning P-35, shirts, gloves, and an officer's hat. Chauncy began to lay out the major's uniform for that evening. To ensure that it was perfect, he measured the spacing of the badges, insignia, wings, and Military Cross ribbon. A retired sergeant major, late of the Green Howard's Regiment, organizing his own officer's uniform was a task he himself had always enjoyed.

Exactly two hours after arriving at the hotel, and after an hour-long nap, Major John Randal stepped out of the shower. He had just put on his pants and boots first, like a typical cavalryman, when there was a knock on the door. Thinking it was room service, he shouted to Chauncy that he would get it.

Still buttoning his shirt, Major Randal opened the door. Standing there was Lady Jane Seaborn dressed in a simple, single-strap black sheath that left one tawny shoulder bare. Major Randal could see that all her secret agent training had kept her in very good shape.

Looking at her, he felt as if he had been stabbed in the chest with a frozen icicle. For a moment, he was not sure if he was going to be able to breathe. In that regard, at least, Captain Lady Jane Seaborn actually did remind him quite a bit of his old high school English student teacher. She'd had that exact same respiratory effect on him.

"No need to rush," Lady Jane said casually. "I only came by to keep you company until it's time to leave."

"I like company."

Later on, when Lady Jane Seaborn's entourage arrived at the swanky nightclub called the Moonlight Terrace, within walking distance of the hotel, the band was in full swing. The Seaborn party was cordoned off behind velvet ropes in a reserved section near the orchestra. Since the ballroom was located in what amounted to a giant subterranean cave, in the event of an air raid they could simply party on without the inconvenience of having to interrupt the revelry and retire to a bomb shelter.

Hundreds of men in uniform, a few of them, quite senior in rank, and women wearing evening dresses were doing their dead-level best to party like there was no tomorrow; for some of them, there just might not be. The attitude in beleaguered London seemed to be a blend of "Live for today, who knows what is going to happen next" and "Anything goes, no regrets," with a tinge of "Eat, drink, and be merry, for tomorrow we may die" thrown in. And there was the distinct feeling that they were all in it together.

The atmosphere reminded Major Randal of a fraternity party at UCLA or the stag bar at the Army-Navy Club in Manila on a Friday night . . . only much, much bigger. There was a constant roar of sound, and a blue haze of cigarette smoke draped the revelry in a low-level cloud. Major Randal felt stress begin to melt away.

The band was laying down the boogie-woogie; men and women were shimmying out on the dance floor while a muted spotlight played over the scene. A saucy hostess costumed in a very short dress, fishnet stockings, ridiculously high heels, and a tiny cigarette cap led them to their table.

Lieutenant Randy Seaborn's mother, Brandy, turned out to be a stunner on the order of Captain Lady Seaborn. Brandy Seaborn was a vivacious golden girl with hair the color of ripe wheat and a glittering smile. She seemed perpetually happy, to the point that she practically never stopped laughing. The woman certainly did not look old enough to be the mother of a Royal Navy officer.

Captain Lady Jane Seaborn made the introductions. "Brandy, I would like to introduce you to Randy's commanding officer, Major Randal. John, this is Randy's mother, Brandy. She made several trips to Dunkirk in the family houseboat to evacuate troops. Brandy's quite the heroine."

As Brandy Seaborn's eyes flashed at him in instant friendship, Major Randal could not help but notice they were flecked with gold. She was a sparkler. He was impressed to hear about her rescuing troops from Dunkirk.

"John, I am sooo delighted to finally meet you! Randy and Jane have told me so much about you, I feel as if I know you already. You simply must sit here next to me. We have much to talk about."

He found himself wedged between Brandy and Lady Jane. Brandy's girlfriend, Penelope Honeycutt-Parker, who crewed on the Dunkirk missions in the houseboat, and her mustachioed Royal Dragoon husband, Captain Lionel Honeycutt-Parker, sat across the table. Lieutenant Randy Seaborn was there with a doe-eyed beauty, Violet Westinghouse, who looked like a figurine carved out of porcelain.

Lieutenant Percy Stirling had shown up with a luscious, scarlet-haired Australian actress who was wearing a bright yellow sheath dress that fit her like a second skin. *Red and yellow, kill a fellow* flashed through Major Randal's mind, although he knew that only applied to snakes. The young Scot had better watch his step or he would get bitten—which was most likely what Lieutenant Stirling was banking on.

Royal Marine Pamela Plum-Martin made a splash when she showed up with a Royal Air Force wing commander in tow. He was a decorated Spitfire ace, wearing the Distinguished Flying Cross ribbon with two bars. The glamorous bombshell did the Royal Marines proud in a shimmering silver evening gown with a long slit up one shapely leg. She gave Major Randal a toothpaste advertisement–quality smile and a little wink. Marine Plum-Martin was definitely a knockout.

Lieutenant Karen Montgomery arrived looking spectacular and extremely fit. She was with her boyfriend, a Royal Engineer lieutenant who seemed in awe of the new company his girlfriend was keeping. "Commandos!"

"Is she as much trouble as she looks, Lieutenant?" Major Randal asked the young Royal Engineer.

"More, sir."

"I had a feeling she might be."

To everyone's surprise, Captain Terry "Zorro" Stone showed up with his slinky consort, Monica Woodleigh, whose eyes had a glazed look, as if she had just walked away from a high-speed auto crash. Major Randal heard Brandy whisper in protest, "But Errol Flynn never played Zorro!" The dashing Life Guards officer held up the champagne glass he was carrying in salute.

Brandy leaned toward Major Randal and whispered, "Randy is simply walking on air after his unexpected double promotion. I do believe you are his hero, John. Jane tells me we have you to thank for Randy's good fortune."

"Well, not entirely, Brandy. Terry had a vote, as did the sergeant major. We trust your son to bring us home from our missions. He earned it."

"That is simply the most wonderful thing anyone could say to a navy mother, John. I can hardly wait to tell my husband. He and my father should be here anytime now."

Then Brandy Seaborn leaned across Major Randal to say to Lady Jane, "I can see we are really going to like your American major!"

At that moment, Vice Admiral Sir Randolph "Razor" Ransom and Commander Richard Seaborn, OBE, made their appearance at the party. Vice Admiral Ransom, having won nearly all of the nation's decorations, was not wearing a single one on his uniform this evening. Commander Seaborn was wearing the Order of the British Empire, awarded to him for his brilliant work routing convoys during the evacuation from Dunkirk.

The OBE was certainly a prestigious award, but, as Major Randal knew, on occasion it was presented for staff work. In fact, among the ranks of those who earned their living getting shot at, OBE was said to stand for "Other Blighters' Efforts." Lieutenant Seaborn was wearing the coveted Distinguished Service Cross, the navy equivalent of the Military Cross, a highly prized valor medal the Admiralty most definitely did not pass out in Cracker Jack boxes. In terms of precedence, the OBE trumped the DSC. In terms of status within the military, every navy officer wanted to win the DSC; it was the fighting sailor's symbol of excellence.

Major Randal remembered Jane mentioning that the commander might be displeased about his son serving in Raiding Forces. Could he be jealous? Major Randal wondered.

To be fair, the commander was a big-ship man. During the last war he had served as a sub-lieutenant on the battleship HMS *Campbeltown*. It had not been his fault that the ship's captain had entrusted him with the critical mission of going ashore to buy fresh vegetables for the officer's mess the very day the Grand Fleet unexpectedly weighed anchor and sailed for its one and only fleet action of the entire war, the Battle of Jutland. The commander had not been able to return back aboard ship prior to her departure.

Nowadays, he routed convoys. "Sorry we're late, Brandy," her husband said as he leaned over to give her a quick kiss. "I've been tied up arguing with your father. He's gotten his way as usual; the Razor is going back to sea."

"Only as a commodore of merchant convoys making the passage to Malta," Vice Admiral Ransom explained, almost apologetically.

Malta was under siege, and the Germans were doing everything in their considerable power to cut it off and starve the isolated population into submission. The crossing to the island was currently rated the most dangerous voyage on the seven seas, under constant attack from German U-boats, Luftwaffe bombers, and even the occasional enemy surface ship for virtually the whole way. Typically, ten ships might sail in a convoy, and it was considered a huge success if three or four made it through. In the Royal Navy it was unofficially referred to as the "Suicide Run."

"Look out, Adolph, you've had it now," Brandy Seaborn cried, doing her sporting best to hide her concern for her father. "The Razor rides again! Don't forget to take your cane, Father."

Commander Seaborn was the only one present at the table who did not laugh. He raised a glass. "I hope I am in time to propose a toast to my son's advancement, at long last, into the ranks of the regular Royal Navy, his promotion to sub-lieutenant, and his imminent transfer to active service on the pride of the British Empire, the battleship HMS *Hood*."

There was a long, uncomfortable silence at the table. Clearly, Commander Seaborn had not gotten the word. Tonight, apparently, he was part of the proverbial ten percent who don't.

The commander's son disentangled himself from Violet Westinghouse, whose arms had been draped loosely around his neck, obscuring his father's view of his brand-new shoulder board rank insignia. Lieutenant Randy Seaborn stood up, and his father's smile turned into a look of shocked disbelief.

"Sorry, Father. I'm afraid there's been a slight change of plans."

18

HOT TIME IN THE OLD TOWN

DISCRETION, ON OCCASION, ACTUALLY BEING BETTER THAN VALOR, Major John Randal decided that this was a good time to repair to the bar. After he had fought his way through the crowd and elbowed his way, at last, to a place he could lean against, he discovered that Captain Terry "Zorro" Stone and Lieutenant Percy Stirling had been trailing along right behind him.

They all lit up cigarettes and ordered drinks. "I can see both of you two studs are doing a fine job of maintaining the image of intrepid Commando officers at play," Major Randal said. "Better watch out there, Percy: Red and yellow kill a fellow . . . "

"That's only with snakes, sir. Besides, I'm carrying a tourniquet in my pocket, just in case."

"Better slap it on your neck, old stick," Captain Stone advised. "From the looks of those blue marks, you've already been fanged. Does your mother know you go out with women like her?"

"Zorro, Miss Woodleigh certainly looks like she has a good personality and probably makes her own clothes," Major Randal said in an innocent tone. "Do all the girls like her, too?"

"Monica Woodleigh is a carnivore. How goes it with you, John?"

"Shopping all day."

"Called on Chatterley at Pembroke's, I see," the captain said, eyeing Major Randal's uniform. "Nobody does a military buttonhole like Pembroke's. Unparalleled. Lady Jane does like her men groomed.

"Mr. Chatterley told you the complete history of your regiment, I bet," Lieutenant Stirling laughed. "He knows more about the order of battle than anyone in all of England. The Nazis ought to kidnap him and pump him for information."

Major Randal should have guessed that a couple of wealthy young cavalry officers would recognize a Pembroke's-cut uniform. "He told me the Rangers had originally been called 'The Devil's Own.' I don't think even the Rangers know that. If they do, they never bothered to tell me.

"Is it true the king has his uniforms made there?" Major Randal asked.

"Did you happen to notice the coat of arms on the door and the phrase 'by appointment,' John?" asked Captain Stone.

"Yeah."

"That is what is called a royal warrant. Various members of the royal family can issue warrants to selected merchants and tradesmen. Holders of a royal warrant are granted dispensation to display the coat of arms of the person who issued it to them on their front door. In Pembroke's case, it is the king."

Lieutenant Stirling added, "A royal warrant can be withdrawn at any time, should the quality of the workmanship ever decline. They are only slightly less rare than golden hen's teeth."

"Everywhere we went today had one."

"No!" Both the young officers cried in unison.

"Where else did Lady Jane take you?" Captain Stone demanded. "Uniforms, shirts, hats, gloves—boots. Did she take you to Blood's? Not Blood's! Tell me she did not take you to Blood's!"

"Blood's boot makers?" Major Randal asked, swirling the ice in his glass. "As a matter of fact—"

"John, there is a two-year waiting list for a pair of boots from Blood's, and that is if your family has been a client for generations! Blood's has not accepted a walk-in client in my lifetime. Your father has to put you on their list the day you are born—provided, of course, he is on it himself."

"Well, Blood's loaned me the pair of Wellingtons I have on. They promised me mine by the end of the week," Major Randal said. He was enjoying a little payback for not being able to go out and party as the two of them were doing.

"Damn, that's a Blood's Sam Browne belt, too!" Captain Stone cried.

"Yes, it is."

"Did you know the term 'blood red' is not actually a shade of red but the unique color of brown dye that Blood's uses to cure its leather?"

"Didn't know that."

"Unbelievable! She took you to Blood's? You probably replaced her dead husband, Mallory, on the list."

"Where are you staying, sir?" Lieutenant Stirling asked.

"The Bradford. Terry's calling in twice a day to let me know how to get in contact with him in case something comes up. Maybe you'd better do the same thing, Percy."

"Yes, sir. How do you like the hotel, sir?"

"It's fine. The lobby looks like an Indian palace."

"Looks like?" Captain Stone shook his head. "It *is* an Indian palace. The management dismantled one and brought it back from India, piece by piece, two hundred years ago. You should ask Jane. I think she owns it."

"I see."

Royal Marine Plum-Martin's much-decorated Spitfire pilot eased up to the bar and ordered a pair of double scotches on the rocks. Major Randal felt a stab of guilt when he realized he had not offered to bring a drink back to Jane, but it quickly went away when he saw the wing commander toss both of them down, one right after the other, a single gulp each.

The Spitfire ace studied the parachute wings on Major Randal's chest. "I say, old chap, isn't it a bit queer to jump out of a perfectly flyable airplane before it even has any bullet holes in it?"

"Yes, it is."

"How many jumps must one make to qualify for parachute wings?"

"Seven."

"Hmm . . . Three more and I shall have to indent for a pair."

Commander Richard Seaborn walked up to the bar. Captain Stone and Lieutenant Stirling grabbed their drinks and made themselves scarce.

Thanks, guys, said Major Randal to himself.

The commander looked as though he had something he wanted to say but did not quite know how to get started. "I understand I have you to thank for Randy's double promotion," he said finally. "Quite a surprise, that."

"Like I explained to your wife, sir, Randy earned it."

"Yes, she told me what you said. We are both very proud. Nice of you to let us know how you feel—speaks well of you to say so. However, this promotion does create something of a problem."

"I see."

"The *Hood* agreed to accept Randy as a sub-lieutenant. They are not going to take him in the grade of lieutenant. It would not be fair to the *Hood* or to Randy."

"I can tell you're not all that pleased with the idea of Randy staying on in Raiding Forces, sir."

"Major, it has been widely reported that you Commandos have a dash each of the Elizabethan pirate, the frontier tribesman, and the Chicago gangster, all rolled into one. That kind of job description is not likely to enhance one's career in the Royal Navy."

"Commander, are you in a position where you could take off for a couple of days?"

"Certainly."

"Why don't you come down and go out on an operation with us some night, so you can see Randy do his stuff? Your father-in-law did. That way, you can evaluate for yourself if Randy is contributing more to the war effort by serving in Raiding Forces than if he were the junior sub-lieutenant on the *Hood*."

"The admiral mentioned that he had accompanied you on a mission—said the *Arrow* was pretty lively."

"Well, sir, if what you sailors call lively is a forty-foot boat standing straight up on her stern and shaking herself like a wet dog, that's what the *Arrow* was the night the Razor sailed to France and back with us. One of the crewmen was so seasick he passed out."

"She was never meant for that kind of weather. The *Arrow* is a pleasure craft intended for fair-weather sailing," Commander Seaborn said with a rueful shake of his head. "Two days' notice would be best. Randy has my private number at the Admiralty."

"I don't think you'll be disappointed, sir."

On the way back to the table Major Randal ran into Vice Admiral Sir Randolph "Razor" Ransom. "So, you're headed back into harm's way again, sir," he said to the silver-haired admiral. "The Suicide Run. Couldn't you find something a little more dangerous, Admiral?"

"They are bringing some of us retired people back in to act as commodores on merchant convoys. At least I shall not be in a mosquito boat that dances on her tail like a hooked tarpon, dead lost in the middle of the night not more than twenty miles from my home in waters I have sailed a thousand times before," the crusty old admiral said with a twinkle in his eye.

"Stay low, sir."

"That was a fine thing you did for my grandson, John."

"He earned it, Admiral. You saw how he handles himself in a tough situation."

Major Randal slid back into his seat at the table. Squadron Leader Paddy Wilcox had arrived, wearing his black eye-patch and escorting two posh young ladies whose combined age might have equaled his, give or take six months either way. Nobody actually believed they were his nieces. The Canadian pilot, as usual, was having a mighty fine time.

"I'm at the Bradford, Paddy," said Major Randal. "Check in with the front desk twice a day and let me know how to get in contact with you."

"Wilco."

Sergeant Major Maxwell Hicks and his wife, Lorraine, made their appearance. Ramrod-straight as ever, the sergeant major conducted himself with an exaggerated, old-world courtesy: the professional's professional. He could just as easily have passed for a Roman centurion as a British Grenadier Guardsman.

Lorraine Hicks was nearly as tall in her heels as he was and was a patrician beauty. The two complemented each other: She was as charming as her husband was wired tight.

"Sergeant Major, I am staying at the Bradford. Leave a number at the front desk where you can be reached in the event something comes up," said Major Randal after greeting the sergeant major and his wife.

"Sir!"

At that moment, Captain "Geronimo Joe" McKoy made a grand entrance. The cowboy showman was dressed to kill in a fringed buckskin jacket. He was carrying his pearl-gray Stetson in one hand, and his associate, Miss Lilly Threepersons, was on the other arm. She was ravishing in chartreuse.

No sooner had they arrived than the lights in the room went up. The master of ceremonies, clad in a roll-collar tuxedo jacket, took the microphone and said, "Ladies and gentlemen, I hope you are enjoying yourselves this evening."

Polite applause rippled through the crowd.

"I have just been informed that we have an illustrious visitor with us tonight, and I want him to come up here so that I can introduce him. Let's have a warm round of applause for Captain Geronimo Joe McKoy, famed Wild West Indian fighter and hero of the charge up San Juan Hill with Teddy Roosevelt's Rough Riders. Please come on up here, Captain."

As the band broke into "Hot Time in the Old Town Tonight," Captain McKoy pranced up to the microphone to the accompaniment of a ripple of courteous, but not overly enthusiastic, clapping.

"It says here," the announcer read from his cue card, "you were also an Arizona Ranger. Is that like a Texas Ranger?"

"Yep, exceptin' we operated in the state of Arizona."

"What brings you to London, Captain?"

"Tonight I'm at a promotion party for a friend of mine, Lieutenant Randy Seaborn, the youngest full lieutenant in the entire dang Royal Navy." The crowd broke into applause and strained to see the young officer. They did not know much about San Juan Hill or Indian fighting, but they appreciated date of rank; the youngest lieutenant in the navy was worth taking a gander at.

"No sense cranin' your necks, folks. You won't have any trouble spottin' Randy. He just happens to be the very first navy officer ever to complete parachute school and is the only navy officer in the service a-wearin' parachute wings on his chest right now. It's right there above the Distinguished Service Cross he won on a Commando raid a while back."

The crowd immediately responded with a heavy round of applause.

"I meant, what are you doing in England, Captain?" the MC pressed.

"Oh, I'm over here, ah . . . entertaining the troops."

"And how exactly do you do that?"

"Oh . . . a-twirlin' pistols, throwing knives, doing a little fancy rope work."

"Sounds exciting! How would you like to put on a demonstration for our audience tonight?"

"Well, I'd be glad to, exceptin' I don't have my shootin' irons or other gear with me."

"Captain, I am sure there are some pistols in this crowd." Everyone laughed. Every officer in the room was wearing his issue sidearm. "Let's get a couple up here, folks."

Two army lieutenants rushed up and offered their weapons.

It's a setup, Major Randal thought. *They're trying to humiliate the old cowboy.*

"Webley .455s with four-inch barrels," Captain McKoy observed wryly. "Lots of knockdown power, but about as well balanced as a primeval club. I'd rather try to twirl bowling balls."

"Well, old-timer, if you're not up to it . . . " the MC taunted.

The crowd laughed; the Arizona Ranger looked dejected. Accidentally, it appeared, he touched a lever on the side of one of the Webleys; the revolver broke open and the bullets spilled out onto the floor. The drummer hit a cymbal. CRASH!

The crowd started to laugh, but the merriment faded when they saw the white-haired gentleman get down on his knees and start to grope around for the shells.

Major Randal felt a red-hot rage and started to get up, but stopped abruptly when Lady Jane reached over and put her hand on his leg to restrain him.

Captain McKoy struggled to his feet and handed the MC the bullets; then he carefully unloaded the other pistol. The room had grown silent. This bad joke had gone too far.

Somehow, again by accident it seemed, one of the ungainly Webley pistols flipped over on the captain's finger as he handed over the last of the bullets. The drummer did a little roll as a joke. No one laughed.

Then the other pistol did the same thing. Now they were both twirling in slow motion, barely making it up and over.

The band kicked into a slow version of "Hot Time in the Old Town Tonight," and as the twirling pistols on his fingers started to pick up speed, the band increased its tempo. Suddenly, from out of nowhere, a huge, gleaming Bowie knife flashed in the air, and spinning pistols started to fly up and down as the old showman juggled all three.

In seconds, the crowd was on its feet, screaming, "Fire, Fire, Fire!" each time the band came to the end of a stanza. The place was rocking.

Just as suddenly as it had appeared, the knife vanished and the two pistols came tumbling down. The captain coolly caught them, reversed them, and offered both to the astonished master of ceremonies, butts first. When the announcer reached out to accept the Webleys, Captain McKoy suddenly did the "border reverse"—and the startled MC found himself looking down both barrels.

The crowd cheered. Someone yelled, "Shoot the bastard!"

This went on several times before the old Rough Rider relented and allowed the frustrated announcer to reclaim the handguns.

"Ladies and gentlemen, let's have a big round of applause for Captain Geronimo Joe McKoy. I, for one, am convinced he could have taught Wild Bill Hickok a few tricks."

The cowboy showman, not looking so old or pitiful anymore, waved to the audience and shouted, "Support your troops!"

The crowd went wild.

Major Randal was probably the only man in the room not on his feet cheering, clapping, and whistling. This was for the simple reason that Lady Jane had not removed her hand from his leg, even though by now it was clear that he no longer needed to be restrained.

It dawned on him that he was having a really nice evening. He was a little concerned about one thing, though: He was reasonably confident, from the way his leg felt right that minute, that when Lady Jane did take her hand away, there was going to be a scorched handprint on the pant leg of his brand-new Pembroke's tailored uniform. How was he going to explain *that* to Mr. Chatterley?

SECRET SERVICE

19

CLOAK AND DAGGER

MAJOR JOHN RANDAL WAS SITTING ON THE COUCH IN HIS SUITE at the Bradford Hotel. His butler, Chauncy, had thoughtfully provided him with the *Sunday Times*, the *Sunday Dispatch*, and the *Daily Mail*.

The stories were all about the threat of invasion, the dogfights over southern England, the evacuation of children to Canada and the countryside, the hunt for Nazi Fifth Columnists (everyone seemed to be on the lookout for Nazis disguised in nuns' habits, parachuting in to coordinate with the dreaded Fifth Column), the sinking of British ships, and the blackout that had been in effect from the first day Britain entered the war. Citizens throughout the UK were being exhorted to cope and to "just get on with it." There was not a lot of good news.

One writer addressed food rationing, complaining that "the rich could simply go to a restaurant . . . " Apparently, restaurants were not rationed. The Bradford sure did not seem to be.

Which reminded Major Randal: He had to meet Jane downstairs for breakfast. Chauncy helped him into his Pembroke's-cut blouse.

"Beautiful blouse, sir."

"What's your opinion of women in uniform, Chauncy?"

"Ours is not to reason why, sir."

"Been giving it some thought, have you?"

"Have a nice breakfast with Lady Seaborn, sir."

At that very moment, Captain Lady Jane Seaborn was sitting in the morning room off the main lobby with her nephew, Lieutenant Randy Seaborn. The two had always been exceptionally close.

"How are you getting along with the major, Aunt Jane?"

"I am not sure, actually, Randy."

"The two of you seemed to be hitting it off rather well last night. You make a great-looking couple."

"I am not totally convinced he is not simply being polite out of pity to a lonely widow."

"You are hardly pitiful, Aunt Jane."

"You spend a lot of time together late at night on the bridge of your boat. What's he really like?"

"The major likes horses, guns, sports, and girls, just like the rest of us. Only, we don't understand his sports, nor he ours," Lieutenant Seaborn said with a laugh. "What we talk about on the bridge at sea comes under the protection of sailor-to-sailor confidentiality. That makes it private, Aunt Jane."

"Randy . . . you know I'm your favorite relative."

"All I can tell you is the men all say the major is a great combat leader . . . and he can surf."

"Whatever does that mean?"

"We are not quite sure, but he mentions it now and again. Sometimes he will say, 'The surf's up,' and that always means we're going on a mission."

"John says that?"

"Not exactly. What he says is: 'Surf's up, boys. Let's go kill some bad guys.' When you do something noteworthy, he calls you 'stud.' My personal favorite thing is when we go on a raid, the minute he comes back on board after being ashore, he always says to me, 'Let's get the hell out of Dodge, Randy.'"

They both laughed.

"Sounds like something out of a low-budget cowboy movie."

"We all like to hear him say it. I have to warn you, Aunt Jane, I think the major may be damaged goods."

"How do you mean, Randy?"

"He brought his men out of Calais all right, but I'm not sure he made it home himself. The major laughs a lot, but not with his eyes. Sometimes he gets this faraway look. Only it is not like he is looking as much as he is listening for something out there."

"Like the Razor when he thinks no one is watching?"

"Exactly."

Lady Jane continued. "Dudley Clarke told me John blew up a bridge outside of Calais that, had the Germans captured it, would have enabled them to roll right over the British Expeditionary Force trapped at Dunkirk before it could have been evacuated by sea. His action saved the army, but a lot of civilians on the bridge were killed when the demolitions went off. Dudley said it was one of the most courageous decisions he has ever known of a junior officer having to make. Do you think it bothers John?"

"The major never mentions Calais," her nephew responded, clearly not wanting to say much more about his boss on that subject. "Now, what I want you to tell me, Aunt Jane, is one good reason why you are not sure if he likes you."

"John keeps saying that I remind him of his old high school English teacher. The way he says it does not sound like a compliment."

Lieutenant Seaborn looked at his beautiful aunt and burst out laughing. Her cheeks turned rose-colored and she demanded angrily, "Randy Seaborn, why are you making fun of me?"

"Did the major bother to mention that his high school English 'student teacher,' whatever that is, was the reigning Miss University of California at Los Angeles, and that he had a terrific crush on her?"

"I love you, Randy."

"I love you too, Aunt Jane. We did not have this conversation."

"What's so funny?" Major Randal asked as he strolled up to the table.

"That is classified information protected under the Marine-to-sailor confidentiality act, or maybe covered by family privilege. Either way, we are not telling you, John," Lady Jane said teasingly.

"I see," he said, which was what Major Randal always said when he did not have any idea what else to say.

"I'm shoving off," Lieutenant Seaborn announced. "Grandfather and I are meeting later for a working lunch."

"What are you and the Razor up to?"

"Sir, we need at least two more watch officers. I am going to solicit Grandfather's ideas on how to recruit. "

"See if you can find a couple who can read a chart," Major Randal teased. "By the way, I think I've come up with a solution to some of our navigation problems."

"Really, sir?"

"What I'm about to say does not leave this table, is that clear? Here's the plan: A few nights before we intend to raid a certain stretch of the French coast, we go over to the general target area and snatch a pilot off the first fishing boat we can find and haul him back to Seaborn House.

"The night of our actual operation, Randy, you sail the *Arrow* to within five miles of the target, then we bring the pilot up on the bridge, put a pistol to his head, show him the chart, and have him guide us in."

"Wow, that's almost better than having radar, sir. Those fishermen know every nook and cranny of the coastline." Lieutenant Seaborn sounded truly impressed. "Are you sure you're not asking too much of me, to be able to navigate within five miles of our pinpoint?"

"I've got a lot of confidence in you, kid."

As soon as Lieutenant Seaborn was gone, Lady Jane gave Major Randal a short briefing on what they would be doing for the next week. "You are entering the clandestine world of cloak-and-dagger, and there is no turning back," she explained. "Once in, never out.

"From this point on, John, everything I am about to tell you is classified 'Most Secret.' It is also restricted to 'Need to Know,' and until I inform you differently, no one other than the two of us has a need to know."

"I see."

"I need to hear you say that these instructions are clear and that you agree to comply with them."

"Wilco. That means I understand and will comply."

"I am perfectly aware of what 'Wilco' means."

"Now, if I had just said 'Roger'—"

"That would have meant you understood but did not give any assurance you would comply. Now, will you be serious—"

"Wilco."

"The names, and even the initials, of the organizations I am going to brief you on are classified. None of them officially exist."

"So we're not officially having this conversation, right?"

"I rather thought you were going to be a fast learner."

"Thank you."

"The first thing I am going to do is introduce you to my boss, Brigadier Collin Gubbins, the director of Training and Operations for Special Operations Executive, also known as SOE. The brigadier is a specialist in irregular warfare.

"SOE was created by combining a group known as EH (for the Electra House, where they previously had their offices), which studied ways to undermine German military morale; a department from the War Office MI(R) that had a mission somewhat overlapping that of Section D; and the original Section D from the Secret Intelligence Service.

"SOE has been given the brief by the prime minister to 'set Europe ablaze.' We are in what might be described as the dirty tricks business. Our mission is direct action, as opposed to intelligence gathering.

"We are going to spend some time with Major Lawrence Grand, the rather flamboyant head of SOE's Section D. The D stands for 'destruction.' I think you're going to like Lawrence. Take note: He's the man we need to make our best impression on—for the present."

"I'm not good with first impressions."

"Do try, John."

"Wilco."

"Thank you. Now, the Secret Intelligence Service, sometimes called the British Secret Service, shall be significantly more difficult for Raiding

Forces to establish a relationship with. I do not expect to accomplish more with SIS at present than a brief introduction. SIS is also known as MI-6, and sometimes we refer to it as the 'Old Firm' because so many SOE people used to work there, myself included. They refer to themselves as 'Broadway.'

"Considerable friction exists between MI-6 and SOE. The Secret Intelligence Service has been conducting espionage for ages; Special Operations Executive has been going only a few months, which makes it the junior service by about three hundred years.

"What you need to keep in mind, John, is that SIS operatives take excessive pride in being the old-school, button-down professionals and tend to look down their noses at SOE, considering it a motley collection of bunglers and amateurs. SOE is composed of barristers, bankers, cat burglars, movie stars, magicians, safe crackers, and snake charmers, with a sprinkling of renegade RAF, Royal Navy, and British Army officers. It is an eclectic gang of cutthroats, by any measure."

"Sounds like a fun bunch of guys."

"And girls."

"They have you, Lady Jane. How are they fixed for belly dancers?"

Humoring him with a much-put-upon smile, she continued, "The various agencies, departments, initials, and numbers can be quite daunting at times. What is important to understand is that although MI-6 and SOE have two completely different briefs, they both operate in the same places at the same times against the same enemy. Occasionally they work together on certain things, but most often they go their own ways.

"As I pointed out, MI-6 is charged with intelligence gathering. Unfortunately, Broadway did not have one single agent in place in France at the outbreak of hostilities."

"I thought SIS was supposed to be the best secret service in the world," Major Randal interjected.

"Well, it seems that before the war, MI-6 had a certain gentlemen's agreement with the French Intelligence Service—the Bureau Central de Renseignements et d'Action—not to spy on each other."

"Lovely."

"Yes. Well, now MI-6 is scrambling to recruit and put intelligence agents into place in occupied France as rapidly as it can. At the same time, SOE is working just as fast and furiously, developing plans to build up arms caches, insert sabotage agents, and organize local resistance movements. Gathering secret intelligence requires stealth, guile, and discretion, and is entirely covert by nature.

"Blowing up a railroad or assassinating a Nazi official, on the other hand, is an overt act designed to destroy a specific target, while at the same time calling attention to the fact that we did it and will do it again somewhere else at a time and place of our choosing. SOE is a bang-crash-wham outfit that likes to advertise. Our operatives do not know the meaning of the word 'subtlety,' and discretion is not in our mission statement.

"So you see, John, what is good for SOE is not automatically good for MI-6. In fact, it can at times be disastrous, and that is cause for some of the friction between the two organizations."

"I know you have a plan," Major Randal said. "Where do you see Raiding Forces fitting into the picture?"

"Even though MI-6 maintains a decidedly low profile, there is, from time to time, the need for it to conduct a 'direct action' mission. Strategic Raiding Force could handle such missions. And SOE will have a lot of tasks that we can perform."

"I see."

"At the moment, however, there's quite a bit of secret-agent, double-agent, and possibly even triple-agent intrigue in play between SOE and MI-6. Both organizations are suspicious to the point of being paranoid about each other, and rightfully so. You and I must always be careful to portray Raiding Forces as perfectly neutral. Our goal is to do business with both organizations."

"Good plan."

"There's a fledgling escape and evasion group, MI-9, just getting going," Lady Jane continued. "Its brief is to set up escape lines for British soldiers left behind in France and downed RAF fliers. While it is not fully operational as of yet, this is a good time to introduce ourselves and explore any possible areas of common purpose. We are also going to meet with an ultra hush-hush organization called the Political Warfare Executive: PWE."

"What could Raiding Forces possibly have to offer an agency involved with politics?" Major Randal asked.

"PWE is charged with attacking economic targets and generating black propaganda."

"What does that mean?"

"They operate against strategic targets that affect the German economy or currency, and they produce portrait-quality, high-grade pornography."

"Let's meet with them first."

"I knew you'd say something like that. What they do is serious business, John."

"Sounds serious to me."

"PWE obtains photos of Germany's most famous field marshals, generals, fighter aces, panzer leaders, and so forth. Then they doctor up the photos to depict the subjects in compromising situations and mail the fake copies anonymously to their wives, girlfriends, or even to their mothers."

"That ain't fighting fair."

"Reportedly, the program has caused a number of unhappy problems for certain hearts and minds belonging to some of Germany's finest," Captain Lady Seaborn confirmed with a chuckle.

"I bet it has. I thought you said undermining morale was the mission of one of the three agencies that were combined to form SOE."

"You *were* listening! Originally it was, but that particular function—psychological warfare—was carved out and transferred to PWE. It is confusing, John, and some of the shuffling of intelligence responsibilities does not always seem entirely logical. Not one of the organizations I have briefed you on has any fighting troops assigned. Our goal is to establish Raiding Forces as the action arm available on call to the intelligence community: ready, willing, and able to carry out their direct action missions. My plan is to set up Raiding Forces as the private army of the secret services. The Germans have one for the Abwehr called the Brandenburg Training Company."

"What do you get out of all this, Jane?"

"A real job," she answered without the least hesitation.

"Don't you have one now?"

"Not really. After Mallory was killed, I was invited to volunteer for the Secret Intelligence Service because of my language skills and my family connections. Naturally, I was accepted and sent through agent training straight away."

"You can throttle a German attack dog with your bare hands, as I recall. How many dogs would you say you have actually strangled, Jane?"

"I got to you with that one, didn't I?" she teased. "John, you're so easy. At any rate, it eventually began to dawn on me that I was never going to be allowed to parachute into France by moonlight on a secret mission, even though I had performed well in training. The training schools were merely a way of keeping me out of harm's way. I suspect MI-6 sent me to every finishing school they have. Then the SOE transfer occurred and the exact same drill began all over again.

"If you and I pull this off, my plan is to serve as Raiding Forces' liaison officer to the intelligence community. I might even talk you into letting me organize your service and support troops, which, in case you have not noticed, I have been doing already."

"Sergeant Major Hicks has informed me, on numerous occasions, that I need a batman."

"I am quite serious, John."

"I know you are, Jane, and I know good advice when I hear it."

"I have desperately hoped you would see it that way. Not every officer in your position would."

"Well, that doesn't mean I'm willing to be responsible for you jumping out of airplanes over enemy territory with a knife in your teeth for King and Empire either."

"All I want is to do something meaningful," she persisted. "It isn't fair to be forced into an inconsequential assignment simply because I happen to be a woman, or to be sheltered because of my social position."

"Here's the deal," Major Randal said. "You can write your own ticket with Raiding Forces just as long as it doesn't involve participation in direct combat operations."

"I love you, John."

"That's probably what you tell all your commanding officers."

"Only the ones with the moral fiber not to let me push them around too terribly much." Lady Jane flashed her best man-killer smile. "You turned out to be a lot tougher than you look."

"Speaking of morals," Major Randal said, suddenly hoping to change the subject, "now that I think about it, don't forget—my picture has been in the newspapers. So if a package of eight-by-ten glossies of me ever turns up in the mail, be advised that the Germans probably play the same exact same 'hearts and minds' game PWE does."

"In your case, Major, sir, they would not have to go to the trouble of faking the photographs. All the Abwehr would have to do is tail you and that alley cat Terry Stone with a camera on any given weekend."

Major Randal was beginning to suspect that Captain Lady Jane Seaborn just might be even more capable than he had originally thought, which, as he recalled from their first meeting, would make her very, very capable. Reflecting on Miss UCLA and Lady Jane, Major Randal realized he'd always been attracted to beautiful, smart women. "Does this conclude your briefing?"

"This concludes my briefing. What are your questions?"

"Can I tell Terry about the PWE porno ring?"

20

D FOR DESTRUCTION

BEFORE THEY LEFT THE RESTAURANT, CAPTAIN LADY JANE Seaborn had a surprise for Major John Randal. Without fanfare, she produced a small, expensive, green leather box from her purse and slid it across the table to him.

"John, I would like you to have this."

"I can't accept any more gifts from you, Jane."

"Yes, you can," she said with a gentle smile.

The green leather box lay there between them.

"Open it, please, John."

At a loss for anything to say, he flipped open the lid. Inside was a rugged, black-faced Rolex Oyster wristwatch with Coke-bottle-shaped, green luminous hands, large green digits, and an adjustable bezel ring numbered ten through fifty. The Rolex was the best military timepiece he had ever laid eyes on.

"Nice watch."

Lady Jane took the Rolex out of the box, popped the steel bracelet, and slipped it on his wrist. "My plan was for it to be a birthday surprise for my husband, Mallory."

Major Randal did not know what to do with that piece of information. It was a real conversation stopper.

"After Mallory saw the Rolexes the Royal Navy purchased for hard-hat divers," Captain Lady Seaborn continued, "he desperately wanted one. Rolex Oysters are waterproof to two hundred meters; salt air will not cause them to rust. He said it was the best sailor's watch ever made. Unfortunately for Mallory, the navy limited the issue to hard-hat divers only, and no matter how hard he tried, he was unable to obtain one. I contacted the Rolex factory in Geneva. This watch is an exact copy of the Royal Navy diver's model."

"I never met your husband, but it sure seems he had world-class taste in all things fine."

"Why, John, I do believe you just paid me a compliment."

"If I accept the watch, am I inheriting it from your husband?"

"No, Mallory never knew about it. His ship sortied the day the war broke out, and I never had the opportunity to give it to him before he was lost at sea. I want you to have it, John."

The Rolex felt really good on his arm, almost as good as the warm glow he was getting from Lady Jane cupping his hand in both of hers.

"I know it seems silly to you, John, but remember: British officers are obsessed with trivial details. Rightly or wrongly, they judge people on trifling, inconsequential things."

"So you've told me."

"This Rolex is sure to catch the eye of every officer who sees it. But John, impressing people has nothing to do with why I decided you should have it. I want you to believe that."

"Why do you want me to have it?"

"Because the thought of you wearing it makes me feel good," she said, sounding uncharacteristically vulnerable.

"You're a hard woman to say no to."

"Does that mean I'm growing on you?"

"Jane, if you grew on me any more, we'd be Siamese twins."

She hesitated for a second, trying to decipher if he was teasing or not. Suddenly, her eyes sparkled with pleasure.

He had to admit, he really liked it when her eyes did that. Spending time alone with Lady Jane always felt like a rare, special privilege, and it gave him a strange, fine feeling . . . not one he had previous experience with.

A short walk from the Bradford Hotel took them to the headquarters of the newly formed Special Operations Executive. The office space where they exited the elevator had once been the head office of the firm Marks & Spencer, barristers during peacetime. The receptionist smiled and said, "He is expecting you."

Brigadier Collin Gubbins, MC, Royal Artillery, stood up the moment the two walked into his large office. He was a soldier with an unorthodox military past. Only recently he had organized the super-secret stay-behind underground sleeper forces, the British Resistance Organization's Auxiliary Units, designed to rise and wage guerrilla war after Hitler invaded England. They were in place now, lying in wait and ready to swing into action in the event of invasion, which could come at almost any time.

A shortish Scotsman in his mid-forties, with clipped speech, the brigadier appeared to have boundless energy. "So, you are Lady Jane's American friend, the pinprick fellow. Congratulations on your well-deserved Military Cross, Major. A nice bit of work, that!"

"Thank you, sir."

"Lady Jane, you are planning to show him around, are you not? Introduce him to a few of our people?"

"Yes, sir."

"Splendid! Nice to meet you at last, Major. We are always on the scout for people who want to do their part—and who have the initiative to actually figure out some way to go out and do it."

The meeting was over almost as fast as it started. Captain Lady Jane Seaborn and Major Randal went downstairs, around the corner, and across the street to No. 2 Caxton Street, next door to St. Ermin's Hotel, to meet Major Lawrence Grand, the head of Section D. He was the man that, as Captain Lady Seaborn had briefed Major Randal, they most needed to impress.

When they walked into Major Grand's office, Major Randal's first thought was that he looked like what you might expect someone in the secret agent business to look like, especially if you watched a lot of campy Hollywood movies. The major was nattily attired in a beautifully tailored Savile Row suit in navy blue pinstripe, with a red carnation pinned to the lapel. In his teeth he was clenching a long, ivory cigarette holder containing a custom-blended cigarette, hand-rolled to his personal specifications. There was a pair of smoked-lens glasses lying on his desk.

This meeting was the opposite of the one with the brigadier, lasting well over an hour. Major Randal was grilled on every aspect of the raising, organization, training, and operations of Raiding Forces.

Major Grand took his time. The questions he asked were penetrating and illuminating. He listened carefully, evaluating every word of Major Randal's answers. The head of Section D was thorough and patient. It was the type of interview, Major Randal realized, in which Major Grand obtained a lot of information but did not give much away in return.

Finally, the debonair spymaster asked, "What is it, exactly, you want from me?"

On cue, Major Randal piped up as if it were his idea in the first place. "We're here to explore the possibility of joint operations, Major Grand. You supply the targets; we hit 'em."

"Are you going round to see Slocum?" the section chief asked Captain Lady Seaborn casually.

She nodded.

"Lieutenant Commander Slocum is our man in charge of the Transportation Section, on loan from the navy," Major Grand explained. "Afraid we have had a rather bad run of luck from the sea side of things. Winds, tides, storms, equipment failures, faulty navigation—all those kinds of things. You name it, we have traveled down the entire gauntlet of nautical misfortune.

"You should be a bit of fresh air for Slocum. He tried sixteen times to insert one of my agents into Brittany by sea before giving up.

"Now that I think about it, actually, maybe it is not such a great idea after all for you to go see the commander," Major Grand said. "He just might tend to view you as a competitor. No good would come from that, what? But not to worry. I think it fair to say you can look forward to Section D finding suitable employment for your services without involving the Transportation Section."

Major Grand beamed a moment, looking off into the distance as if lost in thought, then said, "Now, Randal, old boy, tell me what it is I can do for you as a token of my goodwill—cement our future relationship and all that sort of thing. No one has ever come to see me who did not ask for something sooner rather than later."

Captain Lady Seaborn had specifically cautioned him not to ask for or to accept anything from anyone without a signal from her. Because Major Randal did not get any such signal he dodged the question. "If you have any spare destroyers or a submarine you could loan . . . "

Major Grand laughed. "Afraid we do not even have a canoe at our disposal at the present time. We have to beg or borrow for every operation. Our man Slocum always has to go through navy channels to requisition what he needs. He is a stickler about following navy regulations to the letter. All that takes time, uses up reams of paper, gets us ensnared in miles of red tape, and, as likely as not, results in our being told we cannot have whatever it is we indent for. Dreadfully tedious, that!

"Now, Randal, you waltz in here today, casually mention you have a motorized yacht, a crew, trained raiding men who have actually gone across the blue and carried out several operations, one of which was spectacularly successful—oh yes, and all qualified parachutists to boot—and then you volunteer to work for Section D with no visible strings attached. As an added sweetener, you do not seem to be much concerned about red tape or going through channels. You just go and do it. Truth be known, it is about all I can do to keep from leaping right over this desk and kissing you on the cheek this very instant. Surely I can perform some small service for you in return, as an act of good faith. Everybody needs something, and most seem to think I am some sort of magician."

Major Randal glanced at Captain Lady Seaborn. She gave him a small, almost imperceptible nod.

"Pistols. My men are armed with Webley revolvers originally designed for shooting Fuzzy-Wuzzies," Major Randal said, hoping it was a small enough request. "We could use automatics."

"Fifty do for starters?"

"Perfect."

"You are staying at the Bradford, I presume? I shall have them brought around in the next day or two. Abracadabra! Hey! Presto! See how easy that was? Now I feel much better."

As they were getting up to leave, Major Grand added, "Lady Jane, I must say you do make a smashing captain of Royal Marines. Actually, I was not aware the Marines even had a women's auxiliary. Absolutely marvelous uniform. You two have been visiting Pembroke's, I see. How is old Chatterley holding up these days?"

As Major Grand walked with them out of the building, Major Randal inquired, "Was that true about trying sixteen times to put one agent ashore in France?"

"Yes, absolutely. The navy tried one more time, unsuccessfully."

Once they were alone out on the street, Captain Lady Seaborn explained, "There has been conjecture that Slocum may be putting the Admiralty's agenda ahead of SOE's. The navy wants total, iron-fisted control of all boat traffic across the English Channel, and they are livid about the existence of 'private navies' chartered to operate outside their supervision. If we demonstrate the ability to put agents and military stores ashore in occupied France by sea, Raiding Forces will have inked its first client."

"Can't do any worse than SOE's doing," Major Randal said.

"My thoughts, exactly."

21

NEVER-NEVER LAND

THE REST OF THE WEEK WAS SPENT IN A MIND-NUMBING SERIES of meetings. Captain the Lady Jane Seaborn had done her advance work; her contacts were impressive. She had unrestricted access and knew how to navigate the maze of London's wartime bureaucracy. Officers of all grades went out of their way to treat her as a very important person.

Nine secret intelligence organizations were in operation in Great Britain, and the Royal Marines captain and Major John Randal met with them all, except those engaged in purely signals intelligence gathering. The one glaring exception was that they did not go anywhere near "Broadway," the Secret Intelligence Service, otherwise known as MI-6.

While it was impossible to keep all the players straight, Major Randal was beginning to develop a picture of the shadowy world of British covert operations. What he saw was a fascinating, behind-the-scenes peek into the never-never land of espionage, intrigue, subversion, and black propaganda, rarely seen by outsiders.

The clandestine services had been hurriedly expanded due to the war, with urgent demands pouring in from every direction for intelligence gathering, sabotage, and unconventional special operations. Every intelligence officer they met with seemed to be promoting his own personal agenda; no two organizations appeared to be operating off the same plan. In a couple of cases, separate divisions located in the same building within the same agency were gearing up to fight their own private wars with completely different objectives, clearly at odds with each other.

There was little-to-no interservice cooperation on the military side, and even less collaboration between the clandestine services. Empire building, bureaucratic wrangling, turf wars, and nasty political infighting were much in evidence.

While some organizations had overlapping missions, others did not seem to have a clear idea of what their mission was exactly. A great deal of time and energy appeared to be spent on mystifying, misleading, and confusing one another instead of the enemy. The only common denominator Major Randal observed was lack of experience. The imperial intelligence community in 1940 was a textbook example of government bureaucracy run amok.

One thing came across loud and clear: Great Britain had a considerable amount of catching up to do if it was to have any hope of competing against the sophisticated Nazi intelligence apparatus that had already cast its invisible web worldwide. In stark contrast, the British reveled in a cheery, chaotic, comic opera atmosphere of slapstick, casual, nonprofessionalism, all the while exuding a misplaced confidence in their ability to cope and somehow muddle through.

The Admiralty was an interesting place to visit because it was the Royal Navy's strategic operations center as well as an administrative headquarters. The Royal Navy had undergone a radical change of heart in the relatively short time since Major Randal had accompanied Lieutenant Colonel Dudley Clarke on the first raid, and was now openly hostile to small-scale raiding. The navy had concluded that Commando operations were a drain on its overstretched resources.

After the youngish lieutenant commander they met with stole a peek at his elegant gold Patek Philippe watch for perhaps the third time, Captain Lady Seaborn's eyes blazed and she abruptly stood up. "Quite sorry to have been such an imposition today, Commander."

As they stalked out she drawled, loud enough for the startled officer to hear and in a tone dripping contempt, "The Razor's right. The navy used to have wooden ships and iron men, but now they have iron ships and wooden men."

The Royal Air Force, at one time the most innovative organization of all the British armed services, turned out to be the most egocentric and wrong-minded outfit Major Randal and Captain Lady Seaborn met with all week. The RAF was not interested in cooperating with any other service—army, navy, Combined Operations, or intelligence—and was serenely confident that air power had some mystical ability to win the war all by itself. To be fair, Major Randal concluded, the Royal Navy was defending its turf; the RAF did not have any excuse except self-delusion.

The wing commander of the Air Intelligence Section sniffed dismissively at the idea of Raiding Forces attacking German airfields on the coast of France in order to destroy Luftwaffe fighters on the ground. "Major, there simply is no target a small party of Commandos can attack that we are not able to deal with much more effectively with aerial bombs," he said, cutting another meeting short.

Major Randal wondered if the hard-pressed Hurricane and Spitfire pilots in the Blind Eye would have been as quick to reject the offer.

The top-secret Political Warfare Executive of the Economic Ministry of Defense turned out to be an interesting group of people, composed of academics, scientists, intellectuals, economists, bankers, and captains of industry. There were even a few well-known former pacifists thrown into the mix. About the only criterion for being assigned was that you had to be an acknowledged success in your civilian field of endeavor.

PWE's sole agenda was to win the war as quickly as possible so that staff could quickly get their highly successful civilian lives back on track with the minimum amount of disruption. In short, its mission was to destroy the Nazis' will to fight and to discombobulate the German economy. The personnel assigned to PWE were willing to consider anything: Everything was on the table, nothing was too outlandish, and no idea was off-limits.

At present, PWE was in the earliest, most preliminary organizational stage, and while not ready to begin discussing specific missions, PWE staff indicated that several projects were in development. They were delighted to learn about Strategic Raiding Force's availability for joint special operations and quick to admit they were going to have a pressing need for what they jokingly referred to as "you knuckle-dragger types" to do their dirty work.

At least, Major Randal thought they were joking. He liked the PWE people right from the start. It was a case of opposites attracting.

As an organization, PWE was imbued with an oversized sense of humor. With perfectly straight faces they told Major Randal that the only operation going at the moment—besides the pornography—was a propaganda effort to convince the Germans the Royal Navy had "imported two hundred man-eating sharks from Australia and plopped them into the English Channel to eat Nazi invaders." They were not kidding; that is exactly what PWE was telling the Germans on nightly pirate radio broadcasts.

PWE was the only organization to conduct its initial meeting with Captain Lady Seaborn and Major Randal by committee. Jointly it was agreed to formalize their relationship by having Captain Lady Seaborn appointed immediately to act as liaison between Political Warfare Executive and Strategic Raiding Force. Major Randal volunteered to provide special operations advisers to work in-house with PWE staff, once PWE was ready to begin planning specific direct-action missions.

Walking out of the building, an obviously delighted Captain Lady Seaborn explained, "PWE has an even higher priority than SOE does. Once this mob get their show up and running, they're going to be a law unto themselves. You did very well in there. The idea of Raiding Force military advisors was wonderful."

The next stop was the fledgling Escape & Evasion Organization, located in Room 900 of the War Office. In prewar days, Room 900 was the "Tea Room"—not where they served the tea, but the closet where the service staff mixed it. MI-9's office location explained everything Major Randal needed to know about where it stood on the War Office priority totem pole. The room still smelled of tea.

The officer they met with was a captain wearing the badges of the South Wales Borderers and a thousand-yard stare. The captain had been captured and sent to a prison camp, had managed to escape, and then had made his way across France by a variety of means.

Currently, the entire MI-9 organization consisted of only three people: the officer commanding, who was away at the time on other business, the captain, and one civilian secretary. But it had big plans to bring out the large number of British Expeditionary Force troops still on the loose in France—escapees and evaders from the other occupied countries and downed RAF pilots and aircrews. Additionally, MI-9 was planning to teach escape and evasion techniques throughout the military system to those in occupations that made them the most likely to be captured, and to manufacture escape and evasion aides and devices for those who would be in harm's way.

The problem was, how to get started. No one was expressing much interest in what they were tasked to accomplish—except the RAF, which was actively looking for ways to retrieve highly valuable pilots and flight crews shot down on missions over the Continent in order to return them to flying duty. The general idea was for MI-9 to set up clandestine escape lines in occupied France and other countries, to move evaders overland to the coast for pickup and eventual return to the United Kingdom by sea.

There was nothing MI-9 could offer Raiding Forces in the way of missions, because they did not have any. There was also the rather obvious problem of a conflict in mission statement; they were, after all, lifesavers, not life takers.

Out of the blue, Major Randal interjected, "I think we can help you. When MI-9 is ready to begin extracting evaders from the Continent, Raiding Forces will provide capable men to go along and act as your covering party."

The South Wales Borderers officer looked at him like a man who held the winning lottery ticket. Major Randal continued. "Raiding Forces has a forty-foot, high-speed yacht assigned. In the event MI-9 ever has high-grade, top-priority evaders who need to be brought out of France in a hurry, we'll go over and pull them for you."

When they walked out of the War Office, Captain Lady Seaborn was beaming. "Nicely done, John. Your idea to provide Raiding Forces personnel as security for their extraction operations was an offer MI-9 literally cannot refuse, and the suggestion that Raiding Forces is available to bring out their high-priority evaders on short notice was even better. Now they have something of value to go out and sell to the services. What a marvelous development."

"I like what MI-9 is trying to do," Major Randal said simply, "and I want to be a part of it."

"You will be. MI-9's commanding officer, Major Norman Crockatt, is a dear friend. I know Norman is going to be tickled pink!"

Considering some of the sessions he had sat in over the last few days, Major Randal was not convinced things were all that terrific, but he decided he really liked it when Lady Jane was this happy.

22

ON HIS MAJESTY'S
SECRET SERVICE

FOR MAJOR JOHN RANDAL, THIS DAY'S MEETING WAS THE MOST important of the lot, though there was no way to actually know for sure at the time, since it was an episode straight out of *Through the Looking-Glass*.

In the morning when he came downstairs to link up with Captain Lady Jane Seaborn, he was surprised to find her sitting in the morning room with a spiffy-looking Captain Terry "Zorro" Stone, who was superbly turned out in his best uniform.

"What have we here?"

"Duty calls, old stick."

"Duty?"

"I asked Terry to be here," Captain Lady Seaborn explained. "We have need of his special talents today."

"Does that mean there's some top-secret outfit we haven't met with yet that's headed up by a nymphomaniac?"

Captain Lady Seaborn rolled her eyes. "Hardly. Today you two have a command performance with C, the chief of British Secret Intelligence, MI-6. You will join him at his club, White's, for lunch. Since no women are allowed inside, not even in the club's waiting room, I shall not be tagging along."

"You came in to have lunch with the boys, Zorro? I'm impressed."

Captain Stone humored him with a thin smile.

"Terry is a member of White's," Captain Lady Seaborn explained, "which by any measure is the most prestigious club in London. To become a member, one must be proposed and seconded. Then, once in, a new member is on probation for some period. Everybody is somebody at White's, but being somebody by itself is not an absolute guarantee of membership. To be eligible it is necessary to have power and position or the prospect of having them, as well as money. Most of the Royals belong."

"I know White's. We met Colonel Clarke there for lunch."

"You may have lunched there, John, but I seriously doubt you grasp the power dynamics of White's," Captain Lady Seaborn explained patiently. "The place is much more than just a club. In reality, it is an enormously influential political and social semi-secret society with close ties to Eton and the Life Guards.

"Eton has an ultra-exclusive boys social club called Pop. The boys in it literally go on to rule the Empire. The members look out after one another for the rest of their lives through the Etonian old-boy network. They have a saying at Eton: 'You do not have to be in Pop to be a success in life; simply to know a member is enough.'

"Also, there is a prestigious fox hunting club, the Beaufort Hunt, that's even more select. Like White's, it is not only a sporting association but also a political and social cabal of extraordinarily high influence. The Beaufort membership is quite capable of reaching out to even the most remote corners of the Empire and pulling the strings necessary to stage-manage events. C is a man named Colonel Stewart Menzies, DSO, 2nd Life Guards, Eton, Pop, and the Beaufort Hunt."

"Sounds well-heeled," said Major Randal.

"Terry is a member in good standing in every organization the colonel is, with the single exception of MI-6."

Major Randal gave Captain Stone an amused look. "And all along you've led me to believe you're just a simple, degenerate womanizer! Aren't you the social butterfly?"

"One does have one's responsibilities, old stick," Captain Stone replied dryly. "However, I believe the rather more apt description is 'social lion.' A butterfly, I am led to understand, is what professional ladies of the evening in the Orient—which I do believe includes your old haunt, the Philippine Islands—call certain of their clients who flit from flower to flower instead of landing on just one for the evening. Then, of course, you would know a lot more about that sort of thing than I would, eh, John? Considering you do have a certain butterfly engraved on your trusty cigarette lighter."

"Aaah—"

"Lady Jane is a member of the Beaufort Hunt, one should not fail to point out," Captain Stone continued, unruffled. "Personally, I merely ride after foxes, dally with the daughters of the membership, and look dashing wearing the Beaufort buff and blue riding jacket, set off by the elegant brass buttons engraved GPR, which, for the great unwashed, stands for George Prince Regent, the first gentleman of Europe. Beaufort has marvelous hunt balls."

"So, you two are fraternity brothers," Major Randal said.

"It's not quite exactly like that," Captain Lady Seaborn smiled. "My Uncle Johnny is a longstanding member, and he wanted me to join so I could ride with him."

"Well, yippie-kay-yay."

"Her uncle, Colonel Bevins, is also a member of White's," Captain Stone added, "a graduate of Eton, a member of Pop, and C's longtime friend. And for the record, he's extraordinarily well-heeled, as you so colorfully put it."

"This is the most important interview you may ever have, John," Captain Lady Seaborn said with an imploring look on her face. "If you get on well with Colonel Menzies, the future of Raiding Forces is assured. Do try."

"I'll give my best, Lady Jane. I wouldn't want to be an embarrassment to the Raiding Forces contingent of the Beaufort Hunt."

The Bradford provided a car and driver to chauffeur them to White's. There was a strained silence between Major John Randal and Captain Terry "Zorro" Stone during the ride. Finally, the dashing Life Guards officer said, "I probably should have mentioned the Beaufort Hunt, old stick."

"I was wondering why you didn't, old stick."

"I have not hunted since the war started. Lady Jane was a married woman, though her husband never seemed to be around and she always rode with her uncle. We only vaguely knew each other, and since women like her generally tend to view bounders like me as polecats, I kept my distance. Besides, Jane was officially off-limits to me, since her uncle is a former member of Pop. Even I have certain conventions I will not violate."

"Jane called you a skunk?"

"Well, no, actually. As I recall, it was 'lounge lizard.'"

"You two do know the secret handshake, though?"

"True, I should have mentioned it. But really, I never thought much about it."

"I don't like surprises."

"Sorry, John."

"How exactly do you cook a fox anyway?"

Captain Stone looked at him tranquilly and observed, "Nice Rolex. Navy model?"

Proving to Major Randal once again that if he crossed verbal swords with the scourge of the Life Guards, he had best be prepared to take his share of hits.

White's was an unassailable social bastion where only men of vast wealth, high position, and immense power were welcome. The secure haven was so cloistered, no enemy spy could ever possibly infiltrate it unless he had been born and raised in the British aristocracy. While quite a few of its members were in the Great Game, however, White's was not to be confused with the Secret Services club. That distinction, according to Captain Lady Jane Seaborn, belonged to its rival, Boodles, just down St. James Street.

Colonel Stewart Menzies, aka C, and the executive leadership inner circle of Broadway, the Secret Intelligence Service, had elected to make White's its unofficial headquarters. Everyone at the club knew Colonel Menzies, of course, and most were aware of what he did for a day job. There was not the faintest trace of gossip, though; it just was not done. The head of MI-6 felt so comfortable and secure at White's, he had his most sensitive mail delivered to him there to be read in his personal enclave, the billiards room.

When working at the club, he was never disturbed. C was not the only member who brought his work there to be conducted in comfort and privacy within its hallowed halls at any given time. It was said the officers for one entire Commando battalion, No. 8, had been recruited at White's from among the sons of the ruling generation of the wartime British Empire.

When the two Raiding Forces officers arrived, the hall porter said, "Nice to see you again, Captain Stone."

"Hello, Groom. We have an appointment with Colonel Menzies."

"Please have a seat in the anteroom while I check to see if the colonel is available, sir."

Within less than half a minute, Groom was back. "The colonel will see you now. Come right this way, gentlemen."

When they entered the billiards room, they could make out a slim, courtly man of approximately fifty—whose hair was thinning in front and whose clipped mustache was turning gray—sitting and reading next to the fireplace. Over the fireplace hung a bust of Edward VII and a "Champion of England" boxing belt. Scattered around the room were deep leather armchairs and acres of thick pile carpet. The wood ran to mahogany. No one was playing billiards.

Colonel Menzies rose when they approached and extended his hand. He looked extremely fit. "Terry, how nice to see you," he said.

Major Randal recalled that, by tradition, cavalry officers of the same regiment always called each other by their first names except when they were on parade. The colonel clearly regarded himself, still, as a Life Guards officer.

"Good to see you, Stewart," Captain Stone replied pleasantly to the older man. "I would like to introduce you to Major John Randal, my commanding officer and very dear friend."

"It is a pleasure, John. Your reputation precedes you. Not only did I follow with interest your exploits at Calais, but your great champion, Lady Jane, has also given me an exhaustive report on your raiding operations to date. I must confess to being more than a little curious about the man who can capture her fancy."

Colonel Menzies was a throwback to another age. He had been schooled at Eton, as had Captain Stone, in "God, Greek, and guns." That is, he was taught that those who wanted to rule and command must first become gentlemen and that character was more important than intellect. He had been groomed to be a man of courage, truth, honor, and, last but certainly not least, chivalry. He hated to travel.

These traits were not generally associated with the spymasters of the major world powers—not most of them, at least.

That afternoon the three men sat by the fire, alone in the heavily paneled room, and discussed a number of things. At the end of their visit Major Randal would have been hard-pressed to say exactly what it was they talked about; it was all quite vague.

Just before Major Randal and Captain Stone left, Colonel Menzies commented, "John, it has often been said that on the playing fields of Eton, England wins her wars and keeps her empire. A quaint notion actually, but one rather widely held. What is your take, as an American, on that line of thought?"

"Too bad you didn't just challenge Hitler to a cricket match, sir."

Colonel Menzies was still chuckling when the two Commando officers stood up to leave.

Few people are ever privileged to actually observe how government operates behind the scenes, and many of those who did were not always aware of what it was they were witnessing. It seemed so ordinary.

Is this how Great Britain's national intelligence policy is formulated? Major Randal wondered. One man sitting alone in an empty pool room by a fire, a secret puppeteer masterminding the world's most powerful intelligence organization, making decisions that affected the survival of the entire free world? Apparently so. It was a very heady experience to have been so close to the epicenter of power, even for such a brief time.

Had he passed muster? He had no idea.

C did drop one possible hint, however, when the spymaster offhandedly observed to Captain Stone, "John already knows two of us, Terry, and unless I miss my guess, it shall not be long before he makes it three."

Was he referring to members of the club called Pop? He must have been. Who was the third member? Major Randal did not have a clue.

In the car on the way back to the Bradford, Captain Stone said, "The women ride sidesaddle."

"What?"

"The Beaufort Hunt requires its female members to ride sidesaddle. You should see Jane sit a horse."

"Somebody needs to tell you old boys and girls it's the twentieth century."

"Are you absolutely certain, old stick?"

23

CHINESE FIRE DRILL

LIEUTENANT PERCY STIRLING KNOCKED ON MAJOR JOHN RANDAL'S door at the Bradford later that afternoon. Since he'd had to call ahead first to obtain permission to board the private elevator, his arrival did not come as a surprise. What was unexpected, however, was the slim, towheaded lieutenant he had with him who was wearing the regimental insignia of the Sherwood Foresters, parachute wings, and a maroon flash that read 11 SPECIAL AIR SERVICES BATTALION.

"Major Randal, I would like you to meet Lieutenant Harry Shelby," Lieutenant Stirling said when Major Randal opened the door. "We served in No. 2 Commando together, only it's not called that now. They changed their name."

"Nice to meet you, Lieutenant. Chauncy, would you bring these men something to drink? Beer okay?" he asked his guests.

"Yes, sir," they quipped in unison with big smiles.

The butler appeared shortly thereafter with tall, frosty mugs he kept in the refrigerator at all times for just such exigencies.

"Harry does not want to be in the 11 Special Air Services Battalion anymore," Lieutenant Stirling announced.

"Why not, Harry?"

"Sir, I volunteered for Commandos to get a chance to take part in fast hit-and-run raids on the French coast from small boats. Then the War Department selected No. 2 Commando to become the first paratroop battalion. I was all right with the idea until I found out the RAF does not have enough troop transport aircraft to drop the battalion intact, which means we will not be going on missions anytime soon."

"Harry has a special talent, sir."

"What's that, Harry?"

"I am a big game hunter, sir."

"Tell him about your shooting."

"To keep my skills sharp for my hunting, I compete in long-distance rifle matches."

"Ever win anything?"

"The King's Prize, the Scottish Open Championship, and the Caledonian Shield, sir," Lieutenant Shelby replied with disarming modesty.

"Weren't the Sherwood Foresters in the Norwegian Expeditionary Force?"

"We were, sir, and my battalion also made it to France and came out through Dunkirk. I consider myself something of a specialist in retreats, retrograde operations, and evacuations."

"Well, I heard the Sherwood Foresters gave a good account of themselves against crack German ski troops while covering the withdrawal in Norway. Chauncy, would you get Lady Jane on the horn for me, please?"

The ever-efficient butler quickly brought the phone, trailing a long extension cord, and handed it to the major. He dialed her number.

"Jane, do you have a pen?" he said as soon as she answered. "Lieutenant Harry Shelby, Sherwood Foresters, currently assigned to 11 Special Air Service Battalion . . . Could you have him transferred to Raiding Forces, effective immediately? Thanks!"

He hung up and looked at Lieutenant Shelby. "Welcome to Raiding Forces, Lieutenant." Major Randal handed the phone back to Chauncy. "I take it you did want to volunteer? If not, you just got yourself drafted."

The two young lieutenants looked at each other and grinned. This was more like it!

"Chauncy, see if you can get Squadron Leader Wilcox on the blower."

"Sir!"

While Chauncy looked up the number and dialed, Major Randal continued, "Harry, I have an assignment for you, and I think it's right up your alley."

The young officer looked surprised.

"Sir, I have the squadron leader on the line," Chauncy announced.

"Tell him to be here at 1800 hours for a briefing."

Chauncy murmured into the phone. He looked at Major Randal. "Squadron Leader Wilcox says 'Roger,' sir."

"Now, get in touch with Captain Stone, Lieutenant Seaborn, and Sergeant Major Hicks, and call Lady Jane back to attend as well."

"Right away, sir."

"I'll see you two men at 1800 hours."

The two lieutenants gulped down beers and trooped out the door in high spirits, delighted at being able to serve together again.

Shortly after they left, the phone rang. Chauncy answered. "Sir, the front desk says there is a gentleman downstairs who would like you to meet him in the small bar in the lobby."

"Did they say who it was?"

"No, sir."

When he walked into the bar, Major Randal found Major Lawrence Grand, the debonair chief of Section D, Special Operations Executive, sitting at a table with a cocktail in front of him. The small bar in the Bradford was as good a place as you were likely to find in London to have a discreet rendezvous.

"Hello, Major."

"Hello, Major, to you, too."

"Call me Larry. Care for a drink, John?"

"Sure, Larry. Whatever you're having."

They waited as a lovely waitress dressed as an Indian princess silently glided over with his drink.

"How goes it, John? I understand you've been making the rounds."

"Checking up on me?"

"I am, after all, a spy."

"Is that right? I had the impression you were a pyromaniac licensed to light up Europe."

"You got me there. I hope you will not consider me unwarrantably inquisitive, but I admit to a certain curiosity about your impression of the world of wartime cloak-and-dagger. So . . . soldier to soldier—after all, I am a Royal Engineer, you may recall."

"Looks like a Chinese fire drill to me."

"Quite! Chinese fire drill . . . what a scintillating analogy. I shall have to steal it from you at the earliest opportunity.

"By the way, before I forget . . . the automatics I promised are being delivered to your suite as we speak. Put them to good use, with my compliments."

"Thanks. My men need all the extra firepower they can get."

"Glad to do it. Now, my real purpose in coming here today is to ask you one question," Major Grand said, leaning forward on the table and fixing Major Randal with a direct look. "I want a straight answer, John."

"Fire away."

"Tell me why you volunteered to join the British Army. The real reason, not the fairy tale about saving the world from the evil Nazi horde."

Major Randal looked off into the distance. "On a whim . . . I made the decision on the spur of the moment. After leaving the U.S. Army, maybe I wasn't ready to settle down and go to work at a real job."

"I should say, old chap, you certainly have one now."

"You asked for the reason I joined, Larry," Major Randal said, looking him square in the eye. "It's only fair to tell you; after Calais, I'm in it strictly for payback."

"Quite right." Major Grand stood up. "Perfectly good enough for me. I simply needed to hear it from your lips. Genuine candor is a rare commodity in the sleazy underworld I inhabit. A word of advice, if I might? While you may be completely justified in believing you have stumbled into Cloud Cuckoo Land, bear in mind—every so often even the craziest flaming cuckoo bird lays the odd egg that hatches."

After signing the chit for the drinks, Major Randal stepped out into the lobby. Brandy Seaborn wigwagged him to come over to the corner of the room where she and Captain Jane Seaborn were taking high tea with three soldiers.

He was delighted to discover that the men were Sergeant Mike "March or Die" Mikkalis, Rifleman Tim Authury, and Rifleman Jimmy Castlewick, late of Calais and Swamp Fox Force. Major Randal was amused to observe that, despite self-consciously balancing tiny teacups in their laps, the three combat-hardened veterans appeared to be thoroughly enjoying themselves. Still, no matter how hard the baby-blue-eyed Sergeant Mikkalis tried to appear urbane, he still managed to project the aura of a stone-cold killer.

The last time Major Randal had seen them was the day Swamp Fox Force disembarked from HMY *Gulzar* at Dover. When he walked up now, the three men immediately put down their cups and jumped to attention.

"As you were," Major Randal ordered quickly. "Carry on. How are you, men?"

"Extraordinarily entertaining," Captain Lady Seaborn answered for them. "The lads have been regaling Brandy and me with hair-raising accounts of your exploits at Calais, John. Seems you have been holding back a thing or two."

"What a marvelous story!" Brandy gushed.

"It doesn't count when you're saving yourself, Brandy," Major Randal snapped more curtly than he intended. "What are you men doing here?"

"When it was learned you were staying here at the Bradford, we formed a delegation to inquire if there is a place for your former Riflemen in your current command, sir," Sergeant Mikkalis announced stiffly. "Most Swamp Fox Force men would like to volunteer, Major."

"How many?"

"Eleven of us 60th Rifles and Rifle Brigade men, and Duggan, the Royal Marine who signaled the *Gulzar*. Mickey wants to volunteer too, sir."

"Don't you men think you might be of more value helping to rebuild your battalions?"

"No, sir. They treat us like lepers. No one is interested in the last stand of 30 Brigade at Calais. All people talk about is the miracle of Dunkirk. We want to serve with you again, sir, providing you will have us."

"You're willing to jump out of airplanes?"

"Yes, sir. Lady Seaborn has been gracious enough to explain that requirement to us."

"Can you arrange to have these men brought on board and slate them for parachute school, Jane?"

"Certainly."

"In that case, welcome to Raiding Forces, men. Frankly, I figured you men would be happy to have seen the last of me."

"We liked those jungle tactics you showed us, sir," Sergeant Mikkalis said, his pale eyes gleaming. "We want another crack at your brand of cut-and-run fighting."

"I would have liked to have had you in Commandos from the start," Major Randal told them. "Make sure to tell the others I said so."

"Sir, there is one question," Sergeant Mikkalis said. "That last night in Calais when you ordered us to tear down the wooden fence, you made each man carry a large plank. Since we never used them for anything, the men have been wondering, sir."

"The Channel was only twenty-six miles across to Dover, Sergeant. If there weren't any ships to pick us up, Plan B was to use the planks like surfboards and paddle home."

"Would that have worked?" Brandy asked skeptically.

"We were getting ready to find out," Major Randal said.

"Any way to expedite those transfers, Lady Seaborn?" Sergeant Mikkalis queried. "We'd like to start jump training as soon as possible." The other two Riflemen nodded their agreement.

"Consider it accomplished, Sergeant Mikkalis," Captain Lady Seaborn said. "Orders will be cut and delivered here within the hour." As she said it, she never took her eyes off Major Randal. "The next class at No. 1 Parachute Training School starts Monday, and all Swamp Fox Force volunteers will be in it, on my word."

"In that case, I'll see you when you graduate," Major Randal said. "Good luck, men."

On the way back to the elevator, Major John Randal ran into Captain "Geronimo Joe" McKoy. "New pistols for Raiding Forces have just been delivered to my room," the major informed the old Ranger. "Let's go see what they gave us."

As they were going up, he asked, "How have you been occupying yourself lately, Captain?"

"Well, John, I've been doing some work out in the country at a spook school called Wandsborough Manor. Lady Jane hooked me up with this ex-policeman, Captain William Ewart Fairbairn. They call him the 'Shanghai Buster.' He was on the police force out there, and they say he killed a whole bunch of Chinamen. He's pretty handy with a pistol. You know how I teach you men to watch the front sight close, touch her off, and adios? Well, I never met the man before, but you know what he teaches? Front sight, squeeze, and Godspeed. Ain't that something?"

When they walked into Major Randal's suite, Chauncy informed him indignantly, "These three filthy footlockers arrived while you were out, sir."

"Jackpot!" declared Captain McKoy when he raised the lid on one of the containers. Packed inside were fifty brand-new pistols in Colt factory boxes. "Border Specials, the pistola of choice of the Texas Rangers. FBI issues 'em to its agents, too. As a matter of fact, I've been known to carry one myself on occasion."

"Looks like a standard-issue U.S. Government Model Colt .45 automatic," Major Randal said.

"This here is the Colt .38 Super, John. Built on a .45 frame, it shoots a .45 ACP cartridge necked down to .38 caliber. Colt originally designed the .38 Super for the Mexican trade. Down in Mexico, you can't own any weapon that's chambered for a round their military uses. When Colt necked it down to get around that law, they found out the .38 Super would shoot completely through an engine block. They're extremely accurate once you get the head spacing adjusted right—real flat shooting with fairly mild recoil. Each one holds ten rounds. As a fighting pistol, the Colt .38 Super is just about perfect."

"What would a clandestine organization be doing with Colt .38 Supers?"

"Deniability, probably. A man gets caught with one, it don't automatically look like he has been armed and equipped by British Intelligence."

Major Randal picked up one of the pistols and experienced an instant flash of nostalgia. The finely checkered walnut grip with the oversized diamonds carved at top and bottom felt like an old friend in his hand.

"If Chauncy'll help me tote these footlockers down to my room, I'll inspect 'em all for you and marry 'em up with holsters. While y'all are still on leave, I'll run 'em over to a gunsmith I know at Westley Richards to adjust the head spacing and polish all the parts so they run slick and reliable."

"You're staying here in the hotel?"

"Miss Threepersons and I both have rooms right down the hall, but I've been spending most of my time out at Wandsborough Manor, teaching people with a 'need to know' how to shoot a pistol. It's the dangedest place you ever saw. They got cat burglars, safecrackers, picklock artists, wheelmen, counterfeiters, and all kinds of different people out there a-teachin' every kinda fast and fancy trick you ever imagined to the students, trying to turn 'em into secret agents.

"You go to lunch, and you got these criminals and the policemen that's been chasin' them for years who are also on the teaching staff sitting down at the same table, saying things like, 'Pass the bread, please.' It's a real circus, and I ain't kiddin'."

24

BRIEFING

THE PEOPLE DESIGNATED TO ATTEND THE EVENING BRIEFING assembled in Major John Randal's suite. Present were Captain the Lady Jane Seaborn, Squadron Leader Paddy Wilcox, Lieutenant Randy Seaborn, Lieutenant Percy Stirling, Lieutenant Harry Shelby, Sergeant Major Maxwell Hicks, and, looking as though he had just returned from an extended survival, escape, and evasion course, a hollow-eyed Captain Terry "Zorro" Stone.

"In the strict interest of the health and welfare of our troops, old stick, I highly recommend we cut our leave time substantially shorter in the future," he said with a weak grin.

Royal Marine Pamela Plum-Martin slipped in at the last minute. Major Randal gave Captain Lady Seaborn a questioning look, and she gave him a slight nod.

Major Randal handed Chauncy one of his parrot beak–gripped .455 Webley service revolvers. "Take up a post outside the door and shoot anyone who tries to come through."

"Sir!"

"Before we get started," Major Randal said to the group, "I have a few administrative announcements. First, let me introduce Lieutenant Harry Shelby of the Sherwood Foresters, more recently with No. 2 Commando. Harry doesn't know it yet, but he is going to be Raiding Forces' sniping officer, in command of a special operation we're here to discuss this evening. Harry's seen his share of combat and his shooting credentials are impeccable.

"Next, effective immediately, Captain the Lady Jane Seaborn is appointed to serve as the Raiding Forces' intelligence officer."

There were some shocked looks; none of the officers in the room had ever heard of a woman holding a staff position in a fighting outfit before. On the other hand, they had never encountered as unorthodox a unit as Raiding Forces before in any of their military experiences.

"Stand up and take a bow, Captain."

"Do not panic, boys," she said, flashing her trademark man-killer smile. "I promise it will only be temporary until we can find you the best qualified man for the job."

Everyone laughed.

"Eleven of the Rifle Brigade and King's Royal Rifle Corps men, plus a Royal Marine from the mixed Green Jacket detachment I commanded at Calais who escaped with me, turned up unexpectedly and volunteered for Raiding Forces. They have been packed off to parachute training school and will be joining us just as soon as they qualify.

"Now, let's get down to business."

A hush of anticipation fell over the room.

"For some time Squadron Leader Wilcox, Lady Jane, the Sergeant Major, and I have been quietly working on a project. Now that we have someone with Harry's qualifications on board, all the pieces have finally fallen into place for Raiding Forces to move forward with it.

"The situation is this: There are roughly eight hundred German fighter pilots staffing the Luftwaffe fighter units currently attacking Great Britain. Raiding Forces' mission is to kill 10 percent of them—eighty fighter pilots."

The announcement was greeted by cold, professional silence. Major Randal had everyone's undivided attention.

"To accomplish this task we intend to deploy sniper teams to shoot German fighter pilots at their landing grounds as they scramble for take-off. Consider what I have just told you as classified 'Most Secret'—on a need-to-know basis only. No one outside of this room has a need to know. Do not discuss it with anyone not here tonight. Is that clear?"

"Clear, sir," the men and women chorused.

"Lovat Scouts, the premier stalkers and snipers in the British Army, were recruited by Sergeant Major Hicks with this mission in mind; they will be the designated shooters. We have eight of them completing parachute school this week. Lieutenant Shelby will be the officer in charge of what I intend to call Operation Buzzard Plucker."

Everyone laughed at the name. Sick of hearing Nazi pilots constantly referred to as "eagles," they found the term "buzzards" much more to their liking.

"Some of you may be wondering why we're targeting fighter pilots and not bomber pilots, who do most of the real damage. For the Germans to invade England, they must first establish air supremacy over the Channel. The only way the Luftwaffe can accomplish that is to destroy our fighter command. Operation Buzzard Plucker is intended to help prevent that from happening.

"Squadron Leader Wilcox will now brief you on certain aspects of the operation," Major Randal said. "You will receive a more detailed briefing at a later date."

The former Canadian bush pilot stood up in front of the group. Tonight he was wearing his black eye patch over the left eye. He looked like a rotund pirate in an RAF uniform.

"German industry can build an ME-109 in a matter of days," the squadron leader stated. "It takes a year to train a pilot and at least two years of operational flying for a pilot to become reasonably proficient in the cockpit. It's easy to replace an aircraft; it's almost impossible to replace a veteran combat pilot. The Luftwaffe started out with a huge pool of excellent pilots because of the emphasis it placed on prewar sport gliding associations and the aerial combat experience gained by the Condor Legion pilots during the Spanish Civil War. The Nazis have not capitalized on that advantage, however, by rapidly expanding their military pilot training programs using their combat-experienced pilots as instructors.

"The Germans have foolishly decided to try to win the war with the skilled pilots they have now. That's an incredible mistake the Huns are going to live to regret, I guarantee. Boxers like to say if you kill the body, the head dies. Every pilot we take out is like a body blow to the German war machine.

"The basic plan is to insert a two-man Lovat Scout sniper team by sea, by parachute, or by air-landing them into a preselected target area. The team will proceed, under cover of darkness, to a hide position near the targeted Luftwaffe landing ground; lie in wait until the pilots scramble for a mission; then shoot as many of them as possible, without compromising themselves; while the pilots are sitting in their airplanes queuing up for takeoff. Tests we have conducted at a fighter base have shown that the sound of a squadron of high-performance aircraft running up their engines prior to scrambling will muffle the rifle shots.

"Now, here is where it gets interesting. Instead of returning to the coast for a pickup by sea as the Germans will expect, the Scouts will, instead, move inland to a preselected lake where I will be waiting in a small amphibious aircraft to fly them home."

"Okay, people, that's everything for now," Major Randal said, wrapping up the briefing. "I wanted to introduce you to Harry and get you wired in to Buzzard Plucker before we go off to Commando training in Scotland. Chauncy will show you to Captain McKoy's room. The Captain has a present for each of you, courtesy of Lady Jane. I want Squadron Leader Wilcox, Captain Lady Seaborn, Lieutenant Seaborn, and Lieutenant Shelby to stand fast."

Major Randal then assembled the designated group around the table under the sparkling crystal chandelier in the small dining area in his suite. "Squadron Leader, when will you be prepared to begin Buzzard Plucker?"

"Any time after the amphibious airplane we plan to use arrives at Seaborn House."

"Have you selected a target for our first mission?"

"I have." Squadron Leader Wilcox opened his briefcase, spread a chart of the French coast on the table, and pointed to a spot. "There's a German fighter strip located here, right on the coast. The beach below it is a tiny little slit of hard shingle. There is no coast road to worry about. And there are some fairly rugged cliffs just behind the beach to screen the approach from the sea. Oh, yeah, there is a lake about four miles inland that will be perfect for me to extract the Lovats from."

"Randy, can you get us there?"

"It's a really small pinpoint, sir," the young navy officer said. "There's no way I can guarantee we'll find it in the time frame available if we have any weather at all."

"Do you remember that idea I had for solving our navigation problems?" Major Randal asked.

"Yes, sir, I do."

"Don't you think this might be a good time to put it into action?"

"Absolutely, sir!" HMY *Arrow*'s commanding officer replied with a quiver of excitement in his voice. "With your permission I will cut my leave short tonight and put it into execution straightaway."

"Take Percy with you. He can use the experience."

No one else at the table, with the single exception of Captain Lady Seaborn, understood a word of what they were talking about. Characteristically, no one asked for an explanation.

"All right then, let's do it," Major Randal ordered. "Jane, you and Randy stay here. I have something I want to discuss with you."

Captain Stone came striding in the door as soon as Chauncy opened it. "John, this is, without question, the finest service pistol I have ever seen, and I have handled them all."

"Is that our present, a Colt .45 automatic?" Lieutenant Shelby asked eagerly.

"Negative. This is a .38 Super," Captain Stone said. "You'd better get down there before the supply runs out."

"Hold up, Harry," Major Randal ordered. "Captain Zorro, I'm going to have a quick confab with Jane and Randy, then walk down and introduce Lieutenant Shelby to Captain McKoy. If you can spare a few more minutes before getting back to your debauchery, I'd like a word with you in private."

"Well, all right, old stick. But be advised, I have the Belarusas sisters cooling their heels downstairs in the bar. Probably not such a good idea to leave them to their own devices for very long; they have an enormous capacity to cause trouble."

"The Belarusas sisters?"

"Acrobats. Hungarian, I believe. You should see them knocking down Black Straps—the official drink of the Life Guards, you know."

"Just wait here."

Major Randal huddled in a corner with Captain Lady Seaborn and her nephew.

"Randy, your aunt has some friends who are having a hard time finding a way to supply the resistance forces they're forming in France. If you brought back a fishing boat when you and Percy go over to kidnap an inshore pilot, would it be possible to convert her into a cargo carrier, and do you think you could handle her?"

Lieutenant Seaborn glanced at his aunt. She was staring at Major Randal, clearly intrigued. The Royal Navy officer had never seen her look at anyone like that before—and that included his Uncle Mallory.

"Do you mean, could I sail it on clandestine missions to the Continent, loaded with arms and explosives, for Aunt Jane's unnamed friends, and offload it, sir?"

"That's what I'm asking."

"Piece of cake, sir. I cut my teeth on sailboats, which is essentially what all those French fishermen trawl in."

"Bring one back, then."

"Aye, aye, sir."

"Will that score us some brownie points with your SOE people, Jane?"

Carefully trying to control her mounting excitement, Captain Lady Seaborn replied, "If you pull this off, our future is guaranteed."

Major Randal walked Lieutenant Shelby down the hall. "Harry, you're going to have to run Buzzard Plucker on your own while the rest of us are off on Commando training. Can you handle that?"

"Sir, Buzzard Plucker is a dream assignment tailor-made for me."

"Originally I planned to give it to Captain Stone."

"I shall do my best not to let you down, sir."

"See that you don't."

Captain "Geronimo Joe" McKoy opened the door on the first knock. Major Randal introduced him to his new sniping officer. The two hit it off instantly and were deep in a serious technical discussion about trajectories, muzzle velocities, and foot-pounds before the major had taken three steps back down the hallway.

Back in his suite he found Captain Stone sitting in the middle of the couch with his new Colt disassembled on the coffee table, the pieces laid out on a white monogrammed hotel towel. Chauncy was hovering over him like a mother hen, making sure he did not leak any gun oil on the polished mahogany.

Having been cleared by Lady Jane to do so, Major Randal carefully briefed the Life Guards officer on every detail of the past week. At the end he asked, "Do you think Jane thought this up all by herself—getting Raiding Forces hooked up with all these clandestine organizations?"

"Not likely," Captain Stone answered. "My guess is she had help."

"Who?"

"We may never find out, old stick. It could be Colonel Clarke, possibly that fellow Grand, or maybe even C."

As he stood up to leave, he added: "For all we know, it could be all three. We need to let Jane keep playing out her hand. It sounds to me like you have had a most interesting week, and what she has arranged so far is definitely good for Raiding Forces. By the way, John, why not keep hammering the railroads at the same time we are conducting Buzzard Plucker?"

"Great idea, Zorro."

Captain McKoy was strolling up the hall as Major Randal was showing the Life Guards officer to the door. "I'm bringing your shootin' irons, John," the cowboy called out jovially.

As he came into the suite he said, "When I was logging the serial numbers, I noticed there was a consecutively numbered pair. Thought you might like to have a backup, so I set 'em aside for you."

"Thanks, Captain," Major Randal said, racking the slide on one of the Colt .38 Supers. It opened as smoothly as if it were running on ball bearings. The trigger, when he tried it, broke like a glass rod. "These are the best-tuned pistols I've ever handled. What did you do?"

"Not much. You don't want to be making fancy modifications to a fighting pistol. I just slicked 'em up some."

"Maybe, but the weapon I used on the 26th Cavalry regimental pistol team wasn't this smooth, and it was a National Match target model."

"Glad you approve," Captain McKoy said. "Put 'em to good use. I'm comfortable you will."

25

THE SNATCH

LIEUTENANT RANDY SEABORN GATHERED THE CREW OF HMY *Arrow* on the yacht for a pre-mission briefing. There was quite a bit of good-natured complaining about being recalled from their leave, but the sailors and the Lifeboat Servicemen were all excited by the prospects of a fast, in-and-out operation.

Lieutenant Percy Stirling was also on hand. This was going to be his first mission since his transition to Raiding Forces. In fact, it was his first combat mission ever. Understandably, he felt exhilarated and more than a little bit nervous. Like anyone going into action for the first time, he did not know what to expect.

Standard operating procedure in Raiding Forces laid down the requirement that the commander give a briefing prior to each and every mission. It made no difference if it was a short operation that they had performed many times before. The format was always the same: situation, mission, execution, command and signal, and administration and logistics. Nothing was left to guesswork. Every man was going to know exactly what his duties were, along with those of everyone else.

"Situation," Lieutenant Seaborn began in his usual, somewhat cavalier style. "The enemy occupies the continent of Europe, and we occupy the British Isles. The English Channel lies in between."

The crew laughed.

"Mission: We are going to proceed by the most direct route to this area of the French coast." Lieutenant Seaborn indicated a general area on the map that he had spread out on the deck. "When we arrive in the target area, we are going to board a fishing vessel of our choosing, snatch the skipper, put the crew over the side in their dinghy, take the Frenchman under tow, and return home with all due haste.

"Execution: Once in the target area, we will attempt to locate the local fishing fleet. Once we have located the fleet, we will select a target boat. The two Lifeboat Servicemen who are up next on the duty rotation will row a boarding party consisting of Lieutenant Stirling, Petty Officer Corny, and myself to the target. We will board the vessel and effect the capture. We will then send the French crew ashore in their dinghy and take the boat under tow for the return to Seaborn House.

"Command and signal are per standard operating procedure.

"Administration and logistics: Collect your gear and prepare to shove off."

The men laughed again. They were pretty sure that whoever had invented the five-paragraph order had envisioned a little more detail than that.

"What are your questions?"

There were no questions. Without any fanfare, they prepared to put to sea.

They were headed to the Breton area. According to the *Michelin Guide to Brittany* that Lieutenant Seaborn had consulted:

The Breton Coast is extraordinarily indented. The jaggedness of this coastline with its islands, inlets, and reefs, which is due only in part to the action of the sea, is one of the characteristics of Brittany.

Somber cliffs, rugged capes, islands, rocks, and reefs give the coastline a grimness that is reflected in the local names with a sinister ring: the Channel of Great Fear, the Bay of the Dead, and the Hell of Plogoff.

When the wind blows [which is nearly always] the battering-ram effect of the sea is tremendous. Sometimes the shock the surge gives the rocks can be felt as far off as eighteen miles away.

This was what they told potential tourists!

Lieutenant Seaborn knew that if you factored in magnetic sea mines, E-boats, L-lighters, and the odd Nazi night fighter sweep, there was no such thing as a milk run to Brittany. An unforgiving place to visit at any time, a clandestine nighttime incursion there under wartime conditions could only be described as high risk.

The young skipper also knew that if the *Arrow* so much as touched one of those rocks or reefs, many of which were submerged at various times, they would rip out the yacht's bottom.

Furthermore, should the *Arrow* perchance lose power, be caught in the surf, and get slammed into any of the "somber cliffs" or "rugged capes" by a surge creating a shock that could "be felt as far off as eighteen miles," well, the Royal Navy's youngest lieutenant didn't even want to think about the consequences. The only bright spot would be that if that happened, they would not have to think about their fate for long.

The initial weather report was promising. HMY *Arrow* slipped from the dock at 1600 hours, British Double Daylight Saving Time, and the long passage began.

Halfway to France the wind had increased to Force 5. This was not all bad, since it offered the prospects of working in a weather shore. The night was very dark.

At 2418 hours a violent squall came down and the barometer started falling like a rock. They received a W/T signal that the weather would deteriorate to South-Southwest Force 6–7.

Lieutenant Seaborn ignored the conditions and stood boldly on course.

The fishing industry on the west coast of Brittany was quite substantial. It consisted of vessels of all sizes operating from an array of ports between the Vshant and the Loire. The fishermen were allowed to operate virtually unsupervised by the Germans, though the Kriegsmarine occasionally stationed a guard on board the larger vessels to prevent them from sailing to England.

At 0137 hours three craft were spotted off the port bow. The *Arrow* immediately hove to, and after carefully studying the three possible targets through his night glasses, Lieutenant Seaborn ordered the dinghy put out and the boarding party to assemble.

In the distance, searchlights inland lit up. Tall, pencil-thin light beams pointed at the sky, sometimes swaying back and forth like stately, slow-moving columns, sometimes tottering jerkily and then moving fast, crossing each other's paths. Shell bursts twinkled in the night sky. Red, orange, and yellow teardrop-shaped flashes, looking like the drawings of explosions in a comic strip, erupted from the ack-ack guns on the ground. The crew of the *Arrow* could hear a faint *cruuump, cruuump, cruuump*. The Royal Air Force was giving something near the French coastline a major league pasting.

At 0146 hours the dinghy cast off.

The boarding party had been carefully selected: Lieutenant Seaborn and Lieutenant Stirling both spoke passable French, and Petty Officer Corny was built like an oak tree. All personnel were wearing black knit caps, black turtleneck sweaters, and sand-green Denison smocks; their faces were covered with black greasepaint. Each was armed with a Browning A-5 12-gauge shotgun and a Colt .38 Super automatic pistol. Petty Officer Corny had also stuck a thick, twenty-four inch wooden club with a leather loop on the handle in his belt. The two Lifeboat Servicemen were likewise fully armed and were prepared to board the fishing vessel immediately in the event of any sign of resistance.

All communications would be by hand signals; spoken English was strictly forbidden. Anyone who knew any German was encouraged to say a few words now and then to confuse the fishermen about exactly who was boarding the boat.

The Lifeboat Servicemen closed the distance to the selected French fishing vessel with powerful sweeps of their oars. As soon as they'd pulled alongside the eighty-foot schooner, the boarding party went into action. Lieutenant Stirling ordered forcefully, *"Tout le monde, sur le pont!"* All hands on deck!

When the vessel's captain was identified, Petty Officer Corny unceremoniously hustled him into the waiting dinghy while the two officers covered the rest of the fishing crew with their A-5s.

Then, keeping their shotguns aimed at the sullen fishermen, they ordered them into the fishing boat's dinghy, with instructions to make for shore. As soon as the fishermen rowed out of sight in the dark, the boarding party got back in their dinghy; shortly thereafter, they were back on board HMY *Arrow*.

"Up anchor," Lieutenant Seaborn ordered the instant he came aboard.

The *Arrow* burbled to life—a reassuring sound—then pulled up alongside the fishing boat, transferred Petty Officer Corny plus a skeleton crew on board, and made preparations to take the vessel under tow.

They got under way and headed out into the Channel.

The full impact of the weather hit them once they were in the open. They were soon climbing up the side of one tall, gray-green swell, shooting over the top, and slamming down into the trough. The waves beat on, one after another. The trick was to avoid both being capsized and snapping the towrope. It seemed as if the tiny little *Arrow* would be pounded into matchsticks.

Then the sky cleared and the moon came out bright. The wind did not slack off one notch, however. HMY *Arrow* pounded on, throwing up tall sheets of spray. Towing the French boat dramatically reduced its speed and called for an advanced degree of seamanship.

On the tiny bridge, nineteen-year-old Lieutenant Stirling said to eighteen-year-old Lieutenant Seaborn, "If only our chums back at our schools could see us now! *YEEEEEEHAAAAAA!*"

Lieutenant Seaborn gave him a huge grin and shouted into the ferocious wind, "*YEEEEEEHAAAAAA!*"

The moon went down and the pitch-dark sky eventually began to lighten. Just as a brilliant pastel-pink sun started to come up, they made landfall with their prize in tow and began the run up the river to their base.

Major John Randal was pacing back and forth, waiting for them on the dock. He wore his Denison parachute smock to ward off the morning chill. He had left London the moment he had received word that they had sailed, in order to be on hand for their return.

When HMY *Arrow* carefully pulled alongside the dock, Major Randal called out, "Permission to come aboard!"

Lieutenant Randy Seaborn was a stickler for tradition. He ran a taut ship when it came to protocol.

"Permission granted, sir!"

Not forgetting to salute the ensign flying from the stern, Major Randal leaped lightly aboard.

"Any problems?"

"No, sir. It was a routine mission. Everything went according to your instructions. We have a Plan B on board under guard and, as you can see, a prize fishing vessel, as ordered. She has a spacious hold with plenty of capacity to handle the job of running arms and stores, plus a small crane for loading and unloading. First, though, we shall have to rid it of the awful smell of cod."

"Excellent. Make sure to blindfold the Plan B before you bring him ashore."

"Aye, aye, sir."

"Nice job, men," Major Randall called to the crew.

Then, turning to leave, he ordered, "Leave the rest of this to the navy. Percy, you come with me."

Major Randal and Lieutenant Stirling repaired to the kitchen at Seaborn House, and over mugs of hot tea, the young "Death or Glory Boy" walked him through the night's work. When he had finished, Raiding Forces' commander said casually, "I have a mission for you."

"Yes, sir." Lieutenant Stirling tensed with anticipation, quivering like a bird dog on point.

"I want you and Randy to conduct a demolition campaign against the railroads that run along the occupied French coastline while the rest of us are in Scotland undergoing Commando training. You two work together to select the best places to target. Randy has already been on one of these raids, so he can show you the drill. You will be in command."

Lieutenant Stirling could not believe his ears. He was being given license to carry out his own little private war!

"Had much experience with explosives, Percy?"

"Actually, no, not very much, sir."

"Don't worry about it. Neither has anyone else in Raiding Forces. It's not all that hard to blow a railroad. You plant the charges under the rails with a fuze activated by a pressure igniter, so the next train that rolls by detonates it. Lady Jane tells me there's a territorial engineer unit called the Kent Fortress Royal Engineers stationed not far from here. I'll make arrangements for them to send someone over to show you how to set up your charges."

"That would be helpful, sir."

"The thing to remember is you need to get in, place your explosives, and get out fast without being discovered. I'll rotate a small team of men down here from training at Achnacarry to work with you, but if for any reason they don't arrive, you, Randy, and the Lifeboat Servicemen will have to go it alone."

"How often do you want us to go over, Major?" Lieutenant Stirling asked, fighting back his mounting excitement.

"Shoot for once a week. You'll develop an operational rhythm. Randy's going to have commitments, since Buzzard Plucker has priority. Now that I think about it, I'll send Corporal Merritt down to work with you for a while. Follow his advice and you'll be all right. Think you can handle this, stud?"

"Sir, there is nothing I would rather try."

"Outstanding! Let's call this job Operation Comanche Yell," Major John Randal said, sounding cool and relaxed. "Take it to 'em, Percy. Hit and run."

Major Randal and Lieutenant Stirling went in search of Lieutenant Harry Shelby and the Lovat Scout team that he had taken command of the day before. They found them on the front lawn of Seaborn House working on what looked like adult-sized gorilla costumes.

"These are ghillie suits," Lieutenant Shelby explained. "Each man makes his own. Upon reaching the target area, the Scouts will add bits and pieces of the local flora and fauna for better camouflage. Highland gamekeepers invented the ghillie suit so they could lie in wait for poachers. Then the poachers started using them to stalk game more effectively and to help them hide from the gamekeepers—"

"Have you briefed the Scouts on the mission yet?" Major Randal asked, interrupting him.

"Yes, sir."

Major Randal looked at the young Scouts, suffering from an unhappy premonition that this could all go badly wrong, that Operation Buzzard Plucker might be overly ambitious. Like a lot of Raiding Forces plans, it had sounded like a good idea over drinks in the Blind Eye. But Buzzard Plucker would be the major's first experience of sending men on a mission he had not gone out and done himself—or one where he was not, at the very least, going to be in the field with them, sharing the risks. The Scouts clearly were indifferent to him, and why not? He had done nothing to garner their respect. With men like the Lovat Scouts, respect had to be earned; it was not automatically given.

Major Randal said, "Anyone want to return to your unit now, after finding out what you're going to be getting yourself into?"

"Ach, not on your life sir." Corporal Dickie Whamond spoke for the group. "Now, if you would have asked us that question the day we were up in that wee, wobbly balloon Bessie, Major, you might have received another answer."

"All right then, listen up," Major Randal smiled. "As far as I know, no one has ever tried to snipe German pilots before. I hear you men are the best sneakers and peekers in the business, and some say you're the finest long-distance rifle shots in the army. At Calais, my Green Jackets were getting hits on panzer commanders standing in their turrets at six hundred yards with open sights, so we'll see what you boys can do."

The Lovat Scouts perked up on hearing that. Was their commander issuing a challenge? They liked challenges.

"Lieutenant Shelby, Squadron Leader Wilcox should be arriving at any time now. Have your men saddle up and move down to the boat dock. Stand by there to link up with him to begin rehearsing embarking and disembarking procedures as soon as he lands."

"Yes, sir. Do we have any information on the best way to go about it? None of us has ever even been on a floatplane before."

"No, you're going to have to develop your own procedures by trial and error. Get it right, Lieutenant."

"Sir!"

When they arrived at the boat dock, Major Randal ordered Lieutenant Seaborn to detach the Lifeboat Servicemen from duty so they could take part in the training with the Lovat Scouts. Far off in the distance could be heard the sound of a single-engine aircraft making its approach. It was not clear to Major Randal what the amphibian was going to look like, but the ungainly little biplane that splashed down and taxied to the dock was definitely not it. When Squadron Leader Paddy Wilcox came putt-putting up in a tiny biplane made out of fabric painted a horrible shade of flat black, in an amateurish attempt at night camouflage, the officer commanding Raiding Forces was shocked.

He had good reason to be. The Supermarine Walrus was not very big. It was slow, and it looked something like a ruptured dragonfly. The single pusher-type engine that powered the plane was simply bolted on a triangular iron-strut arrangement between the two wings, above and slightly behind the cockpit. The engine mount looked like a badly improvised afterthought.

In addition to the floats under the wings, the Walrus had fixed wheels mounted on the keel of the fuselage. The wheels were bigger versions of the solid flat type, like the ones boys put on Soap Box Derby racers. The cockpit was constructed of angular, flat glass windowpanes. Charitably put, the ungainly Walrus was definitely no Spitfire, regardless of who had built it.

The Lovat Scouts and the Lifeboat Servicemen were eyeballing the ugly little bi-winged amphibian with mounting apprehension as Squadron Leader Wilcox climbed out of the cockpit, a proud grin on his face.

"What's this?" Major Randal demanded when the squadron leader stepped nimbly from the gently bobbing amphibian onto the dock and tied off the little airplane.

"A Seagull V, the civilian version of the Royal Navy's Walrus. This one belonged to Lady Jane's late husband. Ain't she a beaut?"

"How fast will this clunker fly? The engine sounds like it's powered by a squirrel on a treadmill."

"Nearly one hundred thirty-five miles per hour with a payload of three passengers plus the pilot, Major. After we install the navy-issue bomb racks, she will be able to carry a two-hundred-fifty-pound bomb under each wing. When we fit the gun mount hard points designed for the Supermarine Walrus, they will support four external .303-caliber machine guns. Carrying the guns and the bomb load plus passengers, she's going to lose a step or two."

"I had a flathead Indian motorcycle that could go nearly that fast."

"Major, I can land in a mud puddle. I can take off almost straight up, fully loaded. Since the Seagull has an undercarriage, I can land on a road or in a field as well as on water. I wish I had had one of these during my bush piloting days. This airplane is perfect for what we intend to use it for."

"If you say so . . . Looks like an artifact from the Red Baron's Flying Circus to me."

"The Walrus may be an ugly duckling by day," Squadron Leader Wilcox admitted, "but at night, when she snatches you out from behind enemy lines with the Jerries nipping at your heels, I'll wager she suddenly becomes the most beautiful swan you ever saw."

The Lovats christened her then and there: the Duck—as in ugly.

Training began immediately. Like all good exercises, this one was simple. Squadron Leader Wilcox taxied out and took off with a Lifeboat Serviceman sitting in the copilot's seat. He did a single, short loop and landed.

The Lifeboat Serviceman launched the rubber inflatable dinghy over the side, out of the open-air cupola located behind the passenger compartment, climbed in, and paddled to shore. When he reached the bank, two Lovat Scouts gingerly climbed in, and he paddled them back out to newly named Duck.

They clambered up on the float and lashed the rubber dinghy back to the undercarriage. Then they climbed up a short rope ladder into the open cupola, with the Lovats entering first.

When everyone was on board, Squadron Leader Wilcox immediately lifted off in the shortest distance he could. True to his word, the Duck took to the air fast.

In theory, the plan sounded easy; good plans always do. Considering this one had to be executed at night behind German lines, there were a lot of things that could go wrong.

They practiced the drill over and over and over. Then they practiced it some more.

"Percy, I'm curious about one thing," Major Randal inquired as he stood watching the exercise.

"Sir?"

"Why didn't you go into the Scots Guards like the rest of the men in your family?"

"Sir, the Scots Guards are too intense for me. They have a saying: 'One hundred plus ten percent,' and they live it every day. Besides, sir, I always wanted to be a cavalryman."

"In that case, why'd you volunteer out of the Lancers into the Commandos?"

"That's simple, sir. The romance has completely gone out of the cavalry. Our motto used to be, 'To Love and Ride Away.' Then the War Department armored the cavalry regiments, and we were forced to abandon our horses in order to become mechanized. All Lancers ever do now is pull maintenance on their vehicles. The new motto is, 'Screw and Bolt'—simply not the same, sir."

"I see," Major Randal said. And he actually did.

SPECIAL WARFARE
TRAINING CENTER

26

COHQ TO ACHNACARRY

WHEN MAJOR JOHN RANDAL HAD LEFT LONDON THE DAY BEFORE, the city had been burning. It was still burning when the train pulled into the station on his return. The ugly smell of cordite and smoke hung in the air.

Royal Marine Pamela Plum-Martin was waiting for him when he stepped off the train. She whisked him to the Bradford Hotel in the Rolls-Royce, skillfully navigating around bomb damage, rubble, emergency services vehicles, and firefighting equipment. Military police in their distinctive red hats were everywhere. It was a sobering drive. The Junkers-88 Stukas, Heinkle 111s, and Dornier 17s had done their best work.

"Pretty rough, Pam?"

"Worse than any nightmare, sir."

Major Randal could not help noticing that, like her boss Captain the Lady Jane Seaborn, she was even more attractive when she was serious. Whatever "it" was, Royal Marine Plum-Martin had it. A lot of it.

"Give me a briefing."

"The Luftwaffe has been bombing nonstop since you left. They are trying to wipe London off the map. The Germans are not even attempting to hit military targets anymore. When they come over, it feels like they are aiming right at you, and if they could see you, they would drop a bomb on you just for fun."

"That doesn't make any sense. They've been concentrating on the high-priority docks in the east-end port area. Why would the German High Command suddenly switch to low-value civilian targets?"

"Apparently, sir, the Nazis bombed London accidentally, and the prime minister sent the RAF to Berlin the next night to retaliate, so Hitler ordered the Luftwaffe to strike back and this time obliterate London. Intelligence has reason to believe the Führer is convinced that bombing our cities is going to break civilian morale and force our government to sue for peace."

"How do you 'accidentally' bomb London?"

"I've been wondering that myself. I wish I knew how to fly a bomber so I could wing over and bomb Berlin on purpose!" the Royal Marine exclaimed indignantly. Hitler was going to have his work cut out in trying to break her morale.

When they reached the sandbagged Bradford Hotel, Captain Lady Seaborn was waiting for them downstairs in the lobby. They departed immediately for Richmond Terrace, the headquarters of Combined Operations. Since COHQ was Raiding Forces' parent organization, this should by rights have been the first place they called on during their tour of the wartime agencies, but the meeting had been rescheduled several times. Today they had an appointment with Lieutenant General Alan Bourne, CB, DSO, MVO, Royal Marines, who held the impressive title of Commander of Raiding Operations on Coasts in Enemy-Occupied Territories and Advisor to the Chiefs of Staff on Combined Operations.

Upon arrival they were ushered into the general's office. He could not have been more charming. "We have been following your pinprick operations rather closely around here. COHQ has little to show for its efforts lately. Your small-scale raids have been about the only thing we have had to crow about," Lieutenant General Bourne said sincerely.

"By the way, that was sharp, having your men trained as parachutists. Around COHQ we mostly think amphibiously. Now, thanks to you, we find ourselves responsible for all parachute operations, though there is talk of splitting off Airborne Forces into a stand-alone command to take over that mission from us someday."

"You have to credit Lady Jane for the idea, to be perfectly honest, sir."

"Fancy that. Well, I must apologize to both of you. As usual, I do not have much time today. The chiefs have once again demanded my presence quite unexpectedly. Let me proceed straight to the purpose of our meeting here today.

"I am charged with a four-point brief: coordinate interservice training; run the Combined Operations Training Establishment; advise on tactical and technical research and development; and lastly, devise the special craft needed for all forms of combined operations, from raiding to the invasion of the Continent.

"I have no planning staff, no signals staff, no training staff, and no chief of staff. The Royal Marines are spread out all over the globe, serving on ships and manning shore defense batteries at ports worldwide, so we are forced to use army personnel to staff the new Commando units, which by all rights should be a Marine light infantry mission. Big ideas are all we have around here."

"A formidable challenge, sir," Major Randal said.

"That is the way it always is with us British, I'm afraid, Major. At the beginning of every single war, a cataclysmic disaster occurs and incompetent generals make colossal blunders. The military is always structured, equipped, and mentally prepared to fight the previous war. We are forced to retreat; then, gradually, we begin to put things right. New generals with modern ideas are found; we reorganize and marshal our forces, counterattack, and eventually—slowly but surely—we overcome our enemies and somehow finally achieve victory. It has been said we lose every battle but the last one.

"After Dunkirk, a metamorphosis in military thinking began taking place behind the scenes. A catastrophe seems to be the only thing that can ever wake up the War Office, but that stodgy, old-establishment, barnacle-encrusted firm can, at times, move with surprising rapidity.

"Right now our one and only thought is to return to the Continent, on the principle that it is better to fight over there than over here. However, we have to work up to it. This is the beginning of the era of the swash-buckler and the licensed privateer. Raiding is the order of the day, only how does one get started?

"Everyone has his own thoughts on the subject," the general went on, not waiting for an answer. "The navy—after an initial burst of impressive, selfless, interservice cooperation—is giving Combined Operations only token support these days. The army is actively discouraging its men from volunteering for the Commandos. The RAF is trying to ignore us; we are dead last on its priority list for aircraft.

"There has been more than a little interagency skirmishing over who controls what," the general went on. "Right now, Special Operations Executive has managed to obtain a charter giving them responsibility for raids that number under thirty men. You have never actually taken that many troops on an operation yet, have you, Major?"

"No, sir."

"We are not about to concede you to SOE. Raiding Forces belongs to COHQ, make no mistake. We need—and I cannot overemphasize how great our need is—for you to carry out an operation with more than thirty men as soon as reasonably practical. I think I have something that should help you to go about it. You recall, I mentioned the navy was providing COHQ only token support."

"Yes, sir."

"Strange bunch, the navy. They recently gave COHQ three C-class motor gunboats right out of the blue. Simply gave them to us; we never asked for them, and we have no particular use for them. The navy did not see fit to provide any crew to operate them, of course, nor did they offer to teach our people how to operate them. But now I presume they can honestly say, if queried, that they have provided COHQ with significant materiel support. If I gave you one of the MGBs, could you put it to work?"

Major Randal could not believe what he was hearing. He was not sure of the specs, but he recalled that a motor gunboat was typically about eighty-five to one hundred twenty-five feet long, with an impressive array of offensive weapons. MGBs were fast, powerful little pocket battleships: exactly what was needed for hit-and-run raiding on the French coast.

The general watched Major Randal closely. "Remember, Major, the catch is, there is no crew to man the gunboat, and I do not know where you are going to find personnel. The navy is surely not going to provide you with any sailors."

"Sir, I don't know what to say."

"Do not say anything. Take the boat and go kill Nazis. Furthermore— and this is from the heart—there are some of us that appreciate an American volunteering to serve with British Armed Forces in our darkest hour, and around here, in particular, we are most impressed with your performance at Calais—bringing your men out like that. A lot of us old hands would like to fancy we could have done the same given the circumstances.

"So . . . good luck and good hunting, Major. Now, unfortunately, I really am running short on time."

Captain Lady Seaborn drove Major Randal to the railway station, where Raiding Forces was loading onto a train to Scotland, carrying every piece of equipment the Raiders owned. The group's trip ticket read SPEAN BRIDGE STATION, a place they all knew was located in the Scottish Highlands. But where? Raiding Forces troopers, being known for their enterprise and initiative, broke out a map and, after a great deal of reconnaissance, found that Spean Bridge was in the middle of nowhere.

Fort William, the nearest town, was nearly ten miles away from Spean Bridge, but their destination was not Fort William at all. It was Achnacarry Castle, the ancestral home of Cameron of Lochiel. Achnacarry had been recently selected by Combined Operations Headquarters to be the Holding Unit, Special Warfare Training Center.

The Special Warfare Training Center was where handpicked fighting men were put to the acid test. The training was designed to stretch human fortitude, endurance, and military skills to the extreme. Boys who came to Achnacarry and survived the test left as men—Commandos—changed for life by the experience. Those who did not make the grade were RTU'd, a much-dreaded fate. For some, not surviving the test meant that, literally— the casualty rate was seven percent. The casualty rate, commonly referred to as "wastage," was not to be confused with the failure rate. Casualties meant dead and wounded students. Commando School was not for the faint of heart.

The new "Laird of Achnacarry" was Lieutenant Colonel Charles Edward Vaughan—a former Coldstream Guardsman, a sergeant major in the Buffs, and a veteran of No. 4 Commando. He had been specially chosen to command the Special Warfare Training Center because he was a peerless trainer of men: the proverbial round peg in a round hole, a rare thing in any army.

Lieutenant Colonel Vaughan met Raiding Forces at Spean Bridge Station with a small cadre of his staff, all of whom were wearing forest-green Commando berets. The colonel was a big man who looked something like an elephant in uniform. Standing in the rain with a tall walking stick in one hand, he made an impressive picture. He gave them a little welcoming speech.

"Good afternoon, men. Welcome to Achnacarry, though we are not quite there yet. We shall be putting the polishing touch on your Commando training here in the lovely Scottish Highlands. I trust you will find your stay interesting as well as informative.

"Men, I want to take this opportunity to dispel a certain myth that has been artificially created recently by certain unenlightened members of the national press. Commandos are not a wild, undisciplined mob of cut-throats, thugs, gangsters, ex-gaol birds, and what have you. Commandos are not Greek gods or supermen, either. There is no 'S' on your chest. You are, and always will be, professional light infantry soldiers—the best in the business. Though I must admit, lads, we Commandos are handsome devils, to a man."

The men laughed. Clearly, Lieutenant Colonel Vaughan had a way with troops.

Making his way through the crowd of his Raiders to introduce himself to the commandant of the Special Warfare Training Center, Major John Randal bumped into Sergeant Roy "Mad Dog" Reupart of the Army Physical Training Corps, late of the No. 1 Parachute Training School.

"Fancy meeting you here, Sergeant," he said, feeling his heart sink.

"I told you, you were going to owe me, sir."

"I didn't expect you to transfer all the way up here to collect," Major Randal replied brittlely.

"Oh, no, sir, it's not like that at all. I'm reporting in as your newest volunteer. I've even been practicing my Comanche yell."

"This is a joke, right? Lady Jane put you up to it."

"No, sir. I volunteered, and Lady Seaborn made the arrangements for the transfer."

"Well, in that case, welcome aboard, Sergeant," Major Randal said, sticking out his hand and hoping he did not sound as relieved as he actually felt. The last thing he wanted to find was Sergeant Reupart assigned to the physical training staff of the Commando School on the very day he was reporting in.

The men were ordered to load their equipment onto waiting trucks. There was some initial confusion when a few of the troops tried to climb aboard; they were denied space on the vehicles. When Major Randal finally managed to introduce himself to Lieutenant Colonel Vaughan, the colonel said, "Have your men fall in, Major. The trucks are for equipment only. We shall be marching to the castle."

He gave Major Randal the order cheerfully, as if he were actually enjoying standing out in the cold rain.

"Sergeant Major Hicks, have the men fall in," Major Randal ordered.

There was the usual moaning and groaning as the men formed up.

"It is not far, lads," Lieutenant Colonel Vaughan called out reassuringly, "only seven miles. Forward, march! Route step, march!"

When they stepped out, a small, enthusiastic band of bagpipers—under the command of Pipe Major Johnny MacLaughlin and accompanied by a tall, gangly, knock-kneed bass drummer—struck up "March of the Cameron Men." The band was playing for all they were worth. The Commando instructors had the air of hikers out for a casual stroll.

They soon discovered that the colonel had neglected to mention that the route was mostly straight uphill.

"Seven miles," griped one of the Raiders in formation near Major Randal. "A bloke would have thought they could have brought the blinkin' train a little closer."

The rain stayed constant, a steady drizzle. It never picked up; it never slowed down; it never went away. Soon the new trainees were all soaked through to the skin. Steam rose from the column of marching men. Water ran off their hats, and their clothes were sodden. Raiding Forces leaned into the pace. The band played on.

Tendrils of waterlogged fog swirled around and over the marching column. The rain kept coming down. The slope climbed almost straight up. Water splattered with every step. They marched higher and higher. And the lousy, rotten band played on.

An hour and fifteen minutes later, after what seemed like an *unusually long* seven miles of hard speed-marching, they finally arrived. The band cut out on cue, as fresh as when they had started.

Achnacarry Castle occupied its own private world. Everywhere Major Randal and his raiders looked, they saw men of No. 1 Independent Company—wearing knit caps, with camouflaged faces, and dressed in denim fatigues—on the move. A lot of them had logs balanced on their shoulders. Training was in full swing; the tempo was full speed. No one ever walked anywhere; everyone double-timed, all the time.

"Welcome to Achnacarry Castle, the spiritual birthplace of the Commando fighting man," Lieutenant Colonel Charles Edward Vaughan announced.

"You will always have a home here, men. When you go off on operations and get yourself wounded, there will always be a place here on our staff for you to return to and recover until you are able to go back on active service again."

Captain Terry "Zorro" Stone turned to Major Randal and complained, "I feel dizzy."

"Do you think it rains much here?" Major Randal wondered out loud.

As they would soon find out, it always rains at Achnacarry.

Commando training was ten times harder than anything the Raiding Forces troops had imagined. On their first morning at Achnacarry,

Lieutenant Colonel Vaughan announced, "Today, I have laid on a nice little get-acquainted outing for you. You will all hike over, climb the hill of Ben Nevis, and be back here in time for a fine lunch. You are going to discover that the food here is excellent." (He failed to mention, however, that they would not be eating much of it.) "How does that sound, lads? Any questions?"

"How far away is Ben Nevis, sir?"

"Eighteen miles. Have a nice day, then."

Only the cadre at Achnacarry would have called it a hill; Ben Nevis was 4,406 feet high, and the route they took to the top was almost vertical. They did not make it back to the castle in time for the lunch.

During the first week, out of seven days, it rained all seven. The men averaged four hours' sleep per night. And one meal per day.

At first the training was of the "welcome to the Commandos" variety. Most of the calisthenics were done with logs: team runs carrying logs on their shoulders, sit-ups holding logs, team log presses above their heads, and other diabolical exercises like cross-country speed-marches with the logs balanced on their shoulders. The training was round-the-clock. No soldier ever really likes that sort of thing, and the men of Raiding Forces were no exception. They put up with it for a few days, then they did what men of a certain caliber often do when faced with that kind of training situation: They attacked the problem.

As a group they came to an unspoken decision to see if they could actually kill a Commando instructor by walking, running, or climbing him to death. They had plenty of time, the means, and the opportunity to find out.

By the end of the second week, the Commando staff was beginning to show some concern. They were being gradually ground down, since, by tradition, they did everything the students did, while the Raiding Forces troopers appeared to be gaining momentum. It was not supposed to work like that at Achnacarry.

Each Commando student was ceremoniously issued a toggle rope. The rope was four feet long, with a wooden handle on one end and a loop at the other. The toggle rope was carried on their persons at all times and soon became like an extension of their bodies. It turned out to be an extremely useful piece of equipment for a soldier in the field.

Used by itself a toggle rope was a wonderful aid for scaling a wall. Several could be linked together to form a rope chain. The ropes could be interlaced to form a toggle rope bridge . . . There was no end of things they were handy for. After a short time, Raiding Forces began to wonder how they had ever managed to survive a single day without one.

A permanent rope bridge was strung between the beech trees that lined a beautiful, scenic spot along the River Arkaig. The instructors took great delight in watching their students gingerly make their way across as they mischievously tossed grenades into the water. One little misstep, and all sorts of acrobatics were performed fast, with the usual result of plunging everyone on the bridge at the time into the icy river.

"Cat-crawling" was another favored spectator sport—with the training cadre as the spectators. Spider webs of ropes were strung tree to tree across gullies or ravines, and one line even ran across the mighty Arkaig. In order to perform the cat crawl, a trainee Commando lay on the single strand of rope, torso flat, and pulled himself forward, with one leg dangling down for balance. The cat crawler had to pull with his arms and push with the one leg curled around the rope behind. While it was not as difficult as it sounded, it did take some practice, and the crawler had to focus his mind on the job at hand rather than the dangers that lay below, or he could lose his balance.

Along the way, the cat crawler encountered several small, wooden platforms to be negotiated. Nearby, a rope was tied to a limb. The cat crawler wiggled by, grabbed the rope, and swung to the platform, then let go and grabbed a rope boarding-net ladder. He climbed the ladder up to another rope and started cat-crawling again.

This made for a lot of climbing, crawling, and swinging. Because it was called the Tarzan Course, and the training was referred to as "Tarzan Training," the Commando students were encouraged to periodically shout vigorous, Saturday-matinee-movie-type Tarzan yodels as they trained.

The officers and men of Raiding Forces refused, to a man. What they did instead was give vent to loud, enthusiastic, high-pitched, ear-shattering Rebel yells at every opportunity, which they doggedly persisted in erroneously calling "Comanche yells."

While the Comanche yells did not produce the same instantaneous outrage from the Special Warfare Training Center instructors as they had from the parachute school instructors, the cadre did make note of the rebellious nature of the Raiders for redress at a later time and place of their own choosing. Instructors on tough military courses are wont to do things like that.

Naturally, Raiding Forces knew that would happen going in. In point of fact, they expected it. War had been declared. Things would have all been so much easier on everyone if Raiding Forces had just given those Tarzan yodels.

27

NOT MUCH SHINE

AT ACHNACARRY CASTLE IT WAS UP THE HILL AND DOWN THE HILL for Raiding Forces—in the rain, all day, and most of the night. The instructors fed them one meal a day and used sleep deprivation as a weapon, giving the Raiders a mere three or four hours of shut-eye per twenty-four-hour time period while they rotated in relatively fresh instructors. It soon became apparent to the staff, however, that the Special Warfare Training Center had only so many instructors to rotate, and the hard-charging Raiders were gradually grinding them down.

To make the job even trickier for the instructor staff, the Raiding Forces men were all qualified paratroopers, which gave them a self-anointed moral superiority over lesser men. Not one single Commando instructor at Achnacarry had ever jumped out of an airplane.

School cadre always had the advantage in a training environment, but in this case, it was not a big one. Esprit de corps could sometimes offset the instructor edge.

Commando training became a grim battle of survival, a relentless test, a marathon: brutal, ugly, and desperate, while at the same time wonderful. The war of wills between the Special Warfare instructors and the Raiding

Forces students became the stuff of legends. Comanche yells rang in the glens and valleys; they echoed from the foggy hilltops.

The men of Raiding Forces gradually figured out that they were capable of doing many, many times more than they had ever thought was humanly possible, which, when all was said and done, was the purpose of the exercise. That lesson could only be learned the hard way. *Crack on, Commando! Continue the mission.*

In time, the Raiders began to feel as if they could go on forever: No food, no sleep, soaking wet, straight up a mountain in a dense forest at night in a pouring rain, stopping only occasionally to huddle under a poncho and read a topographical map by flashlight fitted with a red lens filter . . . all in a day's work. Then, after planning it on the move, conduct a raid on an enemy position . . . piece of cake. When they did get a short break, the Raiders lay down and slept on the wet ground in the rain.

Raiding Forces did not even consider stopping the Comanche yells, though they curtailed them during tactical exercises. The instructor cadre never considered cutting them one inch of slack, not for one minute. There were no days off, weekend passes, or holidays. At Commando School they drove on, regardless.

No one realized it at the time, but a tradition was in the making. A standard of training was being laid down for all future generations of Commando students who passed through Achnacarry. Excellence was the standard for every task, and it was expected that every action would be performed at full speed. Nothing less than excellence was acceptable, nor was excellence deemed remarkable or even noteworthy; it was simply the minimum performance acceptable.

One instructor particularly impressed the raiders: Lieutenant Jeb Pelham-Davies from the Duke of Wellington's Regiment was a dark, good-looking, cigar-smoking officer who had been awarded the Military Cross. The men had a word with Major Randal, and Lieutenant Pelham-Davies was asked to become a member of Raiding Forces, the only officer to be invited in by the other ranks.

Early during the third week of training, Captain "Geronimo Joe" McKoy and Captain William Ewart Fairbairn arrived with a small contingent of

Royal Engineers. Being the old military salts they were, it took about ten seconds for them to recognize what was happening. They made themselves scarce, except for Captain Fairbairn's hand-to-hand combat class each day, not wanting to get caught up in the mad contest of wills. Occasionally, the two could be seen working with the small crew of Royal Engineers around an old, abandoned hay barn in a remote glen.

At the end of the third brutal week, the training had gradually shifted from such personal skills as map reading, signaling, rappelling, hand-to-hand combat, and combat shooting to small unit tactics. Compass and map work continued to be phased into all aspects of training.

The Raiders practiced map reading individually and in small teams, day and night, over wide distances, across the roughest terrain imaginable, in all weather conditions. Tactical exercises were incorporated into everything they did; every move they made was tactical. They ate, drank, and slept tactically. They always operated as if they were behind the lines in enemy territory.

The Special Warfare Training Center was the only place in the British Armed Forces where a daily training schedule was not posted for the students to read in advance, and their training missions changed frequently without warning. The idea was to keep the students off balance by constantly surprising them, thus adjusting them to rapid changes of mission. As Lieutenant Colonel Charles Edward Vaughan often liked to point out, "There is no training schedule in combat."

The school commandant could be fiendishly imaginative. One day he simply stopped issuing the troops their one meal per day. Instead, he had the rations hidden on remote compass points deep in the forest, one tiny food cache per team of student Commandos. Either read your map or starve.

It was good training.

In fact, it was superior training, the best in the world. It took a brave leader to break the news to a team of wet, hungry Raiders who had not eaten for a day and who were lost in a damp, dark Highland forest in the middle of the night that he could not locate the grid coordinate where their food cache was located. Before long, out of sheer necessity, all the Raiding Forces personnel had developed into competent map readers.

Captain Fairbairn became a daily fixture in their lives. Among international police officers and fighting men, the Shanghai Buster, a former assistant commissioner of police in Shanghai, was a legend in his own time. A pamphlet he had written called "Get Tough," outlining in simple, easy-to-understand steps what he described as "gutter fighting," became the Commando Bible.

The fiftyish, gray-haired captain wore round wire-rimmed glasses and looked more like a bishop than the killer he was. His philosophy was to "have a strong attacking manner."

He loved the Raiders' Comanche yell. "That's the spirit, lads! Your only purpose in life is to kill or disable your enemy; kill or be killed!" he shouted in his first of many bloodthirsty lectures on hand-to-hand combat. "There is no such thing as fair play; kill 'em all!"

"Never hurts to throw a scare into 'em while you're doing it, either, boys!" Captain McKoy chimed in.

The waterlogged, starving, exhausted, sleep-deprived men of Raiding Forces followed every word of the Shanghai Buster as if they were hypnotized zombies.

"There are five things you have to master: the edge-of-the-hand blow; the tiger's claw, which is a heel-of-the-palm strike; the chiu jab, a heel-of-the-palm strike used as an uppercut; the knee to the testicles; and the thunderclap, which is a strike with both palms held flat to the opponent's ears."

Captain Fairbairn demonstrated each move, and then he had the men pair off and practice each technique on one another . . . and practice and practice and practice. Raiding Forces worked on hand-to-hand gutter fighting at least two hours per day, every day.

One day Captain Fairbairn called them into formation. He held up an elegant, double-edged dagger with a six-inch blade and a checkered metal handle shaped like a Coke bottle. "Men, this beauty is a stiletto I designed in conjunction with my associate, Captain Sykes. We modestly call it the Fairbairn-Sykes Fighting Knife.

"The look and feel of this weapon is that of a surgical instrument. You should use it as delicately as an artist uses a paintbrush. The world famous sword-making firm of Wilkinson produced the first consignment. Each knife has a serial number, and one is going to be issued to each of you. Use it well, with my compliments."

One evening near the beginning of the fifth week of training, the commandant of the Special Warfare Training Center invited a battered Major John Randal to his private quarters in Achnacarry Castle for a drink.

"I understand more of your men will be joining us shortly, John."

"Yes, sir, nine men from the 60th Rifles and the Rifle Brigade, one Royal Marine, plus a lieutenant from the Blues that Captain Stone recommended. We were hoping for more Riflemen, but we lost a couple in parachute school."

"Good! Good!" Lieutenant Colonel Charles Edward Vaughan commented absently. The time had come to call off the war between his staff and Raiding Forces, but it had to be handled diplomatically. The situation was delicate; neither side could be seen as having given in.

"John, I received a rocket from Combined Operations that authorizes graduates of the school to wear the green beret as a symbol of achievement and excellence. Since the Commando Depot, as we will soon be called, will not officially be open for another six to nine months for individual students, and since you are training here as a unit, this ruling may or may not apply to Raiding Forces personnel."

"I see," mumbled a sleep-deprived, hungry Major Randal.

"My thought is, why not agree between the two of us that it does apply and award your men green berets when they complete the next week of training? In that way, as we move into the advanced tactical phase of unit training, your lads and my staff can approach the program more on the level of colleagues."

"Sir, that sounds like a really good idea," Major Randal agreed readily. He was not sure how much more punishment Raiding Forces personnel were going to be able to take. "Why don't we keep this a secret, though, so it's a surprise to my Raiders?"

"Capital idea," Lieutenant Colonel Vaughan boomed, much relieved. He was not sure how much longer his staff were going to be able to keep up with this insane pace of the training. Besides, the advanced tactical phase was all going to be done with live ammunition; the students would have loaded weapons—something that had been giving the "Laird of Achnacarry" plenty to think about in the wee hours of the night.

And so it came to pass that a message was dispatched to Captain Lady Jane Seaborn. In a feat of marvelous legerdemain, she somehow obtained the hat size of each man in Raiding Forces, procured a green beret to match, had the Raiding Forces flash sewn on, and had each individual Raider's appropriate regimental badge pinned under the flash. Each and every Raider's name was typed on a small strip of paper that was placed inside each beret to identify its owner, and then the berets were boxed up, placed on the train to Spean Bridge, and finally trucked from there up to Achnacarry—all in the utmost secrecy.

On the big day, a formation was mustered in front of the mist-shrouded Commando Castle. Lieutenant Colonel Vaughan took one of the new green berets sporting the King's Royal Rifle Corps bronze Royal Crown badge and placed it squarely on Major John Randal's head. Then the instructor staff moved in and walked down the ranks, presenting each Raider with his own personal green beret.

It was the finest of days . . . even though it was raining.

28

FIRST BUZZARD PLUCKER

THE LITTLE WALRUS AMPHIBIAN SPLASHED DOWN INTO THE SMALL bay at Seaborn House like a plump greenhead duck following a long cross-country flight. Tonight, weeks behind schedule, the first Buzzard Plucker mission was going to be launched. Squadron Leader Paddy Wilcox had flown partway up to the Commando Castle to pick up Major John Randal, who had come down on the train to meet the plane in order to go along and observe the team insertion.

The rules of the pinprick raiding game laid down that only people with a need to know were told the details of any operation. While on paper this was a good and militarily sound rule, in practice it was virtually impossible to accomplish in a small unit. It was particularly difficult when you also had powerful outside agencies looking over your shoulder with an intense interest in everything you were doing, planning on doing, or even thinking about doing someday in the future.

Thus, it was not a complete surprise when Major Lawrence Grand, the dapper leader of Section D, Special Operations Executive, arrived unannounced to observe the night's operation. He was not wearing his trademark Savile Row suit with a red carnation in the lapel or his smoked glasses. For this visit he was attired in battle dress uniform, sporting the regimental badges of the Royal Engineers.

All security was not lost, however. Neither Major Grand nor Commander Richard Seaborn, who was also in attendance, had any idea of the true nature of the mission being undertaken. They only knew that it possessed the colorful name "Buzzard Plucker" and consisted of a two-man team that was being put ashore on the enemy coast to be extracted later, at an unspecified time and place. Both officers assumed, wrongly, that it was a reconnaissance job.

Major Grand was aware that the team would be recovered by floatplane, but he kept that piece of classified information strictly to himself.

Neither of the two officers really cared what the Buzzard Plucker team's mission was. Major Grand wanted to see if Raiding Forces could actually put a team ashore at a specific point, and Commander Seaborn was there to observe his son in action.

There was no reason for the SOE officer to believe that the Raiders could successfully put a team ashore as planned. SOE's Naval Section, run by an experienced lieutenant commander on loan from the Royal Navy, had experienced an unbroken string of failures while trying to do the same thing. Since the war began, SOE had not been able to land a single agent by sea, and had not been able to establish even one cache of arms and explosives for the underground guerrilla army they were charged with raising to "set Europe ablaze."

No one in SOE's Transportation Section had any idea that Major Grand was observing the night's mission or that it even existed; he intended to keep it that way.

As the sun began to set, various parties trooped down to the dock and boarded HMY *Arrow*.

The last to board was Major Randal. He arrived at the dock accompanied by Captain the Lady Jane Seaborn. She surprised everyone by suddenly planting a huge kiss on his cheek. The sailors immediately stopped doing whatever they were doing and responded with a rousing cheer. Major Randal stumbled aboard the *Arrow* with scarlet lipstick on his face, and they set sail for the enemy shore.

The night was beautiful and clear. Commander Seaborn had impulsively volunteered to act as navigator. He had been the Navigating Officer on HMS *Hood* on one of her around-the-world goodwill cruises, showing the flag. The Royal Navy does not trust just anyone to navigate one of its capital ships.

Nevertheless, Commander Seaborn blanched when his son showed him the tiny pinpoint they had to find on the rugged coast of Brittany. Then, to his horror, he learned that the *Arrow* had not been fitted out with an echo finder, a range finder, or any other type of navigational aid. Navigation was going to be by chart and compass: dead reckoning the whole way.

A tiny chartroom about half the size of a typical water closet had been constructed under the bridge. There was barely enough room inside to turn around. The chartroom was claustrophobic with the door closed, and the commander would have to keep it closed the whole way in order to turn on the red light enclosed in a wire cage so he could read the chart. The minuscule space had the ambiance of the Black Hole of Calcutta.

Lieutenant Seaborn's voice called down the tube, "Did you note the sailing time, sir?"

Commander Seaborn had forgotten, badly distracted by the sight of his dead cousin's wife kissing Major John Randal. It had been a while since he had done any serious navigation. The chartroom was rolling madly and they were still in relatively calm waters. He did not want to think about what it would be like in any kind of a sea. Commander Seaborn reached up to adjust the red light, lost his balance, and banged his head.

Before long, the breeze stiffened and spray broke over the bow. Major Randal was wearing every piece of wet-weather gear he owned. Over his parachute smock he wore his Commando rubber rain jacket, and over that he wore a set of Royal Navy oilskins. He had a towel wrapped around his neck to keep the water out.

None of it worked. Those on the bridge quickly got wet and stayed wet.

Once at sea, they were on their own. Even though HMY *Arrow* carried a radio, the crew was forbidden to use it. The only time the signalman was authorized to break radio silence was to report the sighting of a major enemy warship under way. All hands unanimously hoped they did not find any reason to use the radio tonight.

Because the yacht was not configured to carry torpedo tubes or guns, if she did encounter enemy ships, she would have to rely on nimbleness, speed, and the skill of her young skipper to carry her through. The *Arrow* did carry a smoke-making apparatus, for what it was worth.

Dark nights always seemed best for this sort of clandestine operation, though there was some disagreement on that subject, it not being very easy to find one's way around once on land during a moonless period. Everyone topside was relieved when the sky clouded over. The water turned black.

In mid-channel the tidal streams were notoriously fickle. Although those within ten to fifteen miles of the Brittany coast were not overly strong, they did run at a right angle. Wind blowing in from the Atlantic could reach gale force in a surprisingly short amount of time.

HMY *Arrow* rolled alarmingly. The ocean boiled; lightning flashed. St. Elmo's fire danced in the aerial riggings, giving the illusion that they were sailing in a ship outlined by neon lights—the last place anyone on a surreptitious mission to an enemy-occupied shore wanted to be.

Most of their charts were out of date, having not been revised since the last war. This contributed to making navigation to a pinpoint on the rock-infested coast of Brittany extremely difficult. Considering that even a two-degree compass error could take them five miles off course, or that a slight miscalculation of the tide rates would put them on the rocks— meaning they would be dead—some might well have regarded the night's work as a suicide mission.

Cooped up in the coffin like chartroom, with ice-cold water leaking on his charts from the voice tube while he was being pounded against the sides of the narrow compartment, Commander Seaborn felt as if he were trapped in an elevator in a building that had been hit by a tornado. This was undoubtedly his worst night at sea ever. At times the *Arrow* actually did stand up on her stern and shake herself like a wet dog, exactly as Major Randal had described her. He silently cursed his father-in-law for giving the *Arrow* to his wife as a present. Then he cursed himself for having joined the Royal Navy in the first place.

There was no way he was going to find any pinpoint tonight. Commander Seaborn was cold, wet, battered, lost, and humiliated. He was also bleeding from a cut on his head. Probably it was just as well that he did not know about the St. Elmo's fire.

"Navigator, report to the bridge, sir," Lieutenant Seaborn cheerfully called down the voice tube many long, desperate, gut-wrenching hours later.

When the commander crawled dejectedly up on the deck ready to publicly admit defeat, he found every man of the crew scanning the port side through binoculars. No one even bothered to ask him their location. His son handed him a pair of night glasses and assigned him a sector.

"What are we looking for?"

"A white flare, sir."

Right at that instant, Major Randal called out, "White flare, Green three-zero-zero."

All hands immediately swung their glasses to the compass point.

"Steer Green three-zero-zero," Lieutenant Seaborn ordered as every pair of binoculars locked in on the azimuth.

"What is that flare?" Commander Seaborn inquired.

"The flare marks a point approximately three miles out, directly opposite our pinpoint, sir. Squadron Leader Wilcox has just dropped it for us from the Duck."

"You mean you never really expected me to be able to find the pinpoint all along?"

"No, sir," Lieutenant Seaborn admitted. "We simply hoped you could get us close enough to see Paddy's flare . . . and you did, Father."

"Won't the Germans see it, too?"

"They might, but they will not have any idea what it means. There are strange lights and sounds at sea all the time these days, sir."

Commander Seaborn felt a wave of relief flood over him. "I was never going to be able to find your pinpoint in this sea, and without being able to take a fix on the stars, I would have felt lucky to hit Brittany. If I had known I was ever going to have a night this bad, I would have gotten out of the navy after the Armistice."

"We have never found a pinpoint either, Father. I think it is practically impossible."

"What about the night you captured your German general? The newspaper said you acted on advance intelligence, enabling you to land with split-second timing and precision."

The young skipper gave his father a sheepish look. "A happy accident, sir. We—I mean, I—got lost. The general was in the wrong place at the wrong time. There was no advance information. Made a rather good story, though. That is classified by the way. Father, are you bleeding?"

"I did bang my head on the light cage."

Major Grand offered him a white monogrammed handkerchief. "You do appear to have a small gash, sir."

"Whoever came up with the idea of using an aerial flare to mark a pinpoint for small-unit operations deserves to be knighted. Capital idea, positively brilliant." Commander Seaborn put the handkerchief to his head.

"Randy suggested it in the Blind Eye one night a while back," Major Randal said, never lowering his binoculars. "Tonight is our first chance to try it out."

"You don't say!"

"The major says, 'It never hurts to cheat,'" Lieutenant Seaborn said. "One of our rules, Father."

Major Grand looked puzzled. "Am I missing something? The flare being dropped—is that not standard procedure?"

"I doubt it has ever been done before, Major," Commander Seaborn said, handing him back his handkerchief. "I have certainly never heard of it, and I keep up with all new developments in navigational aids. The concept is simple but revolutionary, which translates into pure, inspired genius."

"We came up with it out of desperation, Father."

"Execute Plan B," Major Randal ordered briskly.

Lieutenant Seaborn called down the voice tube, "Escort the Plan B topside."

Shortly thereafter, two armed Raiders brought a scruffy man in dark fisherman's clothing up on deck to the bridge.

"You showed him the chart?" Major Randal asked.

"Yes, sir."

"Good."

Major Randal pulled his Colt .38 Super from beneath his parachute smock, cocked it one-handed, and placed the barrel against the back of the man's head. Things got very still on the bridge.

"*Guidez-nous lá-bas, Louis,*" Lieutenant Seaborn ordered in fairly good schoolboy French.

Finding the pinpoint was one thing; actually reaching it was quite another. In many ways this was, in fact, the most hazardous phase of the mission. Every man on board, with the exception of Major Grand, who was not an experienced enough sailor to appreciate the degree of danger, peered hard into the dark waters, looking for the telltale sign of a white foam feather indicating a hidden rock or other submerged peril—all while coping with the effects of the onset of gripping fear. All it took was one little touch from a submerged rock, and *au revoir.*

Acting on the instructions of the fisherman with the pistol to his head, in no time at all the *Arrow* sailed with unerring accuracy to the small isolated beach predesignated as their pinpoint. A dead-on hit! Lieutenant Seaborn and Lieutenant Percy Stirling's snatch mission had paid off handsomely. HMY *Arrow* nosed in to shore as close as they dared.

Lieutenant Harry Shelby was summoned up on deck with the two Lovat Scouts, who were both barefoot, their pants rolled up to their knees. He helped them over the side into the dinghy manned by a Lifeboat Serviceman, then climbed in. The dinghy set out for shore.

"Why were those men barefoot?" Commander Seaborn demanded.

"That's classified, sir," Major Randal replied, though he had no clue why the Lovats were going in without their boots on.

Twenty long, drawn-out minutes later, the dinghy was paddled back, minus the Lovat Scout sniper team. Lieutenant Shelby came back on board and reported that the two men had made it ashore without any problems.

Operation Buzzard Plucker had now commenced.

"If that's what you call cheating on the navigation," marveled an impressed Commander Seaborn after his son explained exactly who the

Frenchman in the dark fisherman's clothing was and how he had been "recruited," "I heartily recommend you cheat every chance you get!"

"Let's get the hell out of Dodge, Randy," Major Randal ordered, interrupting him.

HMY *Arrow* arrived home just as dawn was beginning to break.

Major Randal was pleased that the night's work had gone exactly as planned. Lieutenant Seaborn—whose crew had tagged him with the nickname "Hornblower," after the famed fictional hero created by C. S. Forrester, following the mission to kidnap the inshore pilot—and his partner in crime, Lieutenant Stirling, had certainly done well. The two young officers had clearly demonstrated they could be counted on to carry out independent operations.

Walking off the dock, Major Grand managed to arrange a private word with Commander Seaborn. "I say, was what we did tonight rather all that difficult, sir?"

The Royal Navy officer looked at the engineer in unqualified surprise. "What you witnessed, Major, was nothing less than a masterpiece of navigational improvisation. I like to pride myself that I am one of the most capable navigators in the service, but when I came up on deck, I would have bet you the chances of finding our pinpoint were precisely zero."

"They made it look easy, Commander."

"Quite!"

"Not very sporting, what?"

"Devastatingly effective is the way I would categorize it."

"Interesting."

"It most certainly was for me."

29

BIRD BOMBS

FORTY-EIGHT HOURS LATER, IN HIS LIVING QUARTERS AT SEABORN House, Major John Randal was standing in the shower, head down under the jet. He let the water run a long time. There had not been any hot water at Achnacarry, and he was taking every opportunity to indulge himself during his short time away, though he did feel a pang of guilt that the rest of Raiding Forces was hard at it up in Scotland.

"Sir," Chauncy called through the door, "Lady Seaborn has sent me to inquire if you would be so kind as to join her."

"When?"

"At your earliest convenience, sir."

"Is fifteen minutes okay, Chauncy?"

"I shall inform Lady Seaborn, sir."

Captain the Lady Jane Seaborn opened the door to her suite on his first knock. Major Randal decided, once again, that she was the most attractive woman he had ever seen, in real life or in the movies. The effect she had on him was not wearing off with time, and that definitely was not a good thing.

"Hello, John. I have had dinner served over here for us tonight. Paddy took off two hours ago. We can expect him back with the Scouts any time."

Normally there was a panoramic view of the English Channel out the big bay windows. Tonight, because of the Blitz, the windows were covered in blackout curtains. Although the spectacular view was eliminated, the effect was to make the small, candlelit setting especially cozy.

Captain Lady Seaborn had a surprise she had been saving. "John, we are conducting two PWE operations in conjunction with Buzzard Plucker. They are, in effect, separate missions within our original mission."

He clicked on.

"I briefed PWE on Buzzard Plucker, and they had a suggestion for a cover operation they had been contemplating as a stand-alone operation but had not put into execution because the RAF are being difficult about supplying aircraft. When Paddy either inserts or extracts the Scout teams, whichever best fits the mission profile, he is going to drop two parachutes weighted down by blocks of ice in a preselected area away from the actual target location. The parachutes will float down to the ground and the blocks of ice will melt. The idea is that when the German Security Forces find the empty chutes, they will be forced to conduct a search in the wrong location for what they believe are two British parachutists."

"Beautiful!"

"Mystify and mislead. It should tie up quite a lot of German troops on a fool's ploy. And it will force them to conclude we have agents on the ground, up to mischief."

"What's the second operation?"

"You are going to laugh."

"Can't be worse than the man-eating sharks."

"Yes, it can. Paddy is also dropping dead pigeons."

"You're kidding."

"I am not," she said, laughing. "The dead pigeons have little capsules attached to their legs with fake messages in them."

"What kind of fake messages?"

"The one they mentioned to me was that Combined Operations is dropping hundreds of ghost troops with completely silent weapons into

France to kill Germans. The idea is to provide additional cover for Buzzard Plucker and to frighten the occupation forces at the same time. No doubt there will be other clever little messages we do not have any need to know."

"PWE hopes the Germans find the dead pigeons and read the messages?"

"That is the plan."

"Paddy is bombing occupied France with dead birds?"

"And we can never tell. Are we having fun yet?"

"I sure am. I love those Political Warfare guys."

"Dropping the ice blocks and parachutes is called Operation Limelight, and dropping the dead pigeons is Operation Whistle. Both are classified 'Most Secret—Need to Know Only.' PWE has even assigned a liaison officer here at Seaborn House for the duration of Operation Buzzard Plucker. We are off to an extraordinarily fast start with PWE."

"Can I go along some night and chuck out the dead birds?" Major Randal asked.

"PWE is running one other deception to cover Buzzard Plucker."

"I hope it's as good as the other two."

"They have supplied the Lovat Scouts with standard-issue German Army boots—"

"Oh, that's beautiful," Major Randal interrupted. "Now I get it. The Scouts go ashore barefoot; no one can tell the nationality of one set of bare footprints from that of another. Once the Scouts get off the beach, they put on jackboots. No cause for alarm if a German patrol stumbles across the footprints because there have to be at least a million pair of jackboots marching around France."

"Even better," Captain Lady Seaborn explained. "If the security forces do find any Lovat Scout's tracks—and they probably will, at least in the hide position outside the perimeter of the landing grounds—the Jerries will be forced to draw the conclusion that rogue elements from within the German Army sniped the pilots."

Major Randal looked at her blankly.

"The idea is to create the false impression that there is an active anti-Nazi resistance movement within the German military," Captain Lady

Seaborn went on. "Trust me, John, PWE revels in this kind of mind game. The idea of Germans shooting Germans is going to drive the Nazi internal security services mad."

"All I wanted to do was shoot a few bad-guy fighter pilots."

"The gentlemen of Political Warfare Executive are literally beside themselves," Captain Lady Seaborn continued. "Buzzard Plucker has evolved into an extremely sophisticated intelligence operation."

"You've got to hand it to those PWE studs," Major Randal grinned. "They keep it short, but it sure ain't simple."

"And we get the credit."

Chauncy appeared. "Lieutenant Shelby directed me to inform you that Squadron Leader Wilcox has radioed he is inbound and will be arriving in approximately thirty minutes, sir."

Major Randal threw his napkin on the table and let out a whoop. He had been more anxious about the outcome of this first Buzzard Plucker mission than he wanted to admit. He couldn't wait to get down to the dock.

When he and Captain Lady Seaborn arrived, Lieutenant Harry Shelby was already standing on the dock next to a stubby, sawed-off telephone pole with a flat, red wooden box mounted on it. Inside the red box was a sound-powered field phone. Shortly after the Rolls had pulled up, the phone in the wooden box clattered. Lieutenant Shelby answered it. After a brief conversation he hung up and then threw a switch mounted next to the wooden box. A string of floating landing lights came on out in the bay. The lights were low-powered globes that reflected a golden glow on the water.

In the distance it was barely possible to hear the soft, muted droning of the little Walrus pusher biplane making its final approach. Before long, the ungainly aircraft appeared out of the dark indigo night sky and splashed down. The landing lights were immediately extinguished. After a short run, the plane turned and taxied to the dock.

Two snipers in long-haired ghillie suits climbed out of the back compartment of the Walrus, their headpieces removed so the major could see they were really men and not gorillas. True to form, the two Lovat Scouts were already wearing their distinctive dark blue Scout bonnets with the blue and white dicing.

Scout Munro Ferguson, the shooter, was cradling his .275 Rigby rifle in his arms as if it were a natural appendage.

The other sniper, Lionel Fenwick, who in Lovat Scout nomenclature was described as the "glassman," was wearing a 20X Ross spotting telescope in a leather case hung over his shoulder and carrying a Browning A-5 shotgun. The men were dirty, unshaven, tired, and happy.

Captain Lady Seaborn produced a large thermos bottle and poured them each a steaming cup of tea.

"How'd it go, men?" Major Randal asked.

The Lovat Scout with the rifle did not say anything; he just stood silently, looking off into the distance, sipping his tea. The glassman held up two fingers. "Two buzzards plucked, sir."

"Nice work!"

"Give us a good night's sleep and a couple of warm meals, and we want to get back over there," Scout Fenwick stated in no uncertain terms. "Buzzard Plucker is the mission we Scouts have been preparing for our entire lives, sir."

The shooter blew the steam on his mug of tea and gave an almost imperceptible nod in agreement. These two young Scouts were ruined men; hunting the wily Highland red stags would never be the same for them. Now they knew what their grandfathers had discovered in South Africa while stalking Boers, and their fathers had learned in France while sniping Huns. The Lovats had gotten a taste of it and wanted more.

Major Randal caught the night train back to Achnacarry right after the debriefing.

30

SWAMP FOX FORCE TO ACHNACARRY

A WEEK OF INTENSIVE COMMANDO TRAINING LATER, MAJOR JOHN Randal and Lieutenant Colonel Charles Edward Vaughan were standing outside the Spean Bridge railroad station in the rain, waiting for the train. Major Randal was wearing his forest green Commando beret with the regimental crest of the King's Royal Rifle Corp centered over his left eye and pulled down low, just above the eyebrow. Stitched above the regimental crest was the silver-threaded Raiding Forces flash.

Raiding Forces' training program was progressing exceptionally well. Captain "Geronimo Joe" McKoy was teaching snap-shooting techniques to the Raiders with their A-5 Browning shotguns as well as deliberate and instinct shooting with their Colt .38 Super automatics. His mantra was, "Watch the front sight close, touch her off, and adios! Take your time in a hurry."

The mystery house that the old Arizona Ranger, in collaboration with his associate Captain William "Shanghai Buster" Fairbairn, had designed out of an old barn in which to teach close-quarters shooting techniques and house clearing had become the Raiders' second home. Raiding Forces personnel fired colossal amounts of ammunition at the pop-up targets the two trainers had devised; they had become deadly accurate marksmen. A considerable amount of training was devoted to familiarizing themselves with handling and shooting foreign allied and enemy weapons.

The last phase of the training consisted of pure tactics and covered the complex problems of small-scale raids and ambush and counter-ambush techniques, with heavy emphasis on all types of patrolling and night operations. There was no blank ammunition to be had at Achnacarry. Every drill was live fire.

Amphibious training was a part of virtually every exercise. Raiding Forces would land by boat somewhere—under fire from the school instructors, who were in concealed positions ashore—then the problem would start from there.

Today, Major Randal was at the railroad station to meet the newest recruits to Strategic Raiding Force. Arriving direct from the No. 1 Parachute Training School would be nine Riflemen from his old Swamp Fox Force at Calais, plus one Royal Marine. A tall cavalry officer whom Captain Terry "Zorro" Stone had recommended for Raiding Forces, Lieutenant Taylor Corrigan of the Horse Guards Regiment, who had completed the parachute school in the same class, accompanied them.

The plan was for Major Randal, along with Lieutenant Colonel Vaughan, to lead the new arrivals on what was becoming the traditional "Welcome to Achnacarry" speed march up to the castle. Then he was going to immediately return to Spean Bridge Station and catch the overnight train back to Seaborn House.

Major Randal was going down to inspect operations that had occurred since the initial Buzzard Plucker mission. He wanted to see for himself how the Lovat Scouts were progressing and to check on Lieutenant Percy Stirling's railroad-busting mission, Operation Comanche Yell. Also, he had to admit he was looking forward to a chance to spend more time with Captain the Lady Jane Seaborn.

The train pulled into the station, hissing steam. Eleven newly minted parachutists stepped off, followed by Major John Rock, RE, and Squadron Leader Louis Strange of No. 1 Parachute Training School. Both officers were carrying bulging briefcases.

Lieutenant Corrigan called the small formation to attention, saluted Lieutenant Colonel Vaughan, and reported as if he were on guard mount at Buckingham Palace. "Sir! Lieutenant Corrigan and ten volunteers reporting for Commando training, sir!"

"At ease!" Lieutenant Colonel Vaughan bellowed back in his face from a range of about six inches, nearly blowing the Blues officer backward off his feet. The colonel heartily approved of all things done in a vigorous military manner, though he harbored the innate infantryman's suspicion of cavalry officers. "Have your men collect their bags, stow them on the truck, and be ready to move out in five minutes, Lieutenant."

"Sir!"

As soon as the formation broke up, Major Rock and Squadron Leader Strange approached Major Randal.

"What are you two doing here?"

"Hoping to have a word with you, Major," Squadron Leader Strange responded.

"Bad timing, I'm afraid," Major Randal answered in a brittle tone. He still hadn't forgotten the turret jump at parachute school. "I'm getting ready to speed-march seven miles to Achnacarry Castle, change clothes, come back here, and catch the train to my headquarters at Seaborn House. What's this about?"

"We have a proposition we hope you may find interesting."

"Well, you can come along and brief me on the march if you like, though I must warn you, it's straight uphill the whole way, and it's not going to stop raining."

The two officers from No. 1 Parachute Training School exchanged unhappy glances. A forced march in the rain wearing their walking-out uniforms was not exactly what they had in mind.

"Or, you can make arrangements to travel back on the train with me. I have a private compartment. It's only a single sleeper, but there should be enough room for us to sit and discuss whatever it is you have to talk about in private, without being rushed or disturbed."

"That sounds like the better plan," Squadron Leader Strange agreed.

"In that case, you two can wait here in Spean Bridge or ride up to the castle in the truck that brought us down and take a quick tour of the Special Warfare Training Center."

"We would appreciate the opportunity to visit the Special Warfare center."

"See you at the top of the hill, then. This won't take long. Somehow, Colonel Vaughan got it in his head that a Commando can march seven miles in one hour if he wants to. We won't go that fast today, but it will be pretty close."

Lieutenant Corrigan re-formed the troops. Lieutenant Colonel Vaughan ordered, "Pipe Major, 'Blue Bonnet.'" The bagpipes launched into a tune that sounded something like the wail of a cat whose tail has been run over by an armored car. The knock-kneed drummer banged his drum and wobbled off, giving false hope to the troops that followed. Surely the man could not make it farther than fifty yards without keeling over? He could. When they reached the castle at the top of the hill, the drummer would be as fresh as a daisy and still pounding away like there was no tomorrow.

As their boots crunched in unison over the bridge spanning the Caledonian Canal, Lieutenant Colonel Vaughan commented, "These Riflemen will make fine leavening to your force, John, what with cavalrymen being a bit high strung at times. They shall make an excellent mix. Were they all with you at Calais?"

"Yes, sir, including Corporal Duggan, the Royal Marine." The formation was going at a terrific pace now, almost double time.

"All volunteers for Raiding Forces?"

"Yes, sir."

"Outstanding! Speaks well of you, young Major."

Major Randal dropped back to introduce himself to Lieutenant Corrigan. Captain Stone had said simply, "Tay plans to go to parachute school and then transfer to one of the Commando battalions. Look him over, John, and if you like him, keep him."

Lieutenant Corrigan was a handsome, self-assured young officer who seemed to wear the mantle of command effortlessly. Major Randal had carefully noted how the Swamp Fox Force men responded to his orders. It was obvious the Calais Riflemen respected the lieutenant.

"Thanks for the opportunity, sir," Lieutenant Corrigan said when Major Randal pulled in alongside him.

"How'd you like parachute school?"

"Good training, sir."

"Get ready. The first two weeks at Achnacarry make parachute school seem like kindergarten."

"Splendid," the Blues officer said, deadpan.

"How'd my Riflemen do?"

"Outstanding . . . A tad cynical about that business at Calais . . . Have quite good things to say about you, sir."

"I can see how they might be a little cynical."

"Sir, something came up during training concerning Comanche war screams. Do you have any idea what that was about? We could never quite cipher it out."

"You will, Lieutenant."

Major Randal dropped back and marched alongside Royal Marine Corporal Mickey Duggan.

"Top o' the morning to you, sir."

"How was jumping from an aircraft while in flight, Corporal Duggan?"

"I am not an altitude man, sir."

"Neither am I," Major Randal laughed. "You don't have to like it; you just have to do it."

They marched along in silence for a while. "You're a school-trained signaler, not just a Marine who knows how to signal?" asked Major Randal.

"Yes, sir. Semaphore, naval signal flags, telegraph, and wireless. I used to be a ham operator when I was a lad, and I can build a radio out of a fountain pen and a ball of string. Communications is my hobby as well as my military specialty."

"You saved us at Calais, Duggan. I learned a valuable lesson from that experience."

"What lesson was that, sir?"

"Every Raiding Forces trooper needs to know how to send and receive Morse and semaphore. You're going to be my chief of signals. A promotion goes with the title. There's a catch, though."

"There usually is, sir."

"You have to teach Morse and semaphore to every man in Raiding Forces, including me."

"If you make the training time available, I can teach them, sir."

"You'll get the time."

Major Randal continued to drop back in the column, enjoying brief talks with each of the Green Jackets. Spending time with the troops was what he enjoyed most about being a commanding officer.

Bringing up the rear was Sergeant Mike "March or Die" Mikkalis.

"Any problems at parachute school, Sergeant Mikkalis?"

"No, sir. The Riflemen took to jumping out of an airplane like ducks to water. We lost two men, though. Rifleman Finley suffered a severe ankle sprain on his fourth jump. He plans to heal, finish the course, and marry up with us later. Rifleman Moore washed out. Moore claims he will recycle and be back."

"We can use them. You can't possibly have any idea how happy I am to have you men here, Sergeant Mikkalis, you especially."

"Thank you, sir." The sergeant sounded pleased.

"You can expect me to really be leaning on you once we go operational again. We're having to make this small-scale raiding stuff up as we go along."

"I'm looking forward to it, sir."

"Tell the men to get ready for some really rough training."

"We concluded that after we saw you at Spean Bridge Station, sir. None of us remembered you as being quite so lean and hard."

"Sergeant Mikkalis, you never got around to telling me how you came to be in the KRRC after leaving the Foreign Legion."

"After my tour in Africa with the Legion, I never wanted to serve with zombies again. I joined the regiment because the King's Royal Rifles have the most intelligent individual troops in the army, led by the most forward-thinking officers in the world, sir."

"Good reason."

The rain came down. The bagpipes wailed. The drum boomed. And the hill got steeper and steeper.

"That's Ben Nevis, men," pointed out Lieutenant Colonel Vaughan for everyone's edification. "My staff like to trot over there, run up the hill in the morning, and be back before lunchtime."

"How far is it from the school, sir?" Lieutenant Corrigan inquired conversationally.

"Eighteen miles, but Ben Nevis is only a little more than four thousand feet high."

After that it became quiet in the ranks for the rest of the march.

"Welcome to Achnacarry Castle, formerly the clan seat of Sir Donald Cameron of Lochiel and now the home of the Holding Unit, Special Warfare Training Center," Lieutenant Colonel Vaughan announced grandly when they marched through the gate. "Here, we are going to teach you how to employ every art of Commando warfare known to the Boer, the Chicago gangster, and yes, men, even the wily Comanche . . . "

Major John Randal's bags were already packed. He quickly showered and changed into service dress uniform, linked up with Major John Rock and Squadron Leader Louis Strange, then drove back down to Spean Bridge Station in the commandant's car.

When they reached the village, the three officers proceeded to the lobby of the quaint old Spean Bridge Hotel, where they waited out of the rain for the night train to arrive. Over tea, Major Rock and Squadron Leader Strange continued to discuss the training they had observed. Major Randal could tell they were simply marking time; the two officers were quite obviously champing at the bit to get down to the real purpose of their visit. He wondered what it was.

When the whistle sounded, the three officers paid their tab, walked over to the station, and boarded the southbound train.

It was still raining.

31

FROGSPAWN

THE TRAIN WAS PRACTICALLY EMPTY. AS IT MADE ITS WAY DOWN
the length of Scotland and most of England to London, it would gradually
become full to bursting with soldiers, sailors, airmen, and Marines.

Once on board the train, the three officers repaired to Major John
Randal's tiny overnight sleeper compartment. It was small but opulent,
with prewar mahogany-paneled walls and a miniature crystal chandelier.
There was barely enough room for the three of them to squeeze in.

Steam hissed loudly, the whistle blew, the conductor called, "All
aboard," and the train chugged out of the station.

Once they were under way, Squadron Leader Louis Strange cut
straight to the main point. "We have a proposition for you."

"Shoot."

"Everything we are getting ready to tell you is classified 'Most
Secret.'"

"Wait," Major Randal ordered, standing up from his miniature leather
club chair. "Give me your pistol belts."

The two officers looked startled but unbuckled their canvas web belts
and handed him their side arms.

Major Randal slung the two pistol belts containing two new-issue .38-caliber Enfield revolvers over his shoulder, left the room, and made his way, swaying through the mostly empty train, to the club car, where he found a mixed assortment of troops drinking, relaxing, and shooting the breeze.

Sitting at the bar were two rugged-looking Royal Marines with their side caps stuffed jauntily under the epaulets on their shoulder and their ties loosened. They each had a beer mug in one hand and a cigarette in the other.

Major Randal signaled them to come to the door of the car. With looks of undisguised disdain, they slowly stood up from their stools, ground out their cigarettes, and sauntered over to where he stood. The Marines took their time about it. They had come aboard from the Amphibious Warfare Training Center at Inveraray and were headed to London for some hard-earned shore leave. Army officers were not high on their list at the best of times, much less when interrupting their holiday.

All three stepped out on the walkway between cars.

"Men, I have a mission for you," Major Randal said.

The two Marines exchanged unhappy glances. "Sir?"

"Put these pistols on. I'm going to station you at both ends of the car where my private sleeper is located. If anyone tries to listen in at the door of my room, shoot 'em."

"Shoot them? *Bang*! Just like that, sir?" one of the Marines asked, skeptically.

"Actually, it would probably be better if you detained 'em so I could conduct an interrogation, but if anyone tries to eavesdrop and resists you, shoot 'em, *bang*, just like that."

The two Royal Marines looked at each other and perked right up. "Aye, aye, sir!"

"Good. After my meeting, I'll buy both you men dinner in the first-class dining car for disturbing your leave."

"Thank you, sir!" they chorused. No officer had ever made them an offer like that before.

Major Randal walked back to his sleeper and disappeared inside.

Shortly after the door closed shut, one of the Marines drifted silently down the narrow corridor to have a word with his mate. "You know who that is?"

"Just some bloody Yank officer, probably has a woman stashed in there and does not want her bloody husband to crash the party."

"That's Randal, the pinprick raider. You know who he is, mate, the one what went over and snatched a blinkin' Nazi general, that's who."

"Back to your post, then; this might actually turn into something."

Squadron Leader Louis Strange began his briefing as soon as Major John Randal returned, minus the pistols. "You already know I command No. 1 Parachute Training School, and Major Rock, among his other duties at the school, is responsible for developing and testing equipment for airborne operations.

"What you most likely are not aware of is that we are also members of the syndicate charged with developing national airborne doctrine. Right now the book on airborne doctrine is almost completely blank. All we know is that you can use parachutes, gliders, or in certain cases, conventional, powered troop transport aircraft for the purpose of aerial envelopment.

"Aerial envelopment basically means you fly over the hardened edges of an enemy force and drop by parachute or land in their soft rear areas. Or, it can mean that you unexpectedly strike a hardened target from above. Probably it can also mean quite a few other things we have not figured out yet.

"There are currently two schools of thought on aerial envelopment. One idea is to do it en masse, with clouds of parachutists smothering a target. The other concept is to use parachutists or glider-borne troops, like Commandos, to attack small, point-type targets and withdraw or be quickly relieved.

"The debate boils down to big versus small, parachutes versus gliders. The extreme end of the big concept is to land entire airborne armies, complete with artillery, tanks, and all supporting arms. The extreme end of the small concept is to limit airborne operations to dropping individual saboteurs.

"Within the framework of the big versus small debate there is another burning question to be resolved, and that is, which delivery method is more effective: parachutes or gliders?

"Since he is a sport glider pilot, Rock is a convincing champion for our airborne forces to be composed completely of glider-borne troops. In a nutshell, his argument is that you can take any ordinary infantryman, simply stick him in a glider, and presto, you have created an instant airborne trooper.

"When a glider lands, you have the advantage of the troops on board having unit integrity. Gliders can carry fairly heavy equipment, which means glider troops land as a team, armed and ready to fight as a cohesive unit.

"The argument for a parachute force is more difficult to make. I am not even going to attempt that today. In any event, Rock always wins. On paper, he has the superior argument."

Major Rock, who had not spoken a word this whole time, permitted himself a big smile.

"Are you two planning to settle the argument?" Major Randal asked.

"Absolutely!"

"How?"

"Rock and I propose to pick two point-type targets and attack them. We will attack one with a parachute force and the other with a glider-borne force. Then we will have actual results to evaluate, instead of pure theory.

"Where do you intend to conduct this experiment?"

"For the initial raid we have selected an isolated target on the coast of France. The plan is to go in by parachute and to withdraw by sea."

"So you're pretty far along with this?"

"Oh, yes."

"Why are you telling me?"

"We want you to command the operation."

"You want Strategic Raiding Force to conduct a test-tube experiment against a hard target in order to prove a theory? I hope you noted the word 'strategic' in our name, Squadron Leader. We picked that word to specifically discourage wild-goose chases."

Major Rock spoke for the first time. "This mission *is* strategic, John. It will be the test bed used to refine the tactics and doctrine shaping the development and deployment of airborne forces for the rest of the war. We had hoped to appeal to your American pioneering spirit."

"Do you know how you recognize pioneers? They're the ones with the arrows in their backs." Major Randal took out a Player's Navy Cut and lit it with his old, worn Zippo. "Why don't you tell me what this is really about?"

"I was afraid you were never going to ask," Major Rock said, pulling out his bulging briefcase. "What I am going to show you now is quite probably classified above 'Most Secret.'

"When the German High Command designed its plan to attack France, it had to find a way to move swiftly through Holland into Belgium. The plan was for two panzer corps to make the assault. However, they could only cross the Albert Canal by way of three bridges. Capturing the bridges did not pose a military problem the Germans couldn't overcome; however, the Belgian fort that covered them, Eben Emuel, was thought to be invulnerable from ground or air attack.

"Eben Emuel was constructed to be an impregnable fortress consisting of nineteen casements, containing cannons ranging from 30-mm to 120-mm and manned by six hundred fifty elite Belgian artillerists, backed up by twelve hundred support troops. It was a given that the artillery would be able to pick off the attacking German tanks like clay pigeons as they crossed the canal.

"On 10 May 1940, a party of sixty-five German assault engineers in eleven gliders towed by JU-52s cast off and landed directly on top of Fort Eben Emuel, blew in the exits to prevent the troops inside from escaping or coming out to counterattack them, then leisurely went round and destroyed the guns in the casements that covered the bridges.

"The initial phase of the operation lasted less than five minutes. Victory was assured in that period of time. And by that, I mean the victory that ended up with you escaping off a pier under fire at Calais one dark night."

Major Randal studied the photos and diagrams of Fort Eben Emuel. Most of the fort was underground, with heavy concrete cupolas peeking up that contained the cannons. The fort was surrounded by a moat backed up by a twenty-foot wall and certainly looked impregnable. The German glider-borne assault engineers appeared to have accomplished the impossible—in under five minutes.

"Well, I'm impressed."

"We have to learn how to carry out the same kind of unorthodox operations," Major Rock explained. "British Armed Forces have never contemplated anything like Eben Emuel."

"Then why don't you start with a glider raid first, and mirror what the Germans did?"

"Because there is not a single military glider in England," Squadron Leader Strange said in a sardonic tone. "Only recently we had to put on a glider demonstration at Ringway for the prime minister utilizing single-seat sports gliders flown by civilian pilots. There were, as I recall, a Mini-moa, a Rhonbussard, a Condor, a Viking, and three Kirby Kites."

Major Randal looked at the two officers, recognizing them for what they were: dedicated, overworked, under-supported, far-thinking, highly gifted patriots who were doing what a lot of other desperate military visionaries in every branch of the armed forces, including Raiding Forces, were doing all over Great Britain at the moment—sweating bullets, trying to figure out a way to get back in this war without much to work with.

"I hope the target you have in mind for me isn't anything like Eben Emuel."

The two officers from the No. 1 Parachute Training School visibly relaxed. "This is going to be a test, not a full-scale invasion, Major."

Squadron Leader Strange pulled out a map. "We have selected a small Kriegsmarine naval signals station located near an isolated lighthouse on a cliff overlooking a tiny beach as your target. The beach is ideal to withdraw your troops from. Several possible drop zone sites are located near the target. You drop in, raid the signals complex, go down to the beach, board boats that will be waiting for you there, and come home.

"What say you, Major?" Major Rock demanded.

"I say it's going to take detailed study, precise intelligence, extensive planning, and realistic rehearsals. And it must all be done in the utmost secrecy, executed with split-second timing and absolute precision. Home is a long swim if everything doesn't work out exactly the way you two airborne pioneers hope it will."

"You agree then?"

"It's what Raiding Forces is in business for, gentlemen."

Major John Randal then left the compartment and proceeded to do something he would never have believed, even in his wildest imagination.

First he dismissed the two Royal Marines after establishing a time to hook up with them later for their promised dinner, and then he made his way to the very end of the train.

"May I be of some service, sir?" the conductor in the caboose car inquired.

"I need to place a phone call."

"We have a scheduled stop in approximately two hours, Major."

"When do we reach the next station?"

"Sir, we will pass a station in about five minutes, but the train will not be stopping."

"I want to place the call from the next station."

"Major, we cannot stop this train for you to make a phone call," the conductor snapped peevishly, his eyes angry behind his round, wireframed glasses.

"Frogspawn."

The conductor froze. "What did you say, sir?"

"You heard me."

"I shall require some ID, sir," the conductor said in a submissive tone he normally reserved for the peerage.

Major Randal was fairly sure it was not his military identification card the conductor wanted to see. While unbuttoning his magnificently tailored Pembroke's blouse, he made it a point to open the jacket far enough so the man could see the special inside pocket with the two-button security flap and catch a glimpse of the checkered walnut grip of his Colt .38 Super in the shoulder holster.

He unbuttoned the flap, withdrew the credential holder in the pocket, and handed it to the conductor. The small pigskin leather case that Captain the Lady Jane Seaborn had provided him for use in "special exigencies" contained impressive credentials signed by some very important people.

One document was a letter that read:

```
To: British consuls, senior naval, military,
and air commanders, and civilian officials
to whom the bearer may deem necessary to
present this letter:

This is to certify that Major J. Randal,
MC, is on special duty under War Office
direction.

Provide him all assistance in your power,
to include priority transport by sea, land,
or air. Under no circumstance impede this
officer.

J. M. E. Simpson-Smyth, Brigadier G.S. for
Director of Military Operations & Plans
```

The conductor handed the credentials back by two fingers as if they were red hot. "Please keep your call as short as possible," he said pithily. "The line does have a schedule to keep, sir."

"I will be brief."

When the train stopped, the conductor accompanied Major Randal off and led the way into the station to supervise arrangements for him to make his phone call in the utmost privacy.

"Captain Lady Seaborn," the smoky voice at the other end of the line announced.

"Hello, Jane."

"John! I thought you were on the night train," she responded in a tone not quite so official.

"The train stopped so I could call. Can you meet me at Seaborn House?"

"Is this business, John, or do you simply wish to see me?"

"It's not all business."

"Pam and I can leave right now. We shall meet you at the station in the village when your train arrives."

"Perfect."

"Question before you ring off?"

"Better make it quick."

"Do I still remind you of your high school English teacher?"

"Roger that!"

On the other end of the line he could hear her deep-throated laugh.

Major Randal tried to rationalize what had just happened by telling himself he had only been testing the credentials to see if they worked, in case he ever needed them in a real emergency. He could almost come up with a legitimate reason to justify what he had done . . . the operative word being "almost."

All of a sudden, Major Randal was struck by the nearly uncontrollable urge to walk back to the caboose, "frogspawn" the prissy conductor, stop the train, and call Jane all over again just to hear her voice one more time.

THE MISSION

32

TEST TUBE

WHEN THE TRAIN ARRIVED AT THE TINY STATION IN THE CHARMING little village near Seaborn House, Major John Randal was the first passenger to step off. Two husky Royal Marines came right after him, carrying his bags. Squadron Leader Louis Strange and Major John Rock trailed along behind.

When he saw Captain the Lady Jane Seaborn, he kept himself under tight control as regulations prohibited things like overt displays of affection in public while in uniform. In fact, the two acted as if they barely knew each other.

"These two young studs think they want to join Raiding Forces," he said to her, nodding toward the Marines. "Squadron Leader Strange has slots for them at the No. 1 Parachute Training School. Can you arrange the orders?" he asked.

"The Royal Marines will never consent to a transfer," she answered. Then, noticing the crestfallen looks on the faces of the two men, she quickly continued, "However, if you lads are keen enough to volunteer for an organization so secret that I am not allowed to tell you its name beforehand and even its initials are classified, they will cut orders having you reassigned to Raiding Forces before tea time."

"Whatever it takes, ma'am," Royal Marine Butch Hoolihan responded. His mate nodded in agreement.

"Provide Marine Plum-Martin with your service numbers. She will make the arrangements," Captain Lady Seaborn ordered. "Welcome to Raiding Forces, Marines."

"Thank you, ma'am," the two men chorused in bullfrog-deep voices.

Neither man had ever seen a female Royal Marine before, much less such a stunningly beautiful titled officer; they were not exactly clear on the correct protocol. Both men dimly remembered having been briefed in some distant military courtesy class that First Aid Nursing Yeomanry officers were to be addressed as "Madam," while officers in the Women Accepted for Volunteer Emergency Service, or WAVES, were addressed by the less formal "ma'am." To the best of their recollections, their instructor had never mentioned female officers in the Royal Marines.

To add to their confusion, the sight of Royal Marine Pamela Plum-Martin nearly made them swallow their tongues, if their expressions were any clue. "Good luck, men," Major Randal called as he got into Lady Jane's Rolls.

The ride to Seaborn House did not take overly long. No one said very much on the drive because it was not clear to all present—Squadron Leader Strange, Major Rock, Captain Lady Seaborn, and Major Randal— exactly who had a need to know what, making the atmosphere in the luxury sedan a trifle edgy.

Around one bend in the narrow country lane they came upon what looked like a band of refugees from a Gilbert and Sullivan farce, spread out on both sides of the road in ragged column formation. In the group were a combination of white-haired old men and teenage boys, wearing brassards and outfitted in a diverse collection of army and navy uniforms that dated as far back as the relief of Khartoum.

The entourage was armed with a variety of sporting shotguns along with a sprinkling of kukris, assegais, Bowie knives, cavalry sabers, cutlasses, and an assortment of improvised bludgeons. The local Home Guard was coming in from its early-morning anti-invasion/anti-infiltrator sweep, a recently instituted daily ritual blithely referred to by the local wags as the "Dawn Patrol."

Recognizing the Rolls-Royce, they stood aside and let it pass. One "parashot," as the Home Guardsmen were sometimes called because they were expecting to have a crack at Nazi paratroopers, appeared to be a lieutenant general at least eighty years old serving as a private. He signaled for them to drive on.

"Was that man armed with a golf club?" Major Randal asked.

"I believe it was a seven iron, sir," Royal Marine Plum-Martin informed him, never taking her eyes off the road.

"Lucky for you, they chose not to stop us," Captain Lady Seaborn said straight-faced. "The parashots take their work seriously, and they have a pronunciation test for suspects. A list of words like 'soothe,' 'wrong,' 'wretch,' 'rats,' and so forth—words Germans are not supposed to be able to pronounce. I rather doubt they have ever heard a California accent. They might have clapped you in irons, Major."

"It would be easy to write off the Home Guard," Squadron Leader Strange said. "However, within six days of the call going out, over a quarter of a million men and boys volunteered. And by now, I understand, there are well over one million of them patrolling the towns and countryside, with their numbers swelling."

"I hear there is even a Home Guard unit made up of members of Parliament guarding Whitehall," Major Rock added. "Imagine that: armed politicians."

"Lovely," Major Randal said softly.

Seaborn House could be reached only by a single, winding road or by boat. The river-bounded side of the estate was guarded by the Home Guard, which meant, from the looks of things, it was virtually undefended.

As had been the case for months now, a full-scale German invasion of Great Britain was thought imminent, though it was generally understood that this most likely hinged on the Luftwaffe being able to obtain air supremacy first. To date, the Germans had not been able to gain control of the skies, thanks to the gallant efforts of the hard-fighting Royal Air Force Fighter Command (now known to the world as "The Few"), with a little help from an extremely secret Operation Buzzard Plucker, which was aiding the attrition of German fighter pilots.

Major Randal was surprised to see a brightly painted, red-and-white-striped barber's pole blocking the road a mile from Seaborn House. A sandbagged Bren gun position was opposite the barrier, and the gun was out in plain sight, which meant it was a distraction. There was, most likely, another concealed Bren position hidden somewhere nearby, not visible from the road. The roadblock was manned by efficient-looking military police wearing steel helmets and armed to the teeth.

The men were not ordinary MPs. The blue band painted around their steel helmets indicated they were security specialists from the Vulnerable Points Wing. Each man was equipped with a rifle, a pistol, and a baton. At night they patrolled with sentry dogs, Major Randal soon learned.

The tough-looking, no-nonsense guards at the checkpoint did not raise the barber's pole for the Rolls-Royce, even though they had already inspected it when it passed through on the way to the railroad station only a short while before. Instead, the MPs ordered Royal Marine Plum-Martin to stop, step out, and open the boot of the automobile. The detached, cold-blooded professionalism with which they conducted themselves conveyed the impression that they would just as soon shoot you as look at you.

Taking no chances before allowing the Rolls to proceed, they peered inside the windows of the big sedan to make sure there was no possibility of any Nazis being stowed inside. The security detail was very polite, very thorough, very professional, and as detached as a band of serial killers.

"When did this happen?" Major Randal inquired once they were again under way.

"Right after you appointed me intelligence officer. They work for you, John," Captain Lady Seaborn said.

"I see."

"Probably looking for German parachutists disguised as nuns," commented Major Rock, idly. "I should feel sorry for any they apprehend."

As they started up the drive to Seaborn House, Major Randal asked, "What officers are in residence now?"

"Randy is here, as well as Paddy, Harry, Percy, and Karen."

"Have all of them except Lieutenant Shelby assemble in the formal dining room in fifteen minutes."

The domestic staff lined up outside on the driveway to greet the arrival, as was their habit anytime that Lady Jane had been away for more than a day. Major Randal suddenly realized that she had already been to the house, so they must be there to greet . . . him?

He was pleasantly surprised to find Chauncy standing at the end of the greeting line. "Hello, Chauncy. You're looking fit. Been running the stairs at the Bradford to the bunker lately?"

"Yes, sir. At least once a night, sometimes more. Daytime, too, on occasion."

"Air raids that often? I'm going to want a complete briefing." With Raiding Forces isolated in Scotland, Major Randal had not been aware that London was getting pounded so hard.

At that moment he heard, high overhead, the ominous, low-pitched drone of an approaching armada of high-level Heinkel and Junkers bombers. All of them in the car craned their necks and shaded their eyes with their hands to see. In the pristine blue sky, layer upon layer of bombers, looking like Vs of high-flying geese in perfect formation, winged their way toward London with the sun glittering off their silvery fuselages.

As they watched, the RAF arrived on the scene and dived into action. With their high-performance fighter engines screaming and their light, rapid-firing .303 Vickers air-to-air machine guns chattering, the battle was joined. The fighters, probably Hurricanes, though it was impossible to tell at this distance, had little visible effect at first. The massive Luftwaffe juggernaut of bombers continued to roll on toward the capital like an angry swarm of bees with evil intent and deadly precision, looking to be invincible and unstoppable. And in fact, they were.

A few trails of blue-gray smoke intermingled with the white contrails as more RAF fighters arrived on the scene, vectored from other sectors to the aerial battleground. Gaps began to appear in the Vs of the German bombers as one and then another enemy aircraft spiraled down, trailing corkscrew tendrils of dark smoke.

Major Randal and the rest of the spectators were spellbound by the three-dimensional panorama unfolding above. Little puffs of parachutes dotted the sky as some of the German fliers managed to bail out of their stricken airplanes. Several bright flashes of fire appeared in the sky. The thunder of bombs, apparently jettisoned by Luftwaffe pilots desperately trying to lighten their aircraft, could be heard detonating in the distance. Inexorably, the swirling melee kept slowly moving on in the direction of London and finally passed from sight.

"Have the people I designated report to the main dining room," Major Randal ordered curtly.

"Yes, sir," Captain Lady Seaborn replied in a subdued voice.

They were all affected by the sight they had just witnessed. The stark contrast between the omnipotent, robotic military precision of the German Luftwaffe aerial armada and the golf club–toting Home Guardsmen was impossible to ignore.

When the designated officers had assembled, Major John Randal immediately turned the floor over to Squadron Leader Louis Strange. Neither he nor Major John Rock needed any introduction.

"Gentlemen—and, ah, ladies—I am here to inform you that Strategic Raiding Force has been selected to make a night parachute drop to conduct a raid on a German shore installation located somewhere on the coast of France," Squadron Leader Strange began. "The raid is scheduled to take place in approximately three weeks' time, and it will be the first British airborne operation of the war."

He opened his briefcase and withdrew a stack of aerial photos. "The installation is situated on a prominent terrain feature distinguished by a working lighthouse. There is a path running down the cliff from the lighthouse to a small, isolated beach below the objective, where landing craft assault boats will be waiting to transport the raiding party home upon the conclusion of the operation.

"Now, at this point I suspect that Major Rock has a few comments he might like to make. Rock is going to be dropping in with Raiding Forces to observe firsthand the operation. Major?"

The Royal Engineer stood up. "We really do not know very much about this Airborne Forces business, actually, having come rather late to the game. Leonardo da Vinci invented both the parachute and the glider over four hundred years ago. Typically, our side has just now gotten around to concluding that the idea may indeed have merit. As usual, we have to learn from scratch and try somehow to catch up.

"The parachute raid we are planning is designed to be a test-tube operation. Raiding Forces has the honor of being the guinea pigs in our little experiment . . . "

33

COMMANDER'S COMMENTS

SEATED AT THE FOOT OF THE LONG, POLISHED TABLE, MAJOR JOHN Randal waited until after Major John Rock sat back down before carefully laying out his directives on how they were to proceed. It was important, he believed, for a commander to set the tone for an operation right from the start.

"While it has been described as a test-tube experiment," he began, "this is a mission worth doing, a history-making event: the first British parachute raid ever. Strategy and tactics for future, larger airborne operations will be developed based on what we do or don't do.

"How we go about planning, task-organizing, training for, and executing this raid will be studied and critiqued by military professionals and armchair experts for a long time to come. So let's get it right."

Around the table it grew quiet. There was electricity in the air: excitement, mixed with apprehension, coupled with dread of the unknown. This mission was the one they had all been waiting for—the one each of them had known would be coming some day.

"Since we don't have a staff, I request that Major Rock be temporarily attached to Raiding Forces to serve as mission operations officer."

"Done," barked Squadron Leader Strange.

"Security is paramount. Captain Lady Seaborn, in addition to being the intelligence officer, is going to be saddled with the additional responsibility of being the mission security officer."

"Yes, sir," Captain the Lady Jane Seaborn responded in her clipped, professional tone.

"To pull this off, we have to get in, execute our operation fast, and pull out fast. Actions on the objective: Rock, I want you to allow each team leader to plan his own scheme of maneuver, subject to my approval."

"Roger."

"Draw up a task list for me as soon as possible. I will make individual assignments."

"A preliminary task catalog is already prepared, but I would like a chance to review it again before I present it to you," Major Rock replied.

"Good. Now, Rock, you'll eventually come up with an air plan. My guess is we'll require at least three jump aircraft for the mission. I want you to have a contingency plan for every possible scenario in the event they do not all make it to the drop zone.

"Squadron Leader Strange, you said Coastal Forces would be responsible for the withdrawal phase?"

"That's correct."

"Let's get a liaison officer from Coastal Forces assigned as soon as possible."

"I will see to it immediately."

"Mission planning and the initial rehearsals can take place at Achnacarry. Our normal routine there should be adequate cover. Captain Seaborn, you and your Marines make plans to relocate to the hotel in Spean Bridge; you can commute to Achnacarry."

Captain Lady Seaborn nodded, rapidly making notes.

"Squadron Leader Wilcox, I want you read into the operation so you can advise me on all air aspects of it. What I do not want is for this mission to interfere with your Buzzard Plucker duties."

"Wilco."

"Squadron Leader Strange, you're responsible for making sure the pilots fly practice missions with the exact same mission profile they intend to fly on the night of the actual raid. I want them to practice this mission until they can fly it in their sleep."

"Done."

"Lieutenant Montgomery, we'll need parachutes for training and the actual jump. Make it happen. As of right now, you are also the assistant intelligence and security officer."

"Yes, sir!"

"Plum-Martin, put a call through to Achnacarry for me immediately after we finish this meeting."

"Who would you like to speak with, sir?"

"Colonel Vaughan."

"Yes, sir."

Major Randal looked around the table. "What are your questions?"

Major Rock inquired, "What is Raiding Forces' troop strength available for this raid?"

Major Randal turned to Squadron Leader Strange. "Can you run Lieutenant Pelham-Davies and the two Marines I recruited on the train through the short course?"

"Should not pose any unusual problem, Major. We can have them back to you within a week with six jumps under their belts. There is no reason their qualifying seventh jump should not be into France."

"In that case, Rock, you can count on twenty-four men and five officers available to make the jump. In a pinch, we have an additional four sailors and five Lifeboat Servicemen available, plus Lieutenant Seaborn, all parachute-qualified and partially cross-trained as Commandos. Don't hesitate to use them. They're all capable men."

Major Rock nodded, jotting down the numbers.

"Sir," Lieutenant Randy "Hornblower" Seaborn said, "I have been sitting here thinking. An amphibious operation is like an onion. You peel the layers off, one layer at a time."

"What's your point, Lieutenant?"

"There are many things that can go wrong, sir, when you get the navy involved."

Strained silence greeted his comment. Finally, Major Randal said stiffly, "Thank you, Lieutenant Seaborn, for the insightful observation on the perils associated with joint operations in company with the British Royal Navy."

"Nothing more can go wrong with the navy side of things than you can expect from the bloody RAF," Squadron Leader Wilcox added, gloomily. "Even with the best Whitleys in the air fleet, it will require a miracle to get all three troop transports over the drop zone."

What they were planning was nothing less than the most complicated combined arms, small-scale raid ever attempted by British Armed Forces. In Major Randal's opinion, it was a healthy sign that everyone recognized the inherent difficulty factors. He was not, however, under any circumstances, going to allow negativity to exert an influence on mission planning.

"People, if this was going to be easy, the Home Guard would be doing it. Anyone else care to comment?"

When no one said anything, Major Randal abruptly ordered, "Squadron Leader Wilcox, Captain Seaborn, Lieutenant Seaborn, Lieutenant Stirling, Lieutenant Montgomery, and Royal Marine Plum-Martin, stand fast. I want to see you immediately after we finish here. This meeting is adjourned."

Squadron Leader Strange and Major Rock obviously were not happy to be excluded from what was clearly a post-meeting meeting. Major Randal pointedly ignored their inquisitive looks as they reluctantly left the room. "Shut the door on your way out," he ordered in a no-nonsense tone.

"Pam, go round up Lieutenant Shelby and ask him to join us," he added, even before the door slammed shut.

"Aye, aye, sir."

When he was alone with his Raiding Forces people, Major Randal said, "Now listen up. There's nothing we can do to keep this mission from being complicated. When I speak to Colonel Vaughan in a few minutes, I'm going to ask him to arrange for a team of climbers to come in by sea and scale the cliffs above the beach simultaneously with the drop. They will be tasked with putting ropes in place for the raiding party to use when coming back down during the withdrawal phase. Randy, your primary mission will be to deliver them there in the *Arrow*."

There was a discreet knock on the door, and Lieutenant Harry Shelby, followed by Royal Marine Pamela Plum-Martin, quickly entered.

"Jane, pull the map of our target," Major Randal ordered, casually lighting a cigarette. He exhaled a stream of blue cigarette smoke while Captain Lady Seaborn riffled through her stack of classified documents. When she produced the topographical map, she spread it out on the table, weighing down the corners with ashtrays.

"Harry, I'm going to need a quick in-and-out reconnaissance of an objective we shall call Target X, for lack of a better name."

Lieutenant Shelby studied the map. "Am I permitted to ask why, sir?"

"No, all you need to know is you're tasked to perform a reconnaissance mission not associated with Buzzard Plucker. I want you to personally take in a recon team to eyeball Target X to confirm that the buildings in the aerial photo are what they appear to be, that there are no other camouflaged structures, concealed weapons positions, hidden equipment, troop units, or anything else we don't know about in the target area. Make a head count of the enemy personnel, but you need to be very discreet. The people on X must never realize you've paid them a visit.

"As soon as you're back, I want a personal report. You'll probably have to come up to Scotland to deliver it."

"When do you want my lads to have their boots on the ground, sir?"

"As soon as possible, Harry, if not sooner."

"I can fly Harry's team in, as well as extract it," Squadron Leader Wilcox volunteered. "There's a lake we can use, less than three miles from the target."

"Okay, then, if there is nothing else," Major Randal ordered, bringing the conference to a close, "you all know what you have to do. Let's get to it."

As Major John Randal strolled down the hall to his next meeting with Captain Lady Jane Seaborn, he was surprised by how much pleasure he got from simply being with her. Real Commandos, being life-takers and heartbreakers, were not supposed to have romantic feelings . . . at least he did not think they were.

Right now, he was heading to a meeting with Lieutenant Percy Stirling for a report on Operation Comanche Yell. Then he was scheduled to inspect the French schooner that Lieutenant Randy "Hornblower" Seaborn was having refitted for clandestine arms-running operations to France on behalf of Special Operations Executive.

Immediately after that, he was due for a detailed briefing on Buzzard Plucker from Lieutenant Harry Shelby. Following the Buzzard Plucker briefing, he was scheduled for a conference with Squadron Leader Paddy Wilcox to discuss the status of Raiding Forces' air operations. By that time it was going to be time to get back with Major John Rock to review his mission task list.

The exigencies of war made time a precious commodity; somehow, war warped the accepted concept of time, causing it at times to stand dead still and at other times to flash by like a movie reel at high speed. Even during the periods when the clock seemed to be standing rock-solidly frozen in place, there was always the uneasy sensation of rushing forward toward something . . . but what?

As they walked, Captain Lady Seaborn briefed him on Political Warfare Executive's Operation Limelight and Operation Whistle.

"Limelight seems to be paying dividends," she said. "We have confirmed reports of massive manhunts in the areas where Paddy dropped the parachutes weighted down with blocks of ice."

"Outstanding."

"Of course, we had hoped that Limelight would be a contributing factor to the success of Buzzard Plucker by drawing the Nazis' attention away from the areas where the Lovat Scouts are actually operating, and that appears in fact to be what is happening. Even better, though, is that it is tying up substantial numbers of enemy forces on fruitless searches for phantom parachutists. PWE is loving it, needless to say."

"How's it going with the dead pigeon bombing?"

"No feedback on Operation Whistle at this time."

"I can see how it might be hard to get a dead bird to report," Major Randal said. Captain Lady Seaborn gave him an indulgent smile.

"John, on another subject, I have a question for you," she said.

"Fire away."

"When you ordered the conductor to halt your train to call me, did you say, 'Frogspawn'?"

"How else was I going to get him to stop?"

"You could have given the conductor a written note and had him send me a radiogram. But . . . I had the impression you simply wanted an excuse to talk to me."

Major Randal looked her square in her beautiful green eyes and said, "That's right, I did. And I nearly 'frogspawned' that little conductor again just to hear you giggle one more time."

"I do *not* giggle!"

"Yes, Jane, you do," he said, feeling as though for once he had acquitted himself pretty well with her.

"And I *still* remind you of your old high school teacher?"

"Roger that."

"How were your grades? One would imagine having a beauty queen like Miss UCLA as your English teacher must have made concentrating during class dreadfully difficult."

Major Randal stared at her, dumbstruck. How could she ever possibly have found out about Miss UCLA?

The brilliant, million-candle-powered smile Lady Jane set off zapped him like a death ray.

"You certainly know how to pay a woman a compliment," she said.

"It's easy. All you have to do is be an idiot."

"You *are* fun, John Randal."

"I can see how you might think so."

34

RANDAL'S RULES FOR RAIDING

TWO DAYS LATER, ALL RAIDING FORCES PERSONNEL AT ACHNACARRY assembled for a briefing at 1000 hours. The air was charged with an electric sense of anticipation, coupled with a liberal dose of suspense.

Major John Randal was standing at the front of the round-topped, tin Nissen hut, next to a canvas-draped, three-legged map easel as the officers and men filed in. A smaller easel that was also covered stood to the right of it. He was idly tapping his leg with a wooden pointer.

Unlike most commanding officers, Major Randal chose not to have his troops assemble, keep them waiting a fashionable period of time, and then make a showy entrance. When the Raiding Forces commander briefed, he preferred to arrive first so he could look each man in the eye as he filed in. His men had learned from past adventures that when that happened, they'd better get ready. The commander being the first man in the room set the tone: It had a chilling effect on horseplay and contributed a certain amount of gravity to the event.

Since the Raiders could also not help noticing the heavily armed, stone-faced squad of special military police, in their first appearance at the Special Warfare Training Center, forming a tight perimeter around the hut, by the time they entered the room they were wired tight with expectancy.

The canvas-covered map board—with the implied seriousness and secrecy of what it might reveal—conveyed the conviviality of a ticking time bomb!

"This is a warning order!" Major Randal barked in a sharp, staccato tone, making it sound like a jump command. The men assembled could almost hear the snap of tension in the room. They could taste it, and it tasted like iron.

"Raiding Forces has been alerted to conduct a parachute raid on a point-type target located somewhere on the continent of Europe. Effective immediately, all training will cease. Mission preparation will commence following the conclusion of this briefing.

"With the exception of Lieutenant Shelby and the Lovat Scouts, who are detached for an ongoing operation, every officer, noncommissioned officer, and man of Raiding Forces will participate, including those personnel who are presently away completing parachute school.

"Our mission is to conduct a parachute raid on an enemy signals station-slash-lighthouse complex, to capture or kill the enemy personnel in the target area, to collect any equipment or documents of intelligence value, and to withdraw by sea.

"This mission will be of short duration. From the time the first jumper exits his aircraft over the target until the last man is extracted by landing craft assault boat and shoves off for home, no more than ninety minutes will have elapsed.

"Here is your target." Major Randal flipped the canvas cover over the back of the easel.

The troops saw a simple schematic diagram of the objective. The drawing showed a point of land jutting out into the English Channel. There was a circle labeled LIGHTHOUSE on the tip of the finger of land. Beside the lighthouse were six small rectangular boxes labeled BUNKERS, four on one side and two on the other.

On the land side behind the lighthouse was a small square labeled COMMAND POST/OFFICERS' QUARTERS. Just past this square and angled slightly away was a square labeled SIGNALS STATION.

To one side of the lighthouse was a larger rectangle labeled TROOP BARRACKS. Running the length of the map was a set of parallel lines labeled COAST ROAD. All the objectives were located between the coast road and the Channel. Off the coast road was a large, flat-bottomed, horseshoe-shaped driveway leading into the target area.

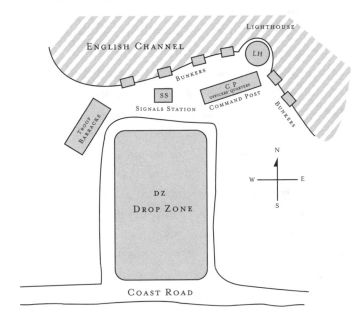

"The area inside the horseshoe is our drop zone," Major Randal said, touching the map with his pointer. "We will begin our attack from there.

"I'm now going to designate the assault team commanders. Each assault team commander will be responsible for planning his own scheme of maneuver, determining how many men it will take to accomplish his individual task, and picking his team.

"Captain Stone: signals station.

"Lieutenant Pelham-Davies: barracks. Since Lieutenant Pelham-Davies will not be back from parachute school until the end of the week, Sergeant Major Hicks, acting as his assistant team commander, will select the men for the team and develop the initial plan of attack on the troop barracks.

"Lieutenant Stirling: lighthouse and bunkers five and six, located here and here," Major Randal said, indicating two bunkers to the right of the lighthouse.

"Lieutenant Corrigan: bunkers one through four, located here, here, here, and here." The pointer touched each objective.

"Sergeant Mikkalis: coast road security. You will place a road interdiction party here and here," Major Randal said, pointing to both ends of the objective. "The two road security teams will fold back and act as rear security as we move down the cliff to the beach for extraction." The tough-as-nails King's Royal Rifle Corps sergeant nodded slightly, locking eyes with his commander, showing no sign of emotion. Sergeant Mike "March or Die" Mikkalis would be the last man out, once again. So be it.

"Lieutenant Montgomery, you are responsible for the parachute rigging detail. Major Rock will act in the capacity of mission operations officer and will be jumping in with us as an observer.

"Captain Lady Seaborn is the mission security officer as well as the intelligence officer. She has prepared a target profile for each of you team commanders. Pick them up on your way out.

"Colonel Vaughan is organizing a cliff-climbing team. This team will land on the beach below the lighthouse simultaneously with our drop. Their mission is to scale the cliffs and put ropes in place for Raiding Forces to have available during the withdrawal phase, in the event the paths down the cliff are too steep to use or are mined.

"Lieutenant Seaborn will have the task of transporting the cliff-climbing team to and from the target area.

"Sergeant Duggan, you will accompany Captain Stone in the assault on the signals station as his assistant team commander and will be responsible for identifying any signals equipment or documents of intelligence value that we need to bring back with us. You will also be responsible for all signals communication between Raiding Forces and the Royal Navy during the withdrawal phase.

"I will personally lead the team that attacks the CP and Officer's Quarters."

Major Randal faced his team. "What are your questions?"

"How many enemy personnel can we expect to encounter on the objective, sir?" Captain Stone asked crisply.

"Good question. There are an estimated thirty Kriegsmarine signals personnel in the target area. Just because they are not Waffen-SS doesn't mean we should take them lightly. Make your plans as if they were."

"Will you be making another turret jump, sir?" Lieutenant Percy Stirling inquired innocently. The room filled with snickers and the tension cracked.

Major Randal wore a bemused expression and studied the troops in the room calmly before he answered. These were the moments he lived for; at times like this he always felt like something of a lion tamer. You had to be very careful or the lions would gobble you up.

"No. However, you may be, Lieutenant, if you ask any more questions like that one." The room erupted in loud guffaws, probably a lot more enthusiastic than the circumstances justified, as the troops let off a little stress. That was a good thing. "Personally, men," Major Randal continued, "I'd rather jump without a parachute than climb out on a Whitley's turret again."

"Yeeeeeehaaaaaa!"

"At ease! Are there any more questions? No? Then I have something else I'd like to go over with you. These are what I call 'Rules for Raiding,'" he said, tapping the second, smaller covered easel with his pointer.

"I don't claim to have thought them up. I did compile them, which means I stole them, fair and square. You'll all be issued a copy."

Major Randal flipped over the cloth cover. There were seven rules. He went down the list.

"Rule 1: The first rule is—there ain't no rules.

Rule 2: Keep it short and simple.

Rule 3: It never hurts to cheat.

Rule 4: Right man, right job.

Rule 5: Plan missions backward (know how to get home).

Rule 6: It's good to have a Plan B.

Rule 7: Expect the unexpected."

The occasional laugh or murmur of approval punctuated the silence in the room as the men absorbed the rules. Rule 5 was clearly a Raiding Forces favorite.

"At this time, Captain Lady Seaborn will conduct the pre-mission security briefing."

The Royal Marines officer marched briskly up to the front of the hut. This was her debut performance as Raiding Forces' intelligence officer. Though she was dressed in a tailored battle dress uniform, no one would have mistaken her for just another one of the troops.

"Beginning this very moment, Raiding Forces is in pre-mission isolation and will remain in lockdown until conclusion of the operation," she said in a no-nonsense tone. "You will not discuss this Raiding Forces mission with anyone. I repeat: Anyone not in this room—with the exceptions of Lieutenant Pelham-Davies, the two Royal Marines he will be bringing with him when he returns from parachute school later this week, and Lieutenant Seaborn and his crew—is strictly off-limits for discussion of any aspect of this mission. Is that clear?" She stared at them long enough to make her point, then continued.

"It has come to my attention that some of you—I shall not embarrass anyone by naming names—have been sneaking into Spean Bridge at night after lights-out to visit your local girlfriends. Do not try it again! If you should, you will be immediately placed under close arrest, held in confinement until the mission is completed, then RTU'd."

A hush of disbelief fell over the room. A few men were thinking, *How in the world could she have found out?* while the others were wondering, *Can that possibly be true?*

"Is that clear, Captain Stone?" she demanded. The Royal Marines captain's eyes were sparkling mischievously as she gazed down at the popular Life Guards officer sitting in the front row with a sick expression plastered on his handsome face. It was a knockout punch.

There was a moment's stunned silence, and then every man in the room was on his feet with a roar, chanting, "Zorro, Zorro, Zorro." They rocked the hut.

Captain Lady Seaborn let them have their fun. She had made her point and at the same time won her spurs. No one present in that room was ever going to see her in quite the same way again.

"Do not, under any circumstance, discuss Raiding Forces' mission with any of the No. 1 Independent Company troops training in the area," she continued. "In fact, do not even talk to them at all. Do not discuss the missions with any of the Special Warfare instructor staff. They have no knowledge of the operation and do not have a need to know.

"If you observe a security violation, report it to me immediately, no matter what time, night or day. Your report will be kept confidential. The lives of the men sitting on either side of you depend on keeping every detail of what we are planning an absolute secret. This operation is classi-fied 'Most Secret.' The Official Secrets Act is in effect."

Then Captain Lady Seaborn rewarded her audience with one of her spectacular smiles and concluded: "I am quite sure the bonnie Scottish lasses are going to be most unhappy with me after today. War is hell, boys!"

The Commandos, to a man, stood up again and applauded her perfor-mance as she marched to the back of the Nissen hut. A sheepish Captain Terry "Zorro" Stone and a few other Raiders were careful not to make eye contact as she went by.

A certain amount of guts was required to stand up in front of the Raiders Forces and threaten them, which is what she had just done. Cap-tain Lady Seaborn had managed to conduct herself with the exact right amount of panache.

As Major Randal passed her in the aisle on his return to the front of the room, he shook his head and tried not to laugh any harder than he already was.

"Never hurts to cheat," she whispered with a wink as they passed each other.

"Thank you, Captain Lady Seaborn, for that most interesting and illuminating intelligence information," he said as soon as he stepped back in front of the room. The Commandos laughed nervously. The troops were not entirely sure how their commander was going to react to finding out that some of them had been going AWOL at night. The major could be unpredictable about things like that.

"Men, it's nearly fifteen miles round trip to Spean Bridge, and it's always raining. You've been averaging only about four hours off to sleep," he marveled. "The march alone eats up most of your time."

"Not if you move on the double, sir," an anonymous voice called from the back of the room.

"Well, it's clear to me that you Raiders have been in these hills way too long. The minute this operation is over, you're all going on a ten-day fur-lough and it's not going to count against your accumulated leave time."

The cheering was loud, long, and straight from the heart. Major Ran-dal let them get it out of their system. Finally he ordered, "At ease!"

When the men settled down, he continued. "Out of admiration for your impressive nocturnal feats of endurance and your unquenchable, ah, spirit, I think it's entirely appropriate that we designate our upcoming mission Operation Tomcat. But hear this loud and clear: From here on, there isn't going to be any of that 'returned to unit' stuff. If I catch anyone sneaking out of camp, I'll just shoot you myself and we'll write it up as a training accident. Is that clear?"

"Clear, sir!" the men of Raiding Forces thundered.

"Now, if any of you know a woman worth getting shot over, let me know. I'll go with you."

Sergeant Major Maxwell Hicks bellowed, "'Ten-shun!" the instant Major Randal started down the aisle for the door. Every man and woman in the room sprang to his or her feet immediately. They remained at a rigid position of attention until the major had left the building and some-one in the back near the door called out casually, "At ease."

The mission clock was officially ticking.

35

PREPARING FOR TOMCAT

AS EVER, THE RAIN WAS COMING DOWN WHEN THE TRAIN PULLED into Spean Bridge Station. Major John Randal was returning from a whirlwind trip to London and to the No. 1 Parachute Training School to brief Combined Operations Headquarters on Tomcat. He had also met with the RAF pilots who would be flying the Tomcat mission. Lieutenant Colonel Charles Vaughan was waiting on the platform in the mist.

Major Randal's first thought was *Oh no, not again*! when he saw the Special Warfare Training Center commander. A seven-mile speed march in the rain was not something he wanted to do every single time he returned to Achnacarry. Today he was in luck; Lieutenant Colonel Vaughan was there to give him a ride to the castle in his Humber staff car.

They rode in the back while the driver, Private Jimmy Wilson, skillfully ran through the gears and the Humber sped quickly out of Spean Bridge, crossed the Spean River, and motored up the hill on the Inverness road, all the way to the top. They went left at the fork, and then Private Wilson downshifted at the bend marking the spectacular rapids called Mucomir Falls.

As they drove up the scenic road in the mist and rain, the colonel briefed Major Randal on developments while he had been away. Before he got started, he barked at his driver, "Wilson, that's a King's Own Yorkshire Light Infantry badge on your beret, is it not, lad?"

"Sir!" responded the puzzled driver, aware that his CO knew perfectly well that it was.

"Do you have any idea where the 1st/4th battalion of your regiment is presently stationed?" the Commando School commandant inquired with all the affability of a Tyrannosaurus rex.

"No, sir!"

"Iceland. Do you know what they have in Iceland, Wilson?"

"Ice, sir?"

"And a lot of it. If you were to somehow suddenly find yourself RTU'd, do you have any idea what battalion you would be going to?"

"1st/4th, sir?" Private Wilson queried in a worried tone.

"Very good, lad. Now, the major and I are going to have a little conversation while you concentrate on keeping us on the road. Everything we say is classified 'Most Secret.' You are not going to hear a word of it. If you do, pretend you do not, because if I find out that you've repeated so much as a single syllable of anything we say back here, that very day you will be on your way to join the KOYL in Iceland before the sun goes down."

"*Sir!*" the driver fairly shrieked.

The imposing colonel turned back toward Major Randal. "John, I have assembled a first-rate team of cliff climbers, under the command of Captain Clive Haig-Tredberry, to land and scale the cliff below Tomcat. Every last one of them is a world-class climber. Haig-Tredberry was in Nepal, training for an assault on Mount Everest, when the war broke out. He is currently helping to organize the Mountain Warfare School. I rang him up and explained our situation, and he volunteered to personally organize and lead the cliff-climbing team."

"Perfect!"

"'Right man, right job,' I believe one of your rules said," Lieutenant Colonel Vaughan quipped. "There is, however, one matter of considerable importance that I feel has not been given adequate consideration."

"What's that, sir?"

"During the withdrawal phase there is bound to be substantial confusion. You will have need of a hard-nosed beachmaster to make sure things proceed smoothly according to plan. Your raiding element is most likely going to be arriving helter-skelter on the beach and possibly under fire. You will probably have some prisoners, and you may have casualties to contend with. Things could get sticky fairly quickly."

"Who do you recommend?"

"Me, of course. Every trooper in Raiding Forces will recognize my gentle voice in the dark."

"Colonel Vaughan, you're far too valuable a trainer of men to risk on operations. COHQ will never agree to letting you go."

"Hmm. Well, we wouldn't actually have to tell anyone until it is all over, now, would we, John?"

"Sir, I can't think of anyone I would rather have watching my back. Don't you go getting yourself killed on me."

"I would not think of it!" The colonel huffed dismissively, as if the very idea were simply outside the pale.

When the Humber arrived at the Commando Castle, mission preparation was in full swing. Machine-gun fire rattled in the hills. Explosive charges were going off in the Arkaig River, sending up tall geysers of muddy water as Raiders cat-crawled across it on ropes stretched from the trees on the banks. Other Commandos were rappelling down the side of Achnacarry Castle. Everywhere you looked, men were on the move.

Two Nissen huts had been bolted together lengthwise, with the two adjoining walls knocked out, to form one long, open, rectangular structure. Inside, hidden from prying eyes, a giant walk-through-scale model of the Tomcat drop zone and target area was laid out on the floor.

The floor model had been constructed based on recent aerial photographs taken of Tomcat at the high oblique by the elite RAF Photo Reconnaissance Unit. It was the grandest, most elaborate sand table Major Randal had ever laid eyes on. He was used to scratching them out on the ground with a sharpened stick or the tip of his Fairbairn-Sykes Commando knife and replicating the objective with broken twigs and small stones.

Individuals, and even complete teams, were able to study the objective by strolling down the path running through the center of the model.

The team leaders used four-foot wooden pointers painted white with bright scarlet tips during the walk-through to point out items of interest. There was virtually always one or another team of Raiders moving through the building.

Outside in a secluded glen, Tomcat was staked out to exact scale with white marking tape and tent poles. This mockup was used for the initial walk-through rehearsals.

In another glen, construction crews were rapidly building a full-scale model of the buildings and bunkers of the objective; this would be the site of the full-speed, live-fire drills. The construction engineers were using the false-front building techniques used to construct movie sets, to make the layout seem as realistic as possible.

Captain Terry "Zorro'" Stone, assisted ably by Sergeant Major Maxwell Hicks, was in overall charge of preparing the troops for the mission. They conducted training to Brigade of Guards standards. Captain "Geronimo Joe" McKoy was detailed to supervise advanced night-firing drills.

Raiding Forces was being primed for Operation Tomcat in minute detail, exactly the way the Guards rehearsed when they were preparing to conduct a formal Palace Guard Mount. Perfection was the only acceptable level of performance, considered no more than ordinary Raiding Forces soldiering.

For the first three days, Raiding Forces practiced during regular training hours. After that, a night schedule was instituted. From that time forward, the troops slept during the day and worked at night.

The training was intentionally repetitious. Repetition, repetition, and more repetition ensured that each of the men could perform his individual task blindfolded and on autopilot, like a robot.

Raiding Forces trained using the crawl-walk-run method. As they trained, they progressively transitioned—becoming smooth first, and then adding speed. After that they worked on becoming fast and smooth, until finally they focused on flawless execution at full speed.

Each man knew every other Raider's job and could perform it if necessary. They cross-trained using different men to carry out different assignments. They practiced using fewer men than they had planned for on a given target, to simulate Raiding Forces personnel being killed, wounded, or mis-dropped.

The teams were intentionally scrambled so they could rehearse unscrambling and attacking on the run. The Raiders practiced every possible contingency, from individuals to entire teams failing to show up at the assembly point, causing those Raiders who did arrive to be forced to readjust their attack accordingly, on the run and without losing momentum.

The only thing the officers and men of Raiding Forces could be absolutely sure of was that the drop on Tomcat was not going to go exactly according to the plan. Chaos was a given, so they prepared for it. The troops trained with intensity, determination, and urgency. There was no horseplay.

Sticks of paratroopers were taught to roll up in the direction of flight. The first man in the team out the door stood fast when he landed, and his team members assembled on him while he marked his spot with a hook-nosed military flashlight fitted with a colored filter. Each team had a different lens color.

Drills were run where the drop was widely scattered. Then they were run with the teams tightly concentrated, though nobody really believed that on the big night, when the balloon went up, it would actually work out that way.

Raiding Forces rehearsed having an airplane shot down. Then they practiced for the contingency of having two planes shot down. The only possible way to reach the beach and the landing craft assault boats that would bring them home was through the target area, so no matter how few men assembled on the drop zone, they had to attack and take down the enemy forces on Tomcat. There was no Plan B that did not require capturing the objective.

New, updated aerial photos of Tomcat were provided by the PRU. Each team was provided a blow-up photo of its individual objective.

Captain the Lady Jane Seaborn, Lieutenant Karen Montgomery, and Royal Marine Pamela Plum-Martin pieced together a giant aerial photo mosaic of Tomcat that covered the entire wall at the far end of the two adjoined Nissen huts housing the walk-through mockup. There was almost always a team leader, working individually or with his team, studying it. In what precious few spare minutes of free time were to be had, the men drifted in on their own to familiarize themselves with Tomcat just that little bit more.

Captain Lady Seaborn placed a desk next to the wall. She, Royal Marine Plum-Martin, and Lieutenant Montgomery, taking shifts, were available around the clock to update the maps as new intelligence information came in and to answer any questions about enemy forces on or in the vicinity of Tomcat.

Lieutenant Harry Shelby arrived, fresh from his reconnaissance of Tomcat, and gave Major Randal and his small mission staff an in-depth briefing on the target area. His report was incorporated into the intelligence profile of the target. There were no major surprises.

Major Randal was pleased with the professionalism of the reconnaissance mission and the high quality of the briefing. He ordered Lieutenant Shelby to stay over an extra day in order for every man making the assault to hear his report firsthand. Raiding Forces personnel were even more impressed with Lieutenant Shelby's target briefing than their commander had been. The troops could see that no effort was being spared to make the raid a success; they liked that. It was good not to be flying by the seat of their pants for a change.

The three female Royal Marines good-naturedly answered the same earnest questions over and over, asked by serious Commandos from the lowest private soldier to the commanding officer. From the multitude of questions asked, they developed a short list of the ones they needed to research the answers to. Captain Lady Seaborn and her Royal Marines took their assignment as seriously as the Raiders took theirs.

Tomcat was an isolated duty station manned by Kriegsmarine signalmen. The nearest garrison of Wehrmacht troops was stationed twelve miles away. Reinforcement of Tomcat was a given, to be expected. The Germans were the world's very best counterattack specialists. It might take the Nazis a while to organize their forces due to the remoteness of the region, but when they did, they could be expected to come fast and to come hard.

Speed, therefore, was of the essence for Raiding Forces to succeed. They had to go in and get out fast, before the enemy forces were able to get a handle on exactly what was happening.

As soon as Raiding Forces progressed past the walk-through phase, all training was live fire.

"Nobody learns faster than a man gettin' shot at," Captain McKoy observed approvingly to Lieutenant Colonel Charles Edward Vaughan and Major Randal during a critique of one of the noisy run-throughs.

The Tomcat Raiders practiced insertion by parachute, rapid assembly, actions on the objective, consolidation, withdrawal by rappelling down the cliffs, and re-embarking on the LCA boats. They ran endless combinations of the drills. No detail, however small, went unaddressed.

Repetition, repetition, repetition—the pace never slacked, never stopped. Mission preparation seemed to go on forever.

When Lieutenant Percy Stirling arrived from Seaborn House, his base for running Operation Comanche Yell—hammering away at the French railway system—he nonchalantly informed Major Randal, "Not to worry, sir, the beach below Tomcat is clear of mines."

"How do you know that?"

"Randy, Harry, and I popped over one night with mine detectors we borrowed from the Somerset Light Infantry and swept it. The beach is completely clear."

"How'd you get the Somersets to loan you the minesweepers without giving away the show?"

"Easy, sir. Randy told their commanding officer that Lady Jane had buried her silver to hide it from Germans and forgotten exactly where. Our only difficulty was dissuading the colonel from coming up to personally supervise the search."

"Nice going, stud!"

When Captain McKoy finally heard the explanation behind Lieutenant Stirling incorrectly calling his incessant screeching the "Comanche yell" instead of the "Rebel yell," he shook his snow-white mane and observed philosophically, "I guarantee you one thing for sure: Young Percy's gonna strike terror in many a heart and make a big name for hisself . . . if he don't go and get killed first."

As it would turn out, Captain McKoy was practically clairvoyant.

36

GOOD NEWS AND BAD NEWS

THERE WAS GOOD NEWS AND BAD NEWS. TO COORDINATE WITH THE Royal Navy ship-to-shore, Raiding Forces were issued a No. 18 radio. The radio worked fine in all conditions.

To communicate with each other, however, the teams and Major John Randal's Command Party were issued No. 38 radios. Most of the time, the No. 38s did not work at all. Sergeant Mickey Duggan, who had saved the day at Calais with his signaling skills, did everything humanly possible to make the No. 38 radios function. Nothing he tried could keep the radios from drifting off frequency.

Major Randal became so frustrated that on one exercise, in a rare show of temper, he actually threw his handset at his radio operator, Corporal Jack Merritt, who dodged. The intrepid Raider showed up the next day wearing a padded jump helmet and a cricket mask. Everyone had a good laugh, but no one thought the radio situation was one bit funny.

Finally, a consensus was reached to leave the No. 38 radios at home. If the sets would not work when being pampered, there was no way to reasonably expect them to function after being violently shaken up while bailing out of an airplane at one hundred miles per hour during a low-level night combat jump.

The Raiders were outfitted with a plethora of special equipment for the mission: compasses, flashlights, black-faced military wristwatches of several different makes, their choice from an arsenal of Webley, Enfield, Colt, and Smith & Wesson revolvers (all superbly tuned by Captain "'Geronimo Joe" McKoy) if they chose not to carry the highly favored Colt .38 Super, scarves made from parachute silk with escape maps silkscreened on them, and a button to sew on their battle blouse that concealed a small escape compass (both items supplied by the budding Escape & Evasion Organization, MI-9), brass knuckles, leather gloves, first aid kits, a variety of folding knives to choose from in addition to their beloved Fairbairn-Sykes Fighting Knives, piano wire garrotes, several types of grenades, guncotton explosives, fuzes, fuze igniters, blasting caps, and lightweight waterproof map cases. For security, maps would not be issued until their aircraft were wheels up for the jump on Tomcat.

Captain McKoy created a stir of excitement when he turned up with twenty-three Thompson submachine guns: the most prized raiding weapon of all. This was a stunning development because it was widely known that there were still only forty Thompson SMGs in all England, and they were kept in a central armory to be shared among the Commando battalions.

"Where did you get these?" Major Randal asked, once again amazed by the former Arizona Ranger's ability to perform miracles.

"The good ole U.S. of A. I wrote a letter to the Southwestern Cattlemen's Association, explaining how there was a bunch of Nazi killers led by a crazy American volunteer that couldn't get their hands on any Thompson guns, and they ran it in their monthly newsletter. The editor stuck on a note at the end, asking for ranchers to donate their Tommy guns so they could be put to use a-killin' Nazis instead of coyotes, and by golly, a bunch of 'em did."

"Ranchers have submachine guns?"

"Everybody used to be able to buy one until those Chicago gangsters got to shootin' at each other with 'em out of speeding automobiles. They're real good for ranch protection and varmint eradication."

"Issue one to whoever wants one."

"What about you, John?"

"I'll stick with the Browning A-5 you built for me. I carried a Thompson in the jungle; it's a trifle heavy for my taste."

"Good choice. Oh, and I have one more little surprise for you, John. Take a gander at this." The cowboy produced a bull-barreled, .22-caliber semiautomatic pistol with an exposed hammer. "This here's the silenced pistol you asked me to get for you all those many months ago. I can't tell you how hard it has been for me to come up with it."

The pistol was a High Standard Military Model D. Major Randal had never seen one like it before. "This is the best .22 pistol I've ever handled," he marveled.

"Squadron Leader Strange found me twenty-five of 'em. The RAF originally contracted 'em from High Standard in the U.S. to teach pistol marksmanship to their aircrews. Apparently, pistol marksmanship ain't real high on their list of priorities right now, and they decided they didn't need 'em anymore.

"I had the silencers made over at Westley Richards, patterned on the one that's on the Colt Woodsman I use." Captain McKoy tossed him a lightweight canvas shoulder holster rig.

"Only issue silenced pistols to the men who can qualify 'Expert,'" Major Randal ordered, strapping on the chest rig. Captain McKoy, how am I ever going to be able to repay you?"

"You let me hitch a ride with Charlie Vaughan and his cliff-climbing boys, and we'll call her even," the San Juan Hill veteran said wistfully.

"Don't even think about it."

"I figured you'd say something like that."

Night after night the rehearsals continued. The Commando instructors played the role of the Germans on Tomcat. The instructors were heavily armed with Bren guns and piles of live ammunition. They used up cases of flash-bang grenades. The rehearsals were scary; tracers cracking by within inches became a common experience. Guncotton explosives and flash-bangs boomed constantly.

The mock assaults were loud, noisy, dangerous affairs. By any measure, they were conducting extremely realistic training. Raiding Forces was lucky no one was injured—seriously, that is. Everyone got dinged by flying gravel or ricochets, was mildly concussed, or something.

Confidence was essential for success in a small-scale raiding unit, and Major Randal knew there were two types of confidence to be found in military formations: hard earned and misplaced. One would accomplish the mission, and the other would get you killed.

Only tough, realistic training—conducted by capable officers, hard-driving, no-nonsense noncommissioned officers, and highly motivated soldiers willing to lay it all out on the line time and time again—could truly achieve the physical and mental level of competence necessary to develop legitimate, hard-earned, professional confidence.

Major Randal knew that many units bragged about conducting Commando-quality mission preparation, and quite a few actually believed they did it. But most did not even come close to the real thing, mainly because they didn't understand what it takes to actually achieve it. There are no shortcuts.

Raiding Forces worked hard. Then overnight, without fanfare, they packed up and moved out to the brand-new home of the Royal Navy Amphibious Training Center for the next phase of their mission preparation—Inveraray, located on Loch Fyne.

37

THE NAVY PLAN

INVERARAY WAS A PICTURESQUE LITTLE TOWN, NOT THAT DISTANT from Achnacarry Castle, that had been invaded by the Royal Navy for the duration, to conduct amphibious warfare training in anticipation of combined operations with the newly formed British Army Commandos and later the retaking of the continent of Europe—an ambitious thought, considering that the most impressive of the British amphibious operations to date had been in the retrograde. Someone in the Admiralty was a far thinker—or possessed of an oversized sense of humor.

The Amphibious Training Center was a laboratory built for only one purpose: to learn how to conduct modern amphibious war, a skill the Royal Navy realized it had lost. In order for the three organizations to become acquainted with one another, the idea was for Raiding Forces to train with the 15th Motor Torpedo Boat Flotilla, the unit responsible for escorting the two landing craft assault boats that would be transporting them home after the raid.

The navy plan called for two LCAs from the Amphibious Training Center to be waiting with their ramps down on the small, cliff-encircled beach below Tomcat in order to extract Raiding Forces, their prisoners, and any enemy equipment they brought out. Elements of the 15th MTB Flotilla were to be standing just offshore, providing local security against E-boats. Farther out in the Channel would be three Royal Navy destroyers on station, prepared to intervene should capital ships of the German navy attempt to interfere. Farther out over the horizon, even heavier units of the Royal Navy would be on call in the event they were needed.

The Royal Navy mission support plan was like an onion that had been cut in half. You could peel it away, layer by layer, starting with the lightest ships and working up to the heavies, exactly as Lieutenant Randy "Hornblower" Seaborn had described. The plan looked good on paper.

The LCA turned out to be a neat machine.

The officer the navy had provided to act as liaison, Lieutenant Richard Eddington, gave Major John Randal and Captain Terry "Zorro" Stone a personal inspection tour of the new landing craft. "Thornycroft built, each LCA is forty-one-feet long with a ten-foot beam and powered by two Ford V-8 automobile engines. Landing craft assaults are capable of ten knots in a fair sea."

"That's not very fast," observed Captain Stone.

The main features of the flat-bottomed boat were a squared-off bow that could be lowered to form a landing ramp, and a low draft that allowed the craft to slide right up onto a beach. Amphibious raiding troops were able to load onto an LCA and land from her in a big hurry.

"Designed as a short-range troop carrier," Lieutenant Eddington explained, "ship to shore, primarily. But we shall not be doing that on this job. A single LCA can transport thirty-six fully armed troops, so one boat is able to lift all members of Raiding Forces at one time. The second LCA on the raid is for redundancy."

The LCAs were commanded and crewed by Royal Navy Reserve officers and seamen. The reservists were learning their trade and writing the book on modern amphibious warfare as they went along. Most of the crew had come into the navy straight from civilian life and barely knew the difference between port and starboard. The LCA crew, officers, and men had all undergone intensive training at their working-up base, HMS *Western Isles* at Tobermory in the Inner Hebrides.

"Why limit command to reserve officers?" Major Randal inquired.

"That's fairly bloody simple. The reason reservists crew the LCAs is because regular straight-ring Royal Navy officers generally have a hard time intentionally driving their boats up on the beach. Throughout their entire professional career, navy regular officers are thoroughly indoctrinated that the worst crime a seagoing officer can ever possibly commit is to run his ship aground; in peacetime that sort of thing is a career ender. An amateur reserve officer, on the other hand, does not seem to mind running his boat aground. Drive up on the beach? No problem!"

"I see."

"Actually, quite a lot of intestinal fortitude is required to intentionally beach a ship on an unknown enemy shore during the hours of darkness, knowing the Germans waiting ashore are possessed of a military doctrine requiring them to immediately counterattack any intruder with all available force," continued Lieutenant Eddington, a Royal Navy regular officer himself.

"Furthermore, beaching is a tricky proposition. The vessel's skipper has to get it exactly right. Run in too hard and he might get stuck and not be able to back off. It is not considered good form to be marooned on a hostile beach with the sun coming up."

"I can see how it would not be," Captain Stone mused. "Embarrassing, quite."

"Once beached, maintaining position in the ebb and flow of the tide can also be a delicate proposition and requires a high level of seamanship. LCA officers and crew epitomize personal daring, ingenuity, initiative, courage, and can-do spirit."

What the LCA officers and crew *did not have* was much actual hands-on, practical, saltwater experience. And they couldn't navigate across a bathtub.

"The landing craft assault is the coming thing in the Commando raiding business, gentlemen," Lieutenant Eddington concluded.

Major Randal was not so sure. For small-scale raiding he still preferred fast boats like HMY *Arrow*, even if the Raiders did have to paddle ashore in dinghies once they reached the target area. However, for Operation

Tomcat's extraction, in which Raiding Forces was going to withdraw by barreling down extremely high cliffs and re-embark at full speed on a dead run, the LCA boats were just about perfect—in theory, at least.

The LCA seemed to hold a strange fascination for Captain Stone. He inspected the boat from top to bottom and stem to stern, and asked a variety of detailed questions. Major Randal had never seen him so interested in a piece of machinery before.

"From the way you're acting, Terry, it looks like you're considering a transfer to the navy," Major Randal joked.

"I never told you the story behind the LCA, did I, old stick?" Captain Stone asked, offering him a Player's Navy Cut.

"No, I don't believe you did," Major Randal replied, lighting his and Captain Stone's cigarettes. Lieutenant Eddington produced his pipe.

"Colonel Clarke and I were having dinner in the Berkeley Buttery before we had to go on duty at the War Office; it was the last night I worked for him, as a matter of fact. The colonel still had his ear bandaged from nearly getting it shot off on that first fiasco of a raid on Le Touquet. Sitting at the next table was a civilian whom I recognized vaguely as the chief of Standard Oil Company's tanker fleet. He asked the colonel how he had been wounded, and from there they started talking. Somehow the conversation worked around to the subject of landing craft.

"It was a chance encounter, a one-in-a-million event. The Standard Oil man began describing an American watercraft designed by the Higgins Company, built in New Orleans, for hauling oil field workers to their rigs in the Louisiana swamps. The swamp boat sounded like just the ticket for amphibious raiding."

"Don't tell me," Major Randal interjected. "Colonel Clarke asked to see the plans, right?"

"Well, when the colonel told the oilman it was urgent, he went straight out, flagged down a taxi, drove to his company office, rounded up the night watchman to let him in, retrieved the plans, and met us at the War Office a couple of hours later.

"The LCA is the Standard Oil boat. This is the first time I have ever actually seen one."

"Let me get this straight: Not only does Colonel Clarke dream up the idea of forming the Commandos, he names them, and then he discovers the plans for the boat that will carry them into action?"

"And became the first Commando wounded in action. You patched him up," Captain Stone added. "Actually, I doubt I would believe the story myself except I was sitting right there when it happened."

"Amazing," opined Lieutenant Eddington as he chewed on his pipe. "I shall have to pass along that story to the crews."

For the next two days, Raiding Forces familiarized themselves with the landing craft assault boats. They ran endless drills rappelling down cliffs, running across beaches, and climbing aboard the ramps of the beached LCAs.

The Raiders became extremely proficient boarders. The rest of the Inveraray experience, however, was decidedly less exceptional, starting the minute Raiding Forces switched to night exercises. Night re-embarkation on any beach under actual wartime conditions is a tricky proposition, even in fair weather. The tide never stands still, and wind and rain can cause complications all out of proportion to the apparent degree of the inclement weather. Raiding Forces knew all about that from the troops' experience at pinprick raiding. The navy, it seemed, did not.

The tide was always ebbing, running, flowing, jumping up and down, or turning cartwheels. Whatever it was doing on a given night was always the wrong thing for what the navy had anticipated.

The 15th Motor Torpedo Boat Flotilla sailors, whose job it was to escort the LCAs, seemed incapable of seeing Very lights, flashlight semaphore signals, handheld flares, or even a large bonfire built out of frustration on one exceedingly unhappy occasion. On another night, the LCAs could not come all the way into the beach and made the Commandos wade out to them through surf almost up to their necks. Then, causing Raiding Forces' lasting ill will, both LCAs somehow became grounded, and the Raiders had to climb back out into the cold water and push the boats off by hand. They were, after all, Leopard/Commandos, and everyone knows how much cats hate to get wet.

The navy plan was for the 15th MTB Flotilla to escort the LCAs in close ashore, provide a protective screen, and then, after Raiding Forces re-embarked, escort them all the way home. All in all, it did not seem like a bad plan, nor was it overly complicated . . . only it never worked in practice. Major John Randal was beside himself, Lieutenant Colonel Charles Edward Vaughan was philosophical, Lieutenant Richard Eddington was apologetic, and the troops were stoic. Randal's Rule 5—"Know how to get home"—seemed to be in some doubt.

Royal Marines signaler Sergeant Mickey Duggan was nonplussed. "The good thing, sir, is that the No. 18 sets have always worked, so we can at least alert the navy when they get lost."

Both the Royal Navy and Major Randal wanted more rehearsals. A site was located on the Dorset coast near Lulworth that had chalk cliffs similar to those at Tomcat. The navy set sail.

Major John Rock arranged for the Whitley troop transports to be available, to make it a full-scale training exercise. Lieutenant Randy "Hornblower" Seaborn arrived for the first time during the rehearsals and picked up Lieutenant Colonel Vaughan and the cliff-climbing team in HMY *Arrow*.

The stage was set. Raiding Forces treated the exercise as if it were the real thing. The plan called for them to parachute into the target area, conduct a mock attack on a simulated Tomcat building complex, rope down the cliffs, re-embark on the LCAs, and sail happily away home.

Only forty-eight hours remained before the actual raid. Time was becoming critically short. Everyone wanted to get it right this time. Raiding Forces staged at a remote airfield. The pilots took off, flew their simulated mission flight profile, and made a textbook-perfect drop, except that the external bundles were slightly mis-dropped and took a long time to be recovered.

This prompted Major Randal to call a hasty meeting of Major Rock, Captain Stone, and Sergeant Major Hicks afterward.

"We're not dropping our individual weapons in the external bundles. I'm not going to have my men on an Easter egg hunt, crawling around behind enemy lines in the dark, armed only with pistols."

"That's how everyone does it," Major Rock protested. "The Germans, the Italians, Russians, even the Americans drop their rifles and submachine guns by external bundles mounted under the wings. We are talking international airborne doctrine here!"

"Come up with something better!"

After much discussion, it was decided that on the big night they would disassemble the Browning A-5s and the Thompson submachine guns, have each Raider place his broken-down weapon into a small canvas satchel, tie the satchel to his left leg with his toggle rope, drop with the disassembled weapon in the bag clutched between his knees, and then let the bag dangle down on the toggle rope once the parachute deployed. The troops would have to reassemble their weapons on the DZ. Raiding Forces personnel were well versed at assembling their weapons fast in the dark. In a pinch, the Thompson submachine guns were designed to be fully capable of being fired with the wooden stock removed.

But solving the problem of the mis-dropped personal weapons was an easy fix compared to the obstacle to extraction they encountered during the withdrawal phase of the final rehearsal.

That night, when Raiding Forces rappelled down the cliff to the beach, the only Royal Navy vessel in sight was HMY *Arrow* bobbing close offshore. The navy was consistent, at least: They never got it right.

NIGHT JUMP

38

MARSHALING

THE NEXT DAY RAIDING FORCES WENT INTO LOCKDOWN ISOLATION
behind barbed wire at a secluded airfield so secret, the RAF did not even
permit Major John Randal to know its exact location. The Raiders had
been brought to the airfield in a convoy of Bedford trucks with the canvas
tops up and a curtain drawn across the back.

Ammunition and hand grenades were issued. Parachutes were drawn.
Sticks of jumpers and their chalk number were married up. They would
be jumping their old nemesis, the rattletrap Whitley bombers, flown by
pilots assigned to No. 1 Parachute Training School because the parachute
school pilots were the most experienced droppers of paratroopers in the
Royal Air Force.

Final orders had been issued and the last briefing concluded. Each
team commander turned in his copy of the written operations order. The
orders had been stamped in bold red ink:

    MOST SECRET
    NOT TO BE TAKEN ABOARD AIRCRAFT
    OPERATION ORDER TOMCAT

By
Major J. Randal, MC, Commanding
Strategic Raiding Force

The pile of operations orders was ceremoniously burned in a metal ammo can.

In order to achieve maximum concentration of the jumpers on the drop zone, the drop would be accomplished in three serials of a single plane each. The first man to jump would be Major John Randal, and he was scheduled to go down at 0215 hours. The three serials would be dropping at two-minute intervals.

The teams were cross-loaded to allow for the interval in the drops and to mitigate the consequences of an aircraft being shot down or failure to reach the drop point for any reason. Just as quickly as a team assembled on the DZ, it would immediately move out independently on its assigned mission.

As the teams moved out, different tasks would be carried out at different times on the objective. The actions on the objective had all been carefully planned, orchestrated, and rehearsed. Raiding Forces was going to move fast and hit hard.

The atmosphere at the departure airfield was resolute. The men were totally focused. On the flight line there came a loud, sharp engine backfire, followed by a high-pitched wheezing sound as a prop slowly turned. Then the engine broke into a full-throated roar: bone jarring and rough, like a giant Harley-Davidson motorcycle.

Tension shot up like the gauge on a pressure cooker. Then other engines began to wheeze and fire up.

The mission was on.

Beside each of the three Whitleys a stick of Commandos was resting on the tarmac, lying back on their parachutes, trying to conserve their energy. The Raiders began to struggle to their feet, shaking out their equipment: Time to saddle up.

Major Randal went around to the other two Whitleys' sticks of troops and shouted over the roar, "You men all know your jobs. I'll see you on the drop zone. Let's go do it!"

He went back to his aircraft and was given a final jumpmaster inspection. The dispatcher on his plane, chalk No. 1, was his old turret jump dispatcher Flight Sergeant Bill Beaverton, on loan from No. 1 Parachute Training School. All things considered, he was probably the most experienced jumpmaster in any armed force in the world. Having him along on the big night was a confidence booster.

"Good to see you again, sir."

"I didn't think I'd live to hear myself say this, but it's good to see you again too, Flight Sergeant Beaverton," Major Randal said sincerely, reaching out and shaking his hand.

"You have not forgotten your promise to keep a slot open for me when I finish my tour as instructor at Ringway, have you, sir?"

"Think they're ever going to let you leave the school?"

"One can always hope, sir."

"We'll have a place for you if they do."

Captain the Lady Jane Seaborn, Lieutenant Karen Montgomery, and Royal Marine Pamela Plum-Martin were standing on the tarmac beside Major Randal's Whitley bomber, on hand to see them off. The three women looked tense. Captain Lady Seaborn seemed to be struggling with her emotions. Lieutenant Montgomery had tears running down her cheeks, and even Royal Marine Plum-Martin looked slightly misty-eyed. Major Randal wondered why. Did they know something he didn't?

There was no time to stop and find out. He gave them a jaunty salute that was really more of a wave as he led his stick on board the aircraft. Major Randal was cocked and locked—dialed in and ready. No more waiting, no more planning, and no more training. Now it was time to go!

Up in the cockpit the lead pilot, Flying Officer Trevor Wainflynn, turned to his copilot and said, "I feel like a Judas goat."

"What?"

"Leading the lambs to slaughter, then turning back."

"Well, we are carrying some bloody dangerous-looking lambs back there."

Neither man had ever dropped anyone on an actual combat mission before. Tonight was shaping up to be a sobering experience.

The lead Whitley's engines came to a full-blooded roar, now running smooth as silk. Precisely to the preplanned second, the airplane began to taxi; it picked up speed and was airborne as it leaped into the night with a lurch.

Major Randal and twenty-nine heavily armed maniacs were on their way to invade the continent of Europe, all by themselves.

On board chalk No. 3, Lieutenant Percy Stirling shouted, "Get ready, Adolf, here we come, you bloody bastard! YEEEEEEHAAAAAA!" The Raiders in his stick shook their heads. What could you expect from a "Death or Glory Boy"?

The flight to the coast of France was uneventful except for the Whitley's rivets and struts creaking and popping as though she was going to split her seams at any second. That may have been a good thing, because it gave everyone on board something to think about besides the mission ahead.

There was no singing or false bravado other than the one short outburst by Lieutenant Stirling—which was not entirely false. The troops were seasoned professionals, even if this was their first combat jump. Each Raider was thinking his own private thoughts. Raiding Forces was a highly trained, tightly knit team—but when it came time to jump, every man had to do that on his own.

The motto of Major Randal's regiment, the King's Royal Rifle Corps, was "Swift and Bold." He was definitely living up to regimental standard this night.

The inside of the plane was extremely chilly. Major Randal ran the sequence of the plan over and over in his head like a broken record. He wondered briefly about the look on Lady Jane's beautiful face when he was boarding the Whitley. He touch-checked—for the hundredth time—his pistols, his Fairbairn-Sykes Fighting Knife, the gravity knife zipped in the collar of his smock, the six grenades he had in his pockets, his compass, his Very signaling pistol and flares, and along with the MI-9 escape kit sewed into the lining of his smock—maps, Browning A-5, ammunition, hook-nosed flashlight with the blue filter screwed on, toggle rope, canteen of water, first aid kit, wristwatch and wrist compass, cigarette lighter, and cigarettes. They were all there, strapped neatly in place or tucked in the correct pocket of his sand-green Denison parachute smock as they had been the other ninety-nine times he had checked.

Major Randal went over the plan again. The three Whitleys would cross the French coast about ten miles above Tomcat, break hard left, and fly straight to the drop zone. He would jump at 0215 hours, and all the troops would have exited their aircraft by 0219 hours.

The instant he landed, he would pop the quick-release on his parachute, drop it right there on the ground, assemble his Browning A-5, and began rolling up in his four-man assault team: his wingman, Life Guards Corporal Jack Merritt, No. 2 Commando Trooper Frank Hawkins, and Royal Marine Butch Hoolihan. Their objective was the Command Post/Officers' Quarters.

There was no hard intelligence, but they did not expect to find more than three or four officers at Tomcat—no more than that in the building when they hit it. Lieutenant Harry Shelby had reported seeing just three officers during his recon mission.

Flying on board his chalk was Lieutenant Jeb Pelham-Davies. The highly competent Duke of Wellington's Regiment officer was slated to attack the troop barracks with a team of ten men.

On the second chalk was Captain Terry "Zorro" Stone, who had the key mission of attacking the Kriegsmarine signals station with a six-man party. The signals station was located on the far side of Tomcat, away from the DZ. It was hoped that high intelligence–value signals equipment, documents, or personnel would be captured at the site.

Bringing up the rear in the third and last chalk was Lieutenant Taylor Corrigan. He and Lieutenant Percy Stirling would roll up their teams and attack the lighthouse and two bunkers located on the cliff on the right-hand side of Tomcat and the four bunkers on the left-hand side, respectively.

Sergeant Mike "March or Die" Mikkalis would drop with a team that would split into two sections in order to establish a road-cutting security party at each end of Tomcat, to seal it off.

Just at that moment the red warning light winked on. Flight Sergeant Beaverton shouted, "Ten minutes!" in a voice that made the two words sound like an entire paragraph. Then he opened the cover of the exit hole in the floor of the Whitley. A loud, piercing, otherworldly noise screamed throughout the plane's belly.

Down below, for anyone who cared to look, were the white tops of gray-green waves. Major Randal stared out, hoping to see some sign of the Royal Navy. No such luck. But looking down did not seem to bother him tonight. He would have really liked to know for sure that the navy was where it was supposed to be. They flew on for what seemed like another hour.

"Action stations!"

Fireworks started going off outside the Whitley. What sounded like a major-league thunderstorm erupted: enemy antiaircraft fire! Shrapnel from the flak sprayed against the skin of the Whitley like hailstones. Colored tracers crisscrossed the night sky. Great orange fireballs the size of pumpkins pom-pommed straight up at the open exit hole, then curled off into the night. Smaller balls of fire that looked like flaming onions streaked past.

The Whitley pilot, to his everlasting credit, did not jink, speed up, or take any evasive action whatsoever. He was a rock solid professional. Having prepared for this type of mission from the day he was assigned to fly for the Parachute Training School, he intended to put his jumpers on target, on time, or get shot down trying. Behind him the other two Whitley pilots followed his lead and pressed on through the wall of flak.

Tucked in the back, the last man in the stick was Major John Rock. He had planned the mission, and now he was tagging along to observe it. Right this minute he was getting his money's worth of observation.

The jumpmaster signaled for Major Randal to take his position sitting on the edge of the exit hole. The big airplane droned on. There was snow on the ground now below, the result of a freak early snowstorm.

The green light flashed on and Major Randal was out of the aircraft instantly, eyes open—the way it was supposed to be done. As he fell he could see the other two giant Whitleys in line astern. They had closed up, looking like two giant flying pterodactyls.

Good, he thought, *there won't be any two-minute interval now.*

He heard the sound of rustling silk as his X-type parachute deployed and opened, and then he was floating instead of falling. Immediately he let go of his kit bag. The bag dropped down on its toggle rope lowering line lashed to his left ankle.

The overwhelming sensation was of silence. Little puffs of white parachutes dotted the clear, blue-black-purple sky. The Whitleys were gone. The parachutists were all alone in the sky.

Tonight, Major Randal was coming in forward for a change, which gave him a brief chance to study the objective. It looked exactly like the sand-table model, except that it was covered in a light blanket of snow.

There was not a person stirring. Viewed from the saddle of his parachute, Tomcat, covered with snow, looked like a children's toy alpine village. The target appeared tranquil and peaceful. He floated down gently, not even bothering to spill any air out of the canopy to control his descent. The night was completely quiet except for the swish of air on silk.

Beneath him the ground seemed to rush sideways. Instinctively, as he had practiced all those thousands of times, he brought his elbows in tight until his forearms were almost touching together on his chest. The last thing he wanted tonight was to bang an elbow. He kept his chin tucked down tight on his chest, and he wiggled his knees to make sure they were together but not locked. His toes suddenly touched the ground; instinctively he swiveled to the right and made one of the best parachute landing falls of his short airborne career.

39

ATTACK ON TOMCAT

FEW THINGS FEEL AS GOOD AS LIVING THROUGH YOUR FIRST COMBAT jump, Major John Randal decided. The only problem was that there wasn't very long to enjoy the thrill and no time at all to celebrate. The instant he was down and sure he was all in one piece, Major Randal popped the quick-release, jumped up, pulled off the parachute harness, retrieved his kit bag, took out the Browning A-5, and, on one knee, swiftly assembled it, then clunked a round into the chamber.

He looked up and saw the beautiful sight of a tight cluster of paratroopers silently descending almost straight down under their silk canopies. The drop had been perfectly executed. Major Randal's team landed so close around him that he did not even have to turn on the blue-tinted flashlight to roll up the stick. Suddenly they were just there.

Quickly he checked to verify that each man in his team had his weapon assembled; then, with his teeth clenched, he ordered savagely, "Let's go get 'em—follow me!"

The Command Post/Officers' Quarters was located in a small, two-story stone villa in the very center of the objective. They went straight at it.

Major Randal had chosen to drop right on top of Tomcat in order to reduce the length of time it would take Raiding Forces to assemble and reach their targets, to increase the speed of attack, and to maximize the element of surprise. Still, the choice of drop zones had been a gamble. The prudent plan would have been to drop one-half mile away, assemble, then advance in a conventional infantry formation and make a set-piece attack. Most officers would have chosen that method.

Special operations based on prudence do not always turn out to be the most successful or even to result in lower casualties, however. In the first place, a prudent person would never have jumped out of an airplane flying one hundred miles per hour at low altitude in the dead of night behind enemy lines, without a reserve parachute. The truth was, no one in the British Armed Forces actually knew how to select a drop zone for a parachute raid, the jump on Tomcat being their very first one.

The gamble paid off handsomely. All raiding parties were on the ground, assembled, and streaking toward their individual objectives in an exceptionally short period of time. Surprise was complete.

The night was perfectly still and silent. The air was crystal clear. Stars twinkled in a beautiful blue velvet sky, and the thin layer of snow on the ground muffled the sound of the Commandos' rubber-soled raiding boots.

Then all hell broke loose.

Tracers crisscrossed back and forth—green-white, red-orange: bright, fast, and loud. WHAAAM! WHAAAM! Grenades began going off, indicating that Lieutenant Jeb Pelham-Davies' team had reached the troop barracks. According to plan, they hit it from all sides at once on the dead run.

Streams of tracers ripped across Tomcat in a vicious crossfire from the direction of the lighthouse, the troop barracks, and the signals station. From the look of things, it seemed as if nothing could survive for an instant in the intense curtain of enemy fire.

BOOM! BOOM! BOOM! A Browning A-5 bellowed, and then a Thompson rattled, RAAAMP-RAAAMP, as Lieutenant Pelham-Davies' team breached the front and rear doors and simultaneously launched themselves through them.

WHUUUMP! WHUUUMP, WHUUUMP! Explosive charges began detonating.

The high-pitched scream of German 9-mm machine pistols, with their high cyclic rate, shredded the night. Tracers ricocheted off the ground and off the buildings; some streams were fired straight up in the air as if in pure frustration—or possibly it was a signal of some kind. The German defenders had been caught off guard and they panicked. Nazis were firing and trying to take cover at the same time. While some simply ran off out into the night half dressed, others blazed away blindly.

Major Randal's party arrived at its objective running flat out. Miraculously, no one had been hit. Major Randal and Corporal Jack Merritt made up the entry team. They crouched on either side of the front door with their backs against the wall of the villa.

Trooper Frank Hawkins disappeared behind the building to take up his assigned security cover position. Royal Marine Butch Hoolihan ran up in a hail of bullets and slammed into the wall next to Major Randal.

"This is almost as bloody awful as Achnacarry, ain't it, sir!" he piped up with a big grin.

"Nothing's that bad, Butch!"

Major Randal gripped his Browning A-5 tightly in the high port position, then made full eye contact with Corporal Merritt and nodded. The tall cavalryman swung around in front of the door of the CP/OQ, squared off, and kicked it as hard as he could. The door slammed open with a loud crash.

As they had practiced, Major Randal stepped around Corporal Merritt and entered the room first, shotgun at the ready on his shoulder. He was clicked on, tuned to a high pitch of readiness.

Inside were five very surprised Germans sitting stiffly around a table in the center of the room. A late-night card game? Who were these men? Visitors? There were not supposed to be this many officers here.

The stated purpose of the exercise was "to capture prisoners who might be in possession of signal information of high intelligence value." The plan called for Major Randal to effect entry and call out, "*Hände hoch!*" then take all offending enemy personnel into custody after they meekly surrendered.

It was probably a good plan. Certainly it had seemed like it all those hundreds of times they had rehearsed it. The problem was that when he stepped into the room and saw five real, live enemy combatants in uniform over the sights of his Browning A-5 shotgun, he momentarily went blank on the German phrase "*Hände hoch*."

Major Randal stood frozen in the doorway, aiming the Browning at the card players, desperately trying to remember the right words, until one of the Germans appeared to make a move for his holstered pistol. He should not have done that.

The A-5 boomed five times very fast, so fast the sound of the shots ran together. The five enemy soldiers were flung all over the room like rag dolls, all of them knocked down before the first 12-gauge shell casing hit the floor. Playing cards scattered everywhere.

"Prisoners, sir!" Corporal Merritt chided as he advanced past Major Randal. Taking the lead as rehearsed, he started moving up the stairs with his Thompson submachine gun locked in tight against his shoulder, both eyes open over the weapon's sights. Major Randal fell in behind him, feeding loose shells from the large billows pocket of his sand-green parachute smock into the Browning A-5.

"Hoolihan, check to see if any of these people are still alive, then move back to your position," Major Randal called out to the Royal Marine who was right behind him, as rehearsed, to secure the prisoners.

"Sir!" Royal Marine Hoolihan shouted. When he saw all the bodies he pulled up short. "Nice shooting, Major!"

"Check 'em out, Butch, then get back outside, fast!" Major Randal ordered tersely, closing up on Corporal Merritt.

"Should have *Hände hoched*," Royal Marine Hoolihan muttered as he bent over the dead Nazis.

At the top of the stairs a half-dressed man suddenly appeared, wildly firing an MP-38 machine pistol.

RAAAMP! Corporal Merritt chopped him down with his Thompson without slowing his advance or lowering the submachine gun from his shoulder.

There were four bedrooms on the second floor. They cleared them one at a time. Three of them were empty. In the fourth they found a middle-aged Kriegsmarine officer hiding under the bed in his pale blue silk pajamas.

Corporal Merritt bent down and looked at him over the sights of his submachine gun. "Did you actually think that was going to work, Fritz?" he asked the trembling Nazi superman—a semi-concussed Nazi superman as a result of the effects of the No. 69 stun grenade that Major Randal had wisely tossed through the door before they entered the room, as a precaution. You cannot be too careful.

"It never hurts to cheat, does it, sir?" Corporal Merritt commented as he pulled the dazed German officer out from under the bed.

Major Randal took that as a compliment.

Outside, Royal Marine Hoolihan resumed his security position. He and Trooper Hawkins each had their backs touching the edge of a corner of the building diagonally, across from each other. A straight line between the two Commandos would have run through the center of the villa.

Their security positions had been carefully worked out during rehearsals. While they could not see each other, each Raider could cover two sides of the building by constantly swiveling his head back and forth. Anyone exiting without calling out "Remember Calais" several times was subject to being shot or otherwise assaulted—which meant they would be.

The volume of firing on Tomcat had dramatically increased as team after team reached its objectives and began to vigorously execute its missions. From inside the CP/OQ, Royal Marine Hoolihan heard the first WHUUUMP! of a concussion grenade up on the second floor. He knew it was a stun grenade, used as Major Randal and Corporal Merritt cleared the rooms upstairs.

Soon he heard a second WHUUUMP! coming from another room. Then he heard a creaking right over his head, on the wall above his left shoulder. Royal Marine Hoolihan looked up. To his amazement, he saw a window open and a dark, shadowy figure silently climb out and, being extremely careful, hang down, dangling by his fingertips.

The Royal Marine watched incredulously as the figure hung there for a long moment, then let go and dropped. Whoever it was, he noted, did not shout "Remember Calais" or anything else. Unfortunately for the shadowy figure, he landed on all fours less than a foot from the alert Royal Marines Commando.

He was too close to shoot, Royal Marine Hoolihan calculated; besides, the orders were to take prisoners when and if possible, so the Commando did what all Royal Marines had been exhaustively trained to do since the invention of the handheld fusil.

In one smooth motion he took a half step forward with his left foot and planted it toward the attempted escapee—who was rising and just beginning to notice the British Commando for the first time—then dropped the wooden stock of the Thompson .45 submachine gun off his shoulder, and, with the weapon held vertically, finned barrel straight up, magazine to the front—with his left hand firmly gripping the forearm and his right clasping the small of the stock—brought the heavy, wooden butt up in a sharp, vigorous, striking motion, completing a short powerful arc. He used a lot of follow-through.

The leading edge of the heel of the Thompson's steel butt plate caught the Nazi flush on the button of his jaw. Royal Marine Hoolihan had executed the classic vertical butt stroke, a movement that had been hammered into him a million times, or maybe more, during countless hours of bayonet drills. A thing of beauty when executed correctly, the vertical butt stroke delivered everything his drill instructors had promised. The short, powerful blow levitated the escapee from all fours to flat on his back, knocked completely unconscious without a sound, unless you counted the ugly, meaty whack the metal butt plate made when it came into contact with the German's jaw.

Royal Marine Hoolihan wished his mates back in the Marines could have seen him do that. He would have sworn the strikee bounced when he landed on his back. Bloody fantastic! All that rifle drill finally paid off.

From the front door, Major Randal called out, "Remember Calais, remember Calais!"

Then he walked around the corner and inquired conversationally, "What you got there, Butch?"

Before the young Royal Marine could formulate an answer, Major Randal whipped out a pair of British Parachute Wings from an inside pocket of his Denison smock. He had brought them along just for a moment like this, and now he nonchalantly pinned them on the surprised young Raider's chest. "Here you go, Butch. I believe tonight was your seventh qualifying jump. Consider yourself badged."

For Royal Marine Butch Hoolihan, getting his wings totally unexpected like that, right there on the objective, was the highlight of his brief but exciting military career thus far. He thought it a really tremendous gesture on the major's part . . . though maybe a bit extreme.

The prostrate German let out a weak moan, putting an end to the little ceremony.

40

CONTINUE THE MISSION

LIEUTENANT JEB PELHAM-DAVIES COMMANDED THE LARGEST party of men in the assault on Tomcat. He was responsible for what was potentially the most difficult target on the raid: the troop barracks. The exceptional young officer had been selected for this vital assignment primarily because of his extensive battle experience while serving in the British Expeditionary Force in France. His regiment, the Duke of Wellington's, was a splendid county regiment that had established a reputation for the high-quality officers it produced. The Dukes' motto was "Fortune Favors the Brave."

After the jump on Tomcat it took him longer than it had Major John Randal to assemble his team, though not by much. Sergeant Major Maxwell Hicks had carefully selected Lieutenant Pelham-Davies' team, loading it extra heavily with battle-hardened Green Jackets from Swamp Fox Force. Major John Rock was also officially attached to his team as an observer. "Fighting observer" was more accurate, as he was armed with a Thompson submachine gun that had an ornate silver concho inlaid on the stock.

As Lieutenant Pelham-Davies and his men raced toward their objective, a spectacular pyrotechnic display lit up the night from all points on Tomcat. The crisscrossing tracers were flying so fast and thick, they seemed to be solid beams of light. It was difficult to believe that there were five standard hardball rounds between every tracer bullet. The 9-mm rounds screaming past made a distinctive loud, snapping, mean sound that cracked like a metal carpenter's ruler being rattled violently, amplified a thousand times louder.

The intense volume of fire, coming mainly from machine pistols, seemed impossible to survive.

Most of the fire was of the "spray and pray" variety: fired in panic and hope from windows and doors, by scared German sailors who had been sound asleep in their beds, safe in occupied Europe one minute and under attack by British parachutists the next. The fire was wildly inaccurate, but it looked and sounded truly awe-inspiring. A great deal of courage and personal fortitude was required for the Raiders not to immediately go to ground and take cover when the Tomcat defenders initially opened up. Every survival instinct in their bodies screamed out for them to do just that.

However, personal fortitude was a common commodity in Raiding Forces. They pressed on, knowing that to slow their attack was the same thing as committing suicide. Getting pinned down in a long, drawn-out firefight was not an option. Besides, the Raiders had trained extensively under live fire at Achnacarry, and the instructors there had consistently come closer to hitting them than the startled Germans on Tomcat . . . so far.

Before reaching the barracks, Lieutenant Pelham-Davies' team smoothly broke into two groups, with Sergeant Major Maxwell Hicks leading one party that flowed down the far side of the barracks and around the back to become the rear-door entry team.

Lieutenant Pelham-Davies and his opposite number, Rifleman David Pettigrew, late of Swamp Fox Force, threw themselves up against the wall of the entrance to the barracks. The Dukes' officer was clenching a thin, unlit cigar in his teeth. Behind them the rest of the barracks assault team took up positions, armed with a mixture of Thompson .45-caliber submachine guns and Browning A-5 12-guage semiautomatic shotguns, all held at the ready.

On the signal from his leader, Rifleman Pettigrew swung around and kicked in the door, then jumped back. While he was still moving, Lieutenant Pelham-Davies rolled two No. 36 fragmentation grenades in the door, then reached out and jerked it back shut. Theirs was not a mission of mercy, and taking prisoners was not on their list of things to do. Tonight they were a kill team.

WHHHHHAAAAAAAAMM! WHHHHHAAAAAAAAMM!

Instantly following the second detonation, Lieutenant Pelham-Davies led his men charging through the door into the barracks, firing left and right alternately as they went in. The rattling noise of the Thompsons, the Brownings' booming, the dust, the smell of cordite, and the eye-burning smoke from the grenades were staggering. A violent steel hailstorm suddenly broke out in the tightly confined space, raged momentarily, and subsided. The fight was over fast.

Three Nazis who beat feet for the back door were cut down before they made it off the back step when they ran head-on into the rear-door entry team.

When the chaos was under control and flashlights came on, it was found that eighteen Nazis were down with varying levels of wounds, and five were dead. With all the explosions and close-in shooting, it would have seemed that no enemy could still be alive.

The Raiding Forces team had one man KIA and four men wounded.

Lieutenant Pelham-Davies took the thin cigar out of his mouth. "That was intense," he remarked to Rifleman Pettigrew.

"All in a night's work, sir."

"Exactly."

Both men exchanged the depleted magazines on their Thompson submachine guns for fully topped-off fresh ones. The Tomcat troop barracks was secure, but at a price.

It was not long before Major John Randal arrived to see for himself how things were going. "Good work, Jeb," he said, pulling out a set of British Parachute Wings from the inside pocket of his Denison smock and pinning them on a bemused Lieutenant Pelham-Davies.

"Interesting qualifying jump?"

Taking the thin cigar out of his mouth, Lieutenant Pelham-Davies responded dryly, "That would be one way of describing it, sir."

"Carry on."

Lieutenant Taylor Corrigan's party was the third one to depart the drop zone. He was tasked with the mission of knocking out the four bunkers located at points beginning behind the troop barracks and running along the edge of the cliff to the lighthouse. It was crucial for the bunkers to be destroyed completely in order to prevent the Germans from reoccupying them later and firing down on Raiding Forces during the withdrawal phase of the operation.

Lieutenant Corrigan, of the fashionable Horse Guards Regiment, was the newest officer and the least-known quantity to Raiding Forces. For that reason, on the suggestion of Sergeant Major Hicks, his team was composed entirely of cavalrymen from the Household Cavalry Brigade, three of whom had previously served with the lieutenant in the Blues. The cavalrymen were old-timers in Raiding Forces, having all been there from the first polo-playing intake. They were not about to let an officer from their old brigade look bad on his first showing; he was one of their own. Taking advantage of little details like that is important in a special operations unit.

British men of Lieutenant Corrigan's class were expected to lead in war, and lead he did—from the front. His plan of attack was simple: He intended to take down all four bunkers simultaneously. In that way, there would not be any opportunity for the German sailors in one bunker to rally to their comrades' aid in the other bunkers, as they might if the bunkers were attacked one at a time.

After studying the aerial photos of the bunkers, he had noted an inherent design flaw in their construction. Each bunker was made out of poured concrete, and all four were identical. The entryway to the bunkers was at the left rear side. You had to go down four steps dug into the ground to reach the door. The bunkers were formidable fighting emplacements— virtually impregnable—provided that they were manned and that the attack came from the sea. From the rear, the bunkers did not have any firing ports.

Lieutenant Corrigan pointed out his discovery to his colleague, Lieutenant Percy Stirling, who was responsible for neutralizing the lighthouse and the two bunkers on the far side of it. Together they worked out a simple scheme of maneuver, designed to eliminate the targets quickly.

Both officers had essentially the same task. Lieutenant Corrigan had to take out the four bunkers before they had time to fire on the cliff-climbing team coming up from the beach simultaneously with their attack. Lieutenant Stirling had to take down the lighthouse fast, because anyone stationed in it could fire down not only on the cliff-climbing team but also on the Commandos from both teams as they were attacking the bunkers, plus anyone anywhere in the entire Tomcat target area.

"Percy," said Lieutenant Corrigan, "If you knock out the lighthouse before a shot is fired at my bunker busters, I will pick up next month's tab at your club."

"Consider it done, Tay."

As mentioned, Lieutenant Corrigan's scheme of maneuver called for him to take on all four bunkers at once. Coming off the drop zone at a dead run, his team skirted around the left flank of the troop barracks, pounding hard yet silently in their rubber-soled boots over the light ground covering of snow. The initial approach was surreal; they felt as if they were in a dream state, dead silent, bounding effortlessly along, almost floating toward the bunkers.

The sensation did not last long, however, because the night suddenly exploded into a massive hail of incoming automatic weapons fire. Luckily for them, the firing was all originating from the far side of the troop barracks building, so they were somewhat shielded from it and did not even break their stride. The Raiders were no longer in any sort of a dream state; the situation had suddenly turned very real.

Lieutenant Corrigan's team skirted around the end of the barracks and came upon the line of bunkers in front of them, perched right on the military crest of the cliff. The English Channel was gleaming in the moonlight. As they closed in on the bunkers, it became more and more apparent how high up on the cliff they were. It felt as if they were running along the roof of a skyscraper with no protective rail. They had jumped from the

Whitleys at just slightly more than the height down to the beach—it was a long, long way down!

Approaching the bunkers, the Raiders peeled off exactly the way they had rehearsed: one man dropping off behind each concrete structure on the run until Lieutenant Corrigan and his opposite number, Corporal Ned Pomptous, reached the last one. While Lieutenant Corrigan provided cover with his Browning A-5, the other Raider eased quietly down the four steps, took a grenade out of his pocket, and made ready to pull the pin.

Lieutenant Corrigan blew three blasts on the silver whistle he wore on a lanyard around his neck, sounding the prearranged signal to his men to toss a No. 36 grenade into each of the bunkers simultaneously. Muffled WHUUUMPH WHUUUMPH WHUUUMPH WHUUUMPH! rippled down the bunker line, as if the detonations were chasing each other. Their attack was over quickly.

When their grenade went off, Lieutenant Corrigan and Corporal Pomptous rushed in and cleared the first bunker. The only thing they found was a dying German sailor sprawled on the concrete floor in a spreading pool of blood.

Lieutenant Corrigan pumped a single 12-gauge round into the Nazi and then ordered, "Set the charges."

He quickly moved back down the line to assist each of the other three Raiders in turn with clearing their bunkers, at a minimum, a two-man job. They did not find anyone else alive. All four of the bunkers had been manned. In all, his team had killed five enemy sailors.

Apparently, the German defenders had reached the bunkers only bare seconds ahead of Lieutenant Corrigan's men, because they never even got off a single round at HMY *Arrow*, the LCAs, or the cliff-climbing party, who could be seen furiously coming up the cliff, climbing hard and fast. The defenders had never known the Raiding Forces team was right on their heels. Even so, it was a close-run thing. The Germans could have caused a lot of damage in short order had they engaged.

When each of the bunkers was clear, Lieutenant Corrigan's men prepared guncotton charges made up of enough explosives to destroy the bunker completely, to prevent it from being reoccupied by the Nazi defenders later as Raiding Forces was pulling out. Down the line, the cry of "Fire in the hole!" rang out three times from each bunker, exactly as if it were a training exercise at Achnacarry.

The four heavily muffled WHUUUMPH belied the damage the explosives were doing inside. Destruction was massive. The bunkers were no longer a factor to be concerned with.

It was a neat piece of work. Mission accomplished.

41

LIGHTHOUSE SECURED

LIEUTENANT PERCY STIRLING'S PLAN OF ATTACK WAS TO TAKE out the two bunkers to the right flank of the lighthouse, followed by the lighthouse itself, in rapid sequence. With only five men, he was going to be spread thin on the ground. Lieutenant Stirling's scheme of maneuver called for three men to assault the two bunkers, much the same way Lieutenant Corrigan's team was handling the other four, while he and his wingman, Trooper Trevor Roper, took down the lighthouse.

Things had to be timed just right. The lighthouse was actually out in front of bunker number five, so if they charged past the bunker before it was cleared, he and his wingman would be subject to being shot down at point-blank range from behind.

On the snow-padded drop zone, the "Death or Glory Boy" rallied his team on the fly and broke all speed records for assembly and departure to his objective. The night was eerily silent when they started out. The only sound was the crunching of their rubber-soled raiding boots in the soft powder of snow.

The popular young officer had been sternly admonished to refrain from any Comanche yelling until after the Germans opened fire. The hope was that Raiding Forces might prolong the element of surprise, not announce their arrival by sounding off like a troop of the Confederate Cavalry or a war party of Comanche Indians.

The plan worked for a while. All was perfectly still on Tomcat, even with the Commandos down and out of their parachutes and going about their appointed tasks.

Then all of a sudden it seemed the whole place literally blew up. Automatic weapons fire erupted from every direction. Angry streams of red- and orange-colored tracers crisscrossed the objective.

The lighthouse was the most distant target from the drop zone; Lieutenant Stirling's team had to pass through the very center of Tomcat to reach it. When the blizzard of German automatic weapons fire erupted, they found themselves taking fire from all sides at once.

Fortunately for Lieutenant Stirling and all the rest of Raiding Forces, machine pistols were not very effective at more than point-blank range unless fired with deliberation. Any submachine gun's muzzle had a tendency to climb when fired fully automatic, which made it difficult to score hits if the shooter did not take the time and trouble to aim and fire it in short bursts. Deliberate aiming was in short supply on the German side tonight, and short bursts did not seem to be in vogue among these defenders. The panicked Nazis were burning up truly impressive amounts of ammunition, putting out a massive volume of fire in a breathtakingly short period of time. Tomcat was a very loud, frightening place to be at that moment.

Though cleared to commence Comanche yelling once the shooting started, neither Lieutenant Stirling nor any of his men made a single sound. To a man, they thought they were all dead, or more to the point, soon going to be. It did not seem possible to run through the heavy wall of fire lacing Tomcat and not get killed.

As Lieutenant Stirling had noted while he floated down in his parachute, the lighthouse was fully lit up. Now, up ahead through all the intense automatic weapons fire, there it loomed, beaming its light out to sea. Lieutenant Stirling's Raiders pounded straight toward the light. The longer they ran, the farther away the lighthouse appeared to be. Time stopped; everything was happening in slow motion. No matter how hard they ran, the Raiders could not seem to get there.

On their left, Major John Randal's team hit the Command Post/ Officers' Quarters. To the far left, Lieutenant Jeb Pelham-Davies' team stormed the troop barracks. Dead ahead, Captain Terry Stone and his men were entering the signals station.

Lieutenant Stirling and his men kept running hard toward the light-house, but it just would not get any closer. He had his Thompson at the high port. The weapon seemed to weigh at least a hundred pounds.

Bullets cracked. Tracers flashed. Grenades exploded. Wait a minute; did he actually see that bullet? In flight, and it was not a tracer! Several large explosions reverberated. Tracers danced around their ankles. The lighthouse was still not getting any closer. Time seemed warped. Sounds were muffled, strangely drawn out and distorted. It was dark around the outer edges of his vision, as if he were looking down a tunnel.

Lieutenant Stirling was huffing and puffing, which did not make any sense; they had only run about one hundred fifty yards, and he was in Olympic-class condition from all the training Raiding Forces had gone through at parachute school and Achnacarry. The blood pounding in his ears sounded like African tom-toms. He did not have any energy and felt abnormally weak.

Suddenly, without any advance warning, everything snapped into tight focus; sounds became extremely loud, his vision became crystal clear, and he suddenly found himself sprinting terribly fast, almost flying-out-of-control fast—the fastest he had ever run in his entire life. He was hauling it! The three-man bunker-busting team pulled out front with a burst of speed as planned, peeled No. 36 grenades out, and pulled pins. WHUUUMP! WHUUUMP!

"Clear, sir!"

"Clear, sir!"

Then, as rehearsed, Lieutenant Stirling and Trooper Roper darted past the two blown bunkers and threw themselves up against the door of the lighthouse. How odd! Had he really seen a bullet in flight? Had things actually been going in slow motion? One thing was sure: Lieutenant Stirling was never ever planning to tell anyone what he had just experienced. They would think he was crazy. "Death or glory" . . . what fool said that?

Lieutenant Stirling looked at his men to see if they were going to mention anything about what had happened—when time stopped. No, apparently not. They were moving around, preparing their guncotton charges, carrying on, business as usual.

All right, he said to himself, *now I know what it's like.* Sneaking ashore behind enemy lines and blowing up railroads had been a piece of cake compared to tonight. No one had ever told him a firefight was going to be like this. And nobody ever would. Combat was one of those things you had to experience for yourself. Lieutenant Stirling did not know it yet, but he was going to be charging that lighthouse in slow motion in his dreams for the rest of his life . . . and he was never going to get there.

The door to the lighthouse was not locked. Trooper Roper jerked it open and Lieutenant Stirling bounded in. He raced up the spiral steps, taking them three at a time. The staircase corkscrewed almost straight up; he never noticed or slowed down. Lieutenant Stirling was totally focused on what he would find at the top; Trooper Roper was right at his heels.

Outside he could hear his men shouting: "Fire in the hole! Fire in the hole! Fire in the hole!" WHUUUMPH! "Fire in the hole! Fire in the hole! Fire in the hole!" WHUUUMPH!

When they reached the top landing, Lieutenant Stirling did not hesitate; he bounded into the room to find a German sailor with his back to him, looking out to sea through a large pair of Zeiss binoculars. A Mauser M-98 rifle with a sniper scope on it was leaning against the wall beside him. Why he was not firing was a mystery.

The German turned in surprise and grabbed clumsily for the rifle.

RAAAAMMMPH! Lieutenant Stirling nearly chopped him in half with the big .45 slugs from his Thompson submachine gun.

Then it was all over. Unlike surviving his first parachute jump, there was no euphoric thrill connected to living through his first combat action. He merely felt dead tired and strangely distracted.

Down below he could see the beach and the Channel sparkling. The two LCAs were nosed in right where they were supposed to be, waiting for Raiding Forces to embark for the return trip home.

Standing offshore was his friend and Operation Comanche Yell railroad-busting associate, Lieutenant Randy "Hornblower" Seaborn, in HMY *Arrow*. Behind her, bobbing in the waves, were the sleek gray motor torpedo boats of the 15th Motor Torpedo Boat Flotilla. From the great height of the lighthouse on the cliff, they looked like miniature toys. It was a beautiful sight. He should have felt like yelling, "YEEEEEEHAAAAAA," but he just did not have the energy.

The view from the lighthouse also revealed every square inch of Tomcat—which was a much smaller place than it had seemed a few minutes ago.

"Search that man and bring me his binoculars and leather case. You keep the Luger."

"Thanks, sir."

Lieutenant Stirling was unaware that he had taken on the persona of a Highland chieftain at war. He was totally in his element, exuding command presence, the absolute master of everything in his immediate vicinity. Life-and-death decisions came as easy as daydreams. When he spoke, men listened and jumped to comply.

"Take up a post here and keep a sharp lookout for a counterattack coming from either direction along the road. Give a shout if you see any enemy activity. When the signal to pull out comes, move out fast! I will delay igniting the fuze on the demolition charges until you exit the door and give me the all clear."

"Sir!"

When he arrived downstairs, Lieutenant Stirling remembered to shout out "Remember Calais" before he came out the door. He exited to find Rifleman Jim Peterson, Trooper Terrance McPherson, and Trooper Bill Loumount crouched down, weapons at the ready.

"McPherson, drop your spare guncotton charge here and go find Major Randal. Give him my compliments, inform him the lighthouse is secured, and say that the LCAs are on the beach right where they are supposed to be. Then get back here to me as quickly as you can."

"Sir!" the Blues trooper shouted in a tone that conveyed how personally pleased he was with the content of the message he was delivering. The navy was on station to take them home; that was nice to know!

"Peterson, take Roper's, Loumount's, and my spare guncotton charges and put them with yours and McPherson's inside the lighthouse while I coordinate with Lieutenant Corrigan. Set the fuze but do not light it. I will personally ignite the charge after Roper gives the all clear when he comes down following the signal to withdraw."

"Where should I place the charges, sir?"

"I have no idea. There is a formula for blowing up a cylindrical structure, but I do not remember what it is and never understood a word of it anyway. Just pack the guncotton in somewhere."

Blowing the lighthouse was not a priority mission. At virtually the last minute while Raiding Forces was at the departure airfield, Major Randal had casually mentioned to Lieutenant Stirling that it might be a good idea to "take it out if you get the chance."

Since they were only a few minutes away from boarding the Whitleys when the major had brought it up, about the only preparation he could make was to have every man in his team strap on an extra twenty-five-pound charge of guncotton. With explosives, a pound in the right spot will blow down a bridge whereas a hundred pounds in the wrong spot barely rattles it.

The lighthouse was a hollow shell. The only solid object in the whole structure was the tall, two-story metal tank inside. It probably would not take much in the way of explosives to bring it down; one hundred twenty-five pounds of guncotton was more than likely overkill. When in doubt, Lieutenant Stirling opted for the "P for Plenty" formula, which is the universal fallback plan for all non-engineers or non-demolitions experts when faced with a hasty demo job they are not trained for.

As he was turning to set the charges, Rifleman Peterson commented approvingly, "You looked pretty good out there, sir—leading the charge."

One of the most combat-experienced men in Raiding Forces, Rifleman Peterson had been at Calais with Major Randal as part of Swamp Fox Force. A compliment from him was really worth something, because he was not noted for passing them out, particularly to green lieutenants.

Trooper Loumount added, "Blimey, sir! That was the longest one hundred fifty yards I ever slogged. Every Jerry in the entire bloody German army was shooting at us. On our next mission, would you try to find us an objective that ain't quite so much like the Charge of the Light Brigade, sir?"

It is one thing to perform well and be a popular officer during training. It is entirely another to transform that popularity into respect from men you have actually led in battle. Lieutenant Percy Stirling had stepped up.

"I will be right back, men," he said.

Rifleman Peterson went inside the lighthouse to hunt for a place to set the charges, as per his orders. His schooling in demolitions had been rudimentary. He knew how to blow up a bunker, a gun emplacement, or a railway line, but he did not have any training at all in blowing up lighthouses.

Generally speaking, he knew it was desirable to have your explosive charge tamped down. That way, the maximum explosive force is created, because the shock waves resulting from the blast are not allowed to dissipate upward into thin air. *You do not want your explosives lying out in the open*, he vaguely remembered an instructor saying some time in the dim and distant past. So he looked for something he could put the charges under to help tamp them down, recollecting that sandbags had been mentioned as working best. Unfortunately, he did not have a sandbag.

His regiment, the Rifle Brigade, had been trained to rove out in front of the army as its eyes and ears. Green Jackets were expected to operate on their own hook and think for themselves. Swamp Fox Force and then Raiding Forces had carried that concept forward, demanding that troops be resourceful and requiring them to act on their own initiative.

Rifleman Peterson used his initiative then and there, wedging the one hundred twenty-five pounds of guncotton explosives up against the giant metal tank—it was at least two stories tall, maybe more. Then he went outside and dragged in a dead Nazi from one of the knocked-out bunkers and placed him on top of the explosives.

That bloody well ought to tamp them down, he thought as he carefully put the time pencil in place, being careful not to activate it—that was the lieutenant's prerogative.

Rifleman Peterson did not have a glint of an idea how a lighthouse worked. If asked what powered the light, he probably would have said, "Electricity." There were, after all, those electrical poles leading up to it.

What he did not realize, because no one had ever briefed him on the subject, was that the lighthouse on Tomcat was acetylene powered and that the tank had recently been topped off.

Acetylene is highly flammable; it said so right on the side of the tank in six-inch-high letters printed in bright red. The warning was in French, however, and Rifleman Peterson did not speak or read one word of the language.

Acting on orders from his team leader, Rifleman Peterson had placed one hundred twenty-five pounds of guncotton explosives under a completely full, two-story-tall acetylene fuel tank—unwittingly creating what might arguably have been the largest incendiary device on the continent of Europe.

Death or glory! YEEEEEEHAAAAAAH!

Only no one actually said any of that at the time.

42

P FOR PLENTY

CAPTAIN TERRY "ZORRO" STONE'S TEAM WAS THE NEXT TO THE last to depart the drop zone. The last team to leave was led by Sergeant Mike "March or Die" Mikkalis, who had the important job of establishing a pair of blocking positions on each side of Tomcat, designed to cut the beach road, the only high-speed route of approach into the objective. When the Germans' counterattack came, they would be traveling down the road, using it as the axis of their approach march from one direction or the other.

Sergeant Mikkalis had the secondary mission of rear security during the withdrawal phase. Every man in Raiding Forces, from the commander down, was hoping he would have a very quiet evening.

Unfortunately, the reason the ex-legionnaire was delayed leaving the DZ was because his men could not find the external bundles with the anti-tank mines packed in them. Too heavy to carry in leg bags, they had been mis-dropped. There was very little chance the Germans could get any tanks to Tomcat in the short amount of time Raiding Forces planned to be on the objective, but if they did, things would get really ugly—fast.

Captain Stone was responsible for the key objective: the signals station. He was hoping to capture a prisoner with knowledge of current Kriegsmarine signals procedures, or some piece of signals equipment that would be of high intelligence value—possibly a codebook or an encoding device. If any high-grade intelligence was to be found at Tomcat, it would most likely be located in the signals station.

By the time he and his men floated down and released their canopies, most of the other teams had already landed and were away. The signals station was the closest objective to the drop zone, only about thirty meters distant. They managed to get to it before any of the other teams had reached their individual designated targets and the general firing had broken out.

Unbelievably, the Raiders managed to achieve the element of surprise. That should not have happened and was hard to explain, but then, Captain Stone had always been a lucky officer.

As rehearsed, he dived through the door; shouted, "*Hände hoch!*" while in midair; and landed on the floor, using the toe of the stock of his Thompson submachine gun to break his fall. He then did a spectacular infantryman's roll, as he had been taught in the Life Guards school for dismounted operations with a SMLE rifle, and very nearly knocked himself out cold in the process.

In rehearsals he had never actually attempted the showy fall and roll; it was something a little extra he improvised, living the moment and operating under the influence of a major adrenalin surge—a hazard of the raiding trade.

The breaking-your-fall trick had always worked just peachy with a .303-caliber Short Model Lee-Enfield rifle, because it was possible to brace your right forearm along the top of the rifle's wooden stock to absorb the shock of the impact. However, the butt of a Thompson, with its finger-grooved pistol grip, has an entirely different angle of drop and was not designed for such gymnastics. It is particularly unsuited when fitted with the heavy metal one-hundred round drum magazine of .45-caliber ammunition that Captain Stone had mounted on his, exactly like ones they used in the gangster movies he loved to watch.

In fact, that was the reason Captain Stone had wanted to carry the big drum magazine; it was a case of real life imitating Hollywood. Somewhere in midair it dawned on him why drum-fed Thompson submachine guns were sometimes referred to as "Chicago pianos"; his felt about as aerodynamic as a baby grand.

Captain Stone ended his roll with his midsection landing on the rear sight of his weapon so hard he bounced just a little bit and let out what sounded like, "*Whoof.*"

Two startled German sailors sat at their duty stations, paralyzed with fear, staring in wonder at the British Commando in the prone position who had so unexpectedly arrived by sailing into their midst armed with a high-capacity, gangster-movie gun, nearly knocking himself silly. The Kriegsmarine signalmen were not so paralyzed, though, that they failed to raise their hands high, double-quick.

The Nazis did not move a muscle. They had seen some of the same movies as Captain Stone and had an idea what those Tommy guns could do at close quarters . . . such as the inside of a Chicago garage on St. Valentine's Day. The two Germans could not help but wonder if he had rubbed the noses of his bullets in garlic, as the criminals did in the movie. They were not about to do anything rash to find out.

Outside, firing commenced, increased quickly to a violent crescendo, and then died down with merely an occasional round popping off. In a matter of minutes Major John Rock showed up to help search the signals station. Not long after that, Major John Randal arrived for a quick situation report.

Radios and other equipment were ripped out of their brackets and placed in Bergen packs for rapid transport to the beach. The Raiders did not take time to evaluate what was what, they just smashed and grabbed. Documents were swept into canvas duffel bags. Time was limited. The intelligence boffins could sort it out later.

Major Randal ordered his signalman, Royal Marine Sergeant Mickey Duggan, to step outside and fire red-over-green Very lights—the traditional signal of success on a Commando raid.

Down on the beach a cheer went up. Lieutenant Colonel Charles Edward Vaughan, who had been pacing up and down the beach, looking like a restless water buffalo in front of the two beached landing craft, ordered, "Stand ready, lads."

He repeated himself unnecessarily to the Lifeboat Serviceman who was waiting with a small rubber inflatable dinghy to take Major John Randal out to HMY *Arrow*. "Stand ready there, sailor."

Then he turned to the silent bagpiper who had been matching him pace for pace up and down the beach and ordered, "Pipe Major, 'Yellow Cock.'"

Back on Tomcat, Major John Randal gave an order to Royal Marine Sergeant Mickey Duggan: "Fire Greens."

The Royal Marines signaler immediately complied, pumping five green flares into the night sky. It was the signal to withdraw; no one could possibly miss it.

While every man on Tomcat immediately began to execute the withdrawal plan toward the cliff rally point, Major Randal turned and walked the other way—inland. He went out to the coast road alone and called softly, "Remember Calais."

Sergeant Mike "March or Die" Mikkalis stepped out of the dark, cradling a Thompson submachine gun, and responded, "Remember Calais, sir." He was surprised and pleased to see Major Randal. His showing up had been neither planned nor rehearsed. The King's Royal Rifle Corps sergeant and his men were waiting for a series of five red flares to release them from their rear security mission and allow them to pull back to the beach.

Theirs was a lonesome vigil.

Major Randal said conversationally, "I've been meaning to tell you; I recommended you for the Distinguished Conduct Medal for your actions at Calais."

"Thank you, sir," Sergeant Mikkalis responded gruffly to cover his pleasure. "I was merely doing my job."

"It's been approved."

"Sir, I cannot possibly accept it unless they give you at least the DSO," the recruiting-poster-tough Commando sergeant protested.

"Sure, you can," Major Randal said. "We all would have been in big trouble without your rock-solid leadership."

"Sir, I had the distinct impression we *were* in big trouble."

On Tomcat, Raiding Forces personnel began folding in on themselves in series of bounding movements, leapfrogging toward the cliffs. Every move was carefully orchestrated. The troops were under tight control.

The Raiders shifted back to where Lieutenant Taylor Corrigan and Lieutenant Percy Stirling had set up security positions around the two sets of ropes that had been carried up the cliff by the hard-charging team from the Mountain Warfare School. The mountaineers had performed an impressive feat of speed climbing.

There had not been time to make a reconnaissance of the narrow path down the cliff. For all anyone knew, it could be mined. All personnel would go down the ropes tonight.

Captain Clive Haig-Tredberry of the Mountain Warfare School established a series of stations all the way down the cliff where the men would have to change ropes. The Raiders from the bunker-busting team and the lighthouse assault team had already gone down, dropping off a man at each station to provide additional assistance to the people who would be following them. Even though everything was running smoothly, it was taking substantially longer to rope down the cliff than anticipated.

There were a total of eight German prisoners. The sight of the ropes going over the edge of the cliff caused them to rebel momentarily. Captain Terry "Zorro" Stone, ribs still aching from his spectacular though painful entry into the signals station, was in no mood to be trifled with at this point in the evening; he indicated his displeasure by loosing at their feet a long burst of fire from his "Chicago piano." They were the first and only shots he fired that night. He felt better for it, and besides, he noticed right away that the Thompson had become substantially lighter. The Nazi prisoners shinnied down the ropes, looking as though they had been mountaineering all their lives.

Finally, red flares were launched, recalling the rear security element. Sergeant Major Maxwell Hicks met the two road security teams when they arrived at the ropes; he was fretting like a mother hen.

Major Randal was the last man down the rope. He took one last look back at Tomcat. The objective looked peaceful in the pale blue moonlight. The signals station was burning merrily. Captain Stone had fired it, hoping to confuse the Germans about the material they had carried off. Down below he heard the sound of a bagpipe shrieking from the beach. It sounded as if a cat had gotten its tail caught in the lowering ramp of one of the LCAs.

When Major Randal arrived on the beach, Lieutenant Colonel Charles Edward Vaughan had things under iron-fisted control, with everything completely organized, running like clockwork. The Raiders were executing the withdrawal plan as if it were a well-rehearsed demonstration. Raiding Forces had never conducted a practice re-embarkation exercise that had worked as flawlessly. All that hard, repetitious training finally paid off.

When Major Randal walked up, Lieutenant Colonel Vaughan snapped to attention and gave him a salute worthy of his old regiment, the Coldstream Guards. "Beachmaster reports all personnel accounted for. We have a good count. You have all your men embarked at this time except for your personal party, which will be going out on the MGB 345, and beach security."

Major Randal acknowledged the salute. "Can you give me a casualty report?"

"One man killed, four wounded. The wounded are on board being treated by a navy doctor. Their wounds do not appear to be life threatening. At least that is the initial indication, John."

"Thanks, Colonel Vaughan. Very nicely done. I doubt anyone will ever do it any better."

"My pleasure—and I can say the same to you, lad. All things considered, militarily speaking, it does not get any better than this."

"Time to go then, Colonel. Pull in your beach security element," Major Randal ordered briskly.

"My sentiments exactly."

Major Randal stepped into the rubber inflatable dinghy. Captain Stone was already aboard waiting for him. As soon as he was seated, the Lifeboat Serviceman shoved off. Major Randal helped paddle with the butt of his

Browning A-5 shotgun. He looked over and saw that Captain Stone had ripped the heavy drum magazine out of his Thompson submachine gun and was using his weapon to paddle just as furiously on the other side. Both men were giving it everything they had. Time to go! They just might actually pull this one off.

Just when it looked like they were going to make it home free, suddenly, horrifyingly, the night erupted into day.

FLASH BANG! A blast blazed, brilliant enough to read a newspaper by. The whole of Tomcat, all the way down to the beach, was magically illuminated; the Raiders could see for miles! The startling white-flash explosion was the most dazzling, mind-numbing event anyone present had ever experienced. It lit up everything.

Then the booming explosion rolled across the water and over them, but compared to the stunning luminosity of the blinding flash, it was a virtual pipsqueak. There was no weapon in the British inventory capable of making a flash like that happen. Was it one of the Nazi wonder weapons? Some gigantic incendiary? The end of the world seemed upon them!

The Raiders and sailors were stupefied beyond description.

"What the bloody hell is that?" screamed a startled Captain Stone.

"How am I supposed know?" Major Randal shouted back.

All three men in the rubber dinghy immediately recommenced paddling like wild men while looking back over their shoulders in terror. They literally could not comprehend what they were witnessing. Nothing in their collective experience had prepared them for the terrible magnificence of what was happening.

On top of the cliff a gigantic tornado of fire spiraled insanely out of control, spinning upward for what looked to be a mile in height and a quarter of a mile in width at the top. The brilliance of the inferno was incredible. They had seen the largest guns fired in action, and they had witnessed bombing raids from up close—on the receiving end and from a distance. They had seen Royal Navy ships explode.

But nothing prepared them for this monster flame.

And then, suddenly, it vanished in a poof, like a candle that had been snuffed out! Night vision was ruined; the men were almost blind from the brilliance. Finally, when they realized that whatever it was was not coming to kill them, the three of them in the dinghy shipped oars and just stared back in awe at the now-smoldering cliff, weak with relief.

"I thought I was going into cardiac arrest. What do you think caused that blast?"

"Percy blew Tomcat's lighthouse to smithereens!" Major Randal rasped, still in a nearly catatonic state of shock. "We're going to need a lot more demolitions training, Terry. We don't know enough about explosives not to be dangerous to ourselves."

"Consider it done, old stick. I shall get on it straight away. I never knew destroying the lighthouse was on for tonight."

"I sort of casually mentioned to Percy it might be a good idea to blow it," Major Randal explained. "I only meant for him to put it out of action. What do you think he did?"

"He complied."

When the two officers arrived on board HMY *Arrow*, they found a badly shaken crew. "What was that?" Lieutenant Randy "Hornblower" Seaborn railed in a high-pitched voice. "For a moment I thought I was witnessing something straight out of H. G. Wells. Did we cause that detonation, sir?"

"I'm not sure. Let's get the hell out of Dodge, Randy, before anything else happens."

"Aye, aye, sir. I *want* to go home."

That night Lieutenant Percy Stirling passed into the military pantheon—forever after to become known as "Pyro" Percy, a true living legend. As Captain "Geronimo Joe" McKoy had predicted, Lieutenant "Pyro" Percy Stirling was responsible for striking terror into the hearts of many brave men—nearly all of them his own.

A lesson learned: It was not always possible to actually expect the unexpected, no matter how hard you try.

Combat is like that.

FROGSPAWN

43

RETURN FROM TOMCAT

THE RETURN VOYAGE FROM OPERATION TOMCAT TOOK NEARLY nine hours. It was a calm passage, though turning to cold. There was no German pursuit. HMY *Arrow* sailed with the two landing craft assault boats in line formation astern. Around them on the horizon, the 15th Motor Torpedo Boat Flotilla ranged in a loose, diamond-shaped defensive perimeter. The LCAs' top speed of ten knots dictated the pace for the entire convoy.

When dawn broke it was a beautiful sight to the men of Raiding Forces. Maybe it was not the kind of beautiful sunrise an artist might paint, unless it was his last day on death row before the hanging: The daybreak was a gray, cold, drizzly, muddy-looking sunrise, but to the men returning from Operation Tomcat it was a beautiful thing, because when the Raiders had taken off last night, none of them had been exactly sure he would ever see another one.

With the sun came a flight of four Coastal Command Hawker Hurricane fighters. They roared in at low level, rocking their wings in a V-for-Victory salute, and blasted by. The troops cheered and waved. In perfect formation the Hurricanes zoomed upward in a lazy curve to take up station, race-tracking over the convoy to provide air cover for the remainder of the trip.

In the far distance the faded purple coastline was an inspiring sight.

The coast of England swam into focus. The convoy paralleled it until it was time to turn and make the run up the small bay below Seaborn House. The 15th MTB Flotilla materialized to seaboard, each torpedo boat flashing dot-dot-dot-dash—again, V-for-Victory—with her Aldis signal lamp as she sailed past. Then the flotilla boats kicked in their powerful engines to "all ahead full," shooting up tall rooster tails of seawater in their wake, and broke off for their home station.

The Hurricanes came down and each plane made a lazy solo pass, doing a slow Victory roll. They, too, broke off and flew out of sight.

Soon the little LCA armada was sailing up the mouth of the river to its dock, led proudly by HMY *Arrow*. Each craft they passed sounded its horn: dot-dot-dot-dash. Every cottage they passed on shore had people standing outside, waving Union Jacks. When the wind carried right, they could hear the faint sound of cheering.

"What do you think's going on, Randy?" Major John Randal asked. "You pick up anything on your radio?"

Lieutenant Randy "Hornblower" Seaborn looked at Major Randal closely to see if he was joking, and when he realized the major was serious, he started laughing. "That's for us, sir."

"Are you nuts? All we did was blow up a lighthouse."

"We really blew the hell out of it," Captain Terry "Zorro" Stone pointed out reasonably.

"Attention on deck!" Lieutenant Seaborn suddenly ordered the crew of the *Arrow*. "Look sharp, lads, we have a side party standing by on the dock."

"Who are all those people?" Major Randal wondered out loud in amazement.

"I have no idea, but they seem glad to see us. Time to get the party rolling. Leave has never sounded so good," Captain Stone exclaimed, with a tingle of excitement creeping into his voice. "I do need my rest and recreation."

"You nearly required hospitalization after your last one," Major Randal said dryly.

HMY *Arrow* eased up to the wharf with its powerful engines warbling. Flashbulbs were popping. The local maritime brass band members were playing their hearts out, blaring "Rule, Brittania." Waiting on the dock were senior officers from all three services, including Royal Marine Lieutenant General Sir Alan Bourne and his new replacement as director of Combined Operations, Admiral of the Fleet Sir Roger Keyes, Bt, GCB, KVCO, CMG, DSO, the legendary hero of Zeebrugge.

A full complement of representatives from the print and newsreel media was present, along with what appeared to be the entire civilian population from the surrounding three counties.

The "Razor" was there, as well as Randy's parents, Commander Richard and Mrs. Brandy Seaborn. Lieutenant Seaborn did his best to ignore his mother during the docking maneuvers. He did not want to make a hard landing with her watching.

Major Randal stepped off the *Arrow* and saluted Lieutenant General Bourne, the man he recognized as his commanding officer.

"Congratulations, Major," the general said to him, returning the salute as one professional to another, ignoring the mob scene raging around them. "Let me introduce you to my replacement and your new commander, Admiral Sir Roger Keyes."

The crusty old admiral immediately grabbed Major Randal's hand and shook it before he had a chance to salute.

"Absolutely capital performance, Major. One of my first official acts is going to be to lavish a shower of medals on your troops. They deserve it. You lads have made us all proud men today."

Then there was a Royal Air Force air commodore pounding him on the back, and a couple of army generals he had never seen before were soon pumping his hand. Major Randal literally had to tear himself away to get back to the dock so that he could be there to greet his troops ashore as the first LCA pulled up beside the *Arrow*.

The men of Raiding Forces were doing their best to affect the look of cool, tough, professional fighting men who had pulled off a highly dangerous mission, while likewise conveying the impression that it was nothing much to get excited about. *Parachuting behind enemy lines? That's what we do.*

The Tomcat Raiders swaggered off the LCA, carrying their weapons casually in one hand and their Bergen packs slung nonchalantly over their shoulders. They were bristling with pistols and fighting knives, wearing their green berets at jaunty angles, having discarded their jump helmets. The men still had streaks of charcoal camouflage on their faces.

The commander of the Special Warfare Training Center, Lieutenant Colonel Charles Edward Vaughan, was fallen on by a mob of enthusiastic volunteers for Commando training the moment he stepped ashore. It appeared as if the Somerset Light Infantry was volunteering en masse.

Major Randal knew he was going to have one very unhappy local commander of anti-invasion troops on his hands. Regiments of the line really hated it when their best men volunteered out for Commandos or Airborne Forces. Up until now he had made a point of not accepting any volunteers from the Somerset Light Infantry in the interest of local harmony, but he intended to give Lieutenant Colonel Vaughan a list of 4th Battalion Somersets he was interested in—if they made it through Achnacarry.

Brandy Seaborn came up and gave him a huge, welcoming hug. "John, I am so very proud. How terribly exciting this is—as ever, the dashing hero."

"Brandy, don't tell anyone, but I've been on more dangerous training exercises," he whispered in her ear. He scanned the crowd. "Where's Jane?"

"She's not here, John," Brandy Seaborn replied. "I thought she would be."

Before he could respond, a clutch of reporters swarmed around and started shouting questions at him as if he were hard of hearing. They wedged themselves between him and Brandy Seaborn. He looked over at General Bourne and Admiral Keyes. The admiral gave a slight nod of approval. For the next twenty minutes, Major Randal patiently answered their questions, making sure not to discuss any operational details.

It occurred to him that no matter which way he turned, standing on the edge of the crowd was always the debonair figure of Major Lawrence Grand, nattily attired in an impeccably tailored navy blue, double-breasted, pinstriped suit. He was chain-smoking his brown, custom-rolled cigarettes in a short ivory holder, wearing tinted glasses and, as usual, a red carnation in his lapel.

Why did Major Randal have the feeling that Major Grand was keeping close tabs on him?

Then Major Randal bumped into an ancient sergeant major. "What am I looking at?"

"I have been recalled to the colors, sir," a slightly embarrassed Sergeant Major Maurice Chauncy explained.

"So, this is what a Green Howard looks like!"

"Sir!"

"Does this mean you're not my butler anymore?"

"Oh, no, sir. I merely have to pull duty in the Operations Room." Looking around to make sure no one could overhear, Chauncy whispered, "Buzzard Plucker, sir."

"I see," Major Randal said, which of course meant that he did not have any idea what his former butler was talking about. "I guess you'll be going to parachute school next?"

"Actually, sir, Lady Seaborn did mention something about balloons."

"You're kidding."

"Lady Seaborn specifically made reference to a short course. I think I might like to give it a go, sir."

Major Grand strolled up and stuck out his hand. "Congratulations, John. You obviously have a talent for fast cutting-out operations. A word with you in private, if I may."

Major Randal turned back toward his butler. "We are not through talking about this, Chaun . . . ah, Sergeant Major."

"Sir!"

They walked off a short distance from the crowd. Leaning close to Major Randal's ear, Major Grand said, "Frogspawn."

Major Randal froze. He clicked on.

"A major crisis of national strategic importance has been brewing for some months, and I have been quietly developing plans for a sensitive military operation to intervene and put things right," Major Grand said. "Imagine my complete surprise to find that the troops I had earmarked for this delicate secret mission were away campaigning somewhere in France at the very moment I needed them. Attempting, I believe, to prove something called 'The Theory of Aerial Envelopment.'"

Major Randal felt the skin on his cheekbones grow tight.

"You know, John," Major Grand continued, "the thing is that the policy of 'need to know' helps keep the enemy from finding out what it is we are up to, but the downside is that 'need to know' sometimes leaves our side in the dark. It definitely kept me out of the loop about Operation Tomcat."

"I see."

"You are going to be staying at the Bradford Hotel two nights hence. I will pick you up in the lobby at 0900 hours the following morning. I have a busy day planned for you, and I promise you will not be bored."

"Lovely."

"By the way, cancel any leave you may have promised your troops. Stand down Operation Buzzard Plucker and Operation Comanche Yell, effective immediately. Raiding Forces will be deploying within the next few days, and you will need every officer and man you can take with you. A sea cruise is in your troops' immediate future."

"I'll put Raiding Forces on alert."

"Be discreet, John. Ah, maybe it would be best if Admiral Keyes and General Bourne do not get wind of this little talk. Everything I have just said is strictly 'need to know.' At this point they do not have any need . . . and they never will."

"Roger," Major Randal said. "We never had this conversation."

"'Those who dare,'" Major Grand continued, quoting Prime Minister Churchill softly, almost as if talking to himself, "'reap great rewards.' Duty calls, Major."

The war marched on.

HISTORICAL NOTES
OF INTEREST

Prologue

The 30 Brigade in Calais consisted of a mixed assortment of units with titles that gave a misleading impression of the brigade's true strength. In the U.S. Army, where Lieutenant John Randal had served for four years previously in the 26th Cavalry Regiment, for example, a "corps" was a major unit of two or more divisions, plus artillery, support, and miscellaneous attachments totaling, at a minimum, 30,000 men. The King's Royal Rifle Corps was but 750 men at full strength.

A regiment in the U.S. Army is approximately 3,000 men strong. The Queen Victoria's Rifles, though styled a "regiment," were in fact a 566-man reserve motorcycle reconnaissance regiment, minus the motorcycles—which, due to a glitch in communications, had been left behind in the QVR depot in England when the regiment deployed to Calais.

The Third Royal Tank Regiment had been ordered, upon arriving in Calais, to burn its tanks in order to keep them from being captured by the rapidly advancing Germans, and some tanks were actually destroyed before cooler heads prevailed and the order was countermanded. Prior to deployment one-third of the highly trained specialist tanker troops had been pulled out to form the nucleus of a new tank regiment and replaced by what was described by their commanding officer as "completely untrained militia."

A "brigade" in the U.S. Army is about the same strength as a regiment. The Rifle Brigade, like the King's Royal Rifle Corps, was a mere 750 men. Unfortunately for the Rifle Brigade, the crew of the ship that transported it to Calais panicked in the confusion on the dock when they arrived, and sailed home with all their heavy weapons and two-thirds of the ammunition still in the hold.

Chapter 1
The Rangers Regiment (territorial units in Great Britain are the equivalent of the U.S. National Guard) had been called up to replace the KRRC losses at Calais, and was activated as the 9th Battalion, "Rangers" King's Royal Rifle Corps.

Chapter 2
What the first Commando operation accomplished under the circumstances was actually pretty amazing. Prime Minister Winston Churchill had been all over the page on exactly what he expected of his Leopards. The PM really wanted a full-scale invasion complete with tanks, which was impossible at the time.

Chapter 5
R.A.M.C. stands for Royal Army Medical Corps.

Chapter 7
In the Great War (World War I), as a cost-saving measure, British pilots were not issued parachutes on the grounds that having one might encourage aviators to bail out when attacked or to elect not to try to land their airplanes when they were damaged because they had the option of parachuting to safety instead of crash landing.

No. 2 Commando, an existing unit, was selected to become the first airborne outfit in the British Army. The men could either volunteer to become parachutists (making them triple volunteers—for the army, for the Commandos, and for parachute training school) or transfer to another battalion.

Chapter 19

Brigadier is a rank in the British Army; however, unlike in the U.S. Army, a brigadier is not a general.

Chapter 32

Coastal defense in the area surrounding Seaborn House rested with the 4th Battalion Somerset Light Infantry. The Somersets were a dandy county regiment that boasted the distinction of being the only regiment in the British Army without the "Royal" prefix authorized to wear blue facings on their uniforms.

Chapter 40

What Lieutenant Taylor Corrigan had no way of knowing when he was developing his plan of attack was that the bunkers were not manned at all times. The German defense scheme called for them to be occupied hastily in the event of an enemy threat. The defenders believed that because the cliffs were so high they were invulnerable to attack from the sea. If there was a raid, they would have adequate time after the alarm had been raised to man the bunkers and fight off the intruders. It was a bad tactical plan, the kind that sometimes happens when sailors are ashore doing soldiers' jobs or when soldiers are manning ships at sea.

Chapter 41

German machine pistols at this time, particularly the new-issue MP-40, were without question the best submachine guns in the world—state of the art. Their high cyclic rate literally spewed 9-mm rounds, creating a distinctive high-pitched screaming sound that had a debilitating effect on the morale of their targets.

Chapter 43

Great Britain had the Official Secrets Act. If Major John Randal had made a slip, nothing he said would have been allowed into print that could advance the Germans' knowledge of Raiding Forces, operations, organization, tactics, weapons, or equipment, or that gave the enemy insight into how the British Army planned or trained. Freedom of the press did not mean the freedom to give the enemy useful information during time of war.

DEDICATION

This book is dedicated to the men of A Company 2nd Battalion 39th Regiment 1st Brigade 9th Infantry Division.

After an intensive six-week campaign of airmobile operations in the Mekong Delta, Alpha Company played a key role in the climatic Battle of the Plain of Reeds, which resulted in the 1st Recondo Brigade, commanded by the legendary Colonel Henry 'Gunfighter' Emerson, being awarded the Presidential Unit Citation.

On 3 June 1968, the third morning of a four-day running battle in the Plain of Reeds, Alpha Company air-assaulted into a hot LZ; charged across one hundred meters of open rice paddy straight into the teeth of a dug-in main force Viet Cong regiment that was throwing everything at them but the kitchen sink; carried the enemy left flank, penetrating their first line of bunkers; and pinned the VC in their emplacements and fixed them in place until the rest of the 1st Brigade could arrive, encircle, and destroy them. This was accomplished despite A Company having landed outside the range of artillery support, with the company commander killed in the first few minutes, and fighting in 110-plus-degree heat—with no shade, no water—armed with M-16 rifles that would not function in those conditions. They were outnumbered more than ten to one. The initial air strike had to be called in on their own position to prevent A Company from being overrun, which was complicated by the lack of even a single smoke grenade or any other signaling device to mark their location.

One senior officer described Alpha Company's charge and refusal to allow the VC to break contact as the "finest small unit action ever fought"—and maybe it was.

Six Huey helicopters flew out all the men in the company left standing.

And to my wife, Lindy.